Glencoe

Glencoe

A ROMANCE OF SCOTLAND

BY
MUIREALL DONALD

Laughing Owl Publishing, Inc.

Glencoe: A Romance of Scotland
Copyright © 1998 by Muriel Donald. All rights reserved.
Printed in the United States of America. No part of this
book may be used or reproduced in any manner
whatsoever without written permission from Laughing
Owl Publishing, Inc. except in the case of brief quotations
embodied in critical articles and review.

Laughing Owl is committed to our Authors and their
Work. For this reason, we do not permit our covers to
be "stripped" for returns, but instead require that the
whole book be returned, allowing us to resell it.

FIRST EDITION
First Printing, 1997

Cover art and design: Laughing Owl Publishing, Inc.
Photograph by Steven E. Donald
ISBN: 0-9659701-3-2
LCCN : 97-073403

Laughing Owl Publishing, Inc.
12610 Hwy 90 West
Grand Bay, AL 36541

Acknowledgements

This book is the result of four years' fascination with the story of the events at Glencoe. It couldn't have been completed without the help of my critique group and their determination to make this book the best it could possibly be: Aleta, Melanie, and Diana – you are the very best friends a writer could have. Special thanks go to Steve and Hamilton, for their unwavering support.

Author's Note

The Glencoe massacre occurred late in the seventeenth century and the event rocked Scotland. Robert Campbell, the Earls of Argyll and Breadalbane, and King William and Queen Mary all are historic personages. Their presence in **GLENCOE, A Romance of Scotland** is in no way intended to reflect the historical accuracy of their roles in the plot surrounding the massacre. All other characters and events in this book are fictional and exist only in the author's mind. For helping me understand the events leading to the massacre, I am much indebted to John Prebble's book, *Glencoe, The Story of The Massacre*.

In 1996, I visited Glencoe and the Clan Donald Center on Skye with my husband, Steve. He is descended from a MacDonald clan, and I from the Campbells of Argyll. We also visited Inverary, the home of my grandmother, Mary Campbell. This book is for Steve and for Mary.

Today, the 14,200 acre wilderness of Glencoe, along with the rugged mountains which are called the Five Sisters of Kintail, are maintained by the Scottish National Trust. Visitors to Glencoe stand silent before a clan memorial to the fallen MacDonalds. It is a proud testimony to the passion and perseverance of a singular people who were Highlanders first, last, and forever.

CHAPTER 1

Edinburgh
January, 1693

A woman's low, throaty laughter drifted down a curved stairwell. In the entryway below, a man named Niall MacDonald paused before ascending the stairs, listening to the admiring murmurs issuing from within the lady's drawing room. Niall indulged himself in the momentary enjoyment of a fragrant scent permeating the hallway, borne by opulent blooms of purple and dark vibrant blue heather stuck casually in cloisonné vases. The lady's hand was evident in the careless arrangement of flowers, similar to her whimsical attitude toward the men she collected.

Niall took an extra moment before announcing his arrival in her home, paying a silent homage to the seductive talents of Maire Douglas. Her receptions were well known throughout Scotland; her power to ruin reputations, legendary.

In Edinburgh, where political liaisons were as changeable as the fierce winds of the Highlands, Maire's skill in being at the center of current intrigues and conspiracies afforded Niall rare access to the secrets of King William's court. The gossip of Edinburgh's noble ladies and the pillow talk of its most powerful men were substantial gifts, dropping like jewels from Maire's soft red lips. There were those who suspected her of being wanton, but no one, so far as Niall was aware, knew her for a spy.

Niall handed his walking stick to the parlor maid and took the stairs with three great strides. He entered the small foyer that led to Maire's rooms and bowed slightly to the gentleman just leaving.

"MacDonald," said the Englishman stiffly, inclining his head.

"Sir." Niall spared but a cursory greeting for the man. His glance went eagerly to the room beyond, where Maire reclined on a chaise. As Niall joined her, lifting her hand to his lips, he heard the Englishman snort.

The departing guest, head held high, took his time descending the stairs. Niall waited to speak until he was certain the Sassenach was listening outside the doorway.

"Lady Douglas, thank you for seeing me. I came as soon as I settled into my rooms."

"How perfectly wonderful of you to visit me," Maire crooned, winking licentiously at him. "Especially since you have neglected me for the past year." She assessed him with pleasure, her eyes lingering on the well shaped calves beneath his red and blue plaid. He had invaded her dreams far too long, and no other man even came close to firing her imagination the way Niall MacDonald did. Maire's catlike green eyes narrowed; it was past time to remedy the matter.

"I could stay away no longer." He cast a watchful glance over his shoulder.

They heard the entry door slam downstairs, and Maire covered her mouth to stave off a fit of giggles.

"Poor Charlie," she said at last. "He so wants to believe that he alone holds my heart." She sent Niall a measuring glance. Perhaps his return signified a desire to take up their alliance where he had left it. Her skin heated at the thought.

"A dangerous desire for a Sassenach," Niall said with an answering grin. "One that will cost him his own heart, should he seek to act on it." He rose and walked to the window, twitching the lace curtains aside to watch as 'poor Charlie' drove away in his carriage.

"Not so dangerous, I think, as the look in your eye." Maire raised a peach colored silk fan to her face and waved it gently. "The English are here to stay, you know, so long as our good king reigns."

"And not a moment longer than that." Niall turned back to face her. "Tell me, Maire, how is it that you alone in all of Scotland are possessed of heather? 'Twill be more than a half-year before the hills are purple."

"Having a wealthy Englishman for a friend has many advantages. My heather comes from a hothouse in France. Dear Charlie knows it is my favorite flower, and he indulges me terribly." The corner of her mouth turned up in a sly smile.

"Enough of Charlie. What news have you?"

She lifted her yellow flounced silk skirt, affording him a glimpse of slender white-stockinged ankle as she stood to pour him a cup of mulled cider. She smelled of lavender scented toilet water and sweet wine, an intoxicating mixture for any man, be he Scot or Sassenach.

"Is it only news that you want, Niall?" Maire handed him the steaming drink. "'Tis a sad remark on my efforts, that you alone of all Edinburgh do not fall at my feet. Tell me, what is it that I do wrong? Only a year ago, you were all afire for me. Given but a little more time..." her voice trailed away in a sigh.

Only a year ago, he thought. Niall studied the woman before him. The passing of time had only enhanced her charm. He spared a moment's pity for poor Charlie, her latest amusement. *Let Charlie have the pleasure of drowning himself in Maire's honey.* Niall had no desire to repeat the experience. *Only a year ago.* He thought of all that momentary dalliance with Maire had cost, and his lips curled back in what might have passed as a smile.

He took the cup from her, sniffing appreciatively at the blend of whiskey and pale cider rising from the brew. "This will chase the shivers away, lass. Here's to the retreat of the English." He drank it down in one large gulp and set the cup noisily upon a marble-topped table.

"Now. What news?" He sat down on the settee across from her, crushing several delicate tapestry cushions in the process.

Maire sat too, and arranged her black curls over one shoulder. "The usual sort of tattle. I do grow tired of hearing about Lord Sinclair's newest horse and Lady Glensin's latest lover." She paused and touched one long, sculpted fingertip to her right cheek. "I seem to recall, though, that your poor dead uncle's neighbor, Robert Campbell, is to receive a promotion soon. He may also be given a wardship over the lands of Glencoe. "Tis whispered that Breadalbane arranged it all."

"With King William's sanction." Niall scowled. His heavy black brows met across his forehead. "They willna find Glencoe so easy a target, even with my uncle MacIaian dead and his sons scattered."

"Perhaps not," Maire said, idly examining the amber and silver ring on her right index finger. "But Campbell of Argyll will be seeking satisfaction for the slight suffered by his ward at the hands of one of your surviving kin. The lass rode alone to the village and was accosted by a man wearing a MacDonald plaid. Argyll's compassion toward your clan stops short when he feels his generosity has been thrown back at him."

"He did help to relocate some of the folk, and has sent several wagons full of provisions. That will cease, if what you tell me is true. Was the girl raped?" Niall asked with a frown.

"I think not, merely frightened. The man asked for alms and she laughed at him." Maire shrugged. "He pulled her from her horse and shook her roundly for her rudeness. To any other lord it would be a small matter, easily resolved. I doubt such an outcome in this case."

"They are starving in the hills." Niall said. He rose from the settee and paced the room, stopping before the mullioned windows that looked out toward Holyrood. His fist closed around the delicate curtains. "Can the Campbells leave us no dignity? It's enough that they slaughtered my uncle in his own hall last year. I've bided hard since, waiting for the opportunity to repay Robert Campbell."

Maire went to him, reaching out to stroke his hand softly, her pale, cool fingers barely grazing the top of his whitened knuckles.

"'Tis not time for you to plan revenge," she argued. "This rivalry between the two clans was ancient before Robert Campbell or MacIaian Donald were ever born. You must let your cousins, John and Alasdair, decide what is best. They have been pardoned. Isn't it enough?"

Niall stared at the dainty hand resting atop his hand. He released the curtains, sliding his palm out from under her touch.

When he did not answer, Maire folded her hands across her tiny waist. It was clear he had not come to Edinburgh simply to be with her. Pride made her eyes widen slightly, her lips curve up in a slight pout.

"Be realistic, my dear," she said, her voice light and indifferent. "Your cousins are no longer outlaws. Wait for them to return home. Let them avenge their father's honor."

Staring into the past, remembering the dead he had buried a year ago, Niall did not answer. The time for waiting was past. King William's infamous oath of loyalty was a matter of strife throughout Scotland. The Highland chiefs were the last ones to hold out against it, the only Scots with any honor remaining. They would have a Scottish king or no king at all. His uncle MacIaian died for his views, speaking out where others reluctantly conceded.

And now Niall's kin were paying the price.

"I canna allow Campbell to ride against the few remaining people at Glencoe," Niall said at last. "The snow is hard upon the Highlands and the clan is hungry. Damn! Why couldna the girl have ridden on past? Is there aught else I should know?"

Maire shrugged again, her white shoulder lifting prettily under its soft pale sleeve. "Campbell of Breadalbane is not a man to play with, Niall. He took oath to the King that he would clear Glencoe of traitors. Now those traitors have threatened the ward of Argyll, the very man who acted as their benefactor. It will not be easy for you there. Few of your kin remain, only a handful."

She turned the full force of her pleading gaze on him. "Think, Niall. Can you lead an attack on Robert Campbell with so few? For you can be certain, Breadalbane will have a hand in this, too. He surely has already sent his condolences to the Earl of Argyll, and Robert is but their poppet, dancing to whatever tune they order played."

She watched Niall carefully, noting for perhaps the hundredth time the graceful strength of his arms and the proud glare of his hooded black eyes. It was difficult to restrain her desire to touch him.

As though reading her mind, Niall stepped away from her and resumed his position on the settee. When at last he looked at her, Maire smiled with sweet tolerance.

"You know that I am right."

"The clan has little left to lose," Niall said. "Such stakes make the possible rewards all the more desirable."

The door downstairs opened and closed again and a draft of cold air rushed up to the small sitting room. Maire shivered delicately. "Arygll is enraged over the insult to his ward. Do tell the men to remember that, Niall. You cannot afford to lose any more of your family."

"Especially over a Campbell brat," Niall agreed. He crossed his legs at the ankle and the heavy plaid settled snugly around his thighs.

Maire looked away from him and fanned herself again.

"She is comely and spirited, I hear, given to riding alone when the mood strikes her. 'Tis said to infuriate Robert, who has been given the guardianship of both her and her sister."

"She is a Campbell," he repeated, "no doubt possessed of bad teeth and a pocked complexion."

"How discourteous of you." She wrapped a lacy shawl about her shoulders. "I will be so glad to see the last of the winter," she vowed, affecting a disinterest in the subject of the feud.

They heard her maid run lightly up the stairs. "Beg your pardon, ma'am," the girl bobbed her head. "But this here's a letter for you from that Lady Cathaleen."

Maire raised her eyebrows. "Do you refer to Lady Cathlan, child? Try to get the name right, details are so important. I should hate to have to send you back to the kitchens." She reached for the packet and the servant dropped it into Maire's outstretched hand.

The maid curtseyed, then ran out of the room.

"I see your attitude toward the servants has not improved," Niall said. He knew her far too well, his questing black eyes missed nothing, and the pretenses that worked so well on other men were wasted on him.

Maire lifted her chin and stared at him defensively. "The girl is English and of little use other than to provide me with occasional bits of gossip."

"Are you going to open it?" he asked, frowning at her delay.

She turned it over in her hands, remembering the last letter she received from her friend. Niall had been attending her then, also. Their delay in reading that letter had cost him dearly. But it had cost her his companionship.

She cast the missive onto her dressing table. "I know the contents of this one. An invitation to her ball. Lady Cathlan feels I am long past the desired age of being married. She continually seeks to help me out of my doleful state."

"And you continually resist her help. How uncharitable of you." Niall smiled. He crossed the room and took Maire's hand. "Thank you for your help. I must leave you now, to arrange for my return to Glencoe."

He smiled wickedly, showing the edges of his white teeth. "As always, it has been a rare treat."

"You might stay to amuse me," Maire pouted. "I shall have to send for Charlie again, I suppose, to divert me from my boredom. Really, Niall, you just arrived and now you are leaving again? It is too bad of you." She sat down on the settee he had vacated, petulance covering the longing in her heart.

"You bored? Never. Not while there's a living man within smiling distance." Niall kissed her hand and returned it to her lap. "You know why I do not stay."

"It was a tragic accident, Niall. You had no way of knowing what lay in that letter. No one could blame you. And you have not censured me for my part in it. Can we not go back to where we were?" Maire counted five heartbeats before he answered. Her beringed fingers clenched the silk of her skirt.

"You were not responsible," he said heavily. "I am Highland. That makes me responsible, and I can never go back. Have a good time at the ball. But don't get married, Maire. Thousands of hearts would break at the news."

Niall turned, ignoring the sudden sadness he saw filling her dark blue eyes. There was nothing he could say to lessen her disappointment, no gesture he could make to put things back they way they were a year ago. He was a different man now, one with no time or inclination for dangerous indiscretions.

He left her house in a swirl of plaid, a heavy dark green cloak thrown over one shoulder to ward off the biting north wind.

Plans for evening the odds against Robert Campbell churned through Niall's mind. The man was only the instrument of his superiors, of course, but it was Robert who had accepted Maclaian's hospitality. He had eaten MacDonald food and slept in the MacDonald hall. Then he had raised his men in the dark of night to run their swords through the clan in the worst breach of Highland honor ever known. Had it not been for Robert's own piper, who played a warning that night, and the personal integrity of a few of his men who helped their hosts escape, the entire glen would have been massacred along with their chief.

There could never be a true reckoning, not with so many dead and dishonored. Retribution was not totally within Niall's grasp, not against the powerful Campbell clan. The best he could do was make them uncomfortable, and prick at their damned crooked-mouth Campbell pride.

Of a certainty, he could do that. And he would start with the Campbell brat who made a habit of riding alone against the orders of her guardian. Holding Robert's ward hostage would insure a fine ransom, one that easily see Niall's clan through the rest of the winter and even beyond, if he were canny enough to strike a good bargain.

CHAPTER 2

Chesthill House
Glenlyon

Meg Campbell dug her heels into her pony's shaggy brown flanks and urged the stolid beast forward through the snow banks.

"Hurry Elizabeth!" she called to her younger sister who rode behind her at a slower pace. "They'll be after us at any moment!"

She spared a quick glance toward her uncle's house of Chesthill, searching the purple and gray hued horizon for the guards who were certain to follow. Her luck held; there was neither sight nor sound of the men Robert Campbell had set to watch over his wards.

Meg reached up to pull the long ivory pin from atop her head, allowing her thick dark auburn hair to spill loose around her shoulders. She cast the pin away, threw her head back, and laughed aloud at the exultant triumph that swept though her.

It was her seventeenth birthday, and Robert was unkind to forbid her riding to the village. The incident last month with her cousin Sarah was an unfortunate error in judgement. Sarah should never have scorned the man who asked alms for his wife and child. It should have been Sarah facing punishment for her conduct, but she was safely back in Edinburgh and far from Robert's grasp. Meg was left alone to face the consequences of the ill-fated adventure.

She set her teeth and scanned the landscape once more. Only rocks and snow banks met her eyes. Somewhere under all that white were the first shoots of deer-grass. In another few months the fiddle-curled ferns would try to push their way through the softening ground. The glen had called her forth from the dark confinement of Robert's house, and with or without his permission, she would enjoy this ride.

It was exactly the sort of day to be spent outside under the wild Highland sky, watching the hawks at their hunt, and feasting on the brown bread and cheese Cook had packed for Elizabeth. A small flask of wine provided by Meg's maid, Dora, would warm them when they grew chilled.

Once out of sight of the house, Meg reined her pony in to wait for Elizabeth. Her sister was the least accomplished rider Meg knew.

"Do hurry, Bess. We must be well away before they miss us."

Elizabeth's breath came in short, shallow gasps. Her fair hair twisted in tiny damp curls around her heart-shaped face. "Meg, oh Meg, we shall be in such trouble when Robert hears of this." She cast a fearful glance backward as though expecting her uncle to ride down upon them. "Should we not go back? Dr. Kincaid will be so worried."

Meg frowned at the mention of their tutor. "We won't go until we are made to go back. Even Dr. Kincaid understands the need to see something besides the inside of a house for weeks on end. The village is only a bit further, and I wish to spend my birthday outdoors, not confined to a stuffy library. We'll stop to eat our meal, then be back before Dr. Kincaid has finished his prayers." Meg kicked her pony once more. "You'll enjoy yourself once you set your mind to it. Come on!"

Secure in his hiding place behind the granite rocks of the Glenlyon Pass, a tall man pulled the hood of his black woolen cloak down snugly to hide his face. His hands twitched as the Campbell girls rode past in careless style, their passing marked in a dramatic splatter of snow and ice shards.

He controlled his anger at the sight of a curved cheek and dainty, kidskin covered wrists. Fresh and innocent of the danger so near, they rode close enough that he could smell the scent they wore. Apple blossom, like the perfume another girl had loved.

The man caught his breath and quelled the ringing inside his head. *Not now, not yet.*

They were younger than he had assumed. Virginal.

So much the better.

He let them ride out of hearing, then he mounted his own horse, a tall rangy black who knew his master's mind without the need for spoken commands. He followed them, these heedless girls who had laughed at the poverty of his kin.

Not now, but soon. Oh, very soon. The taste of Campbell surrender would be all the sweeter for the waiting.

A year was a long time to bide the rage in his heart. It was more than enough to prepare a careful assault on an enemy, to initiate a calculated strike against the house of Campbell.

The hunter raised a long thin whistle to his lips and blew a short signal upon it. In a few moments, he heard an answering note from the trees at the other side of the wood.

He caressed the hilt of his sword as he rode. The clipped hooves of his horse bit neatly into the white-crusted ground.

✦

"Here," Meg said with a shake of her head. "This couldn't be more perfect." She surveyed the tiny clearing with satisfaction. There was even a felled tree upon which they could sit, sparing themselves the discomfort of the cold earth.

They were only a short distance from the village, surely close enough to be safe from the outlaws rumored to be living in the forest. Meg halted her pony and slid gracefully from its back to the ground.

Beside her, Elizabeth jerked her own pony to a reluctant stop, all but falling from its back in her clumsy attempt to dismount. Elizabeth laid one hand to her breast.

"I will never understand your love of horses," she said. "Diarmud does not like to be ridden at all. He fought me every step." She smoothed her black velvet riding skirt, brushing away the powdery traces of snow that clung to it.

"Because he knows you do not like to ride," Meg answered, scratching the gray nose of the maligned pony. "If you were to give him a good rub, and whisper sweetly in his ear, he would welcome your touch."

Elizabeth shivered as she watched Meg dig into her pockets for a tiny wrinkled apple. Diarmud's big lips covered Meg's tiny hand, snuffling the treat up with a smacking gulp.

"Are you not afraid he will bite you?"

Meg kissed the pony's nose and then pushed him away. She laughed when he whickered his displeasure. "He'll not hurt me, not if he wants another treat when he gets you safely home."

"I am hungry, too," Elizabeth said, and reached across the pony's back to untie a sack of food. "It feels as though we've ridden for hours. 'Twas sweet of Dora to prepare our lunch."

She unfolded the sack their maid had provided, then spread the bread and cheese out on top of it. Meg brought out a tiny silver wine flask and opened it. She raised the flask to her lips and drank a long, slow draught. Then she handed the vessel to her sister.

They sat down on the fallen tree, giggling like small children. Meg reached down and formed a tiny ball of snow in one fist. She threw it lightly at Elizabeth, squealing as her sister threatened her in return.

Finally they settled down to their refreshments. The cheese was slightly warm, with a heavy sweet flavor. Meg took her dirk from her boot and sliced off a piece of cheese, fitting a portion of bread around it. She bit into it, savoring the taste.

Elizabeth handed the flask back to her, and Meg drank again. She took her time with her meal; all too soon they would be returning to Chesthill and Robert's restrictive care. A melancholy threatened her, not unlike the lowering gray clouds above her head.

"Are you worried about what Robert will say?" Elizabeth asked. She shivered, and took a small sip of wine.

"I cannot deny it. I wish I were braver, and not so hesitant to stand up to him. But I fear he will forbid us to ride at all. And I should hate that." She sheathed her dirk back against her ankle with a quick, stabbing motion.

Elizabeth took another long gulp of wine, spilling a few drops on her cloak. "You are the bravest person I know," she said. "No one else dares argue with Robert. He hates it when you do. I fear one day he will strike you, Meg."

Meg took the flask from her sister and set it down. "Lightly, Bess. You will be drunk if you are not careful." She thought about Elizabeth's last words and shook her head.

"Robert would never dare to mark either of us. The Earl of Argyll would have him flogged. We are far too valuable as marriageable properties. Still," she said to herself, "'twill not be pleasant when he finds out that we have thwarted his orders again."

She moved to the ground and leaned back against the tree trunk, scratching her back on the deadened bark. "I mean to enjoy this day, because it may be the last free one I get for a long time."

Meg yawned, stretching her arms out above her head. She wanted to close her eyes; the clearing had started to swim in circles around her. *It must be the wine.* Dora had stolen it from Robert's special hiding place, the cabinet where he kept his most potent vintages.

She looked at Elizabeth; her sister seemed to be fighting sleep, too.

"Are you tired, Bess?"

At Elizabeth's answering nod, Meg closed her eyes. "Perhaps we can snatch a few minutes of a nap," she murmured. "We can still be back before they miss us."

Niall MacDonald knelt between the girls. Maire had not lied; both sisters were comely. He wondered which of them had laughed at his kinsman.

The conversation he overheard between the girls led him to suspect the red haired one. There was a clear defiance in the disrespectful manner with which she spoke of her guardian. Niall studied her again, noting the high color in her cheeks, the fine black eyebrows that accentuated her triangular face. She slept deeply, her full breasts rising gently with each breath. She was dressed like her sister, in a matching black velvet riding dress that suited her rosy complexion.

The other girl, the little blond with the pale and pretty face, murmured in her sleep. Niall stilled, watching her cautiously, then he relaxed. She had drunk more of the drugged wine than her sister and was only feeling the effects of it.

He wrapped the leftover food in Meg's leather sack and stuck the flask in the belt of his trews. Then he sat back against the tree trunk to wait for his brothers, his gaze returning often to the girl named Meg.

Meg awakened slowly, from deep within a fog, hearing men's voices close by, and the rap-tap of plodding hooves. She lay on her side, the feel and smell of rough wool all about her. It was heavy, a blanket perhaps, or a musty old cloak, and it covered her eyes so that she could not see. She listened, her pulse beating hard in her chest. The slow creaking that filled her ears surely came from a cart.

She tried to sit up, but her ankles were bound. Her hands, too, were tied. She twisted them behind her back, but the bonds held. A bubble of confusion welled up inside her. She pushed it away and concentrated on her surroundings.

An unpleasant scratch plagued the back of her throat. Her nose itched, and she wrinkled her upper lip in a desperate attempt to control the sneeze she felt building.

When the urge subsided, she listened again for the voices that had awakened her.

Where was Elizabeth? Who were these men? Meg moved her right leg a little and was reassured to feel the weight of her dirk against her ankle. Above all things, she knew she must not give way to fear.

"Stop!" a male voice called. The horses slowed and then came to a halt. The cart lurched to one side and the blanket was tossed away. Meg closed her eyes again.

They lifted her up and out and deposited her upon the ground. She lay motionless, her face pressed against the cold, damp earth.

"All out?" a deep voice asked.

Another man grunted. "Bring the horses. Our guests will give us no trouble for a while, but we need to get on our way. We've a good hard ride before us if we want to reach home without anyone following us."

Home! Meg strained her ears to try to catch each word, but no further mention was made of their destination. Again she was lifted and this time placed across the bony ridge of a horse's back. The animal jerked at the strange burden.

"Easy now, Cailleach, easy sweetheart." The man who spoke was standing right beside her. Close enough to spit on if she had been free. In frustration, Meg kicked her legs out, wishing to hurt him, but he grasped her ankles and held them in an ironlike grip.

"This one's awake, Andrew. What shall I do?"

She had betrayed herself. Meg waited for reprisal, but a new voice commanded differently, in a deep bass rumble that made her heart race once more.

"Leave her be. She's safe enough, trussed like that, and we don't have time to deal with it now." The words were followed by a deep gulping sound.

"Come on, Andrew, pass it over. We're thirsty too," said another voice.

The man beside her added a hearty agreement and Meg's rage overlapped her common sense. She was thirsty too, and cold and uncomfortable. She twisted and writhed until at last the horse she lay across made a sudden bolt, discharging her to the ground.

The men roared with laughter. Someone snatched the blanket off her head and Meg looked up to find herself in the midst of a small circle of men. They were all wearing the infamous MacDonald colours.

MacDonald. These men must be part of the outlaw survivors of Robert's attack on the neighboring keep of Glencoe last year. He warned her only yesterday of their presence in the forest; reminding her that they sought revenge against him and his family.

Meg steadied her trembling mouth. She and Elizabeth were in great danger. Just as Robert said when he set the soldiers to guard the girls. She should have listened. For once, she should have listened.

The effects of the wine were wearing off slowly. Shaky and nauseated, she was unable to deal with these men in the way she wanted.

But if she were a captive, she was not defeated. Not while there was breath in her body. Her thudding heart threatened to falter, but she refused to allow her body to express panic. Meg looked up at the men, her shoulders squared with defiance.

There were three of them looking back at her. The closest one had bright red hair and a reddish-gold beard. He was quite nice looking, standing there with an almost silly grin on his friendly face. She frowned at him for his insolence.

Then she saw the fourth man, wearing green and white trews and a dark heavy cloak thrown over one shoulder. He stood apart from the others, facing partially away.

He was as beautiful as an angel, but with the darkness of a MacDonald devil. Maybe he was a devil, judging by the sense of power that emanated from him. His shoulder length raven colored hair shone and glistened in the late winter sunlight. It was tied at the back of his head with a strip of leather. When he turned to face her, his black eyes were flints of obsidian, cold as the night under thick, straight eyebrows. A devil indeed!

The hair on the back of Meg's neck prickled a warning, but she could not cease her study of him. The tight fitting tartan trews hugged his thighs. She dragged her gaze from his legs, frantic to free herself from the fascination with his body.

He wore the MacDonald sash proudly across his chest, over a well worn white shirt, and though she saw no sign of a powerful chieftain's badge of authority, in truth there was no need of such a symbol.

His dark eyes pinned her to the ground, dissecting her every feature. Awareness fluttered deep within her, like a small bird caught in a snare.

Then he turned to look at his companions, exposing the right side of his face to her, and Meg's breath stopped.

A jagged scar ran from the corner of his brow to just below his ear.

Meg found her breath again, and closed her mouth, silently cursing her lack of composure.

The other men stared down at her, arms folded across their chests, feet planted firmly apart. The stance afforded her a great view of three well muscled pairs of hairy legs. She blinked her eyes in confusion and averted her gaze.

The black haired man wore an disdainful expression, but none of them had yet spoken. Apparently deciding to torture their prisoner sprawled on the ground, they all shared a refreshing drink, passing a leather pouch back and forth. Meg's eyes burned from holding back tears and the thought of cool water nearly drove her mad. Finally she gritted her teeth, unable to withhold her frustration. She tossed her head to clear the tangled hair from her eyes.

"Will one of you *gentlemen* give me a drink?"

They blinked in surprise, but no one moved to grant her request. The tall redhead with broad shoulders held the drinking horn and Meg's gaze fastened on it. He looked at the dark haired man who had backed away and now stood leaning against his horse. She could see the two warrior's braids now, hanging on either side of his tense face.

"Niall?"

The dark man nodded, still not speaking. Looking at him, trying not to react to the aura of wildness and danger that surrounded him, it was easy to understand why the old Highland chiefs had gained such a fierce reputation.

He gave silent permission for her to drink, and the red haired man knelt beside her, lifting her up to place the horn at her lips.

She took two great swallows before the whiskey choked her, causing her to splutter and cough. Alarmed, her benefactor pounded on her back furiously. Her throat burned, her eyes teared, and a momentary weakness infuriated her.

When she could breathe again, Meg glared at him. "I don't drink whiskey!"

He had the grace to look ashamed. "Er, well we haven't much water with us, you see, and it's for the beasts and all. My name is Ian," he added, an engaging smile broadening his face. He gestured toward the other men. "These are my brothers, Jamie, Andrew, and Niall."

Slightly recovered and angry again, Meg looked around for the leader of the group. "Who is in charge here?" she demanded. "Where is my sister and why have you taken me?"

The dark man, Niall, turned away then, and mounted his horse. He sat there watching her, his face as cold and lifeless as the statue she had likened him to earlier.

The biggest man stepped forward, his face stern and his voice was rough. "Andrew MacDonald, at your service, mistress. As to the reason you are here with us for this grand adventure, well, we thought to give the Campbells a taste of our hospitality in return for the memorable experience we had at their hands last February." He gestured over to another horse, and Meg saw Elizabeth draped over the back of the animal.

Noting her horrified expression, Andrew laughed. "You and your sister are our guests, you see, although not exactly honored ones. Ian, gag her and we'll move on. We want to get home before the snow starts again."

Before Meg could react, a strip of cloth was thrust into her mouth and she was once again tossed on her stomach over the back of the horse.

"'Tis not much further, lady," Ian whispered in a ill fated attempt to soothe her.

Disgusted, Meg glared at the ground beneath her and prayed that the infernal horse would stay steady on its feet. Interspersed with her prayers were fervent curses on the heads of all greedy, thieving Highlanders.

They pounded away through the afternoon, and after what seemed an interminable period of time, the riders stopped and dismounted. Ian pulled Meg down from the back of his mount. His almost flirtatious expression made her want to swear.

Ian released the ropes about her ankles but left the one on her wrists in place. As he untied the gag, Meg twisted her head around, and bit him on the hand as hard as she could.

In one quick movement, the man named Niall jerked her around to face him and shook her soundly.

Meg twisted in his angry grasp, feeling the bruises already rising on her arms. She opened her lips to denounce him, but her words failed at the raw resentment she saw in his eyes and the angry lines around his compelling lips.

She swallowed the moisture that flooded her mouth.

For the first time in her life, she was afraid.

CHAPTER 3

"Mother of Christ!" Ian bellowed in shocked pain. He gazed in astonishment at the trickle of blood seeping from the wound on his hand.

Meg cried out as she struggled for freedom from Niall MacDonald's grasp. But he stood staunch as an oak tree, holding her until she fell limp from the struggle and began to weep.

"'Twould seem she has the hunger of all her kin for the taste of Donald flesh," Andrew called out, and Niall's expressive face contorted at the words.

He released his hold on Meg, stepped back and folded his arms over his chest. The black brows met in a scowl across his forehead and the skin around the scar on his cheek paled.

"You can make this easy or you can make it hard. You are here and here you will stay, so make your mind up to that now. There is no escape and no one to rescue you. No one knows where you are." He spoke with a measured patience, as though explaining to a small child, and she resented him for it, even as the bile of fear flooded her mouth again.

She hated them all and wished Robert Campbell in the deepest regions of hell for bringing this misfortune down upon her. She rubbed her arms where Niall had gripped her, and stared back at him.

There was a groan behind her, and when she turned she saw Elizabeth being carried into a small thatch covered croft.

"Has she been harmed?" Meg asked. She forced herself to meet Niall MacDonald's gaze, unflinching, and as hard as the front he presented.

His well defined lips stretched in amusement at her defiance. She wanted to hit him.

"Nay, she hasna been harmed," said Andrew from behind her. "We are not Campbells, ye ken."

The sarcasm stung but she didn't care, so happy was she to see her sister. Niall nodded to Ian and remained outside, watching as his brother led Meg inside the small shelter.

It was no bigger than a shepherd's bothy, really, only a crude structure that gave limited protection from the weather. The smell of sheep dung that wafted from the grass covered dirt floor was overwhelming, and Meg wondered if they used the building for lambing.

Ian warily untied her hands and Meg rushed over to where Elizabeth lay motionless. Bending down, she placed her ear at the other girl's face. Reassured by the steady rise and fall of breath, she looked at Andrew.

"Why have you brought us here? She is likely to die from exposure and fear." She heard the shrillness in her voice and winced.

Andrew did not even glance at her as he unloaded his pack. Ian and Jamie were building a fire in the pit at the center of the tiny room, and they, too, ignored her questions.

Meg took a deep breath and stood up. MacDonalds they might be, and motivated by a blood feud, but they owed her an explanation.

"Answer me at once!" She spit the command out in a hiss.

Still the three men went about their work, laying out bread and water. The woolen plaids that had been used to cover the girls were folded and piled on one side of the room. Even in the uncertainty of her situation, Meg was impressed with the precision with which they carried out their actions.

Elizabeth moaned and opened her eyes. "Meg," she said faintly. "My head aches so." Her delicate features were drawn with pain.

Meg sat down on the earthen floor beside her sister. "I know, sweetheart, but just be quiet for a few moments and it will pass. We will be all right." She burned inside at her words, but her sister was still a child to be protected at all costs.

"My throat hurts." There were tears in Elizabeth's eyes.

Meg looked around for water, and was gratified to see Ian moving toward them with a wooden cup.

"Not whiskey?"

Ian shook his head in denial. Meg took the cup from him and held it to Elizabeth's mouth. She brushed her sister's mussed blond hair from her face.

Elizabeth drank in greedy gulps. At last she pushed the cup away and lay back down.

"Thank you," Meg said, holding the cup out to Ian. He winked at her and smiled before moving back to the other side of the room.

The men spoke in whispers to each other and Meg strained to hear what they were saying. But Elizabeth, beginning to cry, demanded her attention.

"What is happening?" the younger girl moaned. "Who are these men? Meg, what is happening to us?"

Meg swallowed her own trepidation. Now of all times in her life she must try to garner the inner strength that had always comforted her in the past. But she would not lie to Elizabeth. Their situation was very serious, indeed.

Mentally beseeching Heaven to help her, she laid a cool hand on Elizabeth's forehead and met her sister's frightened gaze. "We've been taken prisoner by enemies of our clan. I do not think they mean to harm us," the alarm on Elizabeth's face quickened Meg's words, "but we must be careful to do just as they say and not cause them any trouble."

"Wise counsel, mistress." Andrew towered over the two girls and Meg caught her breath. He was the largest man she had ever seen, and his wild red hair looked as though it had never felt a comb. "You should follow it yourself instead of trying to give orders the way you did earlier."

Meg stood up to face him, drawing herself up to her full height. The top of her head came barely to the middle of his chest, but she was past being concerned with personal danger.

"I asked a civil question and you ignored me. I shall ask it again, and then again until I receive an intelligent answer from you, uncivilized though you may be. Who are you? Why have you taken us and what do you plan to do with us? You must have poisoned our wine! There is a traitor inside my guardian's house!" Her voice quivered with the rage that fueled her words.

Andrew stared at her. She heard him mutter a low curse in Gaelic, and he took a step toward her.

"Hold!" called Jamie, moving to stand beside Meg.

"No harm comes to them, Andrew, remember? We all agreed."

The big man nodded unwillingly, and Meg sensed the temper in him. "Aye, Jamie."

"Besides," Ian put in, "there's no reason not to answer her. We are, as you have seen, of Clan MacDonald. As to what was in the wine, I do not know, but we were assured that its effects are brief. Why? Well, that's a bit harder to explain. We were following orders."

Meg whirled on him, narrowing her eyes. "Indeed? Why, those are the words used by my guardian when last I spoke with him about you MacDonalds. He claimed to have been carrying out 'orders'. Perhaps you've heard of him. Robert Campbell of Glenlyon? Nephew to the Earl of Argyll?"

Andrew MacDonald's eyes narrowed to slits at the mention of the Campbell colonel. The two other men went still and Meg felt the tension increase in the small room. She looked from face to face, finding no warmth anywhere.

With an instinct born of fear, Meg thought of her dirk, which was still strapped to her right boot. She would bide her time and find a means of escape. Elizabeth's honor, as well as her own, dictated that they must not remain with these strangers.

Ian MacDonald answered her with stiff politeness. "We have good reason to know the name of your guardian, lady. 'Tis one that drives us like beasts. Indeed, it is Robert Campbell we seek to trouble, not you and your sister." His fists clenched with tension. "God willing, you will soon be out of it."

Big Andrew seemed to be having trouble breathing and Meg looked at him. "Are you so afraid of my uncle? You should be. He will have you carved up and served for his dinner if you harm us."

His face turned purple at her scornful words and he started toward her again, but Ian grabbed his arm. "Nay," the younger man said. "Let it bide."

There was a murmur of agreement from Jamie and then, one by one, they all sat down beside the fire and began eating a meager meal of oatmeal and warm water. Meg was left, bewildered, to try to comfort her sister.

"Why is this happening?" the younger girl whispered, her thick brown eyelashes shining with tears. Though Elizabeth wept beautifully, her fair skin was enhanced by a becoming pale shade of pink.

Meg sighed. Her sister was not to blame that her eyes were the color of Loch Awe at high summer, or that her delicate tears would move a heart of granite.

"Surely they realize that we were not involved with the deaths at Glencoe." Elizabeth looked up at Meg for reassurance.

Meg shook her head. "No more than the women and children who died in their beds that night at the order of our dear uncle." She reached for one of the folded plaids and wrapped it around Elizabeth's shoulders to act as a blanket against the harsh cold. For once, she would have liked to carry a sporran of her own, packed with oatmeal and dried fruit to ease the cramping of her stomach. At least Elizabeth had not complained of hunger thus far.

"But he acted on military orders! We are not to blame for Robert's actions. We are innocent of any blood."

Meg sighed and put her arm around her sister. "That doesn't matter. We are Campbells, and everyone in Scotland knows that Robert and his men broke bread and feasted with MacIaian, slept in his bed, and then rose up and slaughtered his clan. I honor my clan, but I am not blind to our sins or to the breach of honor committed against the MacDonalds last winter."

Elizabeth was quiet for a few moments, her wide eyes focused on something only she could see. She turned to look at Meg and her lower lip trembled. "Are they going to kill us, too?"

Andrew, who was closest to the sisters, heard her question and came to kneel beside her, reaching out to touch Elizabeth's hand. "I swear by all the saints, lady, you are in no danger. You were taken for ransom only." He patted her in a clumsy attempt to soothe. "All will be well." He ignored Meg, his attention focused on comforting Elizabeth.

Elizabeth smiled at him like a child and Meg had to fight the nervous laughter that threatened to spill from her rigid body. She hid her face in the folds of Elizabeth's blanket until she was sure Andrew had left. Then she looked sternly at her sister.

"I would appreciate it if you could manage not to be quite so friendly to our captors."

Elizabeth cringed at the sarcastic remark, and Meg was suddenly weary, her energy seeping away from her with the lengthening shadows. "Never mind, Bess, I'm sorry."

The two girls huddled together on the floor, sharing the hated MacDonald blanket between them. It was more for the sake of comfort than for warmth, although the leather flaps covering the windows of the croft were open in the rising wind, but at least they were together and for the moment, unharmed. The crude hut, though sturdy and dry, was one of numerous shepherds' huts scattered throughout the Highlands, intended for only brief and primitive shelter, not for prolonged occupancy.

Elizabeth stopped shaking, forestalling a crying fit, and Meg offered silent thanks to whatever guardian angel was watching over them. At least she wasn't dealing with Elizabeth's hysterics in addition to everything else. Meg felt a bit guilty, and she took Elizabeth's hand in hers, squeezing it.

"'Twill be all right, you'll see. Robert will come for us," she murmured. She ran her other hand through the tangled mess of her hair and wondered just how long rescue would be in arriving.

Elizabeth nodded, her great blue eyes wide with apprehension. "And what then?"

Meg knew her sister's real question. Robert would be honor bound to retaliate against the men who had stolen them and it was to be expected that he would take deep pleasure in it. She shivered. It was not a pleasant thought, to be the cause of more fighting and killing.

Andrew stepped outside the doorway and stood talking to Niall. After a moment, he gestured for Jamie and Ian to join them.

Ian cast an apprehensive look at the two girls, his usually cheerful face revealing a sudden agitation.

"You will wait here, mistress. 'Twould do you good to eat. We've a long ride yet before us."

How dare he give me orders? Meg glanced at her sister, who stared back at her with a frightened expression.

When Ian left the hut, Meg moved on quiet feet to the doorway and stood listening to the conversation of the men. The late afternoon sun was falling swiftly, casting long shadows beneath the tall pine trees that surrounded the croft.

"We should take them to Blackwater," Andrew was arguing, his deep voice rumbling amidst the softer tones of Ian and Jamie.

"Nay," said Jamie. "When we began this, we planned for one girl, not two. I say we should return one of them. Finding a safe place to hide them both will only slow us down."

Ian shook his head. "I disagree. Double the girls and double the ransom. The two of them should bring enough money to carry the clan through the spring and well beyond."

They were discussing her and Elizabeth as though they were stolen cattle instead of human beings! Meg narrowed her eyes and stepped through the doorway.

"Since everyone else seems to have an opinion, perhaps you would be so good as to let me state mine."

Niall MacDonald smiled slightly and accorded her a mocking bow. "By all means, Mistress Campbell. I am breathless to hear what you have to say."

"You will not mock me when you are fleeing for your life from the sword of Argyll," she told him, fitting her hands against the swell of her hips.

He rubbed his hand over the scar on the right side of his face. "I have never yet run from one of your kin and have no plans to begin such a habit."

Meg smiled back at him and lifted one eyebrow. "Do you not? Then you have put yourself in a most precarious position, sir, for without a doubt you will soon be designing a plan to avoid that same kin. Once my guardian and the Earl of Argyll discover that you have stolen my sister and me from our home, you will be outlawed."

He bowed again. "I am already named outlaw, mistress. Another crime added to my name can only enhance my reputation. Now tell me," he drawled, his dark gaze lingering on the soft velvet bodice of her black dress, "what, in your educated opinion, should we do with you and your sister?"

Her palm itched for the feel of her dirk. She almost bent to retrieve it, to bolster her flagging courage. Somehow he divined her thoughts, for his eyes went to her skirt and fastened on the shiny black toes of her boots.

Instead Meg clasped her hands in front of her waist and smiled at him. "I suggest that you return us at once to Glenlyon. Else Robert will have your head cut off and mounted on a pike," she said sweetly. "And the heads of your men as well."

"I wish him luck in the attempt," Niall MacDonald said grimly. He pointed a commanding finger at Jamie. "Take her back inside, give them something to eat, and make ready to ride again. We will decide later what is to be done. This place," he looked around the small clearing, "will not be safe for long."

"Aye, Niall." Jamie reached to take Meg by the arm.

She pulled away from him. "Do not touch me, outlaw. You, Niall MacDonald, as leader of these men, should act honorably at least. I demand that a letter of ransom be sent to Robert at Fort William."

Niall MacDonald raised one black eyebrow at her. "Thank you for that information, Mistress Campbell. If Campbell is indeed at the fort as you say, it gives us more time to secure our plans."

Jamie dragged her into the cottage, ignoring her protests. "You will sit, m'lady." It was said politely, but he thrust her down beside Elizabeth. "Nay," he warned as Meg started up again, "do not try it. My brother has little liking for Campbells."

There was nothing to be gained by further argument. Meg sat down beside her sister and watched Jamie cut a slice of bread to offer them.

Elizabeth's fear was palpable. Clutching Meg's arm, she whispered, "Who is that man you were talking to?"

"He seems to be both their leader and brother. They are discussing how best to dispose of us. It appears," her voice took on a scornful tone for Jamie's benefit, "that these powerful warriors do not know what to do with us."

The sisters rejected the fare Jamie offered, and huddled together in the deepening gloom of the hut. The scraping of boots at the stone threshold made Meg look up just as Ian and Andrew entered the room.

"Are we to keep them both?" Jamie inquired, looking at his brothers.

Ian nodded and Andrew examined the backs of his hands minutely.

"Then we're going ahead with the plan," Jamie said, and Ian nodded again.

Jamie motioned for Elizabeth and Meg to rise. "It seems we've another long ride ahead of us."

"Why?" Meg demanded. "Where do you take us?"

It was Andrew who answered. "We ride to Glencoe, and we ride hard and fast. There will be hard snowfall tonight and we must stay well ahead of it."

Elizabeth gasped in terror, certain that the MacDonalds meant to kill them, but Andrew went to Elizabeth and said, "We have no provisions here. You will be more comfortable at Glencoe, while Niall decides how best to handle this situation."

Elizabeth looked up at Andrew with complete faith, and Meg chewed the inside of her cheek with suppressed irritation.

"I'm surprised he decides anything," Meg said. "I thought you made all his decisions for him. And I thought your precious Glencoe had fallen. How is it that you think to shelter us there?"

"There are a few cottages left." For the first time Ian did not sound at all cordial. "Of course it will be nothing like the luxury you are used to. We are, you understand, in the midst of hard times." His formerly merry eyes held a warning.

Meg wanted to cry at her thoughtless words. These men had lost their homes, their families, everything that was dear to them. Under similar circumstances she wondered how the men of her clan would act. She shivered at the images that thought conjured up, remembering the stories of violence that had swept through Edinburgh after the massacre.

✧

They followed the men back to where the horses waited. Andrew lifted Elizabeth to the back of his brown mare, then vaulted up to sit behind her on the animal's broad back.

Ian moved behind Meg, to help her mount his horse. He placed his hands on her waist. Just before he lifted her, Niall interrupted him.

"Nay, Ian. Mistress Campbell rides with me."

He was already mounted on his tall black steed, looking down at her with a superior expression. Ian guided her over and raised her up as Niall extended his gloved arm.

He pulled her up with a quick movement, turning her sideways to sit before him on the horse. The warmth of his body against her own stirred her pulse, and Meg fought to resurrect her disdain for the outlaws who defied the king's law.

Her own body betrayed her; it struggled to nestle against him, to cocoon into his strength and his hard-edged maleness. Meg twisted in his arms, fighting to find a space to put between them, to shut out the tremulous longing that threatened to destroy her anger.

Even as she identified the framework of her erratic thoughts, he began to laugh aloud; a great ringing laugh that rocked her soul. He dug his boots into the black's haunches and tightened his hold on her. And they rode on.

✧

Glencoe. As they traveled ahead of the approaching snowstorm, Meg wondered what she would find there. By all accounts it had been a mighty keep before the massacre, surrounded by the smaller cottages of the clan. Her kinsmen burned and destroyed everything they could, and stole jewelry and clothing, silver and weapons. They murdered women and children. One report even said that a Campbell soldier had gnawed the rings off the finger of Lady MacDonald.

If that were true, she could expect no mercy from the men who had kidnapped her.

It was almost too much to comprehend. Her head ached from the constant battle of wits against the outlaws. Meg closed her eyes in a surrender to the weariness of the day. The steady gait of the horse lulled her and soon she was dreaming lightly, her head resting against Niall's shoulder. Somehow her sleeping consciousness was aware of the power of his arms, and images of his face moved in and out of her awareness. She wondered if he was aware of just how devastatingly handsome he was and reproached herself for traitorous thoughts.

Sedated by the steady rhythm of the horse beneath her, and the beat of her enemy's heart so close to her own, Meg fell deeper into drowsiness. Somehow, she would deal with all these issues later when she was rested and warm.

A light snow started to fall when they reached the Glencoe Pass and the MacDonalds urged their horses forward.

"Only a bit farther, mistress, and then we will rest." Niall's breath was warm on her neck, provoking again that treacherous response of her body. She feigned slumber, keeping her eyes open just enough to see the passing terrain.

Glencoe was renowned for its desolation; high snowy passes that led unsuspecting strangers to their doom when the rest of Scotland was green and verdant. Even in high summer the moor resembled a dead thing; a dark deceptive floor of matted heather and brittle moss that held ancient secrets. Only those born there knew the safe ways in and out of the glen; and the only path to Glencoe from the north was named the Devil's Staircase, because of its twisting, treacherous ridges that wound snakelike through the high hills.

But the MacDonalds rode fearlessly through the preternatural landscape, facing head on the impenetrable Highland mist that came down from the passes to embrace and shield its own.

Against her will, Meg straightened and pointed to a giant outcropping of granite in the distance, rising in a forbidding mass from the cloaking clouds. "What is that?"

Niall held her close against him, and she heard him chuckle again. "Even your Campbell blood, it seems, recognizes the power of Signal Rock."

Meg caught her breath at the words; the ancient landmark was well known throughout the Highlands, used for more than two centuries to host messenger bonfires during times when neither man nor horse could carry the tidings. "Even a Campbell understands the needs of an isolated people," she answered, shouting the words into the biting wind. "We are no less mindful than you of the importance of contact between our kin."

Niall shook his head at the farcical situation he had undertaken. This was no timorous, shrinking young girl he held in his arms, no untutored woman he could intimidate through implied threats. She was vocal and sarcastic, and contentious.

She was nothing like Laurie, whose changeable moods had echoed the shifting winds and fickle skies of the Highlands. In Meg's place, Laurie would have wept and pleaded for release. All the while she would have fondled the dirk that she would employ against her enemies.

Instead Meg Campbell railed and accused, and trusted to her guardian for deliverance. That was but the smallest difference between the two women, however.

Laurie was dead.

✧

It was night, and a light snow had started to fall when the horses slowed and came to a stop. Niall handed Meg into Ian's arms, then jumped down from his steed. To her surprise, he held out his arms, and Ian handed her over without comment.

Niall carried her into a small stone cottage where a peat fire blazed a welcome, its musty smoke disappearing through a tiny hole in the center of the thatched roof. There were two rough benches against one wall, and a rusted cooking pot near the fire. Sleeping pallets were piled atop each other across the room. It was a rude but warm shelter that promised, at the least, a dry night and a semblance of warmth.

Niall laid her on the rush covered floor beside the fire pit. She shivered from the wetness of the melting snow on her hair, and turned toward the fire. When he placed a dry plaid around her shoulders, she clenched her fists in the rough cloth.

"Elizabeth?" she asked in a quiet murmur.

"She rests, mistress, as should you." There was an odd timbre to Niall's voice, an unexpected softness that seemed foreign to his earlier manner.

Tension coiled in her belly and she sat up to look at Niall. "Have you brought us to Glencoe?"

"Hush," he said, and began to unwrap the dark plaid from about his chest. He looked down at her and smiled mockingly.

Meg stifled a little cry of dismay. Niall lifted the worn lawn shirt over his head, exposing a broad scarred chest. He placed the wet shirt close to the fire, then bent toward her, bronze muscles gleaming in the firelight.

Now it comes, she thought, moving her hand toward her ankle. *Blood for blood.* Her fingertips touched the sheath of her dirk.

CHAPTER 4

"Lie back down," Niall said, as she started to sit up in protest. When she didn't move, he pushed her down flat. He moved beside her and lay down, pulling a heavy dark gray blanket over them. His arm went around her waist and she held herself rigid against it.

"I have no plans to dishonor you tonight," he told her in a bored voice. "Be still and try to rest. It's been a long day."

Across the room, on the other side of the fire pit, she saw Andrew covering Elizabeth with a similar blanket. Then he lay down next to the girl, his huge body acting as a wall of physical warmth.

Meg's heartbeat slowed. The MacDonalds were only trying to keep their hostages from freezing during the long night. But how could the man think she would lie here with him so close to her? There was no reason for him to take off his shirt. Lying so close to the fire, it would dry on his body. And it was indecent for him to press against her.

His thighs cupped her bottom, enfolding her in an unwilling intimacy. His hand was only inches from her breast. Meg closed her eyes. He might not plan to dishonor her in reality, but she and Elizabeth would be ruined all the same if anyone learned of this.

His body was so warm and relaxed. If only she could surrender to that warmth, lose her fear in it. She would never be able to accept lying so close to him, but the initial fear was diffused in a mellow haze as she watched the hypnotic dance of the flames. A strange buffer descended on her mind, insulating her from the emotions of the day. Against all logic, Meg closed her eyes.

Niall listened as her breathing settled and her heartbeat slowed its nervous fluttering. His arm remained rigid around her softness; with each breath of his own he inhaled the snowy scent on her dark auburn hair.

He wanted to bury his face in that hair, to feel the silky strands fall across and into his mouth. Would her dark gray eyes lighten in passion? They had glinted like silver daggers when she believed her sister to be in danger. A thread of tension coiled downward from his belly, enticing him to press closer against her.

He felt her relax, escaping like a child into the safety of unconsciousness. She turned a little, the motion positioning the curve of her breast under his hand. He gritted his teeth and inched himself away from the pliable flesh that warmed him through the armor of her heavy clothing.

Niall did not delude himself. It was only her name that kept her safe. Temptation, born of almost a year's self-enforced celibacy, was not strong enough to camouflage the reality of who she was and why she was here. They were ancestral enemies, with generations of spilled blood between them. He turned, and lay on his back facing the darkened peat ceiling above him.

It was a long time before he slept.

Pale fingers of daylight peeked through the thin leather flaps at the windows. Meg lay still, slowly realizing that she had indeed spent the night next to the outlaw. Sometime during the long hours of darkness, their fire had died to a mere simmering hiss. She looked around the room for her sister, but Elizabeth and Andrew were gone.

Where were they? She must find Elizabeth. Did Niall still sleep?

He was turned partially away from her, his breathing coming in a light rhythm. She moved her body a tentative fraction away from him. When there was no response, she began to push herself slowly up from the floor.

His hand tightened over her waist in an iron-like grip. "You wouldn't be leavin' without us, mistress?"

He had been awake the whole time.

She made her eyes narrow as she smiled at him. "Why, I merely thought to explore your Glencoe. I have heard so much about it, you see."

He stared at her. He did not breathe, or blink, or move in any way.

Meg drew a deep breath. "You do understand that it is my duty to try to escape you?" Her voice was under control now, pleasantly courteous as though she were inquiring after the man's health.

Ignoring the question, Niall released her and yawned, stretching his arms out lazily. He threw off the blanket and got up, leaving her curiously chilled by his absence.

She watched him walk to the door of the cottage and open it. His chest was still bare, his nipples hardening from the cold. He stood at the threshold, apparently gazing at the sky. Then he came back and picked his shirt up from beside the fire. He pulled it over his head, then offered her his cloak.

Standing, she took it from him and draped it about her shoulders. She was trembling from much more than the cold, but she stiffened her back against the betraying shivers.

As though he read her mind, Niall smiled at her. "We will ride to Blackwater today." He walked from the cottage and whistled for his horse. The creature reared and pawed the air several times in a magnificent flurry of hoof flung snow before Niall swung onto its bare back.

Outraged, Meg vented her emotions on Jamie and Ian, who had awakened and were watching the scene with great interest.

"How dare he not even respond to me?"

Jamie stiffened at the shrillness of her voice. "Niall does not have to respond to you. He does not have to explain."

"I see," she said venomously. She mimicked Niall's arrogant attitude, squaring her shoulders and lifting her nose in the air. "The mighty MacDonald issues his orders and you all obey like trained pups, is that it? Have you no self respect? No minds of your own? How can you blindly follow a man who will not even grant you the train of his thinking?"

"You misunderstand, lady, " Jamie's voice was curt and he took her arm roughly. He put a hand on her arm and escorted her to the doorway. "It is only you to whom he will not give explanations. We have no need of them."

Realizing her mistake in criticizing the older brother, Meg changed her tactics. She smiled at Jamie pleadingly.

"I beg your pardon. It is my fear that causes me speak so, fear for my sister and myself. I do not even know where she is at this moment. Think for a moment, how you would feel, taken from your home and not told what will happen to you?"

She turned the full force of her entreating gaze on him, and Jamie swallowed hard. Meg's breath quickened, but her face was sweetly earnest and distraught as she continued her ambush.

"You and your brothers are good men," she flattered him with a lift of her eyes. "I can see that by the way you care for each other. This was indeed a mistake, unfortunate for us all. Will you not help us to return to our home, Jamie?" His name was a caress on her lips and the young boy blushed.

Well pleased with her work, Meg smiled deeply at him. "Every moment we stay here places you and your brothers in greater trouble. Would it not be best for all of us if we were to have the use of two fast horses? My guardian need never know that we did not lose our way in the forest. You have only to tell me where my sister is, and we shall be on our way."

Jamie opened his mouth to respond, but Ian reached out and removed Meg's arm from his brother's grasp.

"Idiot!" he scoffed good-naturedly. "She is trying to use you for her own ends. Niall has said we ride today and that is what we do. Keep your eyes in your head and your foolishness to yourself, else Niall will be sending you back to old Annie for more schooling."

Abashed, Jamie allowed his brother to propel Meg out the door ahead of him to where Andrew was standing with the horses. Elizabeth was already mounted on Andrew's beast, and the big man had his hand on the horse's flank.

The snow had stopped during the night, and the small clearing where the cottage stood glistened like crystallized sugar in the rosy daylight that peeked through drooping white branches of fir and pine. If this is Glencoe, 'tis a fairyland, Meg thought. *Nay, not now,* came the quick answer in her mind, *but it was.*

She gritted her teeth in frustration at her own perfidy. *I must remember my plans.* The only hope was to continue on her present course of flirtation. Sooner or later one of these men would succumb to her. She had no doubt of it, having seen the same game orchestrated in Edinburgh many times. Niall would surely exact a terrible price from whichever of them betrayed him and helped her and Elizabeth to escape. That, however, was not her concern. Getting back to Glenlyon and Chesthill was. And preferably, getting back before any more innocent people were punished over this ill conceived episode.

Once Robert Campbell returned to Glencoe, more bloodshed would befall the MacDonalds. Additional lives would be lost at the hands of her clan and they would never recover from the infamy or regain their once honorable standing in the eyes of other Highlanders.

"Not at my hands," Meg vowed to herself, and allowed Ian to lift her to the back of his horse.

Niall broke the silence. "Nay. The lady will ride with me again. I have no mind to let her try her wiles on any but myself."

Meg's mouth dropped open in surprise. The oldest brother would not prove to be as easy a mark as the others might. More to the point, she did not relish another long ride as the partner of Niall MacDonald. The memory of his body heat still stung her in too many places.

Ian lifted Meg down from his horse and walked her the few steps over to where his brother waited. Sensing her distress, he whispered in her ear, "Keep your own counsel, Meg, and strive not to anger him further."

She felt a genuine flash of gratitude for his manner. "Thank you." Her voice was gentle and soft, and Ian stared at her, bemused by the change.

Above them Niall observed the little exchange. "There was never trouble in Scotland without a Campbell to lay the fire," he said to Ian. "Remember that, brother, lest you find yourself standing in hot boots. She rides with me because I will not have you sacrificed to whatever scheme she has in her head."

Ian's face paled at the rebuke, but he knelt on the ground and he clasped his hands together for Meg's foot. It left her no choice but to take the hand that Niall bent to offer. She shifted her weight to Ian's hands, and raised her arms. Niall swung her up before him on the great horse, his strong arms holding her steady.

"I trust you do not mind riding with me?" his voice was excruciatingly polite, a devastating mimicry of the cultured tones she had used but moments before.

Meg tossed her head, whipping her long auburn hair against his face. She was determined not to let her nervousness show. "I am sure, sir, that with such fine gentlemen as escorts, I need have no fear at all." She smiled over at Jamie, now mounted and waiting beside Ian for the signal to ride.

The boy flushed, making his freckles stand out starkly against his white face as the blush receded.

Niall kicked his horse. The black started off at a run, and Meg found herself forced to rely on her captor's arms for steadiness.

The men had not taken provisions this time, she noted as they rode away under the parting clouds. Their destination must be close by. The snow curtained everything so that she could fix no landmarks in her mind, and the trails they followed were little more than cattle paths, but that was of small concern. She had ridden through vast stretches of forest in Argyll with little problem. Glenlyon lay behind them, to the south. When the time and the opportunity came she would be able to make her way home.

They had only ridden for about an hour when Meg's body began to ache from the repeated exercise. Accustomed though she was to riding, she thought that in the past two days she had done more riding than ever in her life. She wondered if her backside would be bruised at the end of the adventure and gasped at the thought.

Niall tightened his hold on her. Embarrassed by her thoughts, even though he could not have perceived them, Meg pulled the collar of his cloak up about her face.

He spoke to her, his words disappearing into the wind. "Only a few more miles, mistress. Do you need to rest?"

Wanting no courtesy from this man, she shook her head to signify that she did not, and he spurred his horse on, heading straight into the snowfall. Once again, Meg felt herself lulled by the motion and gait of the horse. Niall's closeness was unsettling and she closed her eyes to shut out his nearness. But the image of his darkly fascinating face rose to dominate her thoughts.

Her emotions rebelled at her attempts to regiment them, and Meg found her imagination tracing the shape of his mouth and his chiseled profile. Only the sword scar on his cheek kept him from being perfectly beautiful and even that was compelling, a mysterious complement to his otherwise flawless face.

She reproached herself again. He was an enemy, as were his brothers, even though she and Elizabeth were innocent of any crime against them. Only their names made them foes, and that was a truth that could never be altered.

Meg thought about the other men too, wondering how they might best be used in her scheme. Andrew, she dismissed. The giant was too smitten with Elizabeth and too loyal to Niall to fall for any flirtation. Ian had possibilities though, as did young Jamie. Both were obviously attracted to her, Meg thought, and although Ian was interesting and flirtatious, the less experienced Jamie would come closest to falling for her plan.

Meg wrinkled her forehead in thought. If she could manage to engage the affections of both brothers and somehow play them against each other, she would have a better chance of escape. It was not a pretty idea. But in this situation anything, short of murder, was acceptable. She shivered at the thought of more killing. But her mind was made up. She would continue her mild flirtation with Jamie while complimenting and flattering Ian as much as possible.

There was a good possibility that one or both brothers might be persuaded that they stood a better chance of winning her regard if she were no longer a prisoner. Perhaps the hope of negotiating with Robert and thereby preventing another massacre would be all the weapon she would need. She must grasp and use whatever tools Fate put before her, and if the hearts of the MacDonald brothers happened to be those tools, she would use them, or else they might lose more than their hearts.

"Enough people have died already."

Meg did not realize that she had spoken aloud until Niall responded.

"You are not, I am sure, speaking of Campbell deaths."

Her cheeks stung at his rebuke. "I did not mean to speak at all, but if I must defend my thoughts to you, then know that they were on the lives of all the good people, both yours and mine, who must pay for the greed and ambition of our chiefs."

"Why should you regret MacDonald deaths?" he asked.

"I regret any stupidity fostered by arrogant men who require the less fortunate to carry out their plans." Her pointed chin lifted.

"Then you are saying that your guardian acted out of greed and ambition?"

"Aye!" she spat, furious at his goading. "He did. And I have told him so and anyone else who would listen."

"And yet you do yourself reap benefits from the rewards granted him by your king."

His inference was logical, but Meg shook her head in denial. "Nay, sir, although I would remind you that William is your king as well. My sister and I live under Robert Campbell's roof for the moment, but we do not look to him for our board. Our grandmother," her eyes filled with tears that she quickly wiped away, "our grandmother left her estate in trust for us, administered by the Earl of Argyll until we are of age or married."

"And are you approaching either state?" He sounded truly interested rather than argumentative.

"Elizabeth is but fifteen and so will be under the care of our guardian much longer than I. Argyll is not unkind to us, merely indifferent. At least that was so until he sent us to Glenlyon." Meg realized that her words might sound ungrateful and hurried to explain. "He is quite busy with his affairs, you see, having so many holdings to manage."

"Indeed," Niall MacDonald's tone was wry. "And he adds to them constantly, I am sure, enjoying the rewards of Robert Campbell's activities."

Meg cursed her runaway words. Why did she feel compelled to explain her life to this outlaw? Was it his nearness, his authority, or his strange magnetism?

Was his behavior deliberate, forcing inane chatter from her against her will and invading her private thoughts with his brooding eyes? Meg took a deep calming breath. He was baiting her, hoping she would reveal her plan for escape. He would be disappointed.

"I do not approve of what my guardian did at the order of the king, sir. Nor do I approve of the crimes committed by your kinsmen in the past." She heard him growl and hurried on before her courage failed. "But you have unfairly taken revenge on my sister and me, who had no part in the matter of Glencoe. I beg you," and she turned halfway around in his arms, fixing him with her gaze, "release us at once so that further deaths will be averted."

He did not take his eyes from the path. "The matter of Glencoe, mistress, is the matter of a massacre. Revenge and death are inevitable results from this 'matter' as you name it. Honor demands a righting of the wrong done us."

"Honor will not fill your bellies or bring your dead back to life."

"You are right there. But you and your sister offered yourselves up in this game by ignoring your guardian's orders, and we will garner every bit of fortune possible from the hand you have dealt us. Ransom. Enough to feed my kin for the next few months."

Meg's anger unleashed itself full force. "You damned arrogant thieving raider! Do you know how Elizabeth and I responded to the news of the massacre? We gathered food and blankets for the survivors! We sent supplies out with the help of our minister. How dare you say we offered ourselves up to your rude savage tactics?" She caught her breath and jerked away from the warmth of his body.

The other men heard Meg's outburst and almost as one unit, their horses fell back, allowing the black to outpace them. It was obvious that they wanted no part of this argument.

But the argument had stopped, it seemed, for Niall did not speak again until they topped a hill, entering a thick wood. Then he reined the black in, motioning his brothers to stop. When all had reached the edge of the wood, he dismounted, keeping one hand on the black's halter.

"This is Blackwater. It is not on any map, and the Campbells have no hint that it even exists." He looked at them all in turn, his gaze coming to rest on Meg's face. "You will be introduced as visitors. There are children here and I will not have them alarmed. Do you understand?"

A knifing pain went through Meg's heart. Children. Survivors of the massacre. God help us, she thought. How can we face them?

She clenched the black's mane between her fingers.

CHAPTER 5

Niall's meanness was surely deliberate. For a hate wrenching second Meg wanted to bury her dirk deep in his chest. Time dropped away; she was aware only of the warning radiating from his probing eyes. At last, forcing her heartbeat to slow and willing her cheeks not to flush with anger, she lifted her head.

"I assure you, sir," she said, "my sister and I are quite fond of children and do not make a habit of taking revenge on helpless little ones."

"I will hold you to your word, Meg Campbell," Niall said. His deep voice sent a chill cascading up her spine. "I will not have them frightened or harmed in any way."

She gave him a short nod to signify her understanding. "Why have you brought us here, if you are so worried about these children? Why did you keep us at Glencoe for only one night?"

"The keep is fit only for ghosts to inhabit now," he said, and turned his head away. "You will be safer here at Blackwater. It is unknown to our pursuers."

He led the way into the forest, guiding the black upon which Meg rode. She watched the dark man before her curiously, trying to understand the fascination he held for her. Of a certainty, he was attractive, intelligent, and powerful. There was something more, something she glimpsed in his face as he spoke of the children.

Meg wondered whose children they were, and how many of them were living in this woodland hiding place. She guessed that they were survivors of the massacre, innocent victims whose parents had been cut down in defense of their homes and their lord. Oh Robert, she thought, we will never be able to atone for this.

They rounded a curve in the path and heard the high pitched laughter of children. Meg's attitude softened, and she glanced back at Elizabeth, who had begun to smile in anticipation.

Before them was a tiny thatched cottage with a thin wisp of peat smoke rising from the chimney. There were two small girls running merrily in front of it. They looked up as the horses approached and with a united shriek of joy, ran toward Niall and his brothers.

Laughing, Niall went down on one knee, gathering both girls to his breast. Ian and Jamie dismounted and joined the merry reunion.

"Bad uncles! You've been gone forever!" exclaimed the tiniest girl.

"What did you bring us?" asked the other, possessively beginning to search Niall's sporran.

"Give us a kiss, sweethearts, and say good afternoon to our guests first. Presents come later."

Obediently the two girls stopped their plunder and kissed each of the men full on the mouth. Niall swept an arm around them both and lifted them up so that they could see Meg, and Elizabeth, who still sat with Andrew on his big brown horse.

"Good afternoon!" they chorused.

Meg heard Elizabeth replying to the children, but she was so astounded at the difference in Niall MacDonald that she found herself unable to speak. Obviously there were many facets to this man. Not for the first time, she regretted the enmity that stood between them.

The female replica of Andrew was named Beth, much to Meg's amusement, and Elizabeth was very taken with the child. The oldest girl, Flora, was sturdy and brown and resembled no member of the family that Meg had yet met. Both children seemed hearty and happy and both obviously adored their uncle Niall.

Niall reached deep into his sporran and brought out two candies, marzipan, perhaps, although from a distance Meg couldn't be certain. The little girls crammed the sweets into their mouths, squealing with delight at the surprise. It was evident that candy was an unusual treat for them.

Andrew jumped to the ground and assisted Elizabeth in dismounting. Niall, alert to the movement, relaxed his hold on his nieces. He walked over to his horse and offered his hand to Meg.

Refusing to thank him for his assistance, she dismounted and shook her skirts out, trying to look anywhere except into his eyes. When it became obvious that he was waiting for some response from her, Meg said, "The children are lovely. Do they live here?"

Niall smiled at her and his voice was as cold as the wind that swept over the glen. "Aye, Mistress Campbell, this is their home. They are the daughters of my twin sister, Laurie."

"And is your sister here also?" inquired Meg, looking about curiously.

"She is not. She died in the snows the night of the massacre, protecting the body of her dead husband. And the babe in her belly died with her." He turned away from Meg, and walked back to where the children stood watching.

"Come girls," Niall scooped a child up under each arm, "let's go inside and you can tell me about the tricks you've been playing on Duncan." He cocked an interested ear as Beth began to recount each and every activity of the days while Niall was gone.

Meg remained where Niall left her, standing very still on the path. Speechless from his curt revelation, she looked over at the brothers who were busying themselves with the horses.

Elizabeth walked over to comfort her sister. She offered a stained handkerchief, but Meg brushed it aside.

"I heard what he said," the younger girl's voice was soft. "I do not believe he meant to be so harsh."

"He meant it," said Meg. "He intended to shock me and he succeeded very well." She shook her head. "I do not know what will become of us in this place. Anger and bitterness are all around us and we are hostages against a pain that can never be healed."

Elizabeth took Meg's hands in her own. "With the grace of God any pain can be healed, Meg. You must remember that He has a reason and a plan behind everything that happens."

Meg looked at her sister, the pleading face, the earnest eyes. What if it were Elizabeth whose blood stained the snow that night?

"Where is God's hand in the massacre, Elizabeth? How can you say God had a reason for that atrocity? Only a devil could have conceived such a scheme. A devil named Campbell of Breadalbane. I renounce any God that could have a part in it and I would almost renounce my own clan!" She wrenched her hands from Elizabeth's grasp and covered her face.

Obviously shocked at the blasphemy, Elizabeth paled and would have swooned had not Andrew moved to assist her.

"We'll go in now, " Andrew told them, and put a hand over their arms to guide them to the cottage.

"I cannot go in there!" cried Meg. "I cannot face those children!"

He looked at her gloomily. "We face them every day, mistress, and it gets no easier. So come, and we'll have some hot cider. Duncan will have it laced with usquebaugh, good Scottish whiskey, and it will be just what you need to take the edge off your nerves."

There was nothing Meg could do but follow them inside. Jamie and Ian walked behind her, and she could not look at them, either, as she entered the home of their dead sister. To herself, she cursed Robert Campbell, King William, and everyone else who had anything to do with the massacre. This could never be atoned for, not by tears or prayers or blood.

Different measures were called for in this situation. Shoulders straight, she entered the tiny dwelling with a smile on her face.

"What a lovely home you have, mistresses," she told the two little girls. "I would love to live in an enchanted forest like this. Do you often see fairies hereabouts?"

Beth turned sparkling blue eyes upon the strange lady in the torn riding dress. "Fairies?" the little girl asked excitedly. "Have you ever seen a fairy?"

"Oh yes," Meg assured her, "why, when I was your age I used to play with the fairies in my grandmother's garden. There were ever so many of them." She looked around the croft admiringly. "And this is just the sort of place they love to visit. There are probably two or three hiding now, watching us."

Beth clapped her hands in delight and Niall looked down at Meg with a strange expression on his face. Both fists were planted on his hips, and he was looking at her as though she had suddenly sprouted two heads.

Solemn eyed Flora removed her thumb from her mouth and said, "Father Michael said there's no such thing as fairies."

"That's probably just because he's never met any," Meg answered. "You know how some grown ups are, unless they see something with their own eyes they can't believe its real." She sat down on a short stool next to Flora. "Who is Father Michael?"

"Our priest," answered Ian when it became apparent that no one else was going to speak. "Of late, he finds it politic to visit friends in other areas."

Elizabeth, taking Meg's cue, also sat down with the two small girls. "My name is Elizabeth, which is very like unto your name," she smiled at Beth. "Isn't that nice?"

"Umm humm," Beth nodded and proceeded to climb up onto Elizabeth's lap. "You have pretty hair." The child ran her fingers through Elizabeth's long blond curls, still glossy even after two days of harsh weather, and Meg saw Andrew smile in approval.

"Will you tell me about yourself, Mistress Flora?" asked Meg. "And what it is like to live in an enchanted forest?"

The brown haired girl shook her head and twisted away, burying her face against Niall's leg.

A new voice spoke up from the other side of the cottage, startling Meg.

"Ye talk a good one, lass, but ye'll not get close to our Flora with your fairy stories."

The speaker was an old man, she saw, with a twisted arm.

"How do you do, sir," she said. "I am Meg Campbell and this is my sister, Elizabeth."

The old man hobbled over to get a good look at them. "You'd never be needing to tell me that you're Campbells. I can see it in your faces and your crooked mouths." He spat into the fire. Then he raised a fist at Niall. "Why have ye brought them here?"

Niall remained where he stood, eyeing Meg. "Why indeed," he muttered so low that she was not sure she heard. But to the old man he said, "We will ransom them, Duncan. They left the protection of their guardian and rode straight into our hands. I brought them here for safety."

The crotchety old man glowered a moment longer before turning his back on the two girls in a display of contempt. "And how long must the wee ones suffer this insult?"

Niall laid a gentle hand on Duncan's shoulder. "I will send word to Glenlyon as soon as the weather permits. Until then, they will remain here. They can help with the children, Duncan. It will be a pleasant change for the little ones."

"Excuse me," Meg interrupted, causing Niall to frown slightly. "I believe your story has a few holes. First of all, you obviously arranged for us to drink poisoned wine. Otherwise we'd not have been so easily taken. And now you say that you will send word to Robert when the weather permits? That could take days."

"Or weeks," muttered Ian.

"We cannot stay here that long." She looked at Elizabeth. "We have no other clothing, you surely do not have enough food to sustain us all, and this place is so tiny."

It was the wrong thing to say, she saw. The men all looked at her as though she were an unfamiliar and unwelcome intrusion.

She hurried on with her protest. "Robert will come looking for us. You place yourselves in jeopardy to keep us here."

She saw Ian nod in agreement and she moved to take the advantage. "Duncan," Meg addressed the sour old man, "You must know what will happen if we are found here."

"We all know very clearly what the stakes are in this game," Niall replied as Duncan MacDonald raised his fist again. "But our options are limited. The weather does not permit any changes to my decision. You will stay here until Andrew can ride to Glenlyon or to Fort William with the letter of ransom."

Elizabeth gasped. "He will surely be killed!"

Andrew looked gratified at her concern, but agreed with his brother. "'Tis only to deliver the demand," he explained. "They will not harm a messenger when your safety depends on it." He folded his arms across his chest and stood solidly in the center of the cottage.

Meg could only fume at their unreasonable attitudes. "Is death such a desirable state?" she demanded. "So much that you will place these innocent children in danger to court it?"

Niall bowed to her. "It would seem so, mistress. You and your sister will stay here as our guests. Jamie and Ian will remain also, to be sure that you continue to enjoy our hospitality.

"Andrew," Niall directed his attention to the big man. "You and I will return to Glencoe."

Andrew's disappointment was almost laughable, if Meg could have summed up any such emotion. She was exhausted by the argument and the situation, and had to struggle to keep herself from sagging the moment Niall and Andrew left.

The little girls, Beth and Flora, followed their uncles outside, begging to be taken along. Andrew's deep voice rumbled comfortingly, promising to take them for a ride very soon, but Niall did not speak. Meg imagined him bending to kiss each little forehead before swinging up on his great horse. Then she heard the horses move away and the children calling out their good-byes. What now? she wondered. How long before the soldiers come?

"How will ye explain this to the clan?" Duncan's faded blue eyes were curious as he faced Ian. "They'll have heard ye arrive. Ransom two Campbells? 'Tis a dream! The clan will kill them."

Ian shrugged. "Nay. The clan isna to be told. These ladies are our guests for a time. Jamie and I will take care of any questions." He looked at his younger brother. "In fact, we'll take care of it now, before anyone comes calling."

Jamie nodded and walked outside, his thick red curls lifting in the stiff wind. The belted kilt he wore lifted slightly about his knees, but he seemed unbothered by the chilly air. Meg watched him distractedly, wondering if all

Highlanders were so casual about the cold. She had heard stories that the warriors of old bathed in frigid streams and ran about unclothed so as to be hardened against harsh weather. From what she had seen of the MacDonald brothers, she was well inclined to believe it.

"The other crofts are not far away," Ian broke in on her thoughts. "The people will doubtless wish to see you. We have been isolated from news and friendly faces. When they come, you are not to give your name. Should anyone ask, you are of the Cameron clan, and here at Niall's request to help with the children."

"You give orders as well as your brother does," Meg tensed at his careless command. "Why should we lie to them? Is it a habit with you MacDonalds?"

He looked at her calmly, refusing to rise to the insult. "You will do yourself no good by admitting who you are, and you could do great harm. Think for a moment, mistress, what the response would be if you go smiling among our people and introduce yourself as the ward of Robert Campbell?"

She felt the color leave her face, and Ian nodded.

"So my brother and I will spread the news of your coming before they meet you. It will give you time to prepare yourself for the habit of lying." He nodded to Elizabeth and followed Jamie outside.

Duncan settled himself on a long bench close to the fire, and Elizabeth sat gingerly on the rush-covered floor. Meg could hear the voices of Beth and Flora outside as they played. Even the children of Highlanders, it seemed, were immune to the cold.

Meg tightened her borrowed plaid about herself and thought longingly of her grandmother's comfortable town house in Edinburgh. Chesthill, as unhappy as she had been there, was at least warm and dry. How did these people survive in such primitive conditions?

The scent of a pungent herb drifted from Duncan's pipe as Meg sat down beside her sister. When the old man took a sip of whiskey from a jug, she turned her eyes away. The whiskey was undoubtedly a good way to ward off the effects of the harsh weather, and she didn't begrudge the man his drink. But it was hard to sit there, in silent shivering fear, and feel charity in the face of his dislike for her.

She wanted to be gone from this place, safe and removed from all the ugly reminders of hate and poverty. She wanted to be at home. But she and Elizabeth had no home, not really. No more than these people did, a similarity that only made her heart ache right along with her freezing fingers.

✧

Robert Campbell stared with hardly concealed excitement at the messenger who stood before him. The man had obviously ridden hard and fast to deliver his urgent news; the sweat and stains on his clothing and heaviness of his breathing vouched for his haste. But the information he had just presented from the Glenlyon minister, Dr. Kincaid, was intriguingly full of possibilities.

The colonel motioned to one of his men to bring a drink of water to the fatigued messenger. He waited for the man to slake his thirst and then Robert said, "Tell me again just how it is that my wards are in the keeping of the MacDonalds."

The exhausted man straightened at the words and the sarcastic tone in which they were spoken. He wiped away the tiny bead of sweat that trembled at his temple.

"The two girls evaded the company of the minister, sir, riding out without permission. He said they apparently stopped to partake of refreshments and were resting when the MacDonalds came upon them. The minister said the girls were given poisoned wine, no doubt from some traitor in your own household. The empty flask was found, and Dr. Kincaid said the smell from it was bitter."

"I see," Robert mused aloud, turning to study the elaborate display of swords which hung on the wall behind his chair. "Dr. Kincaid allowed my wards to go riding for the afternoon, unguarded, to the very borders of my lands. And while they were resting, a band of outlaws attacked them and took the girls hostage. Do I have it straight?" He turned quickly, catching the messenger off guard.

Nervous now and uncertain how to proceed, the man nodded. "I...ah, suppose that is it, sir."

"You suppose?" The colonel's voice was hard edged. "Or you agree this is the message Dr. Kincaid told you to convey to me?"

"Yes sir! That is exactly the message."

Well pleased, Campbell smiled and tossed a coin to the messenger. "Your service has been invaluable."

The man bowed and left the room as quickly as possible. His part played, he was eager to put as much distance between the commander of Fort William and himself as possible.

In his office, Robert Campbell sat unhurriedly at his table and penned a letter to his commander, Robert Duncanson. He read over it only once before signing his name with a flourish and sprinkling powder over the ink.

With a peremptory gesture he placed the sealed missive in the hand of his personal servant. "See that this is delivered at once."

The servant slipped soundlessly from the room, leaving the colonel to his satisfaction at the way Fate continued to place the unruly MacDonalds in his path. Of course, finally getting rid of that prating minister could prove to a minor problem, but overall, Robert was certain that King William and his Secretary would be supportive of his efforts to regain his kidnapped wards, no matter what the cost. And when the last of the rebellious MacDonalds of Glencoe had been wiped out, His Majesty would be grateful for Robert's help in restoring the royal reputation.

He opened a drawer in his desk and pulled from it a creased, stained letter. Robert's hands trembled as he smoothed the wrinkles from the paper. His orders of last winter from his commander; a mandate to exterminate the MacDonalds of Glencoe.

Composure failed him as he stared at the words. He was no more than a failed lackey, hired by the powers behind the Crown to do their dirty work. It was a position he had put himself in, he knew, and the bitter taste of it would haunt his dreams for the rest of his life.

Gambling away his lands, and squandering his money on whiskey had put Robert squarely into the hands of Argyll and Breadalbane. When the orders came, he had no choice but to carry them out, no matter that his own niece had married into the clan at Glencoe. In one wretched night, he lost niece, honor, and pride.

Now perhaps he could redeem some of his pride, at any rate. Robert stuffed the order back into his desk, and shoved aside his memories along with it.

A map of the Highlands hung in the office and Robert went to it now, studying the areas which were currently held by his clan. For King William to enrich those holdings by granting Glencoe to Robert for his loyalty would naturally impress Robert's uncle, the Earl of Argyll. In addition, there were the two girls in whom Argyll had a very personal interest.

Robert had long wished to become close to his uncle, and willingly volunteered to take on the guardianship of the two daughters of the Earl's favorite cousin. He hoped that action alone would be enough to place him in a favorable position with the Campbell, but Argyll was one of the old tough Highlanders, who trusted no one, especially family, until they had proved their worth to the clan.

Although Robert's part in the Glencoe affair the previous winter won him a promotion, Argyll was critical of the breach of tradition. Robert had accepted MacIaian's hospitality before slaying him in his hall. No mention was made of the king's order or of the part played by the Earl of Breadalbane.

It was not only Argyll who criticized him, and Robert's mouth tightened as he thought of Meg, his seventeen year old ward. The arrogance of the girl was beyond belief. She presumed on her distant relationship with Argyll at every turn, defying Robert's least command. It was, he thought, just recompense for her to now be at the mercy of the very renegades she so outspokenly defended.

If only Meg had been abducted, he might be slower to think about revenge. But Elizabeth, the younger sister, was another problem. Robert knew that Argyll had plans for Elizabeth that did not include death or dishonor by reivers. The young girl with her sweet face and gentle ways was being groomed to take her place at court, to one day become Argyll's eyes and ears.

The Earl had even sent his personal minister to Glenlyon with the girls, installing Dr. Kincaid as a watchdog to report each and every movement of the household. Under Kincaid's castigating eye, Robert became forced to enjoy his whiskey and his maids at the Fort rather than in the comfort of his own home. Now, with the minister's own admission of failure in his duty, the way was clear to be rid of all of them.

Robert rubbed his hands together in satisfaction. It was a nice, almost perfectly wrapped gift that Dr. Kincaid had placed in his lap. One that Robert would take great pleasure in unwrapping.

✧

The scar on Niall MacDonald's face was white with tension and his jaw clenched against his unrest as he led his brothers to his primitive camp beside the banks of the frozen Coe river. Everywhere he looked or walked or slept, he encountered the faces of the dead.

They called to him in his dreams and haunted his waking hours with equal persistence, reminding him of his failed duty. He held their censure possessively. It was all he could do for them now.

He could not turn time back to that day almost a year ago when he had been so determined to satiate himself with his mistress. The letter of warning had come in the morning and lain unopened on her dressing table until late evening. Too late for Niall to send word to the glen, too late for him to do more than ride like a madman straight into the face of the blizzard that blocked the pass and kept Glenlyon's reinforcements away. Robert Campbell's soldiers had been equal to their task, however, and left only a few survivors to spread the tale throughout Scotland.

Niall's strides lengthened, as though to leave the specters of his failed duty behind him. He could never change what happened, no matter how many private vows he made. The empty keep of Glencoe reminded him daily of his loss. There would be no respite for him until Campbell blood mingled with the snow where MacDonalds had fallen.

And never again would a woman come between him and his honor.

Niall shook his head to clear it of the tormenting images. The coming conference with his brothers was of paramount importance now, memories could be dealt with later.

Ian and Andrew squatted down next to the small fire that burned in a tiny ring of gray stones. The night was black and heavy. It closed around them like a shroud, shutting out the reality of the scorched walls and devastation of MacIaian's once proud home.

Niall spared a brief glance toward the ruined chapel, and nodded slowly. *The Campbells will answer,* he promised the dead who watched him. *You will be avenged.*

"Where is Jamie?" Andrew asked.

"He is watching the pass." Niall gazed into the fire. "'Tis only a matter of time before we have visitors and I want advance warning this time."

He looked his brothers up and down, resolution keen on his tanned, rugged face.

"You have told the others?"

Ian nodded. "Aye. Rose, I think, suspects something. But she will keep silent. We have said that the girls are Camerons, visiting until summer. No questions were asked."

"Good." Niall nodded. "Curiosity is inevitable, and they must eventually meet. 'Tis lucky the cottages at Blackwater are so scattered. My only concern is old Annie. It will be difficult for her to hold her tongue once Duncan tells her the real story. And he will tell her."

"Aye," Ian agreed. "For all the bad blood between those two, they've no secrets. But Annie will be thinking of the ransom and the food that will fill our bellies. She will be all quiet."

"Have you a plan, brother?" asked Andrew, fidgeting with his sporran.

"Aye, of a sort," Niall answered. "We must be ready to die if need be. "Robert Campbell will come and we must be ready for him. I will not let him escape a second time." He stroked the scar on the side of his face.

Ian's handsome face wore an unsettled expression. "I thought we would just ransom the girls."

Stubbornness sharpened Niall's tone. "The plan has changed. Do you really believe Campbell will be content to let it go at that? By now he has sought royal approval to avenge this insult. He will carry Argyll's authority with him as he rides."

"That old fox would never put himself in danger," Andrew shook his head, sending the red braids swinging about his face. "He'll stay well out of the way until 'tis all finished."

"I agree," Niall said. "And for the moment, that is indeed what I hope will happen."

Ian and Andrew looked at Niall curiously.

"Robert Campbell, now a colonel in His Majesty's service, is quite confident of his ability to rout the MacDonald dogs." Niall's even white teeth flashed humorlessly. "He will come with his contingent of men, thinking to use the force of many to eliminate the problem of a few renegades living on his borders."

"Niall, we planned a ransom only. Now we are planning an ambush? How will that help us? If he brings all his men —" Ian's bewilderment was clear.

"We will lure him back to Glencoe like a fox into a sheep herd, using his wards as the enticement. Then we will scatter, Jamie taking one girl to Laidon and you, Ian, will take the other toward Skye. Campbell, if I guess rightly, will choose to follow the easiest path, to Laidon, and when he divides his men, we will be ready to greet him there."

"'Tis suicide, unless we can send word to Fergus for help." Andrew's voice showed eagerness at the thought of battle.

"Aye," Ian murmured, shaking his head.

"Perhaps," Niall's black eyes sought the ghosts in the shadows behind his brothers. "We shall see. Fergus and Alan planned to arrive soon anyway, to aid in the rebuilding. Any road, with the two girls split up, Jamie will still have at least one hostage to bargain with even if Campbell should succeed in retrieving the other. You will go over the plan with Jamie tonight. This is the last word I will say on it, Ian. You are either with me or against me."

Ian chewed his lower lip for a moment. "I am always with you, Niall. But the older girl, Meg, may be a problem. She'll need to be guarded every moment."

"Are you volunteering?" Niall's sardonic question made his brother flush.

Opting not to answer directly, Ian rose and winked at his brother. "Meg Campbell is an interesting proposition for any man."

"She is a Campbell and your sworn enemy," Niall reminded him.

Andrew had obviously been wrestling with an uncomfortable thought during Niall's proposal of his plan. Now he spoke. "'Tis not the fighting I mind, ye ken, but I suppose we— that is, do we have to give them both back?" he asked hesitantly.

Niall's snapping black eyes almost knocked Andrew down. "In the name of God, did any man ever have such a family? I cannot tell where your loyalties lie today, Andrew. Have you lost your senses entirely?"

Stung by the accusation, the big man tried to defend himself. "She is so small and delicate. I feel responsible for her."

Ian laughed and rapped Andrew on top of his head. "You are indeed a great imbecile. There is nothing delicate about Meg Campbell."

"Of course not," the wounded Andrew tried to explain. "I was speaking of Elizabeth."

Niall and Ian looked at each other and shook their heads.

The three brothers walked back along the path that led from the ruined keep toward the river, Ian and Andrew laughing and teasing each other about their two winsome hostages. But Niall was silent. He, too, regretted the circumstances that had delivered these girls into his hands. Another time, another place, and even he might be inclined to pursue an acquaintance with Meg Campbell. Now, Niall had the specter of his tarnished honor to protect him. But a man's needs were powerful. Ian would bear careful watching.

CHAPTER 6

The survivors were a subdued group as they trickled into Duncan's cottage, even in the midst of their curiosity about the new arrivals. It was customary, Meg learned, for everyone to gather with the old man each evening for a bit of song and prayer. The clan restrained themselves, waiting until nightfall to approach Meg and Elizabeth but now they arrived with warm smiles for the two Cameron girls.

Elizabeth's natural talent for conversation eased the first awkwardness, and the people accepted the strange story of unannounced visitors with the normal graciousness of the Highlands. Soon they were talking like old friends, although with strained speech and faces full of the grief of the past year.

Meg found it a bit harder to handle the questions than her sister did as she turned her attention to the interest of an older woman named Rose, whose husband had died in the massacre.

Rose was a tired looking woman with a soft mouth that looked as though it had struggled against sadness one too many times. She wore a white *arisaid*, the plaid favored by Highland gentlewomen. The deep red sleeves of her dress were shiny with wear. A moss-green colored shawl of soft lamb's wool covered her bodice for warmth. Rose was eager for news of the outside world, asking fervently if the Cameron clan planned to come to the aid of the MacDonalds.

Meg bit the bottom of her lip as she looked at Rose. "I think Niall would have more news than I about that," she replied honestly, "he has not told us of his plans."

"Are you from Lochaber?" Rose asked, referring to the chief branch of the Camerons. Her dark eyes were wistful. "James and I visited there once, when we were newly married."

"Um, no," Meg answered quickly, "from Erracht. I have never been to Lochaber." She looked about for something to distract Rose's questions, and spying Beth and Flora in a corner, excused herself to go check on them. It was much safer to be playing with the children.

Sitting with the girls, she was able to observe the MacDonald clan closely. There were five men besides Ian, Jamie, and Duncan. They were all older than Niall, and were obviously closely related. Every man wore a kilt, and as she found herself surrounded by so much MacDonald plaid, Meg's nervousness grew.

She watched the three women shoot quick, appraising glances at her and Elizabeth. One in particular, a red haired girl with slanted green eyes, eyed Meg with open curiosity, and after the first quick greeting, did not speak to either sister.

Meg watched the girl flirt first with Jamie and then Ian, and against her will, felt a slow quivering of what might have been jealousy rising in her heart. Determined to shake the feeling, she left Beth and Flora and walked outside to look up at the sky. Behind her, Duncan struck up a tune on an old fiddle, and the mournful strains of an old Scottish lament issued from the cottage.

Meg shivered, wrapping the MacDonald plaid closely about her shoulders. No wonder everyone looked so sober, if all they did was pray and sing doleful songs about the past. It was a far jump from the evening entertainments in Edinburgh, and the sophisticated attentions of the gentlemen she knew there. That life seemed distant, and slightly unreal. She walked along the narrow path from Duncan's cottage to the edge of the forest, looking up at the stars that shone in a surprisingly clear sky.

Her thoughts were far from Blackwater, and a sudden rustle in the woods startled her, causing her to slip on some small rocks. With a cry of pain, she went down, landing on her side with the rocks pressing into her thigh.

"How stupid." She rubbed her ankle, responding to the shooting pain. Now she'd have to hobble back like a careless child. Meg grimaced as she tried to put her weight on the sore ankle. Easier thought than accomplished.

A dark shape stood before her, blocking out the stars, and she saw Niall MacDonald holding out his arm in assistance.

"Thank you," she said, lifting her chin at an angle, "but I am fine."

His voice held a tinge of humor. "'Twould seem that you are not, mistress. May I help you?"

She gripped his hand and rose. Then she took a step forward to demonstrate her independence, and the offended ankle turned with a wrench.

Meg sat down in an inelegantly heap, and looked up at him. "That really hurt." Her tone gave no hint of her pain.

He shook his head and reached to help her stand. "It is not necessary for you to refuse every offer of help."

She bit her lip against the effort it took to stand beside him. "You're correct of course. Thank you." She took a step forward with her good foot and dragged the other behind. Pain shot through her ankle again and tears sprang to her eyes.

She turned her head away, but not soon enough. Niall reached to take her in his arms and lifted her as easily as he would have lifted Beth. He smelled clean and sweet, a testimony to strong herbal soap, and Meg was angry at herself for noticing.

"Please let me walk." She would not look at him, afraid that the anguish in her voice would also show in her face. God in heaven, she did not want to be in this man's arms.

Niall chuckled, his deep voice vibrating against her. "You would not get very far, I'm afraid. I'll take you to old Annie's cottage, 'tis but a few steps away. She is grandmother to all of us, but she's away just now on business of her own. The cottage will be quiet."

How could he know that she dreaded facing the clan again? But even as she questioned his perception, she was glad of it, although meeting the as yet faceless Annie while in his arms was only slightly less daunting a prospect.

He carried her across the half frozen burn, and into Annie's cottage. Its owner was absent, and Meg sent a silent prayer of thanks to Whoever was in charge of the reckless and careless.

It was a comfortable home, with sheep rugs scattered across the floor and a tiny fire smoldering in the hearth. Carefully trimmed pieces of leather covered the two windows of the cottage, secured by wooden pins stuck into the chinks between the stones of the unstreaked wall. Clearly, Annie was a good housekeeper, unlike Duncan, whose cottage walls bore testimony to the ashes and soot from many fires.

Niall settled her down in a creaky rocking chair and turned to light the low candle on the worn oak table. He knelt before the smoldering fire and touched the wick to one of the banked clumps of peat. The thin flame struggled valiantly for a moment or two before it flared. Niall set the candle back on the table, and before Meg had time to react, he untied her laces, then removed her boot in one swift action. Tossing it aside, he sat back on his heels to regard her ankle. He ran one hand over it, and looked up at Meg. His expression was impersonal, as though he were inspecting a wounded animal and Meg was glad of the formality and the shadows in the cottage.

"Does this hurt?"

He was hardly touching her at all, but she was forced to nod. "Yes."

Niall frowned, the cleft in his cheek deepening. "'Tis beginning to swell. Don't move from here," he warned, rising in one quick motion, "I'll be right back."

Meg leaned back in the chair. Her ankle throbbed with the slightest action and there was no way she could even think of going anywhere. A tear trickled from the corner of her right eye and she brushed it away lest he see the evidence of her discomfort.

He was back before she heard him, with a handful of snow that he placed in a cloth and held against her ankle. "We'll just sit here for a bit," the unreadable black eyes held her with their authority, "and give it time to rest."

The freezing snow felt wonderful after the initial shock, and she welcomed its numbing effect. After a few moments, she looked down at him, noting the comfortable way he squatted before her. His hands held her foot and ankle gently, and his touch against her bare skin frightened her in some unnamable way. His shirt sleeves were pushed back, and the sight of the thick black hair on his arms made her breathing quicken.

"Thank you." She didn't quite meet his eyes, but she felt his amusement at her predicament. "It is kind of you to go out of your way to help me."

Niall shrugged, a slight smile showing on his lips. "I am expected to go out of my way when one of my people needs help."

He sounded like some feudal lord. But she was not about to let him play that role. Meg smiled pointedly at the warrior kneeling before her.

"I am not one of your people." It was gently spoken, but she said it to underscore the differences between them. She did meet his gaze this time, unflinching in her resolution to maintain the distance between them.

Niall's eyes flickered, but his words were as quietly uttered as her own. "I am Highland, and you are my responsibility. That makes you as much one of my people as Annie, who is now elder to us all."

If it was a provocation, she was too weary to take it. She closed her eyes, rebelling against her carelessness, against the pain, against him. "Who is Annie, exactly?"

"She is a cousin of MacIaian's", he answered. "A loving old granny who helped raise us all. Annie kept us together after the massacre. She won't like you at all."

"None of them will," Meg said. "And I imagine they will be less than happy with you when they learn of your deceit. Why have you not sent a letter of ransom?"

He didn't respond right away, and when he did, the strangeness of his voice made Meg open her eyes and look searchingly at him.

"Interesting, is it not, that we can both be Highland and still be so far apart?" he asked.

Meg was not certain how to reply. After a moment, she said, "In values, I suppose you mean."

He nodded slowly. "And in other ways. Has there ever been a Campbell who was not involved with plots and conspiracies? While the MacDonalds — "

"The MacDonalds concern themselves with stealing cattle and innocent young women!" Her eyes flashed in defiance.

Niall massaged the flesh above her ankle. "You and your sister are being held honorably. There is a fine old Highland tradition that requires we return our hostages safely once the bargains are made. Did you know that at one time we were allies, Meg Campbell? That our clans fought on the same side for a brief time? We are all sons and daughters of Alba, of Scotland. Yet we murder each other constantly. 'Tis a sad thing," he looked up at her, "and before his death MacIaian had decided to seek a truce."

She raised one eyebrow. "That was a decision made when he realized he could no longer oppose King William. As for plots and conspiracies, your own MacIaian was as guilty of them as any Campbell. The violence is on both sides. Why should I believe your promises of my safety when you will not believe that I would speak to Robert in your defense? No, a MacDonald and a Campbell could never be allies. Not truly. There is too much bad history between us."

Niall smiled bitterly. "I am not proposing an alliance, mistress. I merely reflect on the irony of our mutual birth and mutual dislike. And the sorrow the differences have cost."

"Yet you continue to feed the quarrels. You have not yet sent a ransom demand, but prefer to keep my sister and me as your prisoners. Can you defend your actions?" She was pleased at her own eloquence. Perhaps he would be swayed yet, and send her and Elizabeth on their way home.

"'I will send it when I am ready." He was gazing at her ankle and the calf of her leg, his right hand inching slightly above the swell of the ankle bone. "You have tiny feet." His fingers moved upward, testing the softness of her skin.

Meg gasped and pulled her foot from his grasp, flinching at the sudden pain. Anger flowed from her in a sudden torrent. She slapped him hard across the jaw. "How dare you. Do not touch me again."

The reddened imprint of her hand was clear against the whitened scar on his face. Her palm stung from the violence of the contact. But she faced him squarely, daring him to touch her again.

Niall stood and folded his arms across his chest. "I wonder," he mused, "were it my brother, Ian, who offered his help, would you be reacting like this?"

"You were not offering help. You were offering something else." Her face felt hot, and she was afraid she blushed. She must have, for Niall smiled at her again with that sarcastic curl to his mouth.

"And if I were, and if the circumstances were of your own choosing, I think you would not be unreceptive." His words mocked her.

He could not have been more clear, and Meg knew that her eyes must be showing signs of the silver rage her friends joked about. He stood waiting for her response, and she wondered if the taunt was a calculated one, chosen to arouse her anger. But, Lord, he was so handsome standing there with his black brows lowered and his mouth a tight slash across his face. Even in sternness, he was magnetic. How could such a man act like such a devil?

"Do you deliberately try to insult me? Or is it your lack of breeding that makes you speak so?" She was close to losing her temper, and the dirk in her left boot rubbed against her leg.

He looked at her for a long moment and then said with a bow, "Perhaps I am mistaken. If so, I apologize for the personal remarks I have made. No doubt it was being so close to your beauty that made me behave so badly."

Meg narrowed her eyes. "It is not necessary for you to be rude. I have thanked you for helping me on the path, and now, if you don't mind, you can leave me here. I ask only that you send my sister to me."

She still sat in the rocking chair, and he was so tall, looming over her like some avenging angel. Or a devil, she amended, trying to negate his air of dominance. The black hair was pulled back from his face, enhancing his cheekbones and long narrow nose.

"At your service, mistress. I shall send your sister to you at once. Keep the snow on your ankle until it melts." He made a half bow and left the cottage, closing the small door behind him.

Meg sat back and closed her eyes again. This constant battling was creating a strain on her nerves that she was most unused to dealing with. Even her sparring with Robert had not left her trembling like this. What was the power of Niall MacDonald, that he affected her so, sending her self-control all awry?

✧

Niall sent Elizabeth to her sister, with Andrew as an escort across the burn. Most of the clan had left for the tiny scattered cottages they now called home. Once serving to shelter only two or three people, the four homes were now crowded with people. It was a situation that must be remedied soon, Niall knew, and the decision weighed upon him.

The men had chosen him to act as their chosen chief, in the absence of John and Alasdair, the direct blood heirs to the position. Duncan, although related to the old chief, was far too old to hold the title. He acted as Niall's counsel though, and wore the chief's dried sprig of white heather in his bonnet religiously. It was a token that Niall would not assume for himself, in spite of the confidence granted to him by the vote of the clan.

Niall felt Duncan's curiosity upon him as Andrew led Elizabeth toward Annie's cottage. The old man lit up his pipe and leaned against the wall, waiting for Niall to speak.

"Am I wrong, Duncan?" Only here, alone with the elder, could Niall relax his position as leader, and he relinquished it gladly for the moment, seeking the wisdom of one who had seen many troubles and joys in his long life.

"To keep them here? I canna say." The old man spoke slowly, his teeth gripping the worn stem of the wooden pipe. "'Tis true enough we have no where to take them at present that would be more hospitable than this. If we can hold on till spring, perhaps John and Alasdair will be successful and a MacIaian will yet return to Glencoe."

Niall knew that Duncan spoke of the clan and of Niall's determination to rebuild their cottages, making Blackwater a secure keep. He intended to hold it for MacIaian's sons, should they ever be able to return. But similar questions could also be asked about the Campbell girls, with no more clear an answer to be found.

He lowered himself to the floor beside the fire pit and leaned back on his elbows. "Perhaps I should see them all safely relocated. At least there would be no more fear of the Campbell. It may be a long time before John and Alasdair are able to leave Appin, no matter how many reassurances the king sends." Niall stared into the fire, as though the dancing flames held the answers he sought.

A thin trail of smoke issued from the bowl of Duncan's pipe. "Aye," the old man agreed. "Perhaps. But they are well hid for the moment, though ill provided. MacArthur and Macintyre will see that they have enough food to last till summer. Then a MacIaian will return to lead his folk to safety."

"Is any place really safer than this? Where the children can grow in peace and women do not bury their husbands so young?" Niall's throat was tight as he thought of the MacDonald heirs who, after watching their father die, had sent their wives and children up the mountain, away from the soldiers' muskets and pikes. "Are even the caves safe from the seed of Campbell?"

"Not this side of Heaven." Duncan turned his chair toward Niall, and sat down gratefully on the cushion Annie had made to soften the seat. He drew a long puff and blew it out noisily. "And maybe not even there, I'm thinking. But that's not what matters, boy."

Niall smiled. No one but Duncan would call him that anymore. "What is it, then, that matters?" Unbidden, the picture of Meg Campbell's face flashed into his mind and he pushed it away.

"Home is wherever you are happiest, lad. It makes no difference whether it be in the house you were born, or the place where you hear your firstborn cry. Ye canna bring the old man back by rebuilding here at Blackwater, nor can you raise Glencoe again. They are gone forever, may the Good God bless them and us. But ye still have a clan and as long as ye hold it for John, the men will follow you whatever your decision."

"Aye." Niall turned to look at Duncan, imprinting upon his mind the image of the old man in the proud plaid, his craggy profile and thin shoulders stark against the fire-lit shadows. "But what is the best decision for them?"

"'Tis easy, lad, do ye but listen to your heart."

Niall smiled, the shadows on his face lightening with realization. "Aye, Duncan, that it is. Wherever we are, so long as we are together, is home. And home should be comfortable and welcoming. So while we are here at Blackwater, for however long God grants it, we shall make it as homelike as possible." He swung himself up from the floor. "Thank you, Duncan."

The elder waved his pipe at Niall. "I did nothing, lad, you made the decision yourself. Now go and fetch yon crooked-mouth lassies before the night grows too long. I would find my bed without being disturbed by their chatter."

Niall glanced up toward the loft where the children slept. "Does it go well, having them here to help with the girls?"

"'Tis a relief to me, I admit," Duncan answered. "But will do no good to make it too cozy, do ye understand?"

The invisible mantle of leadership had fallen upon Niall's shoulders again. "Aye, Duncan, I understand. I have not forgotten and I will not forget. Under any circumstances." He smiled in self-derision, and tiny lines appeared at the corners of his black eyes. "I will be watchful against myself, I promise."

He left the cottage soundlessly, making his way toward the candle lit cottage across the water where Meg sat waiting in Annie's chair.

✧

Elizabeth was massaging Meg's ankle when Niall returned, and he paused in the doorway for a moment, watching them. Meg's eyes were closed, her face reflecting the pain of the twisted ankle. Niall closed the door noisily, and both girls looked up at him.

"Is it any better?" He knelt beside Meg, and examined her foot. "The swelling is not as bad as I feared. Do you think you can manage to walk with the two of us supporting you?"

"I'll try." She wasn't sure herself, but she didn't want to subject herself to another journey in Niall's arms. Meg put her hands on the arms of the chair, and forced the weight of her body up to a standing position.

Elizabeth put a slender arm around Meg's waist. "Can you bear the weight?"

"I think so." She draped one arm around Elizabeth's shoulders and, as Niall turned to offer his own shoulder, leaned into him.

The three took two hesitant steps before Meg crumbled, falling backward against Niall's strength.

"I am sorry," she gasped, her mouth whitening with effort, "I cannot."

"'Tis all right, dear," soothed Elizabeth, "Annie will not mind if you stay here the night."

Niall raised his eyebrow. "I wouldn't be too sure of that, mistress. But it is not important." He lifted Meg into his arms. "We'll manage."

He strode out into the night, and Elizabeth blew out the candle and shut the door behind her. Meg stared helplessly at her sister over Niall's shoulder, her face a luminous mask in the darkness.

"I promise not to wound your dignity any more than necessary," Niall whispered into Meg's ear before Elizabeth caught up with them.

His breath was cool against Meg's face, and she felt tiny goosebumps rising on her neck. "'Tis not my dignity that pains me," she managed to answer, "only the careless damage I have done to my foot."

"Then you don't mind being helped home by an outlaw?"

She looked up at his profile and saw that he was grinning.

"I wouldn't mind at all if the outlaw was truly helping me home." She felt a small satisfaction as he looked down at her. "But Duncan's cottage is not my home, as you well know, sir."

"It is for the moment."

There was no further speech between them until they crossed the burn. He paused then, to be sure of Elizabeth's footing. "Why is Andrew not with you?"

"He was to return with some wine for Meg," Elizabeth said, breathing harshly from the attempt to keep up with

Niall's long strides. "He may be worried when he finds us gone."

"No doubt. But he's a canny lad, he'll soon find you again. Take a good long step over to that large stone, there, and then another. Good," he added, as Elizabeth stood on the farther side of the tiny stream.

He was across in one large step, and smiled at Elizabeth. "In another month, when the Coe is rushing down, 'twill not be so easy to cross."

"By the grace of God, we shall be long gone," muttered Meg.

"Ah, lassie, you wound my heart," Niall winked at her ironically. "Are you so anxious to remove yourself from my protection? I am longing to show you the River Coe in spring."

Elizabeth giggled, and Meg shot her a murderous glance. "The sooner this is resolved the better off we shall all be," she said primly. "I can think of better things to do than walk beside that wild river with you."

As Elizabeth ran ahead to open the door of the cottage, Meg returned her attention to the man who held her so intimately. "Why do you treat this as a joke? It is a very serious matter, and I would have thought that the recent events would have a more sobering effect on your humor."

Niall stopped on the path, tightening his hold on her. "I am fully aware, as you could never be, of how serious the matter is."

Meg frowned at him. "You do not show it, with your remarks about us being under your protection, and your heart being wounded."

She looked up into his eyes and was held by the stark emotion that showed there. The black orbs were brilliant with passion.

"Shall I be stern with you then, and wrathful the way my kindred would be if they knew your name? Would you prefer that I tortured you or raped you while your sister watched? But perhaps, beside the rush of the Coe when it is at its wildest, with the birds singing high around us and the bell-heather blooming, 'twould not be rape."

Meg made a small reproachful cry, but Niall ignored it.

"You are alive tonight because I choose to temper my pain with humor, mistress. And this I do because any harm to you would have repercussions against honorable men who are now in hiding, who must remain exiled from their homes under penalty of death. Never again speak to me of how serious a matter this is."

He walked on, his face grim in the moonlight. Elizabeth waited for them in the cottage, silhouetted in the doorway against the fire in Duncan's hearth. She stepped aside to allow them entrance, and Niall freed himself of his burden with an eagerness that caused Meg to lose her balance. She put one shaky hand out against the wall to steady herself.

"Good night." He left the cottage without another word.

Elizabeth held out her arm to Meg, and they moved slowly across the floor to the pallets where they slept. Duncan was no where in sight, although the cottage reeked with his tobacco, and Meg was glad of the respite from prying eyes and nagging questions.

She lay down, allowing Elizabeth to cover her with the blanket. It was comforting to be ministered to, and Meg smiled at her sister.

"Thank you, Bess. I apologize for the fuss and bother."

"Nonsense, you will be much better in the morning, and if not, I will make a poultice for your ankle." Elizabeth shed her skirt and folded it before setting it beside the pallet. She wrapped herself up in a blanket and lay close to Meg, seeking the warmth of her sister's body.

"Be sure to wake me if you need anything." Elizabeth sounded like a weary child.

Meg smiled. "Thank you," she said softly, and listened to Elizabeth's breathing until it became soft and regular.

Her thoughts were full of the man who had just rebuked her. He had, perhaps unwittingly, just revealed a great deal about himself. Perhaps he was not as indifferent to her as he claimed. Or perhaps he always took refuge in humor and sarcasm when his emotions were involved. It would be an instructive exercise to watch, if true. Just what she could do with the knowledge, was still unclear.

Meg snuggled down into the coarse wool blanket, feeling its fibers tickle her face. She rubbed her nose absently and closed her eyes. If God were merciful, perhaps Niall MacDonald would not haunt her dreams tonight.

CHAPTER 7

"It is like some enchanted dream, Meg," said Elizabeth as they worked side by side in the cottage a few days later.

"A nightmare, more like," grumbled Meg although it was only an outward protestation. The cottage and their adventure did have a sort of fairy tale quality when viewed in an unbiased light. By the end of their fifth day at Duncan's cottage, Meg was beginning to admit, if only to herself, that this particular group of MacDonalds might prove to be exceptional people.

"Oh Meg," Elizabeth scolded, "I see how you look at Flora and even at Duncan while he tells his stories at bedtime. You are enjoying yourself, I know it."

Meg chose not to respond to Elizabeth's fantasies. It was nothing she would give voice to, of course, but the little girls entrusted to her and Elizabeth's care were winning fast places in Meg's heart. Even Duncan revealed a fineness of character that was missing from others of his clan. And Meg was beginning to wonder, if Argyll and Robert had been wrong about that, in what other things might they also have been mistaken? But that sort of thinking was wrong. Generations of Campbell forebears bore testimony to that.

Not getting an answer from her sister, Elizabeth pursued her line of thought further. "Are we not fortunate Meg, for things to have turned out so well?"

"Well? We are being kept as prisoners far from our home. How has it turned out 'well'?"

Elizabeth turned a pretty shade of pink. "I only mean that the children are so sweet and it could have been worse, you know. They have no reason to be nice to us, yet they are kind and gentlemanly."

"Your brains have been addled by the cold," Meg told her sister. "They are not gentlemen, they are outlaws and we are here only because we are providing a service for them. As soon as their ransom is paid, I assure you, they'll have no more use for us and will no doubt leave us in the forest to manage as best we can."

"I don't believe that and I don't think you do either. No real harm has been done to us, and it is no great hardship to care for two little girls and one old man. The others leave us well alone, so the lie is not always in our faces. I think you are wrong, Meg. If the MacDonalds really hated us, we would be in far worse circumstances."

Meg wrinkled her forehead as she considered her sister's words. It was perplexing, indeed, being kidnapped and held hostage against Niall's thirst for revenge, only to discover that the imprisonment consisted of caring for little girls and one crusty old man.

Elizabeth had settled well, playing with Flora and Beth as though she were still a child herself. Only when Andrew and Ian appeared each day to see if any provisions were needed, did Elizabeth remember to conduct herself like a lady. And this was a source of concern to Meg, since no good could come of the infatuation. Robert was sure to come for them. It was his duty and obligation.

Frowning over her thoughts, Meg busied herself at the fire, stirring the huge pot of turnips and broth that she had set to boil for their evening meal. It was a much different supper than she and Elizabeth were used to enjoying, but the stew had a good flavor and the turnips would fill the men's stomachs very well. This was another indication of how quickly she was adapting, Meg realized. Niall MacDonald would be very surprised at the meal she would set before him this evening.

Her thoughts flew back to her afternoon walk through the forest with Elizabeth and the children, hunting for edibles that might lie buried in the snow.

"We'll be sure to find some greens near the clearing," Beth had trilled, "Duncan said that's where the deer go to look for their winter food."

Duncan had been right. When they arrived at the clearing of which he'd spoken, traces of animal foraging were all about. At first, Meg despaired of finding food to take back to the cottage. But after digging just a few inches beneath the snow, she discovered that although the deer loved the taste of slightly frozen leaves and bark, they had left the deeper roots alone. Gleefully, Meg pulled several large tuberous growths from their hiding place and stuffed them in the pockets of her apron.

"We'll eat well tonight," she assured the children, thinking of the dried deer meat that hung in the scullery.

Elizabeth's burst of laughter split the air and Meg looked at her sister questioningly.

"To see you like this," explained Elizabeth, still giggling. "With your hands wet from snow and your pockets full of weeds. 'Tis not you, Meg, not at all!"

But it was. Meg knew suddenly that she was enjoying their adventure and any fears she had harbored about their safety had long since vanished.

She stuck her tongue out at her sister. "Much you know, prissface," she taunted. Stooping down, Meg gathered up a big fist of snow and flung it right in Elizabeth's face.

Gasping, the younger girl wiped the mess away. "Just you wait, Meg Campbell," she threatened, and reaching down, she rolled snowballs one after the other. "Help me girls!" Elizabeth cried to Beth and Flora, and the delighted children joined in.

Soon the air was thick with snow and giggles and shrieks. Meg's hair and cloak were soaked through, as were her mittens and boots. The mock battle raged for several minutes until Meg fell breathless to her knees.

"Enough!" she held her hands up, shaking from the exertion. "I concede."

"Words I never thought to hear you say, mistress."

Startled, Meg whirled around, her mouth falling open in dismay as she recognized the voice. It was the first appearance Niall had made since their frustrating conversation a few nights before. He sat on his horse, his black eyes taking in the four snow dusted girls.

Niall's full lips parted in a genuine smile. "Had I known that a mere snowball fight is all it takes to win your submission, our differences would have been settled days ago."

Beth and Flora giggled, and Elizabeth coughed genteelly into her hand. Meg glared at them and then redirected her energies toward smoothing her ruffled dignity. Damn the man. His blatant masculinity filled the small clearing and she would not, she told herself, react to it.

"We were just having a bit of exercise," she brushed snow from her skirt. "After gathering roots for supper."

"So I see," he said. He looked from her hair to her boots, taking careful note of her bedraggled state.

Meg turned to hurry the children back toward the path. "We must return to the cottage before the children take a chill."

"I think it is you, Mistress Meg, who should guard against the chill. It appears that you have borne the worst of the skirmish."

It was true. She was wet from head to toe while Elizabeth and the girls were only damp. It was galling to admit to him that she'd been bested, even in play.

"They cheated," she said, hands on her hips. "It was three against one."

"It was all in fun," Elizabeth interjected.

"Certainly it was," Niall agreed. "The girls seemed to be enjoying it."

"Wonderful fun," little Beth chimed in, her head bobbing up and down. "Wasn't it Flora?"

Although still flushed from the play, at Niall's appearance in the clearing Flora had once again retreated into her shell. She nodded a silent agreement, her hand holding tightly to Beth's.

Meg looked concernedly at the older girl. Flora smiled so little. "We'll build a snowman if you like, when we get back to the cottage, Flora. Elizabeth and I are champions at snowmen. We build one every year."

She looked up at Niall, still watching from horseback. "If you'll excuse us, we need to get the children back now."

"It's a long walk to the cottage," he responded, his eyes never leaving her face. "You are wet through."

He was provoking her. "I'm fine. Thank you for your concern, but we will walk very fast and will be back in no time."

Niall edged the black horse closer to her. "I think," he said with that infuriating air of command, "that you had better ride back with me."

"Tis not necessary, sir." Her heart quailed at the thought of once again riding with him.

"I think it is." He bent down, holding out his hand and Meg had no choice.

Swallowing down her discomfort, she took his hand and swung herself up onto the back of the horse. "What of the children?"

His arms were strong around her. "Mistress Elizabeth will, I am sure, take them quickly home. By that time you will be dry and warm before the fire." Niall nodded once to Elizabeth and dug his heels into the black's sides.

The ride back to the cottage seemed to take only moments. Meg was critically aware of the man who sat behind her, and of the tingle in her spine as she tried to subdue her unruly thoughts. She wondered if he would stay to eat with them and found herself growing excited at the idea. She squelched it, composing her mind and emotions, so that when at last they dismounted, nothing of her inner turmoil showed in her face.

"Thank you for your assistance, sir," she said, looking up into his dark eyes. "Will you be staying to visit with the children?"

"Not now, mistress, but I will return in time for your evening meal. I find that I'm quite curious as to how a lady such as yourself will prepare a repast from the meager provisions we have at your disposal."

He never lost an opportunity to attack. No matter how hard she tried to keep peace between them, he managed to turn it around on her. "You can have no possible idea of what ladies such as myself are used to doing," she told him, hands on hips. And then she left him, flouncing into the cottage with her chin in the air.

Remembering her earlier anger, Meg frowned while tasting the soup and Elizabeth caught the expression. "Is the flavor bad?" the younger girl inquired.

"Yes, no, that is — taste it yourself." Meg dropped the ladle on the wooden table beside the fire and sank onto a low stool.

"What ails you, Meg?" Elizabeth's soft eyes were full of concern. "You cannot still be worried that we will be harmed."

"Be quiet," Meg warned, "Duncan and the girls will hear you."

Elizabeth cast a glance over to the other side of the cottage where the old man and the children lay stretched out on furs against the wall. "They're still napping. Truthfully Meg, do you still fear their revenge?"

"No. I know that the MacDonalds will deliver us safely to Robert."

"Then what is it?" Elizabeth dropped to her knees beside her sister.

Meg sighed and stared at the earthen floor beneath her feet. "It is just that everything seems to be taking so long. Surely Robert knows by now what has happened. Why hasn't he come for us?"

"I hope he never does!" Elizabeth's voice was fierce, startling Meg out of her emotional fatigue.

Aghast, Meg looked at her. "What do you mean?"

"You said yourself he will be angry. I don't want these people to be harmed. What about the children?" Tears began to well in Elizabeth's luminous eyes.

"Don't you mean 'what about Andrew?'"

Elizabeth stiffened and then covered her face with her hands. "Yes," she whispered, "I am worried for him. Meg, I think I am —"

"Hush! I don't want to hear it. You have no right to any feelings about any of these people and neither do I. Friendly or not, they are still outlaws. The differences between us are insurmountable and we cannot go against our clan. We will still be Campbells when we leave here."

Elizabeth looked up at Meg. "Is that how you felt this afternoon, riding home with Niall? Are the differences so great?"

Meg pushed herself up from the stool and walked away from Elizabeth. She didn't trust herself to answer, she wasn't even certain what the true answer was. "Supper is ready. You can slice the bread." Her hand shook as she began to ladle the soup into wooden bowls.

Mutely, Elizabeth went about the task. Absorbed in their work, the sisters did not hear the men's voices as Jamie and Ian entered the cottage. And neither of them realized that old Duncan had been awake in the shadows for a long time.

"Here's a fine surprise for you!" Ian's voice was merry.

Meg and Elizabeth turned to see a small figure enter the cottage behind him.

"Dora!" Elizabeth ran to the girl and threw her arms about her. "What are you doing here? Who brought you? Are you all right?"

Their former maid giggled and covered her mouth. "Och, miss, 'tis glad I am to see ye here. Mistress Meg," she gave a small half curtsey to Meg.

Elizabeth pulled Dora over to the kitchen. "How do you come to be here?"

Beth and Flora, who had awakened amid all the furor, ran to Dora and embraced her. Dora looked at Meg and Elizabeth with a self-satisfied smile. "As ye can see, these are my kinsfolk. Their mother was the daughter of my gran's cousin."

Meg felt the tiny seeds of suspicion growing in the back of her mind. "Dora," she asked, "did you have aught to do with our arrival here?"

Their former servant looked her straight in the face. "'Twas never intended that you and Mistress Elizabeth should be hurt. That wine was only to ease the way, ye ken. You've not suffered from it?"

Elizabeth's breath left her in a rush and Meg bit her bottom lip. "You helped them plan the whole thing."

"Aye," Dora's curls bobbed as she admitted her part in the abduction. "Me and Andrew put it all together. I was to have the wine ready and to let him know when you would ride out again alone. Dr. Kincaid had somehow become locked in the pantry that morning, so he didna ken yer leaving."

Meg sat down on the low stool and tried to steady her nerves. "What exactly did you put in that wine?"

"Oh, 'twas not me," Dora explained, "me gran fixed the wine up and sent it round to the house for me to keep."

Light was beginning to break over Elizabeth's face. "And your gran of course, is old Annie, whom we have yet to meet."

"Aye. And we just waited a few days to be sure no one suspected. When ye left, I raised the signal, and the lads knew to be waiting."

Meg glared at Dora. "What was the signal?"

The girl chortled. "Why 'twas just a pair of the Colonel's trews, miss. I hung 'em out from his window when ye went on the ride." Her pleasant face fell. "I didna know Cook would dismiss me for my boldness." She turned to the little girls, her hands open in regret. "I have no sweets for ye, today, loves."

Elizabeth was overcome at the idea of Robert's pants being hung from a window for all to see. "Oh Meg," she gasped, "is that not the funniest thing you've ever heard? Oh, I wish we could have seen it!"

Meg strove to keep her face straight. "What about Dr. Kincaid?" she asked. "He was responsible for us and you locked him in the pantry. Is he all right?"

"Oh, aye, the Colonel is in a rare taking, but he daren't turn off the minister without the Earl's permission." Dora assured her.

Elizabeth continued to giggle, and Meg's own indignation gave way to relief that their minister was all right. She allowed the humor of Robert's trews being used to signal the MacDonalds to wash over her, as well.

It was Andrew who broke up the conversation, timidly requesting his supper. Elizabeth scurried to find enough cups and bowls for everyone and Meg tied an apron over her skirt as she prepared to spoon up the stew for their meal.

She had passed several bowls around when she became aware that Niall stood just inside the doorway. He was in his usual role of observer, noting the comfortable camaraderie of the small group. He said nothing as the two Campbell girls set out the evening meal, but sat down next to Duncan and waited for his portion to be handed to him.

Jamie and Andrew watched wide eyed as Meg served up generous portions of thick stew and set it in front of them. Turnips and large chunks of venison floated side by side in the rich broth, and Meg had to work hard to keep her expression bland as the men plunged into the meal. Ian and Niall were more reserved, she saw, but Duncan had no qualms about self-restraint, and attacked his stew as though it might be snatched from him at any moment.

Beth and Flora sopped up their remaining stew with big pieces of the soda bread Elizabeth had baked during the afternoon. Conversation ceased as everyone focused on the hot meal, and Meg was gratified as she watched the MacDonalds consume the food she had prepared.

Jamie and Andrew asked for extra servings, and Elizabeth complied, smiling at their compliments. Ian and Niall, although enjoying the food, were quieter and had contented themselves with the portions Meg had given them. It did not escape her notice, but she did not comment. She thanked them when they praised her cooking, and smiled at Beth and Flora who were too full to talk. Duncan, she saw with amusement, lingered longest over his bowl, smacking his lips with enthusiasm.

Niall watched the faces of his relatives as they relaxed after the meal. Duncan was enjoying a smoke, and Jamie and Andrew swapped hunting boasts beside the fire. Ian had moved to help Meg clear away the dishes, while Dora and Elizabeth played with the little girls in a corner, brushing and plaiting their hair. It was a lovely domestic scene, with no hint of tension in the air.

He watched Meg most of all, watched her grace as she moved about the kitchen, her reactions to Ian's teasing, and the way in which she seemed to content herself with simple household tasks. It did not seem in keeping with her station as the ward of the Earl and Niall wondered how much of her attitude was a performance designed to play on the MacDonalds' good humor.

He knew she flirted with the idea of using Jamie or Ian to her own ends. What her plan might be, he was not sure, but it no doubt was concerned with the escape she kept threatening.

Niall's reverie was interrupted by Beth, who jumped up and ran to his lap. "Tell us a story, Uncle," her tiny dimples outlined her smile as she settled down close to his heart.

Shy Flora joined her sister. "Yes, please," seconded the older girl, "one about the fairies."

Niall rubbed Beth's hair and patted Flora's cheek. "I have no stories tonight."

"Meg knows lots of stories," Elizabeth offered, and the children clapped their hands.

Meg shook her head at her sister. Would Elizabeth never learn to hold her tongue? To the children Meg said, "I am sure Duncan has lots of stories, too."

"We've heard all of Duncan's stories," Beth said firmly. "Want to hear yours."

Ian held out his hand. "Come, Meg, humor us."

CHAPTER 8

Ian winked at Meg, flashing her an intimate smile. "I think you've been caught."

From her seat beside Duncan, Dora agreed with him. "'Twould be a rare treat."

Meg sighed, knowing she had no choice in the matter. She untied the apron around her waist and lay it upon the scarred oaken table. "All right," she conceded, "but first, you wee ones must get ready for bed."

With only a bit of complaining, Beth and Flora complied and soon returned to sit at the fire, eager young faces upturned and expectant. They wore simple white wool shifts that hung down to their small ankles. Someone had embroidered blue bells around the hems. How Laurie MacDonald must have loved these children.

Unable to resist their sweetness, Meg sat down beside them, across from Niall, who settled back against the wall. Ian sat close beside her, and Jamie and Andrew on either side of Elizabeth. Duncan dozed in his chair.

"A long time ago, it was told to me by my grandmother," began Meg, her voice pitched low and soft, "that in the deepest part of the forest, there was a small, beautiful loch where no people ever went."

"Was it this forest?" piped up Beth. "You said our forest is enchanted."

Meg smiled at her. "Aye, I think it probably was."

Beth sighed in satisfaction. "I do, too."

"The loch had a magic spell on it," Meg continued, her memory moving back to the words that Grandmother had used to tell the old story, "that kept away all people. Only the animals could go there, because animals have no wickedness about them but are always the way God made them, which is pure and simple." For a moment, Meg's eyes grew sad as she contemplated the vast differences between humans and animals.

Flora took her thumb from her mouth. "Who put the spell there?"

"Was it a fairy?" Beth's eyes were large with excitement.

"Yes, it was a fairy," nodded Meg seriously. "A very special kind of fairy. It was a kelpie. He had lived in the waters of the loch forever, and it was his job to protect the loch so that the animals would never be hunted or frightened when they came to it."

"What does a kelpie look like?" Beth interrupted again. She leaned into the circle Meg's arm made around her, and looked up trustingly, and Meg's heart ached at the sight.

"They can take any appearance they wish, but this one took the form of a handsome young man. He enjoyed going about among people and pretending to be one of them for awhile. He would watch so that he would know the tricks humans like to use on each other. He didn't like people very much, I'm afraid, for most of the time he only saw them at their worst, quarreling over who would get the last scone or bannoch, or whose horse could run the fastest, or whose whiskey tasted the best."

Flora giggled and cast a sly smile at Duncan, who twitched his whiskers in response.

"Humph!" he said, and bit down on his pipe.

"But one day while the kelpie was returning from the village, he came upon a young maid and her lover, who were sitting in the glen.

"The maid was the most beautiful creature he had ever seen, more beautiful even than the black swan who sailed on the loch each morning, and the kelpie's heart stirred at the sight of her white face and black hair. Her lips were red like the roses in summer, and as the kelpie watched, he fell in love with the human girl."

Beth sighed rapturously. "What did he do?"

"There was nothing he could do. A kelpie and a human cannot be together, for she would drown in the loch where he lived. So he returned to his home, thinking with longing of the beautiful girl."

Her audience was quiet, listening with full attention to the fairy tale. Everyone was focused on the story and the storyteller. Everyone except Niall, who seemed more interested in the contents of his sporran. Determined not to react to his coldness, Meg took a deep breath and continued.

"Every day the kelpie returned to the glen to try to catch a sight of the girl. She was always with the young man, and the kelpie's heart grew jealous as he watched them together.

"One afternoon, the two lovers walked through the forest and came close to the magic loch. The kelpie was so enchanted with the girl that he relaxed his spell, and the two people were able to see the beautiful waters. The girl reached down and touched the surface of the loch, and the kelpie's face appeared as she looked into the deep waters."

"What did he look like?" asked Elizabeth.

Meg smiled. "Kelpies can take any form they choose. This one had beautiful long hair and black eyes."

"Like Uncle Niall," Flora giggled, and Meg started in surprise.

"Well, not really," Meg stole a quick look at the man in question. She smiled at him wickedly. "Kelpies are completely irresistible, not at all like human men."

He studied her with wicked interest, his black eyes alive with the glint of firelight, and Meg's pulse quickened with his attention.

Trying to ignore Flora's comparison, she continued. "They can take the form of the most handsome man in the world. And that is what he did. As she looked into the water, she fell in love with the image she saw there and she reached her arms out to the kelpie. The young human man, frightened and disturbed, caught her by the arm and pulled her from the side of the loch. He whispered sweet love words in her ear and tried to pull her away from the dangerous magic. But she twisted free and went running back to the loch.

"The kelpie lad was triumphant, and he reached up through the waters to touch the girl, forgetting that she was human, forgetting that she could not live in the water. He forgot everything in his great desire for her, and when their hands touched, she stuck fast to him and was pulled down deep into the bottomless waters of the loch and drowned there, never to be seen again."

"What happened to the kelpie lad?" asked Ian softly.

"The kelpie was so sorry over what he had done that he went far away from the loch. He left the magic over it, so that the young man would forget its location and the animals could still come to enjoy it safely. And the young girl waits forever in the loch, lost and dreaming, for her fairy lover to return."

"What a sad tale." The sentimental Elizabeth had tears in her eyes.

Andrew took her hand. "Tis only a story, lass."

Duncan took his pipe from his mouth and pointed the stem at Andrew. "'Tis a good reminder not to go looking for something you are forbidden to have."

Aye," Niall agreed, his black eyes fixed on the sheen of Meg's hair in the firelight. "'Tis a good reminder."

"Any road," Meg finished, "'tis a good reason for little girls to never go near the loch alone. You must always be sure that a grown person is with you when you are around water. Will you promise me that?"

"Yes, yes," the little girls promised.

Meg held out her arms and hugged them both. "Now 'tis time for bed. Off with you."

Giggling to each other, they scampered off with Dora to the narrow ladder which led to the loft where they slept.

Ian rose and held out his hand to Meg, who accepted it gratefully as she stood and stretched. He bent his head close to hers.

"'Twas a sweet story, mistress," he told her, his green eyes holding her own in a long gaze. "You have a way with the words that makes the story seem real."

Flustered by his obvious flirtation with his older brother watching, Meg pulled her hand away. "'Tis the way our Grandmother told it when we were children. I used her words."

From his seat by the fire, Niall gave a low laugh. "Perhaps it was the whimsy of emotion you called up in the telling that moved my brother. He has ever been easily influenced."

Stung by the sarcasm, Ian looked at Niall and said, "Does something ail you tonight, brother? I thought the story a good one, and Mistress Meg's telling of it was excellent. Did you not enjoy it?"

"Perhaps," Meg said sweetly from between clenched teeth, "your brother's meal did not agree with him after all. My grandmother always said that poor digestion is the cause of many a man's foul disposition."

Duncan cackled as he wrapped a blanket around himself. "That's good, lass, that is. You got him there, you did."

Niall bowed to her, in a grand sweeping gesture. "'Tis my turn to concede, mistress. It appears you have won the affection of my family with your fairy story. I applaud your resourcefulness."

She was furious, aware that he insinuated she had sought to influence his family with her simple story. The gray eyes went silver, and Ian, fully knowledgeable by now of that particular signal, moved backward.

"I beg your pardon, sir," Meg's tone dripped with honey. "I tried only to provide your nieces with a bedtime story as they asked. If it did not meet your expectations, that is too bad, but it is your problem, I assure you, and not mine." She tossed her head and taking up a heavy blanket from a peg on the wall, walked to the door. "I'll be back later, Elizabeth," Meg said to her sister. "I need some air." Her back was straight as she strode out into the darkness, her tiny feet making crunching noises in the crisp snow.

Behind her, Ian turned to face his brother. "Why do you feel it necessary to trouble her so much, Niall?" he asked.

"Perhaps because you seem to avail yourself of every opportunity to commend her," Niall retorted, the scar on his face tightening. "Do not think to correct my behavior in this. 'Tis your own that warrants looking after."

Elizabeth gasped and Andrew quickly offered to take her for a walk.

"Jamie will come with us, won't ye, lad?" Andrew shot a pointed look at the young boy.

"Aye!" agreed Jamie with relief. He had no desire to be caught between the two men who now stood glaring at each other. The three left the cottage swiftly as the antagonists began to sort out their differences.

Niall's face was stern as he surveyed the tall redhead before him. Grown man though Ian might be, he had a history of ill timed and badly ended love affairs. Whatever he was contemplating with the Campbell woman must be stopped before it had a chance to take form.

"Well?" Ian finally broke the silence.

"You are falling in love with her." It was an accusation, not a statement.

"Aye," Ian admitted. "I am. And so are you."

Niall's head jerked back in shock. "Never!"

"You are. And afraid to look it in the face and call it by its name. Afraid of breaking your vow over a pair of misty gray eyes. Don't worry that I will press you, brother. I hope you never admit it." Ian's eyes crinkled with the mocking smile he gave his brother. "'Twill suit me well to have the way clear."

"You forget yourself, brother," Niall snarled. "What you suggest is unthinkable. The clan will not allow it. I will not allow it." As his chest began to burn, Niall wondered at the rage filling him. 'Twas only that the clan would never accept such a union, he told himself. Only that. He had no interest in Meg for himself.

"I care nothing about her, beyond what ransom she will bring us."

Ian laughed aloud. "'Tis good news then, and I thank you. As for the clan, since there are currently only nine of us, I see no great problem."

"You will stay away from Meg Campbell." Niall's anger was like quiet thunder in the small room, but Ian stood his ground.

"Nay, brother, I will not. Mistress Campbell herself is the only one who will discourage me. "

"Ian," Niall tried a different method with his obstinate brother. "What is so special about this one? You have had so many, why this girl who is our enemy?"

"I think you could answer that yourself, Niall," Ian's voice had become coldly formal. "And she is not my enemy. She is not to blame for our sorrow any more than are those children lying up there above our heads."

"By the blood of Christ!" Niall reached out to touch his brother but Ian eluded him. "She has won you over with her canny smiles. I have watched her playing her game with you and Jamie, trying to use you to her own ends. I think you do not realize what she really is."

Ian looked at him speculatively. "And I think you see plots and tricks where there is but an innocent girl trying to protect herself and her sister. You take too much responsibility upon yourself, brother. Campbell's soldiers would have come with you or without you that night. 'Tis past time you realized that and stopped denying yourself the grace of forgiveness."

With an oath, Niall turned away from his brother. He left the cottage at a run, thinking to put a safe distance between himself and his brother. Ian was mad, he decided, irreversibly so. It was not his fault. Ian had always been vulnerable to a pretty face and a sad story.

Not this time, Niall told himself. Too much was at stake here. Determined to end Meg's game once and forever, he followed her footsteps in the hardened snow, easily visible under the full bright moon.

She had headed for the small stream behind the cottage, he realized, and quirked his mouth in disgust. A truly romantic stroll and so appropriate after the bedtime story. Perhaps she thought Ian would follow her.

Niall went quickly through the forest, driven by the unnamable emotion that burned in his heart. By God, the Campbells had much to answer for!

Meg stood bathed in the light of the full moon. The tiny burn flowed slowly, its strength still hampered by patches of ice. Her blanket was wrapped around her, and the darkness of her silhouette was stark against the white snow.

He came up behind her, soft-footed and sure. "Are you not afraid the kelpie lad will pull you down into the water, Meg Campbell?"

Her breath caught in her chest, but she turned with deliberate care to look up at him, her eyes distant and hard. "'Twas but a bedtime story to keep the girls from coming here alone. I do not believe in kelpies, Niall MacDonald."

Her mouth drew his attention and Niall felt the beast in his heart stirring again. "Perhaps you should." He pulled her to him in a crushing embrace and his mouth came down hard, bruising her with its assault. Ignoring her resistance, he forced her lips apart and his tongue thrust deep into her mouth.

She fought him, tried to push away, to pull her head from the grasp of his strong hands. Her mind swam dizzily and a tiny sparking current ran up her spine.

Frightened and humiliated, Meg felt her eyes begin to burn with tears. She dug her fingernails into his arms, and when he did not react, reached up to his face to mark him with her fury.

But he broke the kiss and caught her hands above her head, grinning at her like the devil she thought him.

"Remember this when next you seek to play your games with my brother, mistress. This is but a taste of what you can expect when you seek to use men for your own ends."

"Do you threaten me?" she gasped, burning from the taste of his mouth.

Niall still smiled, but his dangerous eyes sent a clear message. "Nay, mistress, 'tis not a threat. 'Tis an example of what you may expect from me if you do not cease your play with my brother."

He stepped back and looked her up and down in an insulting way. "Now I will escort you back to the cottage. 'Twould be a shame for you to become chilled."

CHAPTER 9

The next morning was fair and the clear sky echoed the lifting of clouds in Meg's heart. Visions of Niall's angered face when he kissed her intruded on her thoughts and she caught herself humming as she went about her morning ablutions. She forced herself to control her excitement.

"Never forget" was an ancient Campbell motto. Today the simple precept had more meaning than she had ever imagined.

She could not allow herself the luxury of forgetfulness for even a moment. Niall MacDonald and everything he represented were a dangerous indulgence for a Campbell.

Besides, she reminded herself, that kiss had been intended to taunt, not to woo. 'Twas her own traitorous imagination that threatened her resolve to remain steadfast and loyal to the dictates of clan honor, not the beguiling softness of the dark hair on his arms nor the warmth of his breath on her cheek.

Meg shivered as she realized that once again her daydreams were leading her into dangerous realms. Shaking her head firmly to scatter her wayward thoughts, she picked up a basket from the kitchen floor. She smoothed her skirts before leaving the cottage. Rose and Dora had provided Meg and Elizabeth with dresses fashioned after their own MacDonald style. The unfamiliar plaid kerchief felt strange to Meg, and the patched, yellowed skirt length was a bit short, but the clothing was clean and well cared for.

The night before, as she helped Meg clear away the kitchen, Dora had mentioned that old Annie kept a good store of herbs laid by, and after the heartfelt compliments on the supper of the night before, Meg was determined to follow up that performance with even more tempting flavors for the brothers' palates. Humming softly again she went in search of Dora, who was outside playing with the children.

Jamie and Ian waved cheerfully at her as she walked past the area where they worked. The men wielded heavy axes, cutting wood to the proper length for the small byre they were building for the horses. Meg smiled at them with true pleasure, enjoying their appreciative looks. It was no hardship to be complimented, especially by such interested men.

"I'm going for a walk," she said, stopping for a moment to admire the skill with which Ian labored.

His broad grin made her toes tingle. "Where would you be walking so early this morning? You're not planning another wild escapade?" Tiny drops of perspiration showed on his forehead, dampening the riotous red curls that accentuated his emerald green eyes.

Meg blushed at Ian's teasing question. Just now she felt no overwhelming need to escape, but Ian needn't know that. "Only to Annie's cottage, to ask for some of her herbs," she answered. "I have a bit more sense than to try to escape on foot again, Ian MacDonald."

"Glad to hear it!" he laughed, swinging the great axe upward again. "We've enough work to do today without chasing you down, pleasant though the exercise might be." The muscles in his arms tested the strength of his shirt, and Meg became aware of her too obvious interest in Ian's body.

She looked around for Niall and Andrew. "Are your brothers up and about yet? Surely they should be helping you and Jamie."

The axe split a small tree trunk neatly in half. "Andrew is about an urgent errand this morning," Ian returned good naturedly, "we'll be saving plenty of work for him, never fear."

She didn't want to ask again, but couldn't help herself. "And Niall?"

Ian shrugged noncommittally, but Jamie answered her with a shy nervous smile. "Niall spends his nights at the keep, his days with us. He should be here any time, with rope to lash the end poles together."

Her curiosity aroused, Meg looked back at Ian. "Why does he stay alone at night in the ruins?" Her nails tapped the handle of the basket.

"'Twere best you ask him that." Ian swung the axe again. "Or perhaps not. Niall is not one to give explanations."

As she herself could attest. Still wondering at the oddity, Meg watched them work for a moment longer, then gave young Jamie a sweet smile before continuing on her way.

Dora and Elizabeth were with the children beside the burn, washing the girls' nightdresses. There was much giggling and splashing going on, and no one seemed to mind in the least that the water was still freezing cold.

"Dora," Meg called, "I am going to visit Annie to ask for some herbs. Will you come with me? I've not yet met her."

Dora came with her willingly, the children opting to remain with Elizabeth for more water play.

The path to Annie's cottage was narrow and winding. Located on the opposite side of the burn, the cottage itself stood a good way from Duncan's home, and not for the first time, Meg wondered why the children lived with him and not the old woman.

She ventured to question Dora about it, taking advantage of their easy relationship. Although their clans were enemies, Meg and Elizabeth had always been friendly with their MacDonald maid. In the Highlands, unlike other parts of Scotland, servants were friends.

"Me gran likes her own ways, she's always lived to herself," Dora explained in answer to Meg's questioning. "Even when she was younger and married to me grandad, 'twas so. He was gone most of the time, raiding and all, and she got used to keeping her own house early on. She looks in on the wee ones, sure, but she and Duncan don't get along together so she stays to herself unless we need her." Dora looked up at Meg slyly. "She's something of a wise woman, too, ye ken, with possets and potions for your troubles."

Meg grimaced at the reminder of the wearying draught with which Dora had laced the wine. "I'm well acquainted with her potions," she acknowledged, "but what kind of work does she do? She doesn't, er, do anything bad, does she?"

Dora shrugged. "I ken only the love possets and such. And for curing sick folks. I dinna think Annie would ever bring harm to any soul."

Meg hoped Dora was correct in her assessment of the old woman. But with an old wise or witch woman, as Dora could probably have more correctly termed her grandmother, it was best to remain on her good side. Meg realized she was being superstitious, and hoped that the Good Lord understood. It was just that everything was so confused these days. She didn't truly believe in witches or wise women.

Seen in the daylight, Annie's cottage was small, with beds of carefully tended herbs in neat rows near the door. Even the hibernating plants were well looked after, with blankets of peat laid over them to prevent damage to their dormant roots. Nearer to the cottage, within easy access, lay the perennial herbs of rue, yarrow, and horehound. These were herbs which every household used for stomach ailments, coughs, colds, and digestive complaints.

Dora paused for only a moment at the threshold, calling out Annie's name before entering. Meg followed her hesitantly, wondering against her logical nature if it were polite to thus enter the home of a witch.

Anne stood next to a large iron pot over the fire pit, and Meg stifled an urge to giggle nervously as Dora introduced them. The old woman was bent and hunched, and her face told the story of countless Highland winters. The broth she was stirring with a long wooden spoon bubbled over the fire. It was only a soup or stew, Meg told herself, but when she caught sight of a rabbit's head bobbing around in the steaming liquid, she shuddered.

Annie's sharp eyes caught the mannerism and she laughed out loud at Meg's nervousness.

"Did ye come to sample my cooking?" she jeered at the Campbell girl.

Meg tightened her hold on the basket she carried. "I came to ask for some herbs to flavor my roast."

The old woman looked Meg up and down. "Cooking for my boys, are ye? Thinking to win them over by pleasing their guts, I warrant. 'Twon't work. Ye're still a crooked mouth Campbell and they'll not forget it." She laid the large ladle down across the top of the cauldron. "There's much they won't be forgetting, not for a quick twitch of a skirt."

Flinching at the insult, Meg drew a deep breath, forcing herself to remember her determination to stay in control of her temper. "I cook for myself and my sister as well as for your 'boys'," she retorted. "And they do not turn up their noses at food offered them from my hands. So if you would kindly provide the herbs, mistress, we will be on our way and not trouble you further." She held out the basket.

Annie grumbled to herself but waved at the herbs hanging from a rack overhead. "Take what ye need then, and be quick."

Dora moved quickly to stand on the small table and began untying small bundles of basil and sage. "And here's some fine mint for our brew," she added as she tossed the bundles into Meg's basket. "And bee balm, and, Annie," she asked, "have ye any savory still put by?"

Silently the old woman nodded, her eyes fixed on Meg. "In the back, there," she nodded toward the dark room at the back of the cottage. "Next to the door."

Meg went in search of the savory leaves as Dora continued to fill the basket with the precious dried herbs.

It took a moment for Meg's eyes to adjust to the darkness of the room, and then they widened as she took in the sight of walls filled with small bottles and jars of herbs preserved in oils and tinctures. Annie was indeed more than just an old Highland granny. Meg had never seen such a store of goods outside of an apothecary's shop. And she was certain she had never seen anything like the strange man shaped root that peered out at her from the largest jar.

She didn't even want to know about that, she told herself. Best to conclude her business and leave as soon as possible. The savory hung in a dark corner next to the doorway, and Meg quickly grabbed several leaves and backed out of the room.

Dora and Annie were seated at the table when Meg emerged, with three steaming cups before them. Hesitantly Meg sat down too, and reached for the cup Dora indicated. Tiny flecks of mint floated in the herbal tincture, strengthening the weak flavor imparted from the silvery leaves held within a small linen bag.

After a few sips of the warming brew, Meg grew weary of the lengthening silence. "The drink is bracing."

"Aye," said Dora. "Me gran is famous for her brews. And for her wisdom." She giggled at her own words.

"Her wisdom?" Meg looked at Annie, who only frowned.

"She has the Sight!" Dora confided. "She can tell the past and the future."

Meg stifled another impulse to laugh, and then noticed the bunch of garlic hanging over the lone window of the cottage.

Garlic was often used to ward off evil spirits, and few laughed at such an idea, even in these enlightened times. "Do you tell the future with your potions?" She thought it safer to be polite than to refute the superstition.

"I need no potions to speak to me," Annie muttered. "The future is clear and hard, with many tears and few smiles."

It didn't sound promising but Meg's curiosity was piqued. "Tell us what you see."

Annie grunted. "It takes no sooth to see death in the spring, and betrayal." She drained the last of her cup and set it forcefully on the table.

Meg looked at Dora. "Death?"

Dora, accustomed from childhood to her grandmother's dire pronouncements, shrugged. "It's always death."

They sat in silence a while and Meg watched the older woman attentively. Annie seemed far away, lost in her own world of feyness and mystery. At last Meg summoned the resolve to ask the question she had been pondering all morning.

"Annie," she ventured, "will you tell me why Niall sleeps alone at Glencoe?"

Annie gazed into her cup. "There are demons driving the lad. Dark crying demons, with long fingers and sharp teeth."

Meg felt her heart grow cold. Annie sounded like a maundering old woman. "What demons?" the girl asked abruptly.

"He walks among the lost." Annie's voice was slow and trancelike. Meg was not sure she had heard the words correctly.

"The lost?"

"Aye, the lost ones who died there." Ancient blue eyes looked across the table at Meg. The old woman's expression was clear and devoid of guile. "He seeks absolution among the dead."

Meg looked at Dora, who sat with head bowed. "Absolution? Why?"

Dora met her gaze reluctantly. "'Tis not a happy story, mistress. He would not thank me for repeating it."

Meg leaned forward in the chair; its worn rungs creaked at the movement. "Dora, I very much want to understand this situation and I hope to someday aid in reconciling the hatred between our clans. Please tell me why Niall needs absolution."

Annie pushed her cup away with a clatter. "There can be no thought of reconciliation, Meg Campbell. And my boy will never find the redemption he needs. 'Twas in his hands to avert the coming of the soldiers, or at least to bring warning of their advance. But he lay dozing in a harlot's arms, while the Campbell crept closer and closer to Glencoe." She spat for emphasis, and Meg felt a shiver of foreboding run down her spine.

She looked at Dora for an explanation. "What is she talking about?"

"A friend of MacIaian tried to send word to Niall about the soldiers. But he was with his —" Dora shot a glance at Annie, who sat rocking in her chair, her eyes closed. "Niall was with his mistress, and the message was delivered too late for him to reach the keep. He blames her for keeping him from his duty and himself for allowing it."

"Aye," Annie agreed, her eyes still closed. "And now he stays at Glencoe to remind himself of his kinsmen's deaths and his own dishonor."

Meg was horrorstricken. "But he must realize that the soldiers would have come no matter if he had delivered the message on time."

"He only realizes that he was dallying when he could have been riding," said Dora. "He has sworn never to let another woman mislead him from his duty."

Meg's mind whirled back over the events of the last few days. She began to understand a little better now, Niall

MacDonald's attitude toward her flirtation with Ian, and she felt a flush overtake her at the thought that he equated her strategy with a harlot's games.

The tincture had grown cold, and Meg had no appetite left for it. The man who held her mockingly last night, and fired her blood with his kiss, slept alone with the ghosts of his slaughtered relatives, holding himself responsible for their deaths. She wondered what woman had so enthralled him and felt a stab of bitterness that he was left so scarred.

"It is past time we should be getting back." Meg stood and picked up the overflowing basket of herbs. "Thank you for the drink and the seasonings, Annie," she said courteously. "And for the information."

The old woman looked up at her warningly. "Dinna think to sway him from his atonement, girl. He will not listen to your Campbell blandishments."

"You must not tell him, mistress," pleaded Dora, rising to stand beside Meg. "He would be truly angry. 'Tis never spoken of, ye ken, and we should not have talked of it here."

Meg could vividly imagine his reaction if Niall were to discover that his innermost secret had been discussed aloud. "He will not speak to me at all, so you need have no fears on that score. I would not mention it to him at any price."

The walk back to Duncan's cottage was a silent one, Meg and Dora both busy with their own thoughts. The sound of the axes still rang through the wood, and Meg wondered if Ian and Jamie had been joined by the other two brothers.

The byre was about half completed, with one wall yet to be raised. All four brothers worked together in the winter sun, while Elizabeth and the two little girls sat watching. Folding both arms through her basket, Meg joined them, while Dora continued on to the croft, saying she would fetch water for the men.

Andrew called out a greeting to Meg and she responded, noting with cynical amusement that Niall did not so much as glance her way. He seemed determined to ignore her presence and the thought irked her.

"When you are ready," she called out to the men, "we have hot scones and cream." Their appetites would be great, she told herself, and even Niall would not be able to resist the temptation of fresh scones.

Ian smacked his lips in anticipation. "I'll be joining you in just a few minutes, mistress. And a big cup of cider to go with the scones?" He winked at her in his roguish manner and Meg felt herself responding to him.

She gave a half curtsey. "As you wish, sir." Her smile was dazzling, and she herded Beth and Flora with her as she left, exhorting their help with the impromptu meal. As they walked away, Meg thought she heard Niall say something but no one responded.

In the cottage, Duncan was licking cream from his fingers.

"Shame upon you, sir!" Elizabeth teased the old man. "Save some for those who have been working hard today."

He chuckled, not in the least put out by her scolding. "There's plenty more for those lads, and did I wait for them, 'twould be none at all left for me."

His reference to the hearty appetites of the brothers made the little girls giggle, as Meg and Elizabeth set them up at the kitchen table with their own scones. They had lacked butter in the making and so substituted lard, which Meg did not like at all. A dab of apple jam on top helped the taste greatly. Tepid cider was prepared carefully, so as not to burn tiny tongues, and then the rest of the bounty was laid out for the hungry men who were approaching.

Ian contrived to sit close to Meg, although she busied herself with much running to and fro. Jamie and Andrew laughed and joked throughout the meal. Niall ate quickly and left, with a brief word of thanks which was directed not toward Meg, but to Elizabeth.

Ian and Meg were alone when she said to him quietly, "Annie and Dora told me why Niall sleeps at the keep."

"They should not have done so." His green eyes were serious. "'Tis his business alone and he would not thank you for speaking about it."

"Tell me of the warning letter." She crossed her arms on the table top. "Who sent it?"

Ian's expression was reluctant. "Lady Cathlan sent a letter to Maire, that is, Niall's friend Lady Maire Douglas."

His mistress! thought Meg. But she asked, "Who is Lady Cathlan that she had knowledge of the plan?"

She listened while Ian explained the intricate affairs of the court and their bearing upon the MacDonalds. "Maire and Lady Cathlan are friends and so the letter was sent to Maire's home. It should have worked. It would have worked," his eyes grew sad, "had not the weather worked against the man's desire for his woman."

Ian looked at Meg warmly. One strong hand reached across the table to touch her own and Meg felt the sincerity in the gesture. "The need for a woman is a potent force in a man's life," he told her softly. "A beautiful woman is the most powerful creature in the world."

It was a Heaven sent opportunity to further her plans, Meg knew, yet she hesitated, regarding her own small white hand in Ian's large brown one. That momentary delay defeated her.

A shadow fell across the two who sat at the wooden table. They looked up startled, to find Niall looking at them. A sardonic smile crossed his dark face.

"Have I interrupted a lovers' tryst?" The words were sarcastic and his tone had that mocking edge she hated.

Meg pulled her hand from Ian's grasp and pushed herself up from the table. Not trusting her voice, she turned her back to the brothers.

"I was on my way back to work," Ian said. "You surely do not begrudge me a moment with a lovely lady?"

Meg's eyes widened at his words. How cruel they sounded in view of what Ian had just confirmed to her about Niall and his mistress. She opened her mouth to contradict the seeming inference, but Niall's answer stopped her.

"The world can fall or rise in just such a moment of dalliance, brother. Remember that and let no one use your taste for pleasure against you."

Ian studied his brother for a moment, then turned to smile at Meg again. "My thanks for the scones and the company. 'Twill hold me the rest of the day."

She managed a smile in reply, difficult with his older brother frowning at her. "You are always welcome, Ian."

Niall waited until his brother was out of hearing. He stood between Meg and the door, so that she was forced to attend to his words. Arms folded across his chest, black eyes snapping and flashing, he filled the room with temper and hostility.

"I have warned you against playing with my brother. Did you misunderstand me last night?"

Meg's hands were on her hips, her back stiff as she faced the angry man before her. "I was not playing with your brother. We were having a private conversation which you very rudely interrupted." Her eyes sent silver sparks across the room.

Niall wanted to shake her until her teeth rattled in her head. He could have silenced her easily. All it would take was one blow. Many men ruled disobedient women that way, and it was not taken amiss.

But something in him applauded her courage and boldness. She was all flame and ice, at one moment passionate and feminine; at the next, hardened with a disdain that made him furious. It was hard not to admire such a combination in a woman, even a Campbell woman. His hostage, the instrument of his revenge.

"Stay away from my brothers." He turned and walked swiftly from the cottage.

Meg watched his departure through the sting of swelling tears. His arrogance was unbelievable. She thought of Ian's gentle spirit in contrast to Niall's harsh nature, and her plan to set them at each other's throats crumpled.

She could not play with these men. The honor of her clan dictated that she try to escape, but she would do so honestly, without manipulation, and without causing further damage to the MacDonald brothers.

CHAPTER 10

It had been another day spent trying to avoid contact with Niall. Duncan was feeling the winter chill in his old bones and dozed close to the fire. Just now, Meg thought with a sense of gloom, spring and the thawing of the pass seemed far away. Perhaps tomorrow, the brothers would allow her and Elizabeth to visit Rose, whose cottage was farther down the glen.

It would be good to hear other voices, restful to be out from under Duncan's accusing eyes. The other members of the clan had kept to their own business since the first visit, no doubt sensing something amiss with the visitors. However, the MacDonald brothers seemed more trusting of late, so perhaps a visit with Rose would afford the opportunity for an escape. It would be difficult, on foot through the snow, but not impossible.

Meg looked around the cottage. Beth and Flora were cozily piled in one corner, their small bodies full and warm from the meal they had just enjoyed. Andrew and Jamie had taken Elizabeth walking, to see the moonlight. Only Niall was there to cast a pall over the contentment of the evening. He watched her constantly.

Lengthening shadows played across his face in the firelit room, and Meg felt a stirring wash of foreign emotions within her breast. Her greatest fear was that she would lose the careful control she was cultivating against him. His very presence caused an uncomfortable tingle inside her, that her soul instinctively recognized as being dangerous.

She fought it down yet again, and reached to remove the remnants of his supper, but he forestalled her with words that froze her heart.

"You will not be returning to the house of Campbell for awhile yet." Now he gazed into the fire, as though requiring no response from her.

For a moment she could think of nothing to say at all, only that he had somehow read her mind, and then her chin jutted out defiantly. "You have no right to keep us here. You promised to send for the ransom immediately. It will surely be here any day and you will be forced to release us then."

"Forced?" He turned to face her as he repeated the word.

"Aye, forced! The spring rains are almost here and then the soldiers will come. You will lose all that you have left of your precious Glencoe! Do you not understand that you put everyone at risk by this insanity? The children, Duncan, Annie, your brothers? Even yourself!" Passion overcame her and Meg knelt beside Niall, entreating him to listen.

"We have been gone too long already. They will have started searching and soon or late the search will bring them here. Do you truly think they will show mercy?"

Niall watched her quietly, his face a blank mask. "Your concern for my family does you credit."

"Apparently I have more concern for them than you do!" her voice rose in her anger and fear. "Does your word mean nothing then, to make a promise in one breath and in the next throw your vow to the winds? Every day that we remain here puts us all in more danger."

"And what danger are you afraid of exactly, mistress?"

His voice had become silky and Meg trembled as she looked up at him. She hated the self consciousness that overtook her whenever he was near.

"I do not lightly make promises. And if you recall, my word was to send the news to your guardian as soon as possible."

"And it is not 'possible' now?" she asked.

Niall shrugged and looked back at the fire. "You and your sister seem content with the situation. I see no reason we cannot continue as we are for the while."

Meg's rage broke through her last vestige of self control. "You see no reason? Indeed, sir, reason has no place in your head at all! How dare you assume that we are content with this situation? I tell you and I mean it with my whole heart, if you do not send word to Fort William, I will go there myself!"

She turned to rise, but Niall gripped her arm and drew her to him. His face was mere inches from her own as he pulled her close.

"Do not make empty threats, Meg. You will remain here and follow my orders as do my brothers and Duncan and Annie. You are my guest here until I say you may leave. And you may not leave until I say."

For a moment they stared uncompromisingly into each other's eyes and then he broke his hold on her. "The children have missed the softness of a woman. You and Elizabeth are good for them. They need more than Duncan is able to provide."

His honesty forced her to be honest as well. "We have grown to care for the girls. But that is exactly why we cannot stay here. We must leave. I could not bear it if this place and your family were brought to harm through our leaving. Let us go now, while there is still time to avert trouble. Give us two horses; I will see that they are returned. We can leave in the morning and be at Fort William by afternoon, if all goes well. I swear it."

Niall's jaw clenched as she spoke. He stood up and strode over to the door. Halting at the threshold, he looked back where she knelt beside the fire. "Be warned, Meg Campbell. You and your sister are under my guardianship now and what is mine I keep!" He turned and walked away into the darkness.

The old Highland words stung her, and Meg gasped in dismay. "But I am not yours," she whispered, even as she knew it for a lie.

Angry at herself, at Niall, at Robert, she ran to the door and looked out into the lightly falling snow. "You will not keep me hostage any longer, Niall MacDonald."

His heavy plaid hung on a nail in the wall and she took it up, wrapping it around her shoulders. Her plan only half formulated, Meg went quickly to the crude shelter where Andrew had left his horse.

The mare looked at her quizzically, ears twitching, and Meg fought down the little fear that sought to stop her. "It is all right, friend," she soothed the horse as she reached to untie the loose tether. "'Tis only a little way we'll be going and you'll be back home safe before the sun sets again."

She led the mare quietly outside and then vaulted lightly onto the broad red back. "Now I am turned horse thief," she told the moon, as she kicked her heels in the mare's sides. "So be it."

Their passing made only a faint sound in the snow and Meg shivered, as much at her actions as at the cold. Niall had left her no choice. It was dangerous for her to remain at the cottage and at the mercy of a man who would not be governed by reason. A man she felt herself irrevocably drawn to. No, there was no choice. Regardless of her growing feelings for him, or perhaps because of them, she must go. Tears stung her face as she rode wildly through the night, but they were not caused by the cold wind. Disgusted with herself, Meg wiped her eyes with one hand and tried to keep Niall's face from her mind.

He heard her leave the cottage, heard the sound of the mare's hooves as they scattered snow from the path. For a moment, he toyed with the idea of allowing her to get away, so that his hand would be forced. What stupidity this was, he told himself. Sworn enemies, yet he felt closer to her than he had ever been to another woman. It was impossible. Swearing to himself, Niall went to find the black. At worst they would perish in the snow together, at best he would return her to the cottage.

As Niall mounted his horse, he could barely hear the distant hooves of the mare as Meg rode away into the night. The terrain was treacherous under the heavy snow, and he must reach her before the ground started its familiar rolling and pitching. The cottages were situated in one of the few level spans along the mountainside and Glencoe was famed for its rocky pass and the hidden holes that could break the leg of an unsuspecting man—or horse. Niall had more than once been an unwitting victim of loose stones himself, and he urged Carnoch forward anxiously, hoping to avert the disaster that might await Meg and her stolen horse.

He called upon all his tracking skills to follow her, a talent he had honed during the past weeks of foraging for the clan. It was not the first time he had tracked a

Campbell through the snow, although these circumstances were vastly different. Never before had he felt so powerless.

He knew she had take the mare because it was lightly tethered. But she might not realize that the animal was also tired, winded from Andrew's ride back from his watch post at the pass. It might prove an advantage for Niall since the mare would not be able to travel far without resting.

Niall took a deep breath of the thin night air. Surely Andrew's stubborn mare would stop soon. From the hoof prints in the snow, he could tell that Meg had ridden hard thus far. He would not need to push the black in such a way. It should not be long before he caught up with her. And then his breath caught at a sudden memory.

The last time he had been this way was months before the massacre. He had been tracking a wounded stag when he discovered how well the woods protected their own.

He must proceed after Meg quickly enough to prevent her from coming to harm in a similar way. He pulled Carnoch up to a halt and listened intently, searching through the sounds of the night and the forest.

✧

With her usual self confidence, fired by frustration and anger, Meg was certain she could rely on her senses to get her safely back to Glenlyon. She knew the general direction of Robert's home, and she had turned the mare's nose sternly to the east. For the rest, she would trust in God. But as she rode further into the deepening darkness, she realized that even God may tire of foolhardy adventures. She was becoming worried that they might be riding in a circle, and the mare's pace was slowing as the animal picked its way through the woods.

At first, the rising moon had shed a welcome light over the narrow path Meg followed, but now the moonlight distorted her vision, casting deceptive shadows before her. It might be a hindrance rather than a blessing, she considered, but as long as she kept to the path, all should be well.

She fretted at the necessity for the slower pace, longing to put as many miles as possible between herself and the

MacDonalds. As though in response to the thought, the mare halted, her nostrils flaring nervously.

"Easy now, my lady," Meg crooned to the fatigued creature, hoping to coax her into movement. "What a brave, bright lady you are."

The horse refused to take another step, and Meg peered ahead into the shadows before them, trying to make some sense of the path.

"What is it, my girl? Just take your time, love," Meg urged, her knees exerting pressure on the mare's flanks. "Just one step at the time."

Stubbornly, the mare still balked, and Meg's frustration overcame her. With a loud cry she brought one hand down sharply on the mare's side and the horse jumped forward in fright. They took two steps, no more, and Meg felt the mare's leg give way even as the snap of a bone told a chilling story.

The horse fell full length into a shallow depression, hurling Meg forward. She plummeted to a sickening stop against a large outcropping of small boulders.

Bruised and shaken, Meg felt her head carefully for bumps. There were none, but she would readily swear that every bone in her body had been jolted out of place. As she regained her senses, Meg looked around for the mare, only to see the creature lying motionless a short distance away.

Tears sprang quickly to Meg's eyes as she realized that yet again she had allowed her emotions to govern her actions. The mare was dead, no doubt of a broken neck from the fall. Not only was Meg responsible for the loss of Andrew's horse, she was alone and lost in the wilderness of Glencoe in the middle of the night.

She should never have run from Niall, the bitter insight mocked her. Never have defied his decision. And there was no reason for him to come looking for her. Indeed, there was every reason for him to just allow her to disappear. Facing her ill behavior squarely, Meg welcomed the cleansing tears that washed down her face. Even the Earl of Argyll, she told herself, would have understood the need to weep away her fear and repentance. He however, would never succumb to those emotions.

Meg blew her nose on her sleeve. She was not a powerful Earl. She was a girl of seventeen, lost, hurt, and frightened. So she wept, and somehow the tears made her feel better, lightening the heaviness in her chest as she surrendered to the wraith of desolation.

✧

Not far away, the black horse paused, raising its head high in response to a faint sound just ahead. Its rider stiffened, searching out the darkness for the source.

Ahead of him, lying in the midst of the tiny path, was Andrew's horse. Niall jumped down from Carnoch's back and knelt beside the mare. Dead. Was Meg lying crushed beneath the horse's body?

Merciful God, he thought, let her be safe. *I cannot lose her now.* His fear threatened him, running like cold water through his veins.

For a few seconds he stood with his head thrown back, scenting the wind like a wild animal, intent on locating its prey. Then he caught the pitch of a human voice echoing on the wind.

He was stricken at the pitiful sound. His own selfishness had brought her to this. His own desires and foolish dreams had snared them both in a tightly knotted coil.

In only a few great strides he was beside Meg, lifting her from the rocks and cradling her gently in his arms.

"*Mo crigh*, my heart," he spoke to her in Gaelic, the words carried swiftly away on the rising wind.

He carried her to where the black waited and lifted her onto the great horse. Then he mounted beside her, one arm holding her firmly to his chest. With only a slight pressure, Niall guided the black away from the scene of death and fear. Somewhere close by was an abandoned beehive hut. Niall had sheltered in the decaying structure once before, but tonight it would prove more than merely a convenient place to spend the night. Their very lives would depend on whether or not the hut still stood

✧

A tiny flame rose to life in the middle of the stone ring and Meg sensed Niall's relief although he was characteristically silent. She watched as he stacked a few sticks in easy reach. Feeling useless and in the way, Meg gazed around the primitive shelter for something to do.

The first monks who came to Alba had built many of these structures, called beehives for the spiraling pattern they used with the granite stones. Only large enough for one or two people to live, the huts were sturdy and safe; many had stood for hundreds of years and provided home and shelter for countless shepherds and travelers.

A tiny hole in the center of the cone shaped roof provided escape for the smoke, the only opening in the hut except for the tiny arched doorway. Through this, the wind swirled and moaned, and snow drifted in to cover the hard cold floor.

The hut was empty of food or blankets and against her will, Meg wondered just how long they could survive here.

As though in answer to her thoughts, Niall said gently, "By midday my brothers will have found us. They will not rest until they know we are safe."

Meg swallowed her anxiety. "Aye," she admitted. "I do expect that. 'Tis only that we have no food or water here. And," putting aside the last remnants of her pride, "I am bitterly cold."

He draped the plaid more securely around her shoulders. "The fire will take care of that. As to food and water, we ate only hours ago. Snow can be melted to provide us with moisture."

"And of course, Ian and Jamie will find us soon." Meg's voice trembled a bit.

"Aye." Niall took a step to the door of the hut and stooped down, looking out into the wind and sleet.

Meg wondered at his thoughts. Surely he must hate her even more for placing them in this dangerous situation through her stubbornness and misplaced pride. Meg knew that although Niall would not admit it, they were in serious trouble. His brothers would indeed be searching for them as soon as the weather allowed, but that might not be for days.

She made up her mind. She could not face possible death without setting her conscience to rest.

"I am sorry to have caused this." Meg's voice was quiet but forceful. "If I had not been so determined that I had all the answers, you would not be here. Now the children, your brothers, my sister are all worried and frightened. I should have agreed to your decision."

He had turned from the doorway during her speech and now looked at her in that appraising manner she had come to know. Just when she decided he was not going to respond to her apology, Niall shook his head and moved to sit down beside her.

"If there is to be blame cast, it should fall on me. You and your sister have no business in this. My scheme to feed us through the winter by taking hostages for ransom was the first mistake. I should have sent you back days ago." Niall's black eyes stared into the fire.

"Why didn't you?" Meg asked impetuously.

The scar on his cheek tightened, and he turned to look at her. "Our situation forces me to answer honestly. I did not want to let you go."

Her mouth opened in amazement. What could he possibly mean? And then her common sense clicked in. Of course, when he had discovered her relationship to the Earl, there was even more reason to go ahead with his plan. "You must have hoped for even more payment, once you discovered that Argyll is our uncle."

The dark eyes searched her face. "You misunderstand me. It was not the money I considered when you stood there ranting at me in the clearing. It was the sunlight on your hair and the glint of silver in your eyes."

A thrill ran up Meg's spine. He was admitting aloud the attraction they felt for each other. This was completely illogical, she told herself firmly. In their current predicament, romance was the last thing they should be concentrating on.

Uncannily, he seemed to divine her thoughts again. "Aye," his voice took on a bitter tone. "And here we are, both hostages to arrogance and wishful thinking. I have put you in a very bad position, mistress, and it is I who must beg your forgiveness."

"But what did you think to gain by keeping us, if not more money?" Something perverse made her ask, wanting to hear him speak the words she had fantasized about so often.

They stared at each other for a long moment and then Niall reached out and touched her hair, smoothing it down gently. "I selfishly allowed myself to pretend that we might become friends. And more than friends. I pushed the problem of a MacDonald-Campbell alliance aside."

His breathing quickened as his hand moved from her hair to her face. His fingers were warm against Meg's cheek and she felt herself responding to his touch.

"Perhaps," she half whispered as she looked at the handsome face, "the problems could be put aside somehow."

He laid his hand against her cheek and studied her mouth gravely. One finger traced the outline of her lips. "Nay," his voice was guttural. "Years of raiding and murdering cannot be so easily wiped out." He brought his mouth close to her ear. "Neither clan would accept such an idea."

His breath was warm on her neck, and she felt tiny goosebumps along the right side of her body. Surrendering to her instinct, Meg turned and captured his mouth with her own.

Tiny tremors shot through her at the contact. He was warm, and his tongue searched her out, making her tremble even more. She felt his hands move down her arms and pause lightly upon her breasts. And then he suddenly broke the kiss, pushing her away from him. His breath was ragged, and when he spoke, his voice was hoarse.

"This cannot happen!" He was angry at her, she realized in surprise. "We were blood enemies before we ever met. You told me yourself that it is your duty to escape me by whatever means you can find. And I have my own sworn duty before me that I will not forsake.

His face was hard, and she could have sworn that there was fear in it, had that not been an alien emotion for Niall MacDonald.

Meg wrenched her eyes from the hostile man beside her. She forced herself to look at the fire while she recovered from the effects of the embrace. "Please do not be distressed," her words were carefully thought out before she spoke. "I apologize once more for my behavior. I will not put you in such a position again."

She could feel him looking at her, felt those black burning eyes as though the fire had reached out to place its brand upon her. How could she, how could he, continue to deny the attraction that existed between them? At that moment she had no care in the world for the acceptance of their clans. But he was the only leader his people had now, she reminded herself, and he must consider their safety above his own needs.

"You should try to rest," he said finally, still watching her.

It would be too dangerous to meet his gaze. Better to agree quickly and retain her self control. "Very well," Meg said tonelessly. She offered his plaid, but Niall shook his head.

"Keep it. But those sheep skins in the corner can serve as cover for Carnoch."

At the sound of his name, the black stuck his head in through the doorway and whickered. Niall rubbed the sleek nose affectionately. "'Tis glad I am of your size tonight, my lad."

Meg looked at him questioningly, her gray eyes large in the reflected firelight.

"Carnoch will close the door for us," Niall explained. He gave a gentle push on the horse's withers, and Carnoch sank to the ground, his back forming a warm wall to complete the enclosure of the hut.

Meg understood at once and went quickly about the business of laying the sheep skins over Carnoch's back. The horse was obediently quiet, as though he sensed the importance of the unusual actions.

The snow still fell silently on the drifts protecting Meg and Niall from the savage Highland winds. With the last remaining embers of their depleted peat supply glowing, Niall mentally prepared himself for what promised to be a brutal night. He knew their survival depended greatly upon the black.

The animal lay covered with all available garments to make it as comfortable as possible. Not only was it their only transportation over the rugged terrain, but tonight it would provide heat and windbreak for the two hostages at the mercy of the cruel Highland winter. With blankets a scarce commodity at the best of times, Niall and Meg knew without voicing it that their rough quarters would compel them to be as close as lovers in a farewell embrace. In this way only would they reap the benefits from the weight of the lone tartan plaid.

The night was frigid but the winter sky was clear and illuminated with the essence of the loved ones who were always in Niall's mind, the ones who had gone before into that distant realm. He watched Meg as she prepared the skins which would act as a barrier against the howling wind. This woman had touched his spirit in a way that no one else ever had. Neither snow drifts or blood oaths swayed her from her chosen action, and he recognized in the form of a Campbell woman the answering echo of his own tempestuous nature. But it was a dangerous thought, and this was no night for romantic illusions.

He wrapped a small glowing ember in his sporran and placed it at her feet. Its faint warmth might be the spark that stood between her and the threat of frostbite.

From necessity, Meg lay on her side in order to allow enough room for Niall to stay warm. She acknowledged to herself the strangeness of the forced cooperation even as she shivered uncontrollably in the openness of the rude shepherd's hut.

Niall lay down, pressing his chest against her back. His knees touched the backs of her own, the intimate contact causing her shivering to increase.

Feeling her auburn hair tickling his cheek, Niall listened as the wind slowly set the pace for Meg's breathing, knowing just the moment when exhaustion claimed her.

Only when she was safely at rest, did Niall allow himself to drift into a light doze.

✧

Sometime later Meg became groggily aware of his body lying close to her. Without conscious thought, she reached out and pulled him closer. He turned in her arms and pillowed his head on her breast.

They drifted into deeper relaxation, unknowingly comforted by each other's touch. Then, somewhere deep in her dreams, Meg heard him whisper.

"I cannot let this happen."

She opened her eyes. He was lying cradled in her arms, his head resting against her. Her mind reacted to the impulse of her soul.

"Niall," Meg whispered into his hair. "Men have always warred and reived upon each other and women have always paid the price for the blood. You cannot hold me responsible for the massacre and I do not hold you responsible for the revenge your clan honor requires. If it were otherwise, your dirk would be in my hand this moment, threatening your very life."

His breath stilled as he looked down past the fullness of her breast where his cheek rested. His dirk lay mere inches from her soft small hand. Niall's jaw tightened and Meg felt him go rigid in her arms.

"Strike then, if you will," he said roughly. "But know that my brothers will never let you live after that act."

Her teeth nipped his hair, pulling his head back so that she could look down into his eyes. "It is not fear of your brothers that stays me."

For one intense heartbeat they stared into each other's eyes. Then Niall groaned and reached up to smother her lips with his mouth.

When they finally drew apart to breathe, he asked her hoarsely, "What stays your hand, Meg Campbell?"

Her left cheek dimpled slightly as she considered the straight, firm line of his jaw and the quick rise and fall of his chest. "Name it as you like, MacDonald. Just now the motive is of little importance."

The fingers of her left hand wove a path through the tangle of dark hair at his throat. "The only matters to be dealt with here are of our own making."

Niall pressed her mouth again with a searing kiss. Meg responded wholly to the embrace, and soon they lay entwined on the earthen floor as the dying embers of the fire cast a flickering illumination through the tiny hut.

"This is against all reason," she heard him mutter, and her heart lifted joyfully.

"Reason has no reason to be here," she teased. "I will not allow it to enter."

"Meg, listen to me. We must go no farther or we will surely regret this night." He softened the words with a nibble on her earlobe.

"As long as I live, I shall never regret it."

His eyes rested hungrily on the enticing swell of her breasts. "Nor will I," he confessed, "but answer with the truth, Meg. If this is all we will ever have, will you be content?"

You are Campbell, her conscience mocked, lying with an enemy of your clan. *How can you be content, with the blood of* your *ancestors calling out for honor?* She pushed the thought away, concentrating on the warmth of his touch.

"Ever content," she answered at last, though her voice seemed to come from a far, unknown place. "Even though it is for this one night only."

"I wish it was for a lifetime!" He buried his face in her hair. "God forgive my cast away oath, but were there witnesses here, I would bind you me for all time."

A handfasted bride, she thought, mocked at by family and society. But this was Niall, and they were in a place apart, where nothing else mattered. She licked him lightly, from his earlobe to the tiny pulse that beat at the hollow of his throat. The flesh was salty and she lingered there, nursing with gentle insistence at the beating of his heart's rhythm.

"Then let the fire and the snow and the night be our witnesses, MacDonald, for it is my desire also. Whatever the cost of this oath you fear, by all that is sacred, I would claim you tonight." She reached to untie the leather that bound his hair, and the soft thickness of it fell forward onto her breasts.

He kissed her again, taking her breath into his mouth. His heartbeat hammered in rhythm with her own. Then he broke the contact, throwing his head back for a long, sweetly primitive moment.

"By the forces that grant us passion and life, I claim you, Meg Campbell, as part of my own being, now and for all time. And somehow I will find a way to hold both you and my honor inviolate. This I swear."

Her limbs were suddenly weak, and when his hands moved caressingly over her waist, she shuddered with pleasure. With a gentle hand, Niall untied her laces, pushing the soft bodice of her gown down to expose her breasts. His tongue sent tiny flames of desire rippling down her belly.

"I would have preferred a soft, wide bed for you, my heart, with wine and warmth to celebrate our joining."

"You are wine enough," she whispered as his hands moved to part her legs. "And the warmth of your love makes me mad with wanting."

This is Niall, she thought, *Niall. His hands, his mouth. Oh God, my God, how has this happened?*

He kissed her again before he turned his attention to her breasts. Her muscles quivered and tightened under his power and when he bent his head momentarily to acknowledge the soft curls between her thighs, Meg trembled at the melting wetness she felt gathering there.

Whatever followed, whatever price they must pay, they would have this. The forces compelling her were too strong to resist any longer. Meg looked up at him, wanting to memorize each expression of his eyes. She reached to trace the outline of his lips with one finger.

He was poised above her, ready to enter, his ebony hair flowing down to caress her face. Meg wrapped her legs around him tightly. For a moment he hesitated, holding himself stiff and apart from her.

"Are you sure, Meg? Even now it is not too late. I would not have you regret this in the morning."

An unfamiliar heat cascaded though her body and Meg felt herself opening to him like a flower receiving the touch of the sun. "I am sure," her voice was like the whisper of falling silk. "I am sure."

✧

They lay together before the fire, breath answering breath. The night drifted away as they moved in and out of satiated repose. Meg did not try to put words or reason to what they had shared. It was enough that for this moment, in this place, they were joined. Duty to clan seemed an alien, untouchable thing.

Niall nuzzled her cheek with his own. "If I could take you from here and keep the rest of the world away, I would do it in an instant. But the world does exist, Meg, and we cannot ignore it."

She pulled back to look at him. "Then leash your stubbornness and listen to me. Let me go to Robert and talk to him alone. There is no reason you or your brothers must confront him. Let me take Elizabeth and go to him. I can convince him that we came to no harm at your hands. I will tell him it was a mistake."

He watched her closely. A slight twitching of the scarred cheek made her realize that she had said something wrong.

"Niall, what is it?"

He pushed her away and sat up in one long, angry motion. "I understand now, Mistress Campbell. You did indeed seek any means at your disposal to escape."

He stood up, naked before her, and Meg wanted to scream at the finality she heard in his voice.

He donned the clothes he had shed in his passion, his face becoming granite-like in its lack of expression. He bent gracefully to replace the dirk in his boot.

"What do you mean?" The trembling of her lips almost made her stammer. She bit down on the inside of her cheek to still her fear.

Niall looked at the girl lying at his feet. "Do you deny that you used my affection for you as a means to escape?"

"You are wrong!" she cried. "I did not."

"You did, and most skillfully, too. I cannot blame you. I myself gave you that weapon when I admitted my misplaced reluctance to let you go in the beginning."

"Misplaced reluctance?" Meg's head was swimming with confusion. How could the sweet interlude of a few moments before have turned so shatteringly wrong?

"Aye!" He spat the word at her. "But be assured that any attraction I felt for you has now been completely satisfied. You have proven yourself a fine example of all that is characteristic of your clan. Your guardian is sure to welcome you back with open arms, you are enough like him to be his own daughter."

He strode out into the slowly lightening morning and Meg's heart broke at last. All the pent up controlled emotions of the past few days came pouring out as she wept her grief and frustration into the dirt floor of the hut.

He had left Carnoch for her, she realized through the salty mist that covered her eyes. The horse had risen to its feet sometime during their confrontation, and now stood watching her with same quizzical expression its master so often exhibited.

Meg coughed and wiped her face with the plaid. Elizabeth would be worried about her, and no matter what Niall thought, Meg would not leave her sister in fear for her safety. She would return to Blackwater, and convince Elizabeth to leave with her. The horse could be returned later, somehow.

The black allowed her to mount, and as he turned his head toward home, Meg wondered what she would say to the folk waiting there. Despair threatened to overwhelm her, and tears burned her eyes again. It didn't matter that she couldn't see through them; the horse knew which path to take. Even Niall's horse, she thought, was better able to care for itself than she. She let Carnoch find his way home as she covered her face with her long hair, crying for more than the loss of her maidenhood.

CHAPTER 11

Ian and Jamie were mounted on their horses, ready to ride in search of the missing pair, when Meg arrived at the cottage. Beside them, standing with Andrew, Duncan and Elizabeth, were two strangers that bore a strong resemblance to the MacDonald brothers. They wore dark wool jackets over green and white plaid trews and thick boots lined with fur. Ice crystals shone in their beards, signs of the weather through which they had traveled.

Relieved and thankful for her sister's safety, Elizabeth ran to Meg's side. She reached up to help Meg dismount.

"Meg, we have been so worried! You are all right? The snow was so hard last night, we feared you'd lost your way."

Wearily, the would-be runaway slid to the ground. Carnoch wandered over to the horse shelter to look for his breakfast, unconsciously underscoring his ability to fend for himself.

"We found an old shepherd's hut," Meg explained. "We near froze to death, but there was enough peat for Niall to build a small fire."

Ian jumped to the ground and took Meg by the arm, pulling her to his side. "So Niall left you a fire," he said loudly, squeezing her arm until it hurt.

She twitched away from him in pain. "Nay, he didn't leave me a fire, he built a fire. What ails you, Ian?"

His green eyes narrowed and he looked over his shoulder uncomfortably at the strange men who watched with obvious interest.

Duncan shuffled forward, his rheumy eyes almost twinkling. "And where is Niall?"

Meg pulled the plaid from her shoulders and handed it to Ian. "On his way here, I am sure. 'Twas a miserable night we spent in that tiny hut and we woke early. He left Carnoch to bring me home."

Ian groaned and Andrew began to laugh. An unusual quality of nervousness preyed on the brothers this morning and after the night she just spent, Meg was not inclined to deal with any more MacDonald temperament.

Her irritation rose by the moment and she lifted one eyebrow. "What ails you, Ian?" she repeated, not as politely. "Twas a hard night, we barely slept at all and I want my breakfast. Do not play games with me this morning." She thought of Andrew's poor horse and decided against volunteering that bit of news.

One of the strangers interrupted. "And who is the fair lass wearing our Niall's plaid and riding his great horse?"

No one spoke. Meg looked at them all in puzzlement. Just what was going on here? Surely the MacDonalds had related the fictitious story of their visitors to the newcomers.

The taller of the two strangers offered an apology. "Forgive our lack of manners, mistress. I am Fergus MacAlister of Bute, and this is my brother, Alan. We have come to throw in our lot with our kinsmen, to build a strong new clan in the face of the demon Campbell who thought to finish us forever." The gray haired man spoke with a sense of defiance and determination.

He was older than Niall, and obviously took himself and his tartan pride quite earnestly. Well, so did other clans, Meg thought. And her own was just as significant as the MacDonalds, and probably older. She put her hands on her hips and prepared to inform Fergus MacAlister of just who he stood bragging before.

"I am Meg Ca—"

Ian cut her off quickly, putting an arm around her shoulders. "Cameron. Meg Cameron. From Erracht. She and her sister both have come just as you have, Fergus, looking for a bright future among the MacDonalds of Glencoe." He gave her an affectionate squeeze. "They came looking for husbands."

Meg gasped with shock. "Have you lost what little mind you had?" She looked at Elizabeth for help, but her sister was as dumbfounded as Meg.

The newcomers were interested however, scanning the sisters in an appraising fashion. Meg's outrage grew by the second and her face turned white.

The other man, Alan, nodded agreeably. "Fine lasses, Ian. They look strong." He added to Meg, "Fergus is already married ye ken, but I have yet to take a wife. You are the elder, I take it, and so will marry first?"

Beside Meg, Ian covered his face with one hand. Andrew continued to laugh, a deep rumbling belly laugh that infuriated Meg as it got louder and louder.

Alan turned to Ian. "Are you all laughing at me?" he inquired gruffly. He was shorter than Fergus, and probably a few years younger, with curling brown hair that reached his shoulders. His beard was wild and unkempt as the ice in it began to thaw, and his blue eyes were confused.

"The lass says she stayed the night with Niall," said Fergus, "so perhaps an arrangement has already been made."

"Is that true, Mistress Cameron?" Alan looked downcast. "I would not wish to trespass against Niall's claim."

Meg wasn't sure what he meant, but she would not lie as Ian had just done. "Aye! It is true." The answer was defiant. "And my name is —"

She was interrupted once more, this time by Niall himself who had arrived at the clearing in time to hear Meg's statement.

"Her name is Meg MacDonald."

Like a cat she whirled upon him, ready to strike at the insult. But he silenced her with a quick kiss on her open mouth.

"Quiet," he warned, in a whisper against her cheek. His eyes were dark as cold flint when he turned to face the other men. "'Tis my right to introduce my handfasted bride to my kinsmen."

Meg's mind went numb. Handfasted? He was invoking the irregular marriage laws of Scotland, she realized, but why? He surely must realize the graveness of such words.

But perhaps not.

With one arm rock hard around her waist, Niall grinned at the stunned group standing before him. "Well? Do I have your best wishes, cousins? She brings no bride price but herself, but that alone, as you can see, is more than enough." He pinched her cheek and winked at them.

Fergus and Alan came forward, clapping Niall upon the shoulders and punching him with rough fists on the chest.

Alan apologized for his behavior toward Meg, and Niall accepted it without comment. The would-be suitor looked Meg over carefully and demanded a quick kiss from her for luck.

Still dazed from Niall's announcement, Meg kissed Alan's cheek dutifully, only to realize from the sound of Elizabeth's amazed gasp, that she had just committed herself to an arrangement she had no desire to fulfill. With a wrench she pulled away from Niall's grasp and placed two fists on her hips.

"Have you gone daft?" she berated him. "How can you tell such a great lie to these people?"

"Meg is right, brother," Ian came forward to stand between them, "she did bring a bride price with her, only in your haste to contract the marriage, you neglected to secure it."

Horrified at the mounting lies and humiliated at the leers of the two strangers, Meg felt her face flush crimson. "How dare you?" She took a swing at Niall and missed his jaw by several inches.

Still laughing, he picked her up as easily as he would Beth or Flora and swung her over one shoulder. "As you can see, my bride is full of fire."

The men laughed and wished him luck with the saucy new wife. The last thing Meg saw over Niall's shoulder as he carried her inside the cottage was Ian's dour expression. Suddenly she realized that what she had assumed to be a light flirtation for Ian had in reality masked a much more serious situation.

Niall set her down on the floor. He closed the door before turning to look at her, black brows furrowed over the dangerous gleam in his dark eyes.

"This coil, mistress, like the one last night, is of your own making and none of mine. So you can spare me your righteous indignation and your outraged sensibilities. I am not interested."

"My making?" her voice rose in disbelief. "You just told those men that we are married."

"Aye," he admitted, "I did. Right after you yourself told them we spent the night together alone in the hut."

"But it was the truth —" her voice trailed off and her eyes widened as she realized exactly what she had told the men outside.

"It was indeed the truth," he nodded at her, "and so to prevent them from slaying you where you stood as you compounded the sin by identifying yourself as a Campbell, I chose to explain our relationship."

"Slay me?"

Niall looked at her as though she were a slow minded child. "What would you expect? Campbell soldiers murdered many women that Alan and Fergus knew. And you would stand there and throw it in their teeth that you spent the night with me and your name is Campbell. Not even my sword could protect you if they knew the truth."

She sat down on the kitchen stool. "I am doomed," she whispered. Her shoulders slumped and she fought to keep tears from leaping to her eyes.

"As am I, apparently." Niall looked out the small window to where his kinsmen were laughing and talking. Ian still stood looking unhappily at the door through which Niall and Meg had disappeared, while Elizabeth and Andrew talked with the newly arrived MacDonalds.

Relieved at the peaceful scene outside the cottage, Niall turned back to face Meg. His eyes had resumed their remote shadowy depths and his expression revealed nothing of his thoughts.

"At least for the moment, the danger has been averted. Between us, Ian and I have eased the situation."

"But you have announced us married. You spoke the words in front of witnesses." Married. Her mind refused to take it in.

"In words only, mistress." Niall's voice was unrelenting in its hardness. "I have not forgotten the last words I spoke in the stone bothy. This marriage is to save the soft hairs of your stubborn neck and for that reason only. It will last until such time as I can return you to your home. Be assured that whatever remains of your virtue is quite safe from me."

It hurt to hear him speak so, after the sweet intimacy they had shared in the bothy. Meg blinked her eyes several times to clear her view of the angry man standing before her. When she spoke however, her voice was clear and strong, with no hint of inner struggle.

"My honor does not stand or fall upon your protection, MacDonald. I am quite able to speak for myself and to defend any attacks upon the remnants of my virtue."

"Oh aye, Mistress Campbell, that I can see very clearly." His eyes revealed too much now, accentuating the mockery in his voice. "You would defend yourself and your sister by announcing first that you have spent the night alone with me on the mountain and next by naming your clan before men who have every reason under Heaven to exact revenge on all who carry that name. I agree, you certainly have no need of my protection."

She would not admit her mistake to him, she thought. "I still have my dirk," she reminded him. "And I will not hesitate to use it on anyone, anyone at all, who threatens my sister or me."

Niall crossed his arms on his chest and regarded the toes of his scuffed black boots. "I am certain that the sight of Mistress Campbell advancing with her dirk in hand would give any man second thought before attacking. For that matter, even the sight of her without her dirk should send a sane man running for his life."

Much more of this mockery and she would take her dirk to him. The thought gave her great pleasure and for a moment she indulged herself in the fantasy, her eyes sparkling with relish.

Watching the play of emotion on her face, Niall wondered again at the expansive nature of the woman. Childlike one moment, and intense the next, she was a heady mixture of passion and innocence. But the innocence, he knew, would be extinguished if her true identity was revealed to his kinsmen. He took a deep breath and raised a hand outward, palm open.

"Truce, mistress, for the moment."

Meg watched him warily. She would not trust the words or the man who had held her and invaded her soul so deeply the night before.

He seemed to catch that thought as it flashed through her mind, and he smiled at her, shaking his head.

"Aye," the words were soft, "we both should be suspicious. Would that we had been more so yester e'en. However," his speech was brisk now, "we must go over this marriage arrangement so that no questions arise. You and your sister are Camerons, and we met in Edinburgh at Lady Cathlan's home. You returned to Glencoe with me to try to make some sense of the trouble here." His teeth flashed in a bitter smile and he saluted her with a raised eyebrow. "Outwardly we are husband and wife. Privately, you need not even speak to me. Until such time as my plans can be carried out, this is our situation. Are we agreed?"

She thought he referred to his promise to send a ransom request when the spring thaw came. Surely that could not be much longer, she told herself. And the deception would keep Elizabeth safe for awhile longer. "Agreed."

A thought occurred to her that she voiced before realizing that it would only fuel his anger.

"What if I have a baby?"

Niall stared at her in shock. It struck the pit of his stomach like a sword cut and fear almost made him stagger. His voice grated like steel on steel. "I pray not, Mistress Campbell. Such a child would never be allowed to live."

She stared at him, unable to comprehend the words he had just spoken. How utterly callous was he? She had thought him so tender and giving only a few short hours before. Trembling, Meg rose and faced the man with whom she had found passion and betrayal.

He stared her back, matching her breath for breath, with not a flicker of an eyelash moving in his impassive face. "Did the clan learn the truth of your name, they would cut you down before the babe even quickened in your belly. And if they discover it afterward, I can promise you that it would take an act of the Holy Virgin Herself to stop them from murdering it in your womb and you along with it."

The venom hurt her heart and Meg gasped, putting one hand to her chest. "I am innocent of blood!"

"So were their families."

"You would stand by and let them murder your own child?"

Niall gritted his teeth, and the scar on his jaw whitened with rage. "I said this must not happen and yet I allowed it.

Nay," he swung one heavy fist into the wall, cracking the mud mortar and Meg covered her ears in fright.

Niall turned and looked at her, a haunted soul-wrenching pain in his black eyes. "I did more than allow it to happen. I sought it and prayed for it and reveled in it."

She could not speak, but stood alone in the center of the room, trembling with fear and despair. "What have we done?" she whispered to the man who stood with his head bowed before her.

"We have sinned. Against our clans and against God." Niall's monotone echoed Meg's despair, and she took a hesitant step toward him only to halt when he threw up one arm to ward her away. Somehow that hurt more than his words.

His eyes were bloodshot and wild as he stared at her. "I can promise you this, though, on the small bit of honor I have left, Meg Campbell, that no innocent babe will face the hands of revenge and hate. And as long as I can lift my sword, no one shall touch you. I will make an end of the matter."

"'Twould still be hate, no matter whose hand lifted the sword. To die for honor's sake is small consolation for a woman who will never hear the laughter of her child. And what of you? It might be your son that was cut from me. Have you thought of that? Listen to me. If there should be a babe, you must let me leave. I will go far away so that you need never be troubled by it."

Niall trembled then, and put his hand up as though he would strike her. "You must think me a devil in truth." His anger was a cold thing now, no less burning in its icy flame. "But I care nothing for that, Campbell woman. Will you be content to live in dishonor then? Will you have your child grow up outcast without clan or name to sustain it? Shamed and unwanted?"

"Never unwanted," she whispered. "Never that." Meg lifted her head, the wet streaks showing on her face. "You will have to murder me now, Niall MacDonald, here in this room with my sister and your brothers standing outside. Strike now, because by all the saints you hold dear as well as by my Savior and Master, I swear that I will not allow you or anyone else to hurt my child. Not for the honor of our clans or ourselves."

Niall shook his head in disgust. "These are the last words I will speak on it. I said that I would make an end to the matter myself. Not that I would murder my own child. Only a Campbell could conceive of such a thing. 'Tis not to be wondered at, that they cut down our families with no concern, when even a woman such as yourself can give voice to such a blasphemy."

Dear God, she thought in horror, have I mistaken his words? "Niall," she started toward him, pleading in her voice. "Listen to me, I did not —"

"Nay! Do not touch me." The black eyes were quite human now, she realized, recognizing the disgust in them.

"Niall," she said again, more firmly. "I was wrong."

They were interrupted by a tentative knock upon the door and Andrew stuck his head inside. "Fergus and Alan are wanting to talk to ye," he explained.

Niall started to the doorway. Meg reached her hand out entreatingly. "We must finish this."

He had already resumed the identity of chief which had been temporarily put aside. The man before her was cold and arrogant, from the disinterested dullness in his eyes to the aloof bearing of his proud body. Niall barely looked at her as he turned to follow Andrew away.

"There is no more to be said, wife."

When Elizabeth came to her, Meg smiled to cover her confusion. "It seems that I am now a married woman," she said lightly. "I had not thought to enter the state so soon, but I suppose remarkable events call for remarkable haste."

"Oh, darling, don't," Elizabeth saw through the irony, and put her arms around her sister. "You know why he did it. 'Twas for our good."

"And now I am a double hostage." Meg sighed. "Wherever I turn, more trouble awaits. To be bonded to a man who hates me is not the way I wished to end this."

"He does not hate you. And if you have to be married, Niall is strong and handsome. Is it so bad?"

Meg could not believe Elizabeth's words. "You are not serious. This is not a true marriage, Bess. 'Tis only until we can return to Glenlyon." For the first time, she thought with longing of the gray stone walls of Chesthill. "The marriage will be annulled."

Elizabeth pondered this, watching Meg pace the cottage erratically. "Meg, forgive me but I must ask. Did you and Niall, that is, were you as husband and wife last night?"

Meg halted in her movement, wishing she could avoid the questions of her sister.

"If you were, then the marriage must not be annulled. It would be wrong in the sight of God."

In the sight of God. Meg turned slowly and looked at Elizabeth. The younger girl stood resolute before her, her gaze level. Her hands were clasped as she waited for Meg's answer.

Choosing her words with care, Meg reached out to her sister. She held Elizabeth's cool hand in her own, sparing a moment to wonder at the warmth of her own flesh. "Bess, you must be guided by me in this. Circumstances have arranged themselves so that this marriage must be played out for a time. Eventually, we will leave here and return home. When we do, there must be no hint of anything improper. For either of us. Do you understand? Will you continue to trust me?"

After a moment, Elizabeth nodded. Her blue eyes were loyal. "I do trust you. And I trust that God has a plan for us in this. We must listen for His wisdom and act accordingly."

Meg squeezed Elizabeth's hand, and the two girls walked outside. The men were still under the oak tree, talking animatedly. She caught Ian's eye and smiled at him, but he ducked his head, looking back at Fergus who was waving one hand in the air to emphasize his words.

Niall stood with his back to the cottage, and Meg took the opportunity to steer Elizabeth in the other direction, toward the burn. As they walked away, she could hear Andrew arguing about not waiting until next week for something. Niall's lower tones responded, and the other men quieted instantly, deferring to him.

"He might well be the true chief," Meg said aloud, her thoughts running over the situation. "They hang on his every word."

"Andrew said that Niall was chosen to act as chief until the sons of MacIaian can return," Elizabeth volunteered, swinging her arms out like a child. "He said the men need a leader, and there are clusters of people in hiding all over the glen. They wait for word from the sons of the chief, when they will all come together again as free men."

Meg was amazed at the information. "I did not know this. MacIaian's sons will return? Do you know where they hide? Does Andrew speak to you about their plans?" Her thoughts whirled with the information. Perhaps in this maze of secrecy there was a bargaining point she could use to gain her own freedom.

Elizabeth shook her head. "He would not tell me where they are, only that they are not together. That way, if one should fall, there would still be the other to lead the clans. But he said that powerful people are petitioning the king for restoration."

"Then we must pray for that," Meg answered in disappointment. "Perhaps God will choose to answer this one."

Elizabeth reproved her sister with a frown. "He answers in His own way and in his own time."

"You sound like Dr. Kincaid." Meg smiled genuinely.

"Do I? I don't mean to give you a sermon," Elizabeth giggled. "But I think you forget your faith sometimes, Meg. And we must never stop trusting in God."

"March is almost over," said Meg tiredly, as they came to the stream. "You'd think He would be ready to reward our trust by now."

The clan accepted the news of the handfasting with only a few startled looks. Exactly what Niall told the other men, Meg never knew, but they treated her with a deference that had been lacking before the marriage. It was a time full of strange omens, with late spring coming on, and much was made of the appropriate time the chief had chosen to take a wife.

With the coming of spring, the clan would celebrate Beltane, that pagan holiday which was sacred to the old gods of Scotland. Meg and Elizabeth listened to the stories of past feasts and bonfires that lasted late into the night.

Raised in Edinburgh, the two girls had never witnessed the pagan rites, and Meg's Christian soul was concerned about the rumors of fornication and drunkenness that accompanied the festival.

One night, as they all sat around Duncan's hearth, the talk turned to the meaning behind the upcoming festivity.

Elizabeth listened to the stories with eagerness, learning about the goddess of spring who mated with the green man of the forests at Beltane. It was a sacred joining, Annie explained righteously, and one which the young people of the clan used to mimic in the old days. Any babe born of the Beltane fires would be honored and acknowledged, with no taint attached to its birth.

In the old days, too, cattle would be driven between two large bonfires as the people asked the god for his blessing on the fertility and health of the clan. Cattle at one time had been Glencoe's greatest treasure, but in the pillaging that occurred after the massacre, Annie told them, most of their beasts had been killed or been reived away. The few that escaped had almost certainly died in the snows. She shook her head gloomily. It would be a poor feast this year, if it was held at all.

"But what did the priest think of the Beltane fires?" asked Meg. Even a Catholic priest would know that such things were an abomination before God, heathen symbols of an unchurched people.

"Father Michael himself blessed the cows," Annie answered with a smug smile. "And sprinkled the holy water over the people as they walked."

Elizabeth was entranced with the unusual rituals. "And the goddess comes to bless the land?"

"Aye, lass, always. But this year," Annie sighed, "after so much sorrow and loss, I'm thinking we'll not be celebrating the Beltane fires."

"Never say it!" Duncan shook his stick threateningly. "While there's a MacDonald left to light the torches, Glencoe will mark the feast of Bel."

Everyone looked at Niall for confirmation. He smiled and gestured toward Duncan. "Then we had best start preparing. By my reckoning, Beltane is but one month away."

The women giggled and Annie closed one eye as she looked around the group. "Only the unmarried will partake in the dancing," she ordered. "Not the newly widowed. 'Twould not be seemly."

Meg looked at the agreeable faces around the fire. The only widowed people were Rose and a man named John who lived alone in the forest. Everyone else was eligible to take part in the wilder events of the holiday. Meg shook her head in negation at Elizabeth. When the night came, she would make sure that she and her sister were far from the revelry.

The clan excused themselves early, no doubt to go home and dream of pagan ceremonies and strange gods. Meg tidied up the cottage alone, mulling over the way in which she found herself drawn into the lives of these people.

CHAPTER 12

A patch of pale green deer grass raised tiny tendrils toward the late winter sun. Already the faint promise of lavender was in the air. The narrow burn behind the cottage had thawed, and ran freely down from the Coe, tumbling merrily over the small fall of rocks where Meg's kelpie lived.

It was a good day to be alive. A good day to initiate the firmness and determination of character that the clan had sworn to display together.

Niall watched the men who worked beside him, and offered silent thanks to God that the men of Glencoe still found the strength of purpose to stay on their land.

Counting his three brothers, Alan and Fergus and the men they had brought back with them, there were now fifteen men in the small clan. Annie and Dora had succeeded in convincing the other women to remain, and with small Beth and Flora the total number of women was twelve. The two Campbell women Niall did not take into accounting. They were not destined to long remain in his care, he told himself, and in any case, the clan needed strong women who would work side by side with their men to rebuild and reclaim the land. Hostile strangers would only be a hindrance.

It was a small number on which to found a tenuous hope, but Niall had faith in the will of the people. They had showed their instinct and determination for survival, and he had no doubt that they would succeed. As long as there was a possibility that John or Alasdair might one day return to Glencoe, the clan would continue to have faith. What might happen if King William did not extend the offer, Niall did not ponder.

With his grizzled beard and scarred countenance bespeaking years of experience, Fergus had moved into the position of second hand man to the chosen stand-in chief. All their lives it had been Ian who stood back to back with Niall against the world, but that comforting relationship was now altered, influenced by the light in a pair of scheming gray eyes and the curve of a soft laughing mouth. It was one more stress to an overburdened people, and Niall saw no immediate easing of their estrangement.

He watched as the men worked to raise the small post and beam cottage. Turf would do for the rooftop, as it had for centuries. He was gratified to see that they worked well together, these men from other MacDonald keeps who had come together to aid their unfortunate kinsmen. In the summer, when the weather permitted, they would begin to raise strong cottages of stone. For now, the wooden structures with granite reinforcements were sufficient.

His brothers worked diligently, setting themselves the hardest and most unpleasant tasks. It was an unspoken matter of honor among Niall's brothers, that they must meet high standards and not be found lacking in industry and ambition. All told, Niall admitted to himself, they had achieved much in a short time.

Three new cottages now stood where before there had been dozens. But those three were strong and tight against the high winds and rains, and there was room for growth. He prayed that they would have time to grow and garner their strength before another attack came, yet he knew that such a hope was fruitless.

There would always be raids and killing, it was the way of the Highland clans to thieve from one another to increase their own bounty. There were times when Niall grew weary of it all, and wondered if he was exposing his people to undue danger, yet he could not bring himself to order them to flee this place that so many had died to defend.

In truth, there was no where else to go even if they did wish to leave. They must bide here, awaiting word from Appin and from Edinburgh as to what would happen next. To venture from Blackwater was certain suicide. The borders teemed with patrols who searched for the ragged survivors and Glencoe was bounded on all sides by enemies who would be well pleased to deliver a MacDonald prize into the hands of Robert Campbell.

At the thought of the colonel, Niall's face hardened. Weeks had passed since the abduction of Meg and Elizabeth, and although Niall had set a man to watch the pass at all times, there had as yet been no sign of the advance of the troops which Niall knew were bound to come. He realized it was past time to put his plan into action, separating the two captives so that Campbell would be forced to divide his troops and thus halve his strength.

He would send Jamie away with Elizabeth on the morrow, Niall decided, and in so doing perhaps put an end to Andrew's growing interest in the young girl. Ian's infatuation with Meg was also becoming dangerous. His brother followed the red haired wench around like a starving pup. Ian, too, must be prevented from destroying himself with his shallow dreams. He would appoint Ian to safeguard the children and the elders, thus leaving little opportunity for the two to meet. It would put Meg alone at the cottage, and himself easily able to watch her as he waited for the arrival of the soldiers.

His thoughts stilled momentarily at the idea of guarding her without interference from Ian. Niall, ever alert against the woman's wiles he deplored in Meg, welcomed the opportunity to foil her games. Though to outward appearances, they were living as a married couple, the reality of the situation strained at him every waking moment.

Even his evenings were uneasy, lying next to her for half the night before rising to take his turn at watching the pass. He watched her prepare for bed, combing her dark red hair and donning one of his sister's night dresses. Then when sleep did claim her, it was all he could do to restrain his hands from exploring the sweetness of her relaxed body.

He glanced over to the grove of oak trees where Meg and Elizabeth and some of the other women were laying out a noon repast for the men. As usual, Meg was directing the efforts of everyone else, even as she bent her own energies to the same tasks. He had to acknowledge her skill in domestic matters, even if only to himself. Niall made a wry face, imagining Meg's pleasure were he ever again to fall victim to such a weakness as complimenting her abilities.

The women set out jugs of water with warm bread and cold cheese, keeping the food covered with a cloth until the men were ready for a break from the roofing job.

Dora and the little girls were stacking armloads of turf beside the new cottage. Everyone was helping, and Niall had to admit that even the Campbell women showed a surprising adaptability and aptitude for the work. He had not thought of asking them to help, not considering that they might be inclined to aid the MacDonalds. He had not reckoned on their generosity of spirit.

Niall squelched these thoughts even as they came to his mind. The men had voted him their chief. He must remember that, and act as a chief, not allowing his thoughts to runaway from him like unbridled horses. But as he watched Meg go about her tasks, smiling and joking with the men he led, Niall found the chore he set for himself becoming increasingly harder to fulfill.

Sensing the interest of the chief, one of the women looked up and met his glance with a saucy stare. Her name was Margaret too, but there was no other resemblance between her and Meg Campbell. Margaret had hair as red as Ian's. It swung about her face, framing pert green eyes. Her upturned nose had a piquant quality about it, and as she returned Niall's gaze, she smiled and gave him a bold wink.

For a moment he was startled, then bit his lip as Annie, intercepting the flirtatious advance, began to scold the girl. Margaret Robertson represented no danger. If she persisted in her play she would learn quickly that the new chief was not interested. A commitment to one woman, even though it was not a permanent one, was more than enough for him to deal with.

It was hard, though, to be with a wife and yet not be with her, he acknowledged. Especially when the memory of her body burned him like a torch. Perhaps a dalliance with someone like Margaret was the answer. Certainly his *wife* should have no complaint. Margaret might be just what was needed to keep his mind on track.

Niall's mouth twisted as he reminded himself of how he had indulged himself in the bed of another beautiful woman at a moment when danger was riding toward his clan. He felt that same danger every time he looked at Meg Campbell, every time he thought of her lying beneath him in the beehive hut.

He continued to watch the women under the trees as his memories churned inside him. No woman alive was worth the anguish of neglected duty that writhed inside him. Never again, he vowed to himself. Never again would he put love before honor. Women were important for the survival of the clan, as mothers and wives. And for that role, any woman would do.

There was a hollowness in his soul at the direction his thoughts were leading him. Niall sighed and turned his face to the freshness of a light breeze. It was not Meg's fault, he was honest enough with himself to admit that. She was no worse than any other woman, they were all born ready to distract a man from his obligations. No, the blame rested on his own broad shoulders, and Niall MacDonald wore that blame like a talisman, a shield between his honor and his heart.

He felt a presence beside him and turned to see Margaret coyly offering him a jug of water.

"Thank you, lass," he took the vessel from her hands gratefully. Tilting his head back, Niall drank long and deeply before lowering the jug from his mouth. His black eyes were friendly as they rested on the attentive young woman. "'Twas thoughtful of you."

Margaret dimpled and took the jug back. "You have all been working so hard this morning. We are quite astonished at the results." A small hand waved toward the roof framework now being lowered over the new cottage.

It settled quickly into place and a cheer went up from the team of men who had raised it. Niall smiled, his face reflecting the pride and satisfaction he felt.

"Ye'll be wanting to celebrate?" Margaret's expression was inviting as she tipped her head to one side and considered him with her velvet soft green gaze. Her mouth was pouty and expectant.

Niall's throat was suddenly dry. It had been a long time since a woman had sought his attentions. And the strain of living chastely with Meg was becoming a problem. He felt his body stir at the invitation Margaret so obviously displayed.

With Margaret there would be no question of commitment or promise. It would be a diversion only, and surely a man was entitled to live as a man. He glanced over at the other women under the trees. Meg and Annie had stopped their work and stood watching him with Margaret. Niall felt his face flush in defiance, and he looked back down at Margaret.

Smiling wickedly, he put one hand under her chin and tilted it up toward his own. "Aye, lass," he murmured, "I do indeed feel like celebrating." His lips found hers in a hard emphatic motion and as Margaret threw her arms about his neck, Niall heard the men cheering again as the first support of the new wall was set in place.

When he extricated himself from Margaret's enthusiastic embrace, Meg was occupied with Alan and Jamie, offering them brown bread with thick slices of cool cheese. Annie still watched, however, her face screwed up in a terrible scowl. She pointed her finger at Niall and Margaret.

Niall laughed aloud. "We've been caught, my girl," he slapped Margaret on the backside. "'Tis time for me to get back to work."

Margaret winked at him and picked up the water jug she had dropped during the kiss.

"I'll be back," she promised.

The movement of her hips was exaggerated as she walked away and Niall chuckled at her lack of subtlety.

"I'm sure you will, lass."

He walked over to where Fergus and Andrew were counting out posts. Annie's belligerent tones were audible for all to hear as she chastised Margaret for being a wanton. Fergus looked up at Niall and grinned.

"That's a saucy skirt. I'd hate to be standing where you are, between Mistress Meg and yon teasing lassie."

Niall's face tightened. "'Twas in celebration only, Fergus. There's naught between me and Margaret."

"Do you give her any hint that you're in need, she'll have you between her legs before sundown. She's accommodating that way. If your own lass doesna satisfy the itch, yon Margaret will be glad to."

Niall hesitated to take offense at Fergus' words. Margaret was well known for her open, generous nature where the men were concerned. But he was supposed to be newly and passionately wed. He gazed over at the women again, feeling an ache and tightening in his loins.

Meg felt his eyes on her and looked up to meet them. It was as though he had reached out and touched the very center of her being, and she was confused at the spinning of her head. Did he not feel it also, this invading, torturing heat that weakened her whenever she was near him? The nights were worst, lying so close beside him in the tiny croft, remembering, always remembering, just how close they had been. She prayed that he did not realize how much she craved what he had just given so easily to Margaret, and anger rose in her that he dared to behave so in front of the clan. She fought it down and returned Niall's look. Willing herself to reveal nothing, she picked up a piece of bread and a slice of cheese.

He watched her walk toward him, mimicking Margaret's sensuous movements, and he bit his lip at her irony. By God, she had a sense of humor and wit lacking in other women. What a wife she would have made under other circumstances.

"Are you hungry, husband?" She cocked her head to the side and assumed a flirtatious expression similar to Margaret's. "Such hard labor must cause an emptiness in your belly."

Her tone was sweet, but he heard Fergus snicker beside him. "Aye, Meg, I am hungry." He would play it out any way she chose. He reached out and caressed a dark red curl. "And there is a great emptiness in me that needs to be filled."

Meg smiled and offered him the food. He stayed her hand, smiling back at her with careful control.

"Will you feed me yourself, wife? I crave the touch of your gentle hands at my mouth." By now, everyone around them had stopped working and watched them openly.

Meg's eyes blazed at his words. Then she tore the bread and cheese into two pieces. She looked at him slyly out of the corner of her eye. "As you desire."

Again she offered the food and this time, Niall opened his mouth. Quick as a lightening bolt, Meg crammed the bread and cheese full into his mouth, causing him to choke in surprise.

He spat it out onto the ground before him and the men laughed boisterously. Niall glared at the composed woman before him. "Is that how you think to feed your husband?"

She smiled again, not so sweetly. "I thought such a large portion would suit your — enormous appetite. Did it not?" She cast a meaningful look over at Margaret, who stood with one hand over her mouth.

The humor of the situation overwhelmed him, and Niall found himself laughing along with his men. She was witty indeed, and brave. Not many women would dare to take their men to task thus before the whole clan.

Their men. Suddenly the words penetrated Niall's mind. Was her action the result of jealousy over him? Did Meg in fact consider him to be her man? The speculation sent his pulse racing and he looked at her appraisingly.

She was laughing along with the others, but that determined gleam was still in her gray eyes. Her gaze was wide and fearless as she laughed, and Niall thought again of what a chieftain's wife she might have made.

As the merriment died, he gave her a sarcastic bow. "I fear you have judged the size of my — appetite wrongly, but I thank you for the compliment. In the future, I will take care to give you the opportunity to fulfill my needs before my enormous appetite becomes uncontrollable."

Meg wasn't laughing now, he saw with satisfaction. Her expression had closed up at his words, and the invisible protective shield she could summon so quickly was back in place before he had finished his speech.

Her voice was clipped and precise when she answered him. "I am sure your needs are provided for, sir, as you seem to seek nourishment at different hands than mine. Clearly, there are others who whet your appetite more." She walked regally back to the oak grove.

Andrew and Fergus did not look at Niall as they returned to work, but bent their backs to raising the center post for another small cottage. After a quick exhalation, Niall too, went back to work. For the rest of the day he kept his thoughts to himself, and maintained a safe distance from all the women.

CHAPTER 13

Inverary Castle
Argyll

The Earl of Argyll wrote swiftly, his brow clear, and his manner severe. Righteous anger inspired his words, fueling the orders he set to paper in response to Robert Campbell's advisement of the events at Glen Lyon.

> *"It is incumbent upon you, as my nephew and as the faithful servant of the King, to put a quick and complete end to this troubling affair. I adjure you, by all that your oath has required of you that you act with speed in returning my wards to Chesthill. You must take careful account that all possible avenues of escape are closed off, but no man of the name MacDonald is to be harmed at any cost. Had you succeeded with carrying out Breadalbane's orders in the first instance, we would not now be faced with remedying the ill fated retribution of that undertaking. The hand of God has delivered us this chance to take the survivors prisoner and to make an example of them, thereby clearing the King and his advisors of any infamy from the incident at Glencoe. Take care that our own tarnished name is not further harmed by your actions."*

Argyll's lips pursed as he remembered the tale recounted to him by his loyal men who spied for him at Ft. William. Robert's proclivity for heavy drinking had marred his leadership of the foray into Glencoe the previous year, and could easily have lowered Argyll's standing in the King's eyes. The Master of Stair, Sir John Dalrymple, had made it very clear that another blunder would not be tolerated. It was only by benevolent Fortune that the MacDonalds themselves had now placed Argyll in a highly favorable position.

This time, the Earl vowed to himself, Robert must succeed. A MacDonald prisoner held up to public scrutiny as a kidnapper and thief would do much to restore the nation's faith in the Master of Stair. As the MacDonalds had in their keeping the two wards of the Earl, Campbell was more than justified in retaliating. And in doing so, would help to justify the actions of the King whom most Highlanders called the Usurper.

Argyll paused briefly, his eyes resting on the large portrait of King William which graced his library wall. William was not the first ruler to make the mistake of claiming the Highlands as his own. And this was not the first time a Campbell had worked quietly to ensure his own position and power against such a claim.

It suited the Earl well for King William to think Argyll and Glenlyon loyal vassals of the Crown. The Master of Stair was the real authority in Scotland; Orange William listened carefully to every advisement of his Scottish advisor, and Argyll knew that aiding Dalrymple in restoring the king's standing would yield high returns for all the Campbells of Scotland.

The Earl returned to his letter writing.

> *"See that you do not fail in the careful and assiduous carrying out of your orders. On no account is the safety of the two girls to be risked, but the Crown will not brook another costly mistake. I await the news of your successful campaign."*

The Earl sat back in his chair and smiled with satisfaction. That, he thought, should be plain to enough to let Robert know the plan was to be carried out soberly. Celebrating with whiskey could wait until later.

CHAPTER 14

Spring had finally arrived, and with it the excitement of Beltane. There were no cattle to be blessed, and precious few provisions to make a feast, but the people worked with a new lightness to prepare for the festival. Cream pies and bannochs were baked along with the inevitable scones, newly snared hares were skinned and roasted, then hung to dry over the peat fires. A few of Duncan's treasured jugs of heather ale were uncovered and cleaned up to toast the ancient gods.

From her oak storage chest, Annie provided a bright green square of cloth that she said had done duty many times as a robe for the goddess. This year, as always, they would choose a king and queen to represent the gods, and the queen would wear the green cloth as a royal robe. The color signified fertile land and abundant crops, blessings the clan needed greatly.

Meg watched the activity, relaxing into the spirit of the preparation. It was an unusual way to pass the first of May, but God above knew these folk deserved some merrymaking. She did not, however, forget her original determination to be far from the pagan fires on Beltane night. The stories half frightened her, but the primitive overtones of passion and pleasure also excited her. It was a humbling reminder of her own turbulent nature. She tried to concentrate on the organization of the gathering rather than on its symbolic fertility rites.

Blackwater had no special gathering place for holidays, as the keep had, and so the men took advantage of the still dormant trees and plants, clearing away an area almost big enough to be called a 'down'. Certainly it was elevated slightly, and there had been no massive trees to contend with. But what little grass grew there was straggly and poor looking. Perhaps, Duncan said, it would grow into a proper down by next year's celebration.

"Will everyone be keeping the holiday?" Meg asked him. "Even those in hiding?" Duncan was tasting her cream pies as fast as she could concoct them, and she felt rather like a hardworking mother with three small children to look after on a busy day.

Duncan chortled, and Beth and Flora mimicked him.

"Aye, I dinna doubt they'll keep it in such way as they can. Mayhap with candles instead of bonfires, and a quiet tumble or twa," Duncan winked at her over the children's heads, "but the old ways will be honored. We had no desire to celebrate last year. The year before that, we kept the day at the Carnoch shieling," he spoke of MacIaian's summer home and the thatched beehive shaped cottages that surrounded it, "but 'tis too dangerous to travel there now. The soldiers would pick us off like roosting crows before we made it to the Coe. 'Tis a great shame, it is, for it was the one time when we all came together. From great distances the clan would gather at the shieling, taking the easy hunt from those forests, and feasting on herring from Loch Linnhe." Duncan smacked his lips at the memory.

"How far away is the Coe?" The river should be thawed by now and the idea of a true bath was exciting, distracting her from the picture of idyllic summer life among relatives and friends. Meg waited for Duncan to answer.

He scowled at her. "Too far for a tricky lass like yourself to go alone. Dinna fash about the Coe, ye'll see it when ye see it and not before."

Well, that was most enlightening. Meg repressed her urge to stick her tongue out at the old man. It wasn't likely she'd try to escape now, being publicly wed to Niall. She sighed. Everyone knew about the chief's new wife, even those in hiding, she had no doubt. Such tidings were carried on the winds. If she even thought about trying to leave, someone would be watching to relate the gossip.

Meg tied a dark green kerchief around her hair and picked up the rush basket she used to carry berries. "I'm going to the forest," she told Duncan haughtily, "to look for berries."

He waved his hand at her words and turned to enchant Flora and Beth with more stories of days past. "Our people have gone to summer at the shielings for generations, and there was once a great chief who came to visit there, bringing with him the finest warriors and cattle ever seen in Scotland..." His voice trailed off as the little girls clambered up into his lap.

It was a fine day, one of the last of April, and the sun shone brightly overhead in the bright blue sky. In a few more days, the flowers would start to show, Dora had told her, and she would soon be able to fill her basket with the soft shoots of the first yarrow that bloomed near Annie's cottage. Meg's thoughts drifted as she walked, and she didn't notice the man who followed her, his face alight with pleasure as he watched her movements.

"May I walk with you?" Ian fell in beside Meg on the path, reaching out to take the basket from her. "I have a fancy for fruit, myself."

There had been a tension between them ever since Niall's announcement of the handfasting, and she smiled at Ian with pleasure. "Surely, I am glad of the company. It's been awhile since I've seen you."

"I know. And I've been away for a few days." He did not volunteer more information, but slowed his larger steps to match her own. He had discarded his plaid, she noticed, probably in tribute to the warmth in the air, and wore only a light colored shirt over woolen trews.

"As has your brother." She looked up at him curiously. "Do you know where Niall is?" With Ian, there was no need to hide the relief she felt at not lying beside his brother for the last few nights. But not even to Ian would she admit that the relief came from not having to fight her own desires.

"Aye." Ian's smile did not reach his emerald colored eyes. "He will return tonight. But I did not come to talk to you about my brother."

They had reached the edge of the woods and were shielded from the view of Duncan's cottage by a large elderberry bush. Meg looked up at Ian expectantly.

"What did you come to talk to me about?" It was easy to talk to Ian, there was no tormenting fear of saying the wrong thing or being mocked for her honesty.

He set the basket on the ground and put one hand on her shoulder. "I know you have not reconciled yourself to staying here. Especially since Fergus and the others arrived." He skirted the issue of the handfasting, affording her the opportunity to be oblique as well.

"'Tis true, I still wish to leave. I keep thinking that if I could just get to my guardian first, I could find a way to keep him from attacking Blackwater." She felt the old frustration rising inside. "But Niall has me watched, day and night. There is no way I can leave. And every day brings more danger. The passes are completely open now."

Ian lifted her hand and kissed it. "I would help you." He said it simply, with a noticeable lack of the flirtatious nature he was wont to show.

She removed her hand from his grasp. "Why?" She studied his expression, feeling a warning tingle at the back of her neck. There was a hunger in Ian's face, one she recognized.

He bent his head to place a kiss on her lips. It was sweet and gentle, provoking none of the wild emotions that surged through her when his brother touched her, but Meg broke the contact, stepping backward.

Ian smiled again. "You know how I feel about you, Meg. I think that if you were well away from Blackwater, and felt yourself to be safe again, you might begin to return my feelings." The green eyes glowed with an intense light.

"So you would do this just for me? Run the risk of alienating your brother forever?" It was exactly what she had hoped for at the beginning of this madness, but somehow the winning was not as sweet as she had thought it would be.

"Aye, for you, but not only for you. I am no fool, to think that a few men with rusty swords and big hearts can win over a company of soldiers. If it is possible for you to sway Campbell with your words, I would help you, even if it means I am cast out for doing so."

And Niall was capable of doing just that in his righteous, blind adherence to clan honor. The idea troubled Meg, for it was quite possible that Ian would indeed be giving up everything he held most dear if he did help her escape.

"Do you have a plan?"

He nodded. "The night of the Beltane fires, when everyone is slipping away. 'Twill be easy for us to do the same. My horse will be waiting for us nearby, and we will be at the fort by morning."

It could work. She thought it over carefully. "But Elizabeth?" She would not leave her sister to face Niall's wrath alone.

"She will go as well. I give you my oath." He held her hand. "You said it was your duty to escape."

Did these MacDonalds remember every stupid thing that came from her lips? This was the snare she herself had set, and she must take the prize and run. She pushed the thought of Niall's black eyes away. Things must be clear between herself and Ian, before anything else was said.

"I cannot promise you my affection," she told him, "but you would always have my friendship."

"It is enough for a beginning." Ian's eyes twinkled at last with the familiar conceit. "I never met a lass yet I couldn't win." He ran one finger from the back of her ear in to the base of her throat. "All I ask is the opportunity to woo you without interference."

He bent to kiss her again, and Meg closed her eyes, willing to experiment with the possibility of Ian's wishes. She compressed her lips into a tiny pout, and just before Ian's mouth descended on her own, someone stepped out from the forest behind her.

Ian lifted his head again and his eyes glinted. "Brother."

Meg turned quickly, her heart sick as she saw Niall blocking the path. His black hair was free of its leather thong, and flowed about his shoulders. He wore no shirt, exposing the thick curly black mat of hair covering his chest. Emotion emanated from him, but it was a quietly menacing wave, terrifying in its strength. Meg glanced back at Ian, who looked alarmingly calm.

"Go back to the cottage, Meg." Niall did not look at her, his expression was foreboding as he held his brother's gaze with his own. His dirk was in plain view, held by the belt of his plaid.

"I will not go back." She stiffened her back, a white hot rage building inside her. "You were listening to us, spying on us. How dare you?" Fear for Ian made her incautious.

"Do not order me about like some servant who cannot speak for herself."

Niall didn't waver. "You will go back to the cottage now."

"And if she doesn't? If she chooses to remain with me? To go with me?" Ian was still calm, his voice level. But Meg could hear his rapid breathing and knew that he was not in control of his emotions.

The realization frightened her, and she shook her head to clear her mind. They were quite capable of killing each other right here before her eyes. That was not part of the plan.

"Stop it." She looked at Niall. "If I return quietly, will you let this go?" Her knuckles were white as she pressed her hands to her mouth.

He did not even look at her. "Never."

She picked up her basket, holding it tightly to her breast. "You must not argue. I will go back to the cottage, and we will forget this has happened." She raised her eyes to Ian's face, pleading. "Please, Ian, let's go back. Come with me."

"You have trespassed enough, brother, with your talk and your touching of my wife. Don't add to it." Niall's words were measured and slow. "Meg, I will not tell you again to return to the cottage. Ian and I will settle this." His dirk was in his hand. "I have watched my brother lusting for my wife long enough. While it was only my own honor, I withheld my hand. But now you threaten the safety of the people, Ian, and I will put a stop to it."

Ian lifted one shoulder ironically. "Indeed, 'tis better we settle it now. I am at your service, brother."

"Aye," Meg cried wildly, "settle it with dirks and hateful words, I have no doubt. Will you allow a Campbell woman to be the cause of killing each other? Am I worth that?" In her agitation, the green kerchief slipped to the ground, allowing her abundant auburn hair to swing free.

"Niall, listen to me, I will go back. Ian is not to blame. I sought this, you know that I did. You knew it from the beginning. You must not blame him. I will go back and stay there, I swear it." She was sobbing with fear now, "you must not argue. I will not go to the fort."

Niall looked at her, hard and angry with triumph at hearing her speak her guilt. "I have heard your oath," he said.

"Brother," he lifted his gaze back to Ian. "You are not outcast, but I will not be so lenient a second time. Let me discover you in such a position again and the whole of Scotland will not be wide enough to hide you from my sword. Leave us, now, and in the future, stay away from my wife."

"No," Meg cried. The basket fell to the ground, rolling into the bushes. She clung to Niall's arm, the tears flooding down her cheeks. "He is my only friend here."

"Meg," Ian said softly, "dinna fash yourself, lass." He reached out to smooth her tangled curls but at a low growl from Niall, withdrew his hand. "I will not be far from you, I promise. And when you see the fires, think of me." He turned into the forest and disappeared.

She lay unmoving beside Niall that night, resenting the arm thrown possessively over her. If she so much as changed her breathing, he would know it. The thought rankled, but she expected no less from him. While he held no soft feelings toward her, she was still his hostage, his only weapon against the Campbells. Hard won, he would keep her fast, allowing no opportunity for her to escape.

It was the most painful dilemma of her life. The threat of Ian, cut off from his clan or possibly dead because of his desire to help her, pressed upon her thoughts, preventing an escape into slumber. She lay beside Niall, suffering his embrace until morning came. And then he left her without so much as a word.

There were still two days before the Beltane fires would be lit, but already the men were working to gather the many different types of wood needed to make the ritual fires complete. There were nine kinds of wood used, she learned, as she fought to stay awake in Annie's kitchen later that day. The words to be spoken over the fires were secret, a legacy from the old ways that Annie's grandmother's grandmother had followed.

"It be a recipe for bounty, ye ken," Annie said importantly, "and is never uttered lightly, but only at the holy days."

There was a sacred recipe for everything, according to Annie. Meg's thoughts were resentful as she helped Dora carry the heavy iron kettle from the hearth outside to the cooking spit Andrew had erected over a new fire pit. If the old gods were so powerful, why hadn't they protected the MacDonalds a year ago? But she kept her thoughts to herself, unwilling to rouse Annie's anger.

The fire pit was ringed with the granite stones that Glencoe was famous for, and Annie carefully placed the correct number of sticks in an intricate pattern within the circle. Andrew hung the kettle from three oak branches that formed a triangle over the pit.

They filled the kettle with water from the burn, and Annie threw in some dried herbs. She whispered to the fire as Andrew lit it, no doubt giving it exact instructions on how high and brightly it should burn.

Meg was no longer much interested in the Beltane rites, and welcomed the coming festival only for the rest it would give her. For this one night, she would be alone, and she intended to enjoy herself. A whole evening just to herself, with only Elizabeth for company. The arrogant MacDonalds would be too busy with their heathen rituals to worry about anyone else. Only momentarily did her mind consider attempting the escape Ian had suggested. It would be futile, she realized. Niall would be watching her every move, waiting to catch her.

That night everyone ate together, indulging in their excitement at the holiday which would begin at sunrise. Margaret Robertson was chosen as the queen, and shy Jamie as the young king. They were the subject of many ribald jokes, most of which became louder and more shocking as the night wore away.

"We should go on to bed," Meg whispered to Elizabeth after one particularly vulgar reference that caught her sister's curiosity. She tugged at Elizabeth's hand, and the younger girl rose obediently, her face still pink with blushes.

"I will walk Mistress Elizabeth to Annie's," Andrew volunteered, jumping up from the circle of laughing men. He held out his arm and Elizabeth took it with only a brief questioning look at Meg.

"I trust Andrew's honor above my own," Meg nodded, smiling. She watched the two walk away, and then, with a sigh, she lifted her skirts to start her own trek to Duncan's cottage.

"You have no reason to doubt Andrew's honor." Niall was beside her suddenly.

"Do you make it a habit to frighten people?" She spoke sharply, for he had startled her. "Were you spying on me again?" She didn't wait for an answer but walked away from him without a further glance.

It was no good, he was right behind her. She could almost feel his breath on her neck. Digging her heels in, Meg stopped to confront him.

"It is not necessary for you to follow me. I assure you that I am indeed bound for the cottage where I will go dutifully to bed." She put her hands on her hips. "Go on back to your party."

He looked over his shoulder to where Margaret played at being queen, offering a kiss on the cheek to her eager courtiers. "I dinna think they will miss me. And I would rather see you safely, if not dutifully, to bed."

She frowned in exasperation. "Why not dutifully?"

He smiled at her unpleasantly, mocking her stance. "A dutiful wife would be one who welcomes her husband to the marriage bed."

"I am quite tired of your insinuations. If I were a true wife, and if I had a true husband, I assure you he would be most welcome in my bed." She began walking again, to increase the distance between them.

Niall laughed and followed her. "And I assure you, Mistress MacDonald, that you are indeed a true wife with a true husband."

She would not answer, but strode ahead of him, pausing only to take up a candle which sat on a low stump outside Duncan's cottage. She pushed the door open and went straight to the fire, holding the wick of the candle close so that it would light quickly.

Turning to face her unwanted escort, she said, "Well, I am here safely, if not dutifully, so you can return to the party without fear."

Niall faced the woman he had just called his wife. She was growing too ready to oppose him. His heart hardened. Perhaps a bit of correction was in order, to remind her of the dangerous situation she had caused. He stepped toward her.

"Would you be sending my brother away so soon?" He centered his attention on the curve of her mouth, causing an unsteady flutter to awaken in her stomach.

"We will not speak of Ian." Meg backed away from him, stopping only when she brushed against the square wooden table. "Ian has nothing to do with you and me."

"Agreed." Niall was close now, too close for an enemy, only inches away from her trembling body. His clothing smelled of the smoke from the firepit, woodsy and heavy.

Meg fought to stay focused on the argument. What exactly was the argument? "You agree?" she asked. She couldn't remember what it was he was being so agreeable about.

Niall lowered his head until his mouth was touching her left ear. "You know what tomorrow night is, Meg."

Throat dry, she nodded. Of course she knew. They'd been preparing for Beltane for days. "It's the festival."

Unbelievably, he nuzzled her neck. "Aye" he murmured, "just after midnight 'twill be Beltane. Have you kept Beltane before, Meg?"

Of course not, she wanted to shout at him. She wanted to tell him that she was a Christian girl, raised with good values and strict morals. She wanted to push him away and rid herself of his intoxicating magnetism.

But she did none of these things. Her heart racing like a hunted rabbit, Meg only whispered, "No."

His laughter was a soft vibration against her skin as he touched his lips to her neck. He pulled her into his arms, and she stood there without fighting, allowing her head rest in the curve of his embrace.

The sweetness of it softened her resistance. She leaned against him, savoring his earthy scent and the hardness of his body. *God help me*, she thought, *but I am so weary of fighting.*

Her eyes were closed when she felt his hand cupping her breast lightly, his thumb circling her nipple like a hawk about to swoop down on its unsuspecting prey. "How easily you are won," he whispered, "do you exchange your honor for passion so quickly, Meg Campbell, or will one brother do as well as another?"

She jerked upright in anger and hit him full in the face with the palm of her hand. "You are despicable. I hate you. Never touch me again." She turned away, facing the table so that he could not see the tears.

"I am, as always, at your service, my lady. And now, I believe I shall return to the party. Mistress Robertson will still have a few kisses left to bestow, I'd warrant."

"Go on! Go to your pagan party and your indecent May queen. Never come near me again!' She was blind with rage, and, picking up Duncan's small crockery server of butter, threw it at his head.

He ducked just in time and the server missed, shattering against the door frame into several pieces. Butter splattered on the floor, and Niall sidestepped it.

"But I will be near you again. This very night I will lie beside you, and you will suffer it. Dutifully." He made her an elaborate bow.

Meg raised her chin and put her hands on her hips. "Enjoy my suffering then, MacDonald, for it is all of me you are likely to get."

CHAPTER 15

The day of Beltane dawned clear and fine. Duncan climbed down from the loft with a spryness that belied his constant claims of stiffness and a lame leg. Beth and Flora followed him, rubbing their eyes and clutching their best dresses. Disregarding Meg's repeated reminder that the dresses were to be worn later that evening, the little girls donned the frocks and wore them throughout the day.

No one ate much breakfast. The porridge was hastily spooned down and the dirty dishes forgotten as the old man and the children hurried outside to join in the commotion that could already be heard coming from the down. Meg watched them go indulgently, turning back with a smile and a shake of her head to the washing up that awaited her.

There was a light tap at the door, and Dora looked in. "Annie sent me to ask whether Duncan still has the silver cup from his wedding. If 'twas not lost in the trouble," she referred to the massacre and the inevitable reiving that surrounded that time, "the queen and king will use it to bless the crops."

Meg dried her hands on a square of old cloth and frowned. "I do not know that I've ever seen a silver cup here. Where would he keep it?"

Dora looked around the cottage. "Perhaps up in the loft, hidden in his blanket box?"

"It's worth a look," Meg led the way to the narrow ladder which served as a stairway to the loft. "But you'll have to ask him yourself if you can use it. I cannot lend what is not my own."

"Aye," Dora agreed, "but he will be pleased to lend it. 'Tis a blessing to help in the ceremony."

They found nothing at all in Duncan's blanket box except blankets and a small rectangular box of rowan wood. It was made in two pieces, the lid fitting tightly to the base. Meg ran her hands over the soft finish and fought the urge to open it. It was obviously special to Duncan, to be so carefully put away. She lowered the lid of the blanket box slowly. All she could do was suggest that Dora find Duncan and ask him about the cup. When the other girl left, Meg went back to her cleaning. There was not much to do, the cottage was small enough that just a daily touch was enough to satisfy housekeeping requirements.

It was good to have the cottage to herself for awhile, with no interference or interruption. She paused before the bronze mirror that hung on the wall opposite the door. Her reflection in the dim metal was elongated and made her eyes look slanted. Meg stuck her tongue out at herself and laughed as the strange creature in the mirror did the same.

"You look addled and mazed, making such faces at yourself." Dora had returned and stood laughing at her. "Have a care your face doesn't freeze like that."

Meg laughed embarrassedly along with Dora. "Did you find Duncan?"

"Aye, and he does have the cup still. But 'tis at the keep in a special place, so someone will have to go and fetch it." Dora grinned at Meg, her mouth opening to reveal the missing tooth at the side of her mouth. "I have to help Annie with the queen, so she says, would you please go, miss, and get the cup?"

"I rather doubt she said 'please'," Meg responded, "but no matter. I am finished here, and will be glad to go if you will tell me where to find the cup. Will someone loan me a horse?"

"Oh." Dora's face was suddenly downcast. It was not to be expected that Meg would be trusted with a horse. Then Dora's face lightened as a thought struck her. "I'll go ask Niall, he's over at the down with the others. He'll take you to the keep. You wait beside Duncan's oak tree for him."

"Dora, wait, don't ask Niall!" But the girl was already gone. Meg closed her eyes and gritted her teeth. An uneasy morning ride with her *husband* was just the thing to ruin her day. She looked about the cozy cottage regretfully. She had been enjoying the feeling of lightness and festivity all by herself and now it would be spoiled.

She sat down cross-legged under the oak, relaxing under its cool shade. The tree was massive, with great spreading branches that snaked out like wide arms covered with soft trailing ivy. Duncan liked to doze here in the early afternoons, and Meg herself found it a lovely retreat from the ever-present concerns of her marriage and her husband in name. Perhaps Niall would refuse Dora's request and go alone to retrieve the ceremonial cup.

But he came, most willing to provide the means of transport to the keep. He stood before her like a great dragon, leering at her with his arrogant smile while Dora explained precisely where they should look for the cup.

Her mind a tumult of confusion as she tied her kerchief over her hair, Meg did not hear Dora's directions. It was only when they were mounted on Carnoch's back that she realized she had no idea where to look once they reached Glencoe.

"No fear," Niall answered when she voiced her concern. "Duncan left it hidden at the old chapel. 'Twill be easy to locate."

"But why did he not bring it to Blackwater?" She sat stiffly before him, not daring to relax. At all costs, she would be polite and impersonal in her manner. And nothing more.

"Even the Campbells will not disturb a chapel," he told her. "The cup is safe there, although fire and wind have done their damage to the structure itself."

They rode silently through the forest, listening to the black's hooves softly thudding upon the moss carpeted path. Bracken ferns were beginning to peek out from under the oak trees, and the horse paused briefly as Niall tugged on his mane. Meg looked to where the chief pointed at some bristly pale green fronds that pushed their way out of the ground beyond the forest's edge.

"What is it?"

"The first whin. And the bluebells cannot be far behind." His voice was light and he kicked his heels into the black's sides. Carnoch took off at a brisk run, jostling Meg until she thought her insides would rattle.

They dismounted a short way from the ruins, Niall touching her only as much as necessary to assist her, and walked uphill to the crumbling black stone walls. Meg looked thoughtfully at the cairns of stone that were scattered about, realizing that each pile of rocks marked the place where a MacDonald had fallen.

"Will you move them all to Eilean Munde?" she asked without thinking. Eilean Munde was the sacred burial ground where the people had been buried as far as memory could tell.

"Some think they should lie here forever, reminding all who see them of the treachery that caused their deaths."

It was the first time any of the MacDonalds had spoken directly to her of MacIaian's heir, but she knew from listening to Robert's ranting that the two MacDonalds had been pardoned by the king when his part in the massacre became public knowledge. "There may never be another hereditary chief at Glencoe."

Niall eyed her quizzically. "There are other ways to hold the chieftainship. Bonds beyond those that are known and recognized."

"Being chosen, you mean. I suppose in a way, it may be a greater honor to be chosen than to be born to such a position." She was thoughtful as she picked her way carefully through the new growth of briars that already threatened the pathway to the keep.

"Perhaps." Niall was noncommittal, giving no indication of his own feelings about the matter.

He pointed to a small building that stood to the right side of the keep. "There is the chapel."

The roof, damaged from fire, had fallen in and covered the floor. The altar itself, made from good Glencoe stone, was undamaged save for charred streaks that even the snow had not washed clean. Meg surveyed the small room silently.

"Where would the cup be?"

"Here." Niall went to stand behind the altar and knelt down, pushing at something she couldn't see.

When he stood, he held an object wrapped in a soft blue cloth. He held it out for Meg to take and then he knelt again, and she heard a scraping sound. She thought she heard him mutter something and then he stood up and returned to her side.

"May I look at it?" At his nod, she removed the blue wrapping and gasped at the sight of the ornate silver cup.

It was perhaps twice the length of her hand, the stem curved and swirled like a waterfall. The lip of the cup was beaded, and the cup itself etched with intricate knot work and Celtic crosses.

"How old is it?" she breathed reverently, turning the cup in her hands. "How came Duncan to have such a thing?"

Niall's face also held a look of wonder, she saw, as she glanced up at him. For a moment they were joined in their awe and admiration of the lovely relic.

"Duncan will tell you it came from France, from a cave at the foot of a sacred hill. MacIaian's own grandfather drank from it at his wedding, naming it a treasure without price."

"A cave in a sacred hill! Perhaps it a relic of your faith. It may even have come from the holy city."

"Aye. And the priests say 'tis a mystery of the holy things that we shall never know their true origin. I am content to have the beautiful thing safely kept."

"Aye," she agreed. And then, turning to look at him again, "tell me about MacIaian. What sort of man was he, that even the harpers of his enemies made songs about him?"

Niall gazed somberly at the altar. "MacIaian was one of the last great warriors. He was big, like Andrew, with a full head of white hair that hung past his shoulders and a long beard that covered most of his face. He went about as the old Celtic warriors did, with little clothing even in the winter, and his sword and dirk were always at his side. He reived and raided for the clan, 'tis not to be denied. And so do all the chiefs in this way of life we have built for ourselves. "

Niall's voice faltered for a moment. He stared at the ground. "He loved his wife and his sons, but he loved his people more. 'Twas for them that he humbled himself, going to the Fort and then on to Ardkinglas to throw himself on the mercy of the king. All according to the mandate. He begged for the lives of his clan, whom he thought of as his children, and only when he was assured of their safety did he come back to Glencoe. And when the Campbell came, MacIaian trusted the word of the king's man which had been given him on paper."

There was no emotion in Niall's voice; he might have been reciting a history text. "John and Alasdair showed it to Glenlyon and your guardian lied like the cunning dog he is, and reassured him that no harm would come to the clan. And MacIaian trusted him for the sake of the people. He died under trust, calling for a servant to bring a drink to his murderer."

Meg's head was bent as she caressed the silver cup. "He was a father to you all. 'Tis quite different from the way the Earl of Argyll holds his authority."

"Aye. MacIaian's like will not come again."

She wrapped the cup carefully and said, "We should go back now."

"Aye." The answer was whispered, and shuddered through the stillness of the abandoned chapel.

They walked away and Niall whistled for Carnoch. The black came running, his proud head high and his tail swept out behind him like a flag. Niall leapt agilely to the back of the horse and held out his hand to Meg.

She swung up behind him this time, the cup held protectively to her chest with one arm. She placed it between them, and wrapped her arms around Niall's back, turning her face to the side.

And they returned to Blackwater, each lost in their private worlds of memory and pain.

It was late in the afternoon when they arrived at the down, and Meg took the cup to Annie immediately. It was probable that Annie wanted to perform some sort of arcane ritual over the relic, or at least to clean it, before the fires were lit. Niall went to find Fergus, leaving Meg without a backward glance.

It was as though their quiet talk had not happened, as though his elaborate description of MacIaian had not been uttered. The feeling of understanding and common ground that Meg felt with him in the chapel had dissipated and she was left with a confusion and a slight feeling of depression. The more she learned about these MacDonalds, the less certain she was that the Earl of Argyll was correct in his assessment of them. The situation was a maze of twists and false turns, not the least of which was her own standing as prisoner and yet not-prisoner.

So she gave the cup to Annie gladly, turning off the questions in her mind, and turned to watch as Margaret Robertson preened herself in the green velvet cape.

Margaret was not Meg's favorite of the clan, but she was careful not to let her dislike of the girl show. Meg found her to be shallow and vain, and not at all adverse to flirting with any man who happened to be near. Annie was constantly vigilant, warning off any of the men who seemed more interested than was proper in Margaret. It was difficult work, for the girl flaunted her sexuality.

No one ever spoke of it, but they all knew that the girl often met men at night, long after Annie was abed. Meg wondered at the irony of choosing such a wanton to play the part of the May queen, but perhaps with a festival of such blatant carnality, Margaret was the best suited for the role.

She did look pretty, Meg admitted, as she watched Margaret's animated face. The green cape complimented her slanted green eyes and there was an excited pink blush in her cheeks. If the old traditions were kept up, Jamie would find his hands full dealing with his queen tonight.

Elizabeth helped Annie sew the cape to the shoulders of Margaret's dress. In the dancing that would take place later that night, the cape might fall to the ground if it were not attached, and that would be a bad omen. Only after the queen and king had fulfilled their responsibilities would the cape be spread out on the ground as a blessing for the sowing of seeds. Meg thanked God that Elizabeth's naivete prevented her from knowing exactly what those responsibilities were.

At length it was time for the clan to gather at the down, and Margaret led the women gaily from Annie's cottage, across the burn and toward the heaped piles of wood where the bonfires would be lit. Meg and Elizabeth followed more slowly, not wishing to seem part of the procession.

The men had already been drinking, Meg saw, and she tightened her hold on her sister's hand. Ian and Andrew stood beside Jamie, and Niall had taken a place for himself against the trunk of a rowan tree. The symbolism was not unknown to Meg, and she spared him a quick smile in acknowledgement of the rowan's protection against magic. Surprisingly, he smiled back, and her heart fluttered a bit at the sight.

From somewhere Duncan had procured a small hand drum, and he began to play it now, running a small stick lightly across the skin surface in a sharp rat-tat sequence. Fergus played a steady marching beat on a small pipe that he pulled from his sporran, and Meg's feet began to move in time to the air, tapping the ground in a restrained manner that she hoped would not draw anyone's attention.

Annie jumped between the two piles of wood and held up her arms dramatically. Duncan's silver cup, filled with water from the burn, flashed in her hands.

"Come and take the blessing of the old ones," she shrilled, "let the fires be lit again as they once were, and let the people be happy." With an oddly tender grace, she poured the water out on the ground, saying a prayer in Gaelic.

Niall came forward then, and bent to take a torch from the ground. He put the end of it in the fire that burned below Annie's iron kettle and turned back to face the old woman, obviously waiting for a signal. The torch blazed high in his hand, and Meg caught her breath.

Annie turned toward the setting sun, and just before it sank behind the hills, she brought her arms down in a quick flourish. "Now!"

Niall lit the bonfires, moving from one to the other in silence. As the second one caught fire, he threw the torch to the top of the first pile of wood, the clan cheering madly about him.

Fergus played a faster tune on his pipe now, and Duncan quickened the beat of the drum. Jamie and Margaret stepped between the two fires and held out their arms to each other, beginning to caper around in a spiraling circle. Soon everyone was dancing, everyone except Meg, Elizabeth, and Niall.

A pungent burning scent filled the air, and Meg realized cynically that Annie had primed the bonfires with some type of trance inducing herbs. It was probably done to quicken the women's abandon, as the heather ale would work on the men, although most of the clan undoubtedly did not know of the old woman's manipulation. Meg stepped back, hoping the herbs would not affect her, and she pulled Elizabeth with her, cautioning the girl not to go closer.

The dancing grew wilder, with the men stopping periodically to drink from their mugs of ale. They moved as though they were indeed under a spell, in a sort of weaving pattern in and out around the bonfires. Even Fergus' wife joined the dancing, Meg noted, wondering at the freedom which seemed to be overcoming the married woman's natural reticence. Ian danced with another woman, she saw, and wondered if he would slip away with his partner when the night grew old. He seemed to have forgotten his words to her about the bonfires, and she thought it was a good thing.

Niall's eyes were upon her from his vantage point next to the rowan tree, and Meg knew that he would keep a careful watch over her this night. She tossed her head in response to his critical gaze. *Let him watch then.*

Dora danced with Alan, laughing in the darkness at his bold attempts to pull her away from the circle. The night began to simmer with sensuality. Meg decided it was time for her to return to the cottage, taking her sister away from the rising abandon.

But Andrew came to Elizabeth, holding out his hand, and with a pleading look at Meg, the younger girl joined him, frolicking in the firelight like the others. They were lost in the frenzy that had been so much a part of the lives of their ancestors, Meg realized, and she hoped she would be able to retrieve her sister when the time came.

A hand took her own, and Niall was bowing before her. "Will you dance with me?" Without waiting for a reply, he whisked her into the laughing melee of people, twirling her around and around until she was dizzy from the spinning.

He gathered her close to him, and she felt his hardness pressing against her. Her own body responded and for a moment it was like that other time, in the stone hut during the blizzard. Meg closed her eyes, allowing the wildness to surge through her veins. She moved in time to the music, lost in the closeness and heat of her partner's embrace.

They were parted suddenly by a wave of other dancers, and when she looked around for him, he was dancing with Dora. Panting from exertion, Meg returned to the outer edge of the circle, where Annie and the little girls were watching.

Annie pressed a mug of cool ale into Meg's hand, and she drank it gratefully, uncaring that its potency made her head swim. She watched the dancers, her gaze moving from one couple to another, her breathing altering as she saw the motions become more intimate. She glanced down at Beth and Flora who were also watching with great interest.

"Perhaps I should take them home. 'Tis past their bedtime." Meg looked at Annie hopefully.

"Nay, not yet. The wee ones must also pass between the fires for a blessing." Annie waved her arms again, catching the attention of Fergus, who then blew several short blasts on his pipe.

Reluctantly, the dancers stopped. Annie pushed the children forward to stand beside Jamie and Margaret. "The king and queen must lead the people between the fires."

Jamie took Beth's hand, and Margaret, Flora's. They moved solemnly between the crackling fires, and then the king and queen bent to kiss each sweaty little forehead. Giggling, the children ran back to Meg.

The women now lined up on one side of the bonfires, and the men on the other. Margaret led each man between the fires, and Jamie led the women. Everyone received a kiss of blessing, Meg last of all. The fires were blazing hotly now, echoing the physical heat that had awakened in the dancers.

There was a startled movement at the rear of the group, and Annie set up a wild cackle that made Meg's hair stand up. Pushing her way through the curious people, Annie proudly led a thin, nervous brown cow toward the fire. The creature, apparently drawn to the festivities by the noise and light, mooed questioningly, and everyone laughed. Like a queen herself, Annie pushed the cow between the two bonfires, calling out fervent thanks to the pagan gods who had so obviously blessed the Beltane rites.

Sharing the pleasure of the clan, Meg returned to her safe place of observation to find Elizabeth and the children and take them home. But from the corner of her eye, she saw Margaret Robertson pulling Niall into the circle, and Meg stopped to watch the chief follow the May queen.

He was smiling, his eyes bright with enjoyment, and Margaret pressed her breasts against him wickedly, murmuring something that made Niall throw his head back in laughter. Meg narrowed her eyes as she watched Niall put his arms around Margaret and lift her high in the air, spinning with her in a crazy circle.

The watching people cheered, and Niall set Margaret back on the ground. She grabbed his hand, pulling him through the circle, and stood up on tiptoe, offering her mouth for a kiss.

For a moment he hesitated, then he turned and looked straight at Meg. She compressed her lips. He smiled, shrugging his shoulders.

Then he bent his head to return Margaret's kiss of blessing, and the girl threw her arms around him, molding her body against him. After what seemed hours, they moved apart, and Margaret tugged at his hand, pulling him into the dark shadows away from the fires.

Meg gathered her sister and the children, leading them back to Duncan's cottage for the night. Flora and Beth fell asleep quickly, and Elizabeth sat down before the fire pit, watching its tiny flickering light.

"I had a good time, Meg." She sighed, her voice wistful. "Would it be so terrible a thing, to stay here and one day become one of them?"

Meg sat down on the bench next to the wall she had carefully scrubbed that morning. It was the cleanest part of the cottage, the other walls being covered in peat soot. She leaned against the cool stones. "You could only become one of them by marrying one of them. And that would never be countenanced."

"Yet you have married Niall."

Who even now was undoubtedly locked in Margaret's embrace, Meg thought, closing her eyes. "Not truly, Bess. You know that. And Andrew is not appropriate for you. If you must fall in love with one of them, why not Jamie, who is closer to your own age?"

Elizabeth smiled dreamily. "Jamie will go to France to be a priest one day. It is the dearest wish of his heart."

Meg was shocked. "He wishes to become a priest and yet he takes the part of a pagan king at Beltane?"

"And Andrew is most appropriate. He was schooled in France with Niall and Ian."

"You would never know it," muttered Meg. "But Bess, these folk have nothing to offer you. It would be a sorry existence, fighting for survival every moment of your life. Do you truly wish such a life for yourself?"

"Andrew says the king is sure to make restitution soon. He would take me to Skye, where he has kin and would be assured of a place."

Meg flinched. "You have gone so far as to make plans?"

Elizabeth looked at her sister for the first time. "Aye," she admitted. "Of a sort."

"The Earl of Argyll will never permit such a thing. And you have lost your mind, I think, to make such daydreams. Bess, you have a bright future, why you will be one of the Queen's ladies. Would you give that up?" Meg could not believe her sister's casual attitude toward the wealth and prestige such a position would bring.

"Queen Mary loves the soil of Scotland," Elizabeth said slowly, referring to the dead Stuart monarch, "but she rules with a Dutch king. I would rather live in rags than be daily obedient to such a man."

"You speak treason," said Meg sharply, "and you have been swayed over to the MacDonalds' way of thinking." She rose from the bench and paced the room in agitation. "It is past time we were away from this place. Robert must come soon."

Elizabeth stood up and walked to the ladder. She looked over her shoulder at her sister with a firm glance. "I pray he never comes." She climbed the ladder to the loft and lay down beside the slumbering children.

What do I pray for? Would I stay here too, if Niall asked me? If he looked at me as Andrew looks at Elizabeth, with tenderness and caring? Meg ran her fingers through her hair. She went to the basin on the table and splashed water over her face. Then, resolutely putting her questions from her mind, she undressed slowly, taking care to fold her things and lay them on the bench. Laurie's woolen nightdress was too heavy for such a warm night, so Meg wore only her chemise to bed. She drifted away in her own dream world, and the distant piping and beat of the drum continued far into the night.

Niall entered the cottage quietly. Later he would return to the fires, but now he was drawn to the cottage, to the girl who had danced so willingly with him. He stood looking down at Meg, his eyes drawn to the auburn hair fanned out upon her shoulders, the vulnerable mouth that was slightly parted. She lay on her back, one arm across her middle, the other close to her side. The blanket was thrown off, and in her short undergarment, she was all but revealed to his gaze.

"If I told you 'twas only a kiss passed between me and Margaret, would you believe me, I wonder." He said it in a whisper, not daring to touch her cheek as he wished to do. "But 'tis better for us all if you believe your eyes rather than my wishes. It will make the good-bye much easier."

CHAPTER 16

May descended in a storm and several days of rain forced the women to concentrate upon household tasks, even as the men had gone out to search for game. Although she chafed at the necessity to stay indoors, Meg was relieved that the rains had come. Soon now, she and Elizabeth would be going home.

Elizabeth watched carefully as Dora sat weaving upon the large loom in Annie's cottage. Dora's deft fingers flew over the wool, quickly taming the unruly strands into straight, comely patterns.

"That is grand work," Elizabeth praised. "You are an artist with the loom."

Dora giggled at the compliment. "Not really, mistress. We all learned to weave as bairns. 'Twas the first act of housekeeping taught."

"Because it is the simplest," Margaret Robertson laughed. "Even a child can learn quickly to guide the wool so." She demonstrated as she spoke, and Elizabeth's cheeks turned pink at the implied ridicule.

Meg moved beside Dora. "Here, let me try."

Dora willingly gave up her place at the loom and Meg sat down before the fire. The wool felt heavy and strange to her fingers, but the carding comb fit easily in her small hand. After a few hesitant tries, she caught on to the trick of the loom, and was soon busily running the carding comb.

Elizabeth too tried her hand at the craft, seated beside Jeanne MacDonald, Fergus' wife. Jeanne was older than the other women, except for Annie, and very gentle in speech and manner. Meg was amused, thinking of the Beltane rites where Jeanne had danced with all the energy of the younger women. It was quite a contrast to the decorous appearance she now presented, as with expert hands, she guided Elizabeth's plump fingers along the loom.

"You must control the weave so," Jeanne explained patiently, "never let the loom get ahead of your fingers, else you'll have an unruly tangle."

Meg smiled as she worked, the hum of the loom lulling her thoughts. It was a comfortable morning, even with the flighty Margaret present. Flora and Beth were rolling out barley-meal and dough for bannoch cakes, and Annie knitted quietly in a corner, her eyes intent on the green plaid shawl taking shape in her hands. Meg thought how surprising was that these women had accepted the two MacDonald girls. But then, she reminded herself, they did not know the reality of the situation.

They thought her married to their leader, and her sister merely a non-threatening visitor from another clan. As she worked the loom, Meg wondered what their response would be when they learned the truth.

As if bidden by Meg's thoughts, Margaret Robertson moved nearer, assessing the beginner's work with a grudging smile. It still rankled Meg that Margaret favored Niall, and more than one woman had cautioned Meg to stay close to her husband when the girl was about. After the kiss Margaret had won from Niall a few days before, Meg understood their warnings. She worked to conquer the jealousy that had consumed her during Beltane, as she watched Margaret dancing with Niall. And she refused to wonder what his absence from their bed that night had meant.

Not that she was concerned, Meg tossed her head at the threat of another woman. It wasn't as though she were truly married to the man. Handfast perhaps, but only the birth of a babe would change that, or a joint decision by herself and Niall to exchange vows in a church. Neither of those things were likely to occur, since they were not living together and there was no way Meg would ever take Catholic vows.

Unbidden, her thoughts took life, painting a graphic picture of the one time she had lain with Niall. She never dreamed that the act of lovemaking could be so tender. And the fire of the man. Even now, in her imagination, Meg could feel the same sweet agony that had consumed her when Niall bent his kisses to places other than her lips. Her cheeks stung with the memory.

She yielded her place at the loom to Dora without coaxing, glad of the distraction, and returned to her seat beside Annie. The shirt she had volunteered to mend for Duncan was almost completed, and Meg welcomed the opportunity to concentrate on something other than Niall's kisses. She held Duncan's worn linen shirt in her lap and rethreaded the silver sewing needle that Annie prized. But as the needle flashed in and out of the soft material gathered in her hands, Meg was reminded of another rhythm.

Had he forgotten the intensity of the vows they had exchanged? Meg knew that she never would. They were engraved upon her mind and heart for all time, causing her distress whenever she allowed herself to remember.

In her frustration, she jabbed herself with the sewing needle and cried out with the sudden pain. The other women looked up in surprise, and Meg stuffed her wounded finger into her mouth, sucking on it to stop the bleeding.

Beth rushed over to help, her face and hands spattered with traces of wet flour. "Let me kiss it."

Solemnly, Meg offered her finger for the child's inspection and Beth kissed it. "Our mam used to fix our hurts just so."

"It feels better already," Meg answered with a smile. "Thank you."

"'Tis ill luck to spill blood on a man's shirt."

Meg glanced quickly at Annie and then down at the faint drop that showed on the yellowed shirt before her. "It was an accident. I'm sure I can wash it out."

Annie grunted. "'Twill make no difference an you do. A spark will kindle a fire."

Elizabeth met Meg's glance and rolled her eyes at the old proverb. It was only another of Annie's forbidding predictions and no one paid much attention.

Jeanne said to the old woman, "There have been enough deaths recently to satisfy the Auld Man for years. Let us pray that no more come upon us."

Annie glared at the sweet faced woman across the room. "That will be as God wills."

Dora sucked her cheeks in and blew noisily out. "Dinna try to argue," her words were gloomy. "She's usually right."

Margaret laughed. "The de'il take the Auld Man! We need no talk of death here. 'Tis spring, and we have much to be gay about." Her eyes turned slyly to Meg. "Strong, handsome men and new homes. What more could a woman ask for?"

Jeanne looked at Margaret sternly. "Do not forget the reason those men are here, and why the new homes are being built. We have much to be thankful for, but we have much to remember."

Meg tied her thread into a tiny knot and clipped it with her teeth. "I'll take Duncan's shirt to him, I'm sure he's wanting it." The conversation made her uneasy, with its references to the massacre and the old man of death. Even the soft rain falling outside was preferable to staying in the cottage a moment longer.

She stopped at the water barrel outside the cottage and quickly dabbed a small amount of water on the tiny spot of blood that accused her. It rinsed out quickly, and Meg felt a tiny measure of relief. It was silly to allow Annie's superstition to affect her. But lately Meg was more vulnerable to people and ideas than ever before. It was disturbing.

There was thunder in the distance, high and away to the north. Meg pulled her kerchief tightly about her hair, and ran down the path to the stream toward Duncan's cottage. Andrew and Alan had supplied a wide tree trunk to act as a primitive bridge for the women to walk over. Although not needed now, when the waters were flowing at full capacity, the bridge would be welcome.

Annie had scoffed at the idea, saying she had never needed a bridge before and didn't need one now. But the men insisted, and as Meg gauged the depth of the rising stream, she was glad they had.

She crossed the stream and made her way to Duncan's cottage, holding the shirt close against her breast to protect it from the rain. She rapped twice and opened the door slightly to peek inside.

Duncan was snoring in his rocking chair, his moth-eaten plaid covering him. The fire in his hearth had almost died out and Meg tiptoed over to it, laying the shirt on the kitchen table as she passed.

It wasn't difficult to get the turf embers going again, they were still smoldering from the morning meal. Meg looked around at the disarray of the cottage and felt guilty. With the arrival of Jeanne and Fergus, the two little girls were spending most of their time with the motherly woman. It gave Meg more free time, which she spent as far from Niall as possible. She chastised herself; this was her home for awhile longer, and she should take better care of it. And of Duncan.

He took most of his meals with Jeanne and Fergus, enjoying the easy camaraderie of Fergus' home, and Dora did his washing. Meg took care of the cottage's basic needs, but in her desire to distance herself from her husband, the day to day tidying that was necessary for any house was being neglected.

At least that was something she could do now. Niall was nowhere about and Meg could tell from the loud snoring that Duncan was not liable to awaken any time soon. Determinedly, she donned an apron and set about collecting the dirty cups, bowls and spoons from the morning meal. A pail hung on a nail beside the door and this she filled with water from the rain barrel outside, thanking the heavens that enough rain was falling to replenish it.

Her hands stung from the strong soap, but the dishes were soon clean and dry. She stacked them against the wall and then washed down the old table. There were potatoes set out for their evening meal, so she sat down to peel them, cutting them into fours and placing them over the hearth to boil in the old iron pot.

When the potatoes began to simmer, Meg decided it was time to leave. Duncan would awaken before long and she didn't want to engage in their regular useless argument. The old man still disapproved of Meg and Elizabeth and their presence at Blackwater, especially now that Niall had assumed formal responsibility of her. Although he harbored a valid resentment, his words had grown somewhat softer of late.

Indeed, they were all changing, Meg realized as she left the cottage. Even Annie was not as belligerent as she had been in the beginning. Elizabeth seemed to have forgotten Glenlyon and the surety that Robert would come for them.

Andrew, Ian, and Jamie treated them as relatives and friends. Only Niall remained aloof.

As though her thoughts summoned him, Niall materialized in front of her. He had left silently this morning, not deigning to eat the hot porridge and bannoch cakes she had set before him.

As always, his physical presence overwhelmed her and Meg found herself responding with a chill to his wide shoulders and the thick black hair visible at the open collar of his drenched shirt.

"Where are you going?" There was an unreadable expression in the dark eyes, a tenseness that belied his appearance of authority.

The question was rudely put and Meg resented it. She tossed her hair at him and stared at the scar on his face. "I thought I'd try to run away once more. "Tis a fine day for escape, don't you think?"

Her eyes lingered on his broad chest as she remembered Margaret's taunt about strong handsome men. Even standing there with rainwater running from his black hair and soaking his shirt, he was beautiful. Dear God, what was she thinking? In the moment of confusion, her eyes darkened, and she felt his reaction before he spoke.

He brushed a drop of water from the tip of her nose.

"You shouldn't be standing in the rain."

"I wasn't standing in it, I was running in it." She saw his eyebrow quirk, and said hurriedly, "back to Annie's. I just returned Duncan's mended shirt."

Niall glanced up as a sharp clap of thunder punctuated the sudden flash of lightening. The new bothy for Annie's cow was close by, and Niall took Meg firmly by the arm, pulling her into the shelter.

As they reached the safety of the small building, the skies opened up in earnest, flooding the ground with a torrent of water and sending thunder crashing all about them. Meg covered her ears until the initial raging passed, and when she raised her head, Niall was smiling.

It was so unusual for him to smile, and at her, that she was momentarily confused. "Why are you doing that?"

His expression didn't alter. "Doing what?"

"Looking at me like that."

"And how am I looking at you?" He seemed sincerely curious.

She furrowed her eyebrows. "You seem to be the victim of a strange malady, sir. That could almost be a smile on your face. But no doubt, I am mistaken, as usual, and it is merely a grimace of disapproval." Her gray eyes dared him to respond in kind. In no way did Meg want to engage in serious conversation with him. He was too distracting, and her own desires were too dangerous.

"Disapproval?" he echoed. "Have you done something to warrant censure?" The black eyes watched her quizzically, but his rising tension communicated itself in the rapidness of his breathing.

Determined to be casual about their meeting, Meg removed her sodden kerchief, shaking out the excess water. "I usually don't have to do anything to gain your reproach. It is freely given."

Niall's gaze took in the state of her gown, the damp clinging skirt and the revealing bodice. Her breasts were clearly outlined by the wet fabric, and the nipples were taut from the chilled moistness.

"Just at this moment," his voice was a slow, thickened drawl, "I would have to say that what I feel has absolutely nothing to do with disapproval."

She looked down at herself and realized the source of his amusement. "You are not behaving like a gentleman." But she would not cover herself from his gaze. She stood haughtily before him, daring him to go any further.

The familiar ache enveloped her again, and Niall fueled it with his nearness. He moved closer to Meg, causing her to struggle to maintain her bearing.

"Are you afraid of me?"

Meg stiffened and smiled back at him. "Never."

Niall took another step. "Are you sure?"

She took a nervous breath. "I am not afraid of you, MacDonald."

He laid a hand on the lace in the center of her drenched bodice and felt the heat of her body beneath it. "But a wife should be somewhat afraid of her husband." His hand moved across the front of her gown to gently cup her right breast.

Meg's breathing became shallow. "Perhaps a true wife would have reason to fear a husband. But I, sir, am a handfast bride, taken as a hostage in a game of war to be put aside as soon as my handfast husband tires of the play."

She placed her hand atop his own and removed it from her breast. "You have no right to touch me so."

"According to the laws of Scotland and of God," his hand returned to its former resting place, and squeezed her breast ever so gently, "I have every right."

Her head tipped back as she opened her lips to refute his statement, and Niall covered them, his tongue seeking her own in an intimate caress.

He was so warm, so alive. Uncaring of the results, Meg allowed the kiss, reveling in the touch of his body against hers. She could feel his hardness below, pressing against her own soft place, and a fire ignited along her spine.

Niall broke the kiss and whispered savagely, "I want you now, as before, with the storm wild about us and only the beasts for witnesses. The fires of Beltane still burn me."

His teeth nipped the edge of her earlobe and she winced at the small pain. "I intend to exercise my rights as well as yours." It was a vow and a warning.

She thought of the wild dancing at Beltane, of the way his eyes had glittered as he held her. They had responded to each other that night in the most primal way, and it had been sinful to deny that response.

"Yes!" the word was a long sigh of relief. She was tired of denying herself, of struggling to maintain indifference toward him. For good or ill, they were joined together and she would play out the game as bidden.

He watched as she fumbled with the lacings of her gown, and then a hot impatience took over. Expert fingers accomplished the task quickly, and he pushed the bodice of the gown down to her waist.

Meg felt no embarrassment before him, though somewhere deep within her logical mind, she wondered at her own lack of restraint. She did not follow that thought; Niall was the immediate and very real present, and shyness or remorse had nothing to do with the feelings he roused inside her.

Uncaring of the consequences, she smiled up at him as he traced the nipple of one breast. When he bent to take the tiny bud in his mouth, she almost moaned with the pleasure.

Niall released her slowly after a moment, and stood looking deeply into her eyes. His own were anything but shadowed now, the hotness of black passion was evident within their depths, and the ruthlessness of that power took her breath away.

He raised her skirt above her waist and jerked her linen undergarment down with a quick decisive motion. She could not take her eyes from his face, so alive it was with the blending of barely controlled desire and gentleness.

His fingers found her moistness, and then she did close her eyes, claimed by the rush of warmth between her legs. When she looked at him again, a satisfied smile adorned his face.

"'Tis a compliment you pay me, Meg MacDonald, to tremble thus before me." His eyes were clear and bright, his entire being concentrated on the pleasure he gave her.

Meg whimpered as the fire in her belly began to spread through her body, and, sensing her rising eagerness, Niall guided her to the floor.

Brushing his kilt aside, he pulled her atop him, as he leaned against the wall of the stable, and she trembled as she felt him slide inside her. For a moment she was still, adjusting to the tormenting sensation, and then at his silent urging, she began to move in a rocking motion, controlling the pace and depth of the thrusts herself.

It was a heady feeling of power. Meg threw her head back and her lips parted again with the incredible joy of their coupling. Any thoughts of reluctance or timidity were long gone, and she reveled in the freedom of surrender and control that he was giving her.

She slowed her rhythm and looked down at him. "Is it always like this?" Somehow the differences between them were insignificant now, washed away by the emotional connection she felt.

The black eyes deepened to liquid pools of fire. "It is rarely like this." He reached forward to nibble at her breast. "We are most fortunate in this aspect of our—marriage."

Meg ran her hands through the thick black hair of his chest and took his left nipple between her thumb and forefinger. "I believe that I could begin to like being married."

He sighed as her fingers tightened their grasp.

With a quick sure movement, he raised her up off him and lay her on the ground. He kissed her deeply again and rolled her onto her back. "I have needed this."

She smiled up at him. "Then take it, husband."

He captured her mouth with his own and then entered her again in a quick assault that caused her to arch upward in her reaction. For the space of a heartbeat he paused, and then the thrusting began, carrying her upward toward a rushing, expanding climax.

Her body trembled, her legs quivered, and when Niall pulled out suddenly, she cried aloud in dismay.

"Hush," he soothed her, "lie still for me."

She could do nothing else. Her legs parted and her breasts heaved with the force of her breathing. "Why did you leave me?" she murmured.

He kissed her on one breast and smiled again. "So that I can please you, my lady."

How could he think to please her by removing himself from inside her? And then she gasped as his tongue touched the place he had just left.

"Niall!"

The vibration of his amused chuckle rippled against her softness before his mouth resumed its ministrations. The ache was insufferable, and she pushed herself against him, needing more, seeking a release she couldn't name.

Just when the tide threatened to overwhelm her, Niall slowed the warm probing of his tongue. Meg sighed as he left her on the edge yet again. His fingers pushed up inside her, in a gentle rotating movement and she welcomed the intimacy, moving her hips in a seductive circular motion.

Niall's emotions were turbulent as he watched the woman lying so openly before him. There had never been another like her, nor was there likely to be. The volatile combination of distrust and passion had merged in their relationship, and despite his vow to remain uninvolved, he was dangerously close to forgetting his duty and his plans for revenge.

He raised himself over her and watched as her silver eyes widened with anticipation.

"Do you want me?" he whispered. His smile told her that he knew exactly what she wanted.

The brilliance of her gaze softened. "Oh yes, I want you. Come into me."

"I am your obedient servant." He thrust into her with all his might, allowing himself and his obligations to clan and kin to be submerged in the depths of desire. Within a few moments, he heard her cry out in release, and his own came moments later.

They lay joined for several minutes afterward, listening to the rain against the walls of the stable. Neither spoke, for fear of destroying the sweetness of the interlude.

Meg felt his fingers in her hair and turned her face slightly so that her cheek rubbed against his hand. "We cannot deny what just happened."

He raised himself on one elbow and looked searchingly into her face. "I know."

A thrill ran through her at the simple answer. "You will tell them?"

He knew she referred to the clan, and he shook his head unwillingly. "It is no safer now for them to know who you are than before. Each day the men speak of going against Glenlyon. If they were to discover that they harbor a valuable weapon in their midst, they would rush to use it."

"Is that not what you planned to do? Use us as a weapon, I mean?"

"Nay, not in that way." He shook his head. "I thought to lure Campbell here and execute justice myself."

"But he has not come." Meg watched him curiously, trying to veil her surprise that he was revealing his plans to her. "What will you do?"

Niall turned on his side and wrapped his arms around her. "He will come. The rains have hastened the season, and the pass is completely open. He will come."

"And you will kill him?"

"Aye."

She sighed. "There has been enough killing. The king will not tolerate more of it."

"I am not interested in the king's reaction." He turned to her with shadows in his eyes. "And after I have killed Robert Campbell and revenged MacIaian, what will you do, Meg? Will you stay here with me as my bride or will you scorn me for using you to entrap him and return to your kin?"

"I have no answer, Niall," she told him honestly. "I dread to see his blood on your hands." Hands that have brought me so much pleasure, she added to herself, and shuddered at the thought.

She gathered up her discarded clothing and for the first time would not meet his gaze. "But I think you know that killing Robert will not clear your conscience." The words were out before she could stop them.

Niall reacted swiftly, taking her by the arm and looking directly into her eyes. "What do you mean?"

Meg took a deep breath. "I know why you spend your nights alone at Glencoe. I know about the message from Lady Cathlan. And I know about your mistress."

He was amazed and angry at her words. "Who told you these things?" The old arrogance was back in his voice. "How dare you speak of me to other people?"

"Your people care for you Niall. They worry about you. 'Twas told to me in confidence, and I will not violate their faith."

His eyebrows twitched. "You are a remarkable woman, Meg Campbell MacDonald."

"Aye," she said simply. "To carry those names, I must be. And you are a remarkable man who does not have to kill to gain respect."

"Leave it, Meg." He stood and began dressing. "You cannot change fate."

She let him have the last word, but as they left the stable together, Meg knew she must try to heal the vengeance burning in Niall's soul. It threatened to consume him, and in the last hour, she had accepted the fact that they were joined together in a mysterious and powerful way. Somehow she would save him from himself, and for herself. For she knew without a doubt that if Niall succeeded in killing Robert, the Earl of Argyll would bring the full force of the Scottish crown against him.

Niall helped her across the bridge and stood watching as she made her way back to Annie's cottage. No further words passed between them, but each was aware that a new element had entered their relationship.

She followed the twisting path until the cottage was in sight. The door stood open to the weather, and she could see the bustling activity within.

Jeanne noticed her first and drew her inside quickly. "Oh Meg, where have you been? We thought you were with Duncan."

Meg tensed at the woman's question. "I did go to see him, but he did not awaken. I left the shirt inside, and his supper simmering over the fire. What is wrong?"

Jeanne gestured to Annie's pallet, where Duncan lay covered with a blanket.

"What has happened?" Meg went to kneel beside the pallet.

Annie brushed past her, carrying a bowl of watery porridge. "He was trying to get across yon cursed bridge," the tiny woman fussed. "All alone and in the rain, and he slipped. Dora found him when she went looking for you."

"Oh no!" Meg helped her to prop the old man up so they could spoon the warm porridge into his mouth. "He fell into the water?"

"Aye, the old fool." Annie spoke gruffly, but Meg knew that the woman was worried. And with reason.

Duncan's frail body convulsed in shivers. The shock of the icy stream had caused him to take a chill, and already his skin was beginning to flush with fever.

Meg looked at Jeanne. "How can he be so bad in such a short time?"

Jeanne laid a hand on her shoulder. "He's very old, dear. And it has been a harsh year in many ways."

Meg bowed her head in silence. As she prayed, she felt two small bodies position themselves beside her. She felt comforted in the contact. Flora and Beth were adding their prayers to hers.

Elizabeth helped her sister up and led her away from Duncan's bed. "We should go and let Annie take care of him."

"Aye," Margaret Robertson said with a malicious gleam in her bright green eyes. "Go on back to whatever you were doing when we thought you to be with Duncan."

Meg looked her adversary full in the face. "I was with my husband, not that 'tis any of your concern, mistress. And my sister and I will go. Elizabeth will stay with me at Duncan's cottage so that Annie can have room to care for him here. Come, Elizabeth, girls." She turned on the other woman and walked from the cottage, Elizabeth, Flora, and Beth trailing close behind.

All the way home, Meg held the picture of a worn, bloodstained shirt in her mind. It was only superstition of course, but she could not shake the image.

CHAPTER 17

Duncan was dying.

Meg could see it in his eyes, in the color of his skin, hear it in the rasp of his breathing. She could almost see it in the air around him, a cloudy miasma of vagueness that had begun to envelope his tired body like a soft pensive shroud. Annie had nursed him carefully for several days, with Niall and Fergus sitting vigil each night, but the chill of the icy stream had invaded his lungs, and the clan knew the inevitable result.

There was no logical reason for Meg to feel the approaching loss so sharply. One worn old man, perhaps the last living testimony to a way of life that was quickly passing from view, had no right to inflict pain on the heart and mind of someone he called enemy. But as quickly as she recognized the pain and acknowledged its power, the sharpness of it receded, and she was left with only a wistful sadness that reminded her of the loss of her own grandmother.

In the first days after Duncan had fallen ill, Meg and Niall faced the situation squarely. They had been together, lost in each other, oblivious to anything but their passion when Duncan had his accident. Yet Duncan would have applauded that, Niall told her. The old man knew well the ways of men and women and would have been the first to understand their need.

Accepting that truth, Meg went to Annie's cottage every day, to sit beside Duncan, watching his frail body labor to take the next breath. At some point in the hopeless vigil, she understood that she was witnessing more than just the death of a loved and respected elder.

The strength of the clans was diminishing as the power of England's throne increased. Passing away with that strength was the sense of kinship and respect and history that their ancestors had fought fiercely and died bravely to uphold. Her own clan was a mere instrument of fate, allied always with whoever held the crown. Robert had no choice but to follow his orders, she realized, and the men who followed him had no choice either. Few of them were Campbells, but they must obey the Campbell head of their regiment, never mind the terrible breach of tradition that surrounded their mandate.

Annie sat next to Duncan's head, giving no sign that she thought of any of these things. She simply sat close to him, one hand on the top of his head, crooning to him in Gaelic. Meg thought it was a prayer, but she had long ago forsaken what little understanding she had of the old language, and the words themselves held no meaning. Rather it was the tone of Annie's voice and the softness of her face that reminded Meg of heartfelt supplication.

Ashamed that she had been neglecting her own prayers, Meg took a deep breath and bowed her head. Almost immediately a deep peace enveloped her mind, and her own breathing became easier.

Outside the cottage, Elizabeth and Dora talked to the children, their soft voices rising and falling like comforting whispers on the wind. For once, Meg was glad of the lack of glass in the windows of the cottage. It was sweet to hear the words of the small ones holding watch outside, and important to remember that through their lives, Duncan's own would not be completely lost.

Meg's concentration was broken suddenly and she realized that Annie had stopped talking and was looking at her.

"Stand at his feet," the old woman commanded, as she placed both of her wrinkled hands on the very top of Duncan's head.

Obediently Meg got to her feet and moved around to stand at the foot of the bed.

"Cover his feet like so."

Meg placed the palms of her hands against the soles of Duncan's feet. The air in the room had changed, it felt clear and clean, like the freshness leftover from a sudden rain shower.

"Breathe with him."

Annie spoke surely, and Meg obeyed, adjusting her own deep breaths to the more rapid shallow ones of the old man.

For a few moments they stood that way, crone and young woman facing the ultimate mystery, and then Meg saw that the shadows in the room were gathering and merging into one luminous mist. She glanced at Annie for confirmation, but the old one's eyes were closed as she recited the Lord's Prayer aloud.

They stood that way for several minutes, linked by touch and compassion, and strengthened by the pulsing light which now enveloped the room, until at last the death rattle sounded deep in Duncan's throat. He made a slight shudder and was gone.

Meg released her breath slowly, allowing her hands to return to her sides. Annie, still standing at Duncan's head, finally allowed the tears to come. Somehow the sight of that hurt Meg more than the death she had just witnessed.

She went to the old woman, now the eldest of the MacDonalds of Glencoe, and put her arms around Annie's shoulders. "Come outside."

She led Annie from the cottage and nodded to the waiting group of men and women. The men went quickly inside to carry Duncan to his own home for the laying out. Dora took charge of her grandmother, helping Annie back down the path to the comfort of her home. Jeanne and the other women would provide the last duties Duncan would need before his burial.

"Are you all right, Meg?" Elizabeth patted her sister on the shoulder. "'Twas sweet of you to stay with Annie. But it must have been terrible."

Meg looked at her curiously. "Terrible? It was wonderful." She brushed a lock of dark auburn hair back from the breeze and smiled at her sister.

Elizabeth drew back in alarm. "Are you all right?" she repeated nervously.

Meg turned her face to the distant forms of the mountains. "I hope when my time is over," she said clearly, "that someone will be there to help guide me through the mist like that."

"What mist? Meg, I don't understand you. What are you talking about?"

Meg smiled and touched her sister's cheek. "Dinna fash yourself, sweetheart," she murmured. "I am fine." She sat down carefully on an old tree trunk and looked back out at the bony ridge of mountains in the distance. Even the five sisters, as the old people called them, seemed to be illuminated by the light from Duncan's passing.

"You're not fine, you're talking like Annie." Elizabeth looked around for assistance. The four brothers were walking back from Duncan's cottage and she gestured to them. "Ian! Will you help me with Meg?"

He came quickly, ignoring the warning expression on Niall's face. His expressive face registering his concern, Ian bent over Meg.

"You're a brave lass, Meg Campbell." Ian spoke in a whisper, the words meant only for her. "'Tis not easy to look the Auld Man in the face, even when he has come for another. You were a great help to Annie."

She began to rock back and forth, weeping mutely.

"Ah, lass," Ian put his arms around her. "Go on then and cry if 'twill ease your heart."

Releasing the agony of control, Meg put her head on his shoulder and allowed her tears to flow freely. "Poor Annie," she sobbed, "she had to watch him go. She had to stand there and he went and it was wonderful, and, oh Ian," the sobs were making her incoherent, "he took so much with him."

"Aye, he did, and he'll be missed greatly." Ian's voice was a comforting rumble in her ear and Meg lifted her head from his shoulder to smile at him.

And froze when she saw Niall standing over them. He was frowning.

So easily was the sweetness of the last few days damaged.

"If you are quite through comforting my wife," the words were chilling, "you can busy yourself with fetching the wagon."

Ian looked at his brother insolently. "Send Jamie." He did not move his arms and Meg remained securely held in a position that was growing less and less desirable.

Behind Niall she could see Alan and Fergus and Andrew. All three men looked decidedly uncomfortable, and

Niall's eyes had begun to glow with a hotness that was daunting.

It was time to extricate herself. "Thank you, Ian," she said formally. "I'll just run along and help Dora with Annie now. I'm fine."

Reluctantly, he dropped his arms. "Are you sure?"

"Quite sure." She stood up and looked at her husband. "Should you need me for anything, I'll be with Annie."

"Aye." His voice was almost as sharp as death and she shuddered, moving quickly from the knot of men.

"Why must I go? Send Jamie." repeated Ian.

"I am sending you."

The other men stepped back, distancing themselves from the conflict. Alan fingered his dirk.

"I'll help you," Fergus offered. "Come, we'd best be quick about it." He took Ian by the arm and pulled him firmly away. "My Jeanne will make Duncan a fine shroud."

Niall watched his brother's back as Ian walked away. The redhead's posture was straight as a sapling, arrogance showing clearly in every step.

"I do not like this," Andrew muttered to himself, but Niall heard him and turned the force of his anger on Andrew.

"And you think that I do? Watching my brother make fools' eyes over my wife?" Somehow Niall's dirk was in his hand, and he threw it suddenly at a nearby tree, the violence of his motion cutting through the air like a singing sword. "Ian has forgotten himself and his honor."

Andrew nodded, his long red hair rippling in the light breeze. "You'll go ahead and move one of the girls?"

"Aye." Niall clenched his fists in determination. "I have been wrong to postpone the move so long. You'll go with him and make sure he does not return until the work is completed. Elizabeth may remain here under your eye or you can take her to Skye as we first planned, but when this is all over, I'll take Meg to Loch Trieg."

CHAPTER 18

The old wagon had been pulled in front of Duncan's cottage, and the women gathered outside to watch quietly as Andrew, Alan, and Fergus shouldered the small burden and bore it into the cold bright day.

At least they would not have to contend with rain, Meg thought, scanning the sky. The clouds of the last few days had dispersed, and the air felt almost buoyant in its cleanness. And with the lifting of the inclement weather, Meg knew, would come new problems.

But this was Duncan's farewell, and she banished worries about the future so that she could do justice to the good-bye. A vivid picture of the old man rose in her mind; Duncan smacking his lips over her cream pie, telling a ghost story beside the fire, tipping his head back in laughter over a good joke. So many memories to have accumulated in so short a time. Meg felt blessed to have known him.

Ian and Jamie assisted in lowering the shrouded body into the bed of the wagon, and Alan and Fergus climbed in to sit beside it. The other men would ride alongside, while Ian and Andrew drove the horses.

Niall mounted the black gracefully. He had discarded the trews for this solemn occasion, and wore his kilt unconcernedly as he sat astride Carnoch. His bare thighs were exposed, but he seemed uncaring, caught in the moment. For the first time, the white heather was in his bonnet. His bearing had altered subtly, too, he looked older and in a way, more fearsome.

He looked past the other women to meet Meg's gaze in an acknowledgement of intimacy. For that moment there were only two people in the world, and all their differences and his suspicions were suspended.

I love him, she admitted to herself. *No matter the cost.*

As though he had heard her thought, Niall held out one hand to her.

"Meg," he said, and the sound of her name on his lips was the sweetest thing she had ever heard.

She went forward and stretched her hand out to clasp his.

"When this is over, when we have laid him to rest and I return, you and I have much to talk about and resolve. Duncan's death has cleared the confusion from my heart. There will be no more distance between us, *mo crigh.* Do you agree?"

Her throat almost closed against the sob that threatened to choke her. "Aye, love," she whispered. "No more distance." She released his hand and stepped away from Carnoch, her eyes fastened on Niall's face. *This moment I will remember forever.*

Ian called out to the horses and the wagon started its slow journey to Glencoe. Niall rode at the head of the procession, his black horse setting the pace in a stately gait.

The men were soon out of sight, and Annie, Dora, and Jeanne turned to the task of distributing Duncan's possessions among the other homes. Household items such as basins, dishes, and pots were left to be used by the next occupants of the cottage, but a few blankets and odd items of clothing were passed to those who had the most need. The rocking chair stayed beside the hearth; it was unthinkable to move it from the place where it had stayed for so long.

Even Margaret joined in as they cleaned the cottage from one end to the other, sweeping out the corners and washing down the walls. The pallet on which Duncan had slept was taken outside to be burned. Stuffed with once aromatic rushes and straw, the flames consumed it quickly, releasing a slightly sweet smoke.

The remaining belongings of Flora and Beth were moved to the home of Jeanne and Fergus, who had no children of their own. The little girls, although already spending most of their nights with Jeanne, were eager for the official move.

The women worked quietly. Even the giddy nature of Margaret Robertson was subdued today. Only once did she mention Niall, and that was to question whether or not Meg and her husband would now take exclusive possession of Duncan's cottage.

It was something Meg had not thought of, and the idea thrilled her. Until now, she and Niall had shared quarters with Elizabeth, the children and Duncan. Andrew and Ian slept there too, when not at the camp. It was a cramped situation, but everyone had been pleasant so far. The thought of having their own home excited her even as it frightened her. But then she remembered his plan to take her to Loch Treig and her face fell.

"No doubt Andrew and Ian will move upstairs, taking turns with Jamie," Meg answered Margaret's inquiry. "They have needed their privacy, too." She was concerned about Elizabeth living under the same roof with Andrew, even if only for a fragmented time. Perhaps Annie and Dora could be persuaded to give up some of their privacy.

The stone cairns which sheltered the murdered men of Glencoe were somber in the early spring sunshine. Creaking but steady on its ancient wheels, the wagon bore the body of Duncan MacDonald to his last place of rest, beside the bodies of his kin.

Niall dismounted and allowed the black to roam freely. His brothers helped him dig a shallow, narrow grave. It took awhile, the earth was still partially frozen, although softening somewhat. They used pickaxes as well as shovels to break up the ground and the work was slow and difficult.

Fergus and the other men gathered heavy stones to place atop the grave. It wasn't hard to find enough, Glencoe was covered with boulders of varying sizes. The cairn would keep scavengers away from the body, as well as provide a good memorial to a good man.

When the grave was just deep enough to accept its offering, they laid Duncan's body gently inside. Niall placed the first shovel of dirt over it, muttering a prayer as he did so. The other men then joined it. When the earth had received the old man, the clan placed rocks atop the grave.

Sometime in the distant past, Duncan had told Niall that each rock should represent a prayer for the rest of the dead. Niall reminded the other men of that. And so their thoughts were disciplined as they created the cairn, focused on good and on eternal life, not only for Duncan, but for all the others who lay at rest in the graveyard.

Shortly after the sun passed overhead, they were finished, and they stepped back from the gravesite.

Ian took a jug of water from the back of the wagon, and offered it to Niall first. The brothers stared at each other, Niall recognizing the gesture as both an acknowledgement of his place as chief, and as Meg's husband.

"Aye," Ian spoke low so that only Niall could hear. "I yield, I have no alternative. Watching the two of you together last night told the story better than words."

Relief washed over Niall. He loved his brothers more than he loved his duty, and had spent many nights in the shadow of the keep alone, agonizing over the growing rift between him and Ian. But he did not speak these things aloud, merely accepted the water from Ian and nodded.

They all took time to refresh themselves and then climbed back into the wagon. Niall opted to stay alone for awhile and walk near Maclaian's resting place. The black grazed close by, and the early afternoon felt peaceful.

With brief words the others left, and Niall walked alone through the burned out posts and beams and fallen stones of the keep. The past hung heavy today, and everywhere he looked he encountered regret. The ruined chapel held its own secrets, and it was here that Niall went at last, to be near the burying place of Maclaian.

They had placed him under the altar stone, hoping that no enemy would dare to plunder the holy place. Niall lowered himself to the ground and rested his back against the large slab of marbleized granite. He was usually sad when he came to this place, and today was no exception. It was, however, a bit brighter, as though the shade of Maclaian knew and approved the plans that were hastening toward resolution.

As Niall reviewed his scheme for revenge on Robert Campbell, a faint excitement came over him. He would send Meg and Elizabeth safely away from the center of this bloody business, and then he would repay Campbell's sword stroke with one of his own. Niall ran his fingers over his cheek, feeling the indentation of the scar. "We will meet once more, Campbell," he vowed aloud, "and all the angels in heaven shall not stop me from returning the favor."

Niall had long known that he and his twin sister were MacIaian's children. Not that the father of Ian, Andrew, and Jamie had treated Niall or Laurie any differently than his own children, but Niall knew. Their mother had been a MacAlister of Sleat, who visited Glencoe before her marriage to Arthur MacDonald. She had fallen under the eye of the Donald laird and he had taken her to his bed. There was no shame in that, and Arthur had not turned from her even when they discovered that she was pregnant by the laird. Over the years, MacIaian had come to visit and when he did, Niall and Laurie would be presented for his quiet inspection.

When Laurie had married one of MacIaian's nephews-in-law, it had been an opportunity for the laird to send for Niall, to deepen the relationship with his unacknowledged son.

Niall's shoulders sagged with the heaviness of his thoughts. Here he was, a true son of the fallen chief, standing as chosen leader to the small group of survivors who were fighting so valiantly to rebuild. Fate was ironic in her whims.

He had not told any of them. Annie knew, and Duncan had known. Fergus, he thought, probably had suspicions. But it didn't matter. They had proclaimed him their chosen chief in the absence of John and Alasdair, and that confidence spoke louder to Niall than leadership by birthright ever could have.

His rising need for Meg was another problem. He was too close to holding his sword at the throat of Robert Campbell to allow a distraction now. This afternoon he and Alan would take Meg to the camp at Loch Treig, and he would leave Alan there with her to await the culmination of the plan. Then Niall and his brothers would set up the ambush at Glencoe for Robert Campbell.

In the back of his mind, Niall knew that in this final quest for revenge, he faced the risk of terminating the fledgling love he was enjoying with Meg. But the hand must be played, he reassured himself. He could do no less than retaliate in kind for the executions of his father and his sister and his clan.

Niall sat down on the hard earth and stared at the grave reflectively. MacIaian had been a strong, decisive leader. What he wanted, he had taken with no questions and no regrets. Niall could take Meg the same way, he knew. But the sweetness of the silver passion in her eyes when she kissed him might be vanquished forever if he acted so to her. Choices.

Life was full of choices and a man could never know which choice held success or disaster. All he could do was follow his honor and let it be the guiding beacon.

The peace of the gravesite lulled him, and he was deep in dreams of honor when the soldiers from Glenlyon crept upon him. They left their horses a safe distance away from the keep and moved in silently on foot. Only the clashing steel of suddenly drawn swords alerted him. Niall looked up to see his enemy smiling broadly at him.

Three of the soldiers moved to hold him by the arms as Robert Campbell swaggered within inches of Niall's face. A satisfied smile creased Campbell's face as he tapped his riding crop against his thigh.

He swung it hard, its force laying open Niall's scarred cheek. When he recovered, Niall thought that at least Campbell was confining his bravery to the already damaged side of his prisoner's face.

"It seems you have something that I want." The colonel's voice was pleasant. "I thought I taught you a lesson when we last met, not to provoke me again." He looked appraisingly at Niall's face, using the tip of the whip to prod the wound. "You still wear my mark outwardly. Have you forgotten the schooling I gave you?"

Niall looked above the shorter man's head. A hawk circled high above, and he focused his attention on it, the hunter in the sky who struck only when sure of its aim.

"Where are the girls?" Campbell was already tiring of the situation. His impatience showed in his voice.

Still Niall did not respond. Warm blood ran down the side of his face, dripping onto the collar of his shirt, staining the sash he wore across his chest. The cut on his cheek throbbed and burned as he watched the hawk move in slow, ever-widening circles.

Campbell struck another blow with the crop. Niall's head jerked with the reaction. The wound ripped more deeply, exposing the raw flesh to the warm of the air. Against his will, Niall closed his eyes, sickening with the pain. He strengthened his legs to hold his weight and thought of silver eyes and fox colored hair.

"Where are the girls?"

In his hiding place, Fergus rested his hand upon the hilt of his sword and prayed that his pony would not make a sudden noise to reveal their presence. He had intended only to wait while Niall visited the chapel and now he fretted that he had allowed the other men to leave. They should have all remained with him, to escort the chief back home properly. Now he was alone, one man against many soldiers, with no hope of aiding the prisoner. Fergus steeled his nerve. He would do Niall more service by surviving now, and alerting the clan. He must remain hidden until the soldiers left.

The men holding Niall were averting their faces. It brought the grimace of an amused grin to his face and he winked at Robert Campbell.

The colonel's narrow lips thinned even more. "I assure you, MacDonald, that I have every intention of flaying the rest of your face open if you do not tell me where you have taken my wards." He breathed hard through his thin nose. "You will die anyway, but why make it harder than it has to be? Tell me where you are keeping your hostages." With a savage thrust, he brought the crop down hard against Niall's right arm, ripping the shirt sleeve open and drawing more blood.

"Sir." One of the lieutenants standing beside Campbell spoke respectfully.

"Well?"

"If I may remind you, there are only a few of us here, and our horses are some distance away. We are in a vulnerable position."

Niall smiled. One more day, he thought, and you would have indeed been vulnerable.

Campbell nodded reluctantly. "I agree. I'll take these three," he gestured to the men who held Niall, "and return to Fort William with our prisoner to finish the questioning. I'll send you with orders to the rest of the company. They are to search every part of this God-forsaken wilderness, and put the torch to every building they find. I want those girls found! Leave no place for these outlaws to shelter."

The lieutenant nodded. "Aye, sir."

The wounds on Niall's face and arm were on fire, and they had to drag him to where their horses were tied. They set him backwards on one of the horses, hands tied behind his back. One of the soldiers mounted in front of him, and another tied Niall securely in place.

He did not fear that they would find the clan at Blackwater. It was hidden deep in the forest, and even those who knew of its existence had difficulty finding it without a map. He worried that his brothers would come searching for him alone when his horse returned without him. They would be no match for soldiers armed with muskets and swords.

A fine example of leadership, he told himself. He trusted that Fergus would display better judgement than to allow himself to be taken alone. He hoped Fergus would decide to take the people away, perhaps back to his own clanstead. He prayed that John and Alasdair were still in hiding so that the king's men would never find them.

The blood was clotting on his face as his captors moved at what seemed to be a snail's pace, and a fly buzzed around his head. He did not doubt that Campbell would allow him to die of his wounds. Wearily Niall closed his eyes and an image of Meg formed in his mind. *Now you will not have to choose between love and honor*, he told her. *And finally I will know peace and, perhaps, forgiveness.* His upper arm was flayed open to match his face; but the burning sensation in his heart was more painful.

Her soft silver eyes glistened with understanding. *But I have already chosen love*, she replied in his mind. *And you have no need of redemption or forgiveness.*

He allowed himself to sink into the depths of her eyes. Silver became soothing gray, like a calm, encompassing sea, and the fiery pain of his cuts receded. *Mo crigh, my heart,* he murmured to her. *It saddens me to leave you.* This must the Sight that Annie spoke of, but it was as real as though Meg stood there before him.

She smiled again, but her image was becoming fainter with each breath. *I will not allow you to leave me,* she called. *I will follow wherever you lead.*

Before he could summon the thought to refute her last words, he lost consciousness. The soldiers spurred their horses forward.

Fergus arrived at Blackwater about an hour later. Ian and Jamie looked up from the shelter of the tree under which they were talking when they heard the rapid hoofbeats. Concern lengthened their expressive faces, and when Carnoch ran lightly into the clearing, the brothers looked at each other in fear.

"Call the clan." The command was terse, and Jamie obeyed instantly, pulling his horn from his side and sounding a long note.

They came quickly, men and women, all alerted to the unusual signal.

When they were all assembled, Fergus told them succinctly what had just happened. "They mentioned hostages. They think we have some of their own people here."

Meg felt as though she would faint. Jeanne and Elizabeth caught her as she swayed, and even Margaret looked at her with sympathy. They walked her a short distance away from the men, and Jeanne whispered to her.

"You must not give up so easily. The men will go after him."

Alan, the warrior's son, was livid. "We cannot allow them to kill him too. He is the last, if John and Alasdair do not return."

Ian and Andrew looked at him curiously, even in their fear.

"What do you mean?" Ian looked ready to kill.

"He was the old chief's true son," blurted Alan, amidst the upraised eyebrows of the other men. Shocked and disbelieving, they formed a tight knot around him.

Fergus interjected. "Aye, there is no reason to cover it up now. 'Tis true, lads. MacIaian was his da and Laurie's, by your own mother. Arthur knew it, and loved the boy like his own."

"So he is also the chief's son!" It was a simultaneous cry from the throats of all the men who loved Niall.

"Aye," admitted Alan, "but he preferred the choosing over the birthing."

Ian stood in silence, trying to digest the startling news. But Andrew stepped into the center of the group.

"This can be dealt with later. We must keep it secret still, especially from the women, and we must go after the Campbells. There may be time to stop them before they get too far away."

Fergus shook his head. "There are many soldiers between Campbell and us. He probably left his entire contingent to search the forest for some hostages he thought Niall had taken. There have been rumors of the thing in Appin, according to the news I have been hearing, and I believe this taking of Niall is in response to that. But why should they think we have hostages here?"

On the other side of the clearing, Meg pulled away from Jeanne's grasp. "I must help Fergus make plans. She ran back to where the men stood, arriving in time to hear the last words Fergus spoke. Meg paled and looked back at Elizabeth.

Jamie cast a nervous look at Andrew. With Niall taken prisoner, how would Alan and Fergus react to the news that in their midst stood the two reasons for that imprisonment?

"We have no choice!" Alan argued. "Even now it may be too late."

Ian and Andrew moved closer to the two Campbells. But Meg knew she had to speak.

"Fergus," the words were calm and self-possessed. "I have something to tell you."

As she finished her tale, there were swords drawn all about the group. Ian and Andrew stood before her, while Alan and Fergus faced them in angry disbelief. Margaret and Jeanne had withdrawn in shock. Jamie and Dora stood beside the Campbell girls, offering a semblance of support.

"You can indeed slay us where we stand and no one would fault you," Meg said calmly. "But you will seal his fate if you do. Instead, send me to reason with Robert. It is what I begged Niall to do weeks ago. Perhaps it is not too late."

"You must listen to her," said Elizabeth desperately.

Alan sneered at her words. "You would seize the opportunity to run, how could we be certain you would plead for him?"

Meg lifted her head in defiance, her eyes flickering dangerously at him. "Because I love him."

Alan spat on the ground, but Jeanne stepped forward.

"I believe her," she said quietly. "You have but to watch them together to know their feelings for each other."

"I too believe." It was Margaret, surprising them all with her support.

One by one the other women moved to stand shoulder to shoulder with Meg and Elizabeth. Annie, both hands on her hips, fixed a hot glare on Alan and Fergus. "She is his only hope. Let her try."

Fergus looked like a trapped animal. "She will be the end of him."

"No! Robert will listen to me, because when he hears what I have to say, it will aid him with the Earl." Meg glanced at Elizabeth. "He wants my sister and me at court. And we will go in exchange for Niall's freedom."

Eagerly Elizabeth nodded. "I will leave for Edinburgh at once. Jamie and Andrew can go with me."

"No!" shouted Alan. "Then we lose both bargaining points."

"Don't be a fool, man," hissed Annie. "Elizabeth and Meg know this Campbell dog better than anyone, they have lived with him. Do as she says and cease this arguing."

Fergus looked at his wife. Jeanne nodded. "There is no other way. You must let her try."

Niall's second in command bowed his head. "I will ride with you, though," he told Meg. "And if you try to betray him, I will cut your throat myself."

The sounds of the forest were muted, as though creation itself awaited her answer. She thought of all that her own clan demanded of her. Loyalty. Duty. Innate obligation to hold her name inviolate. But what was loyalty without honor? Duty without love to soften it. For a moment it was as though Meg could see down through the centuries to come, hear the songs and stories that would be told and retold about her clan and its treachery. The name Campbell would never be inviolate again. No action of hers could repair or restore that loss of respect. Her personal honor lay in holding sacred the oaths she had given from her own heart.

And in that moment she knew exactly where her loyalties and duty lay. "He is my husband," she said, her words clear and confident. "No betrayal shall come to him at my hands."

"I take that as oath, Mistress," Fergus answered. "You shall be held accountable to God should your words prove false."

"No reckoning could be sharper than that I give myself. We have argued long enough. I am going to my husband with or without your help."

CHAPTER 19

Meg and Fergus packed only as much as was necessary for the long ride to Fort William. Water, a few pieces of bread, along with the desperate hope that Niall yet lived. The soldiers had several hours head start and the pace would be relentless.

She rode Carnoch, knowing that the black was the most fit of all the horses. Additionally, it imparted a small measure of comfort, a sense of connection to Niall that Meg needed at this moment.

The pass was outlined in brilliant sunshine, and it was obvious from the remnants of prints in the melting snow, that many horses had passed the same way, two by two, only a short time before. Fergus was grimly intent on his mission, sparing no idle talk or hesitance in his riding. He urged his stout Highland pony forward with a recklessness that matched Meg's own, and soon Glencoe and its borders were fast passing away.

Before she had reckoned it, they were on Campbell land, the hours falling away easily behind them. They stopped once, when Fergus sighted a short leather strap on the ground, and Meg's hands tightened in the black's mane as she recognized the thong from Niall's hair.

They passed Glenlyon without more than a brief thought. By now the men and their prisoner would be almost at the fort, and there too would be Robert Campbell, gloating in his accomplishment of the day.

She knew without being told of it that they had used their strength against Niall. But that she, and he, could live with. What she dreaded was the probability of his death. He would never succumb to threats or torture, and eventually Robert would grow bored with the whole affair and put a quick end to it.

Wind roared in her ears as she rode, and it was not a sweet sound. In the voice of the elements were all the calls and cries of the past, and she began to believe Annie's description of curses and apparitions of death. For it was sure that demons pursued her now, in her wild ride to save her husband.

When the night fell, Fergus forced her to stop riding, and they sheltered for awhile under a tremendous oak at the edge of Campbell's land. Fort William lay only a few more hours away, and her spirit chafed at the delay in rescuing Niall. But Fergus was determined.

"We will not go as thieves in the night to steal away a treasure," he explained to her. Centuries of pride and heritage spoke through the concern in his voice. "We must go boldly through the gates, demanding his release. And so we will rest here for the moment, while you gather your determination."

She knew he was giving her the opportunity to calm her thinking before she confronted Robert. Her spirit chafed at the delay, but her mind told her Fergus was right. Emotional attacks would only solidify Robert's control of the situation. A clear headed, logical approach was the best assault possible. Was it not what she had told the clan herself, when she argued for the right to go to Fort William?

She nibbled at the piece of bread Fergus shared, and decided to ask the question that had bothered her all along. "What was Niall's connection to MacIaian?"

Fergus looked at the food in his hands for a long while before answering her. "Lass," he answered finally, "Niall values his privacy. 'Tis enough that the people have named him their chief."

She gazed out into the thick drifting mist thoughtfully. "I suppose that his sister's marriage to MacIaian's nephew-in-law placed Niall and his brothers close to the chief."

"They often visited the keep together."

"But why Niall and not one of the others for chief? Andrew is the most warrior-like."

Fergus shifted his weight and leaned back against the oak for more support. "Ye'll have noticed the lad has a way about him. 'Tis a natural air of leadership, one that many men lack."

She had to agree with that statement, his natural arrogance had been the first thing she noticed about Niall, the quality that set them at odds from the beginning. "He is a good leader for one so young, and he does care for the people more than anything else." That too, was true about him, and even harder to accept. The greater good of his people would always come before her, even if she did remain with him as his wife.

"Aye. And wi' the grace of God, we'll take him back safe to the clan and the two of you can go about the business of raising more MacDonalds for Glencoe."

She blushed at the words, but understood Fergus' sentiment. Of course the clan would wish to protect Niall. He was all that stood between them and total dispersal.

"Why do you trust me now, Fergus?"

"Because I can see in your eyes that you love him," Fergus told her simply. "As Jeanne said. Whatever has passed between you, whatever reason he had for bringing you to us, you love the lad. You are his true wife now, and that makes you one of us. Your own honor will help restore him to us."

There it was again. Honor. It was as much a part of these Highlands as was the mist that came up each night. But she was gaining a new understanding of the word. Although it might not be prudent to tell Fergus that her motivation was due to personal desires rather than family honor.

"We will go now, never mind the darkness." She stood, brushing snow and twigs from her riding skirt. "I am ready to face Robert."

They mounted the horses again and rode straight along the old track toward the gates of Fort William. The night had fallen fully by this time, and the mist was thick. But the horses stayed smoothly on course, and Meg was glad of the veil that hid her face from Fergus.

✧

Robert Campbell took a long appreciative draught of whiskey and set his glass down on the interrogation table with a smile. "Good Scottish usquebaugh," he declared, "is something no Sassenach has yet been able to imitate. Don't you agree with me, MacDonald?"

Niall stood against the wall in the colonel's office, a soldier flanking him on either side in case he attempted to attack Robert. Wrists still tied firmly behind him, his hair hung limply about his blood streaked face. A cut under his right eye evidenced the latest punishment for his refusal to speak, and he wondered if Campbell intended to leave him a face at all. He would never answer, but he was tired, so tired.

"I give you one more opportunity to end this. You have but to tell me where you are holding my wards, and I will send you to the king for a swift trial. Remain silent, and you will die here, a pitiful example for the band of renegades you lead."

Niall returned Campbell's stare without emotion. The smaller man was becoming more excitable with each gulp of whiskey, and Niall wondered how long it would take for the colonel to reach inebriation.

Campbell fingered his the smooth leather of his riding crop lovingly. Suddenly he barked an order to the guards. "Remove his shirt."

Three hours later, Meg and Fergus rode up to the gates of Fort William. The guards lowered their swords to challenge the visitors, but one of the men recognized the ward of Colonel Campbell and waved them through.

"You'll find his lordship in his office, mistress."

Were they too late? They shouldn't have stopped to rest. Meg castigated herself for the delay. Niall might be dead by now, executed at Robert's command. No trial was required for a traitor taken in flight. She had no doubt that Robert would claim resistance on the part of his prisoner to justify the murder. She shuddered.

Robert sat grandly at his writing desk. He did not raise his head when they were announced, but continued writing for a few moments more. Then he lifted his head and gave Meg a welcoming smile. Rising from the table, he walked around to embrace her.

"My dear ward," he exclaimed, "I am so relieved to see you here. Did those outlaws harm you? Or has this one stepped readily into his leader's place?"

The outlaw standing beside her stirred warningly, and she placed a quick hand on his arm.

"I am not in the least injured, Robert, as you can see. And my escort has taken good care of me. This is Fergus MacAlister of Glencoe."

Robert took a step back, an expression of theatrical amazement on his pointed face. "One of the survivors? Can it be possible that there is yet an honest man among them? You have my eternal gratitude sir, for helping my ward escape."

Fergus raised an eyebrow at the exaggerated address. He palmed the hilt of his sword but did not speak.

"I did not escape, Robert. I came freely, with the favor of the clan."

He was curious now, she saw it in his eyes. And then he asked about Elizabeth, as she had known he must.

"And your sister? Is she with you?"

"Elizabeth will journey to Edinburgh, to the Earl of Argyll."

The tip of Robert Campbell's nose quivered.

"Edinburgh." He sank back into his chair. "That is wonderful news, if true. My men are even now searching the forest for the two of you. I will send a message that they need not be concerned for your welfare when they torch the settlement." His face had a vicious pleasure.

"You will never find it." Her voice was quiet. "They have ways and places of hiding that you will never discover. But I am here tonight, Robert, not because I longed to return to your tender care. You took one of the MacDonalds prisoner today, as he stood at the grave of his chief. I wish you to release him immediately."

Robert cocked his head at an interested angle. "He wears a chieftain's badge. 'Tis an act of treason against the Crown to wear the badge of Glencoe. Added to that, he is an imposter, since no seed of MacIaian's has seen fit to reclaim Glencoe."

Fergus made an inarticulate sound and lunged forward. Robert's two guards stopped him, one holding his sword arm, the other placing a sword at the throat of the enraged man.

Meg took a deep breath. "He is not an imposter, the people there have chosen him to act as their chief. And more than that, Robert, he is my husband. I demand that you release him at once."

Robert was delighted at the news. "Your husband? I am most intrigued, dearest Meg. Do acquaint me with the way in which this remarkable event took place." He returned to his seat and leaned back in his chair, lacing his hands behind his head and feigning an air of concern. "You surely were not forced into marriage? I shall have his head if he forced you."

"No, Robert, I was not forced. He did it to protect me and Elizabeth, so that the clan would not retaliate against us as they might have otherwise."

"And you are truly married? Irrevocably, in every sense of the word?" His breath came fast, so eager was he for her answer.

She took a deep breath and met his excited stare "Truly."

The chair crashed down and Robert leapt to his feet. "Then you are outcast from your own clan, my dear ward, and no longer fit to be called Campbell. Argyll will agree with me, and move immediately to remove your name from the family books." His triumph was disgusting. "I will send a messenger to Edinburgh to inform the Earl. You, Meg *MacDonald*," he spat the name, "are no longer my concern. Get you from my presence before I have you imprisoned alongside your husband."

Her heart sank. "Will you not release him now, Robert? He can do you no harm. There are only a few of the clan left, living with difficulty in the forest. Surely enough has been done against them. Show mercy to him and his kin, now and God will reward you for it."

"King William will reward me for bringing a traitor to justice."

The color of Meg's eyes turned to a hard bright glitter. "Release Niall MacDonald and let us leave the fort. We will not burden or trouble you further. You have my word of honor."

"The honor of a Campbell turned traitor? I think not, my dear. Your husband will remain. In the interest of your former relationship to the Earl, I shall allow you and your escort to depart. But my prisoner stays here, until such time as I deliver him to Edinburgh to await the king's pleasure." He poured himself a glass of whiskey and raised it high in a toast. "To King William!"

At a signal from Robert, the guards released Fergus and escorted them to the door. Meg had no choice but to follow them. The door to the colonel's office closed smartly behind them, and she strove to hold her composure.

They mounted their horses again, and Fergus looked at her questioningly. "And now?"

She nodded. "Now we ride to Edinburgh."

CHAPTER 20

Old Towne
Edinburgh

The cobbled streets of the once elegant, oldest part of Edinburgh were filled with every sort of rag-tag refuse and poverty one could expect to find in the slum of a large city. An unending stream of horses and carriages paraded constantly by, and gentlemen of obvious rank stood in street corner conversation with ladies of doubtful gentility. Questionable appearances of humanity abounded everywhere, peering out from alley ways, and assaulting the ears with a discouraged, depressing, whine.

And there were others, better fed, more sleekly dressed and craftier of face than the pitiable beggars who thronged the streets. The others lounged against crowded store fronts and surveyed passers-by, judging from the cut of cloth and style of travel which stranger was best suited to the game of the day. And the game was always won by the others.

Meg had never before entered the part of Edinburgh that constituted Old Towne. Her forays into the city had been confined to her grandmother's town house, which was situated close to the castle, and all her previous travel there had been by closed coach. Now she rode through the open streets on horseback, her nostrils assailed by the dank odor that blew up from the gutters, her face sheltered from view by the cloak which Fergus insisted she pull over her head to protect her identity.

They had to ride all the way through the worst part of Old Towne to find the area frequented by the upper class. Here, amid the hawking vendors who bargained both merchandise and services of dubious legality, and the dangerous outfall of sudden street brawls, were the discreet meeting places of certain influential noblemen who had reasons of their own for maintaining private quarters away from the eyes of the court.

The teeming activity of the streets made it difficult for Meg to ride with her eyes focused straight ahead as Fergus had instructed. He was not anxious to be recognized in Edinburgh, not even in Old Towne where it was customary to turn one's head instead of calling out a greeting to an old friend. He had elected to travel without his MacAlister plaid, deeming it politic not to attract attention in this place where Clan MacDonald was outlawed. Instead he wore a black doublet and tight fitting pants under a long cloak, formal attire that sat strangely upon a rough mannered Highlander.

Fergus called a halt as they neared a tavern at the end of one of the wider alleys off Old Towne's main street. It was situated in the part of the city's maze that lay closest to the castle, and seemed to be of slightly better maintenance than the others they had passed. At least, Meg noted as they dismounted, there were no bodies lying in front of this establishment.

"Keep your cloak pulled tight," Fergus demanded, escorting her into the tavern and seating her at a small table just inside the door. He sat close to her, his back against the wall, his own cloak brushed aside to afford a clear view of the sword and dirk at his hip.

The tavern was comfortably decorated, with dark oak paneling on the walls and exposed beams running the length of the ceiling. A vivid mural on one wall portrayed the royal hunting party as they celebrated a kill. Good quality parquet flooring accentuated the air of comfort, with colorful tile visible in the kitchen entryway. Amid the clatter and conversation of her surroundings, Meg realized that this was more than a mere public house, it was a meeting place, where business of every sort could be transacted with discreet dispatch.

A short man of florid face and obsequious demeanor hurried over with two mugs of ale. He set them down before Fergus, his face carefully disinterested. Nodding his head, Fergus tossed the man a coin and turned a mug up, downing the draught. "Another." He gave the order quietly, and the short man scurried away to oblige.

Meg was consumed with interest; the tavern was a completely unfamiliar scene to her and only the restraint of her escort prevented her from asking question after question.

When Fergus had downed his second ale, and hers as well, a man across the room left his table and walked over to join them. He was tall and broad shouldered, with a red beard and hair. Pulling a chair over, he eased himself into it and raised his mug to Meg in a gallant gesture. He wore yellow and red tartan trews of an unidentifiable clan, and when he smiled, his lips revealed a stunning lack of teeth.

"Any news?" the red headed man asked. His eyes swept the other occupants of the tavern in a constant nervous wave.

Fergus shook his head. "Are my friends here yet?"

"Aye," the stranger raised his eyes to indicate the second floor of the tavern. "And waiting for you."

Fergus pushed his chair back and stood, looking at the man. "You'll be minding our horses." It was a statement of an expected service, and Fergus opened his sporran to produce another coin which he left on the table. He offered his hand to Meg, indicating that the brief conversation was finished.

The stranger pocket the coin and finished his drink. "Aye," he answered, and sauntered outside to lean against the side of the tavern.

"Who was that?" Meg whispered as Fergus led her to a narrow staircase at the rear of the large public room.

He chuckled under his breath. "A friend. 'Tis best if he is not named."

They ascended the stairs slowly, Fergus ahead of her, his right hand just grazing the handle of his dirk. Incredibly, Meg was not frightened by the strange situation. Rather, every nerve was strained with excitement and anticipation. She peered out from under the fold of her hood, sneaking a glance at the crowded tavern. No one paid any attention as she and Fergus climbed the stairs, and she quirked her mouth slightly at the ambivalent attitude of the other customers.

But it was best not to be noticed. The image of Niall's face as she had last seen him on the morning of Duncan's burial, came back to her, and she dug her fingernails into the palms of her small hands. She would succeed in freeing him, would return with him to Glencoe. Somehow.

At the top of the stairs, a door opened suddenly, and Fergus entered without hesitancy. Meg followed him inside and was overjoyed to see Jamie and Ian.

Ian was standing beside the one window of the small chamber, which looked out over the tavern's entrance. "We saw you arrive."

Grateful for the opportunity to relax, Meg threw off the heavy cloak and sank onto a low tapestry couch. Her feet freed themselves from her boots, and she flexed her toes luxuriously. At Jamie's startled glance, she smiled ruefully. "I think better in my bare feet," she explained, and the trace of a grin touched his face.

She curled up on the couch and looked around. The room was small and daintily turned out, almost like a lady's sitting room. The only thing lacking was a bed, but the long low couch on which she reclined could serve a similar purpose. All in all, it was a comfortable place to rest, with candles on the walls and a small brazier of coals providing heat.

"I could like this." She already liked it well enough to fall victim to a drowsy contentment.

"Do not get too relaxed. We have only paid for an hour, and the lady who uses it customarily will soon return to transact her... business." Ian was teasing her, his green eyes turning up at the corners.

But then his serious expression returned and he asked, "Campbell would not release him to you?"

"Nay." Out of the corner of her eye she saw Ian's quick glance at Fergus. "You were all right, and I was wrong. It appears that we must raise the clan and return to Fort William. Force may prevail where reason did not."

"Did you see him?" The abrupt question betrayed Ian's worry for the brother he might never see again, and Meg's heart constricted at the thought.

"Nay." Fergus looked down at the expensive handwoven rug beneath his feet. "The lass is right. We must get word to as many of the clans as we can." He flashed a grim smile at the three who listened. "Being outcast is nothing new for a MacDonald. We'll just go in and take the lad and fade off into the mountains."

It would not be that simple, and Meg knew it. More lives would be lost, either in actual fighting or by execution. Yet the alternative was to leave Niall in prison, and that was unthinkable. Every moment they delayed increased the threat to his life. But Meg would not dwell on that.

She jumped briskly to her feet, determined to appear confident of success. In the absence of her husband, the chief, she must be strong and fearless. "Where is Andrew? Have he and Elizabeth arrived yet?"

"Andrew returned this morning, leaving Elizabeth at the house of Argyll." Jamie sat down on a bench next to the door. "We thought it best to place her out of danger."

"Is the Earl in Edinburgh?" Meg's pulse raced. If she could talk to the Earl, perhaps there was still hope of resolving things logically.

"Nay," Ian dashed her fledgling hope. "He has returned to Argyll. Elizabeth remains under the care of his housekeeper here for the moment, awaiting your arrival." He smiled at Meg wickedly. "You must be anxious to refresh yourself and rest."

"Aye," she said, agreeing with the idea of a bath. But she looked at Fergus. "That can wait, though. We must talk together and decide how best to go about this."

He agreed, rubbing his beard thoughtfully. "Is Andrew near by?"

"Aye," Jamie answered. "Lady Douglas has opened her home to us. He awaits us there."

Meg's attention was riveted by the name. Niall's mistress! She bent her head to disguise her surprise as she retrieved her boots. Slipping them back on her tired feet, she stood up and smiled into Ian's merry green gaze. "Then I suggest we adjourn to the home of Lady Douglas."

✧

The town house of Lady Maire Douglas stood quite near the former home of Meg's grandmother, and it bemused Meg to ponder that perhaps she and her husband's mistress had passed each other in the streets. As they rode, Ian took it upon himself to fill Meg in on the history of the lady in question. Meg had not indicated her interest aloud, and she felt that Ian was enjoying the situation unduly. But she could not restrain her curiosity.

Lady Douglas, Ian explained in great detail, was the widow of a very old man who had died soon after their marriage vows, leaving her with a sizeable fortune and several estates scattered throughout the country. It was whispered that the embraces of his beautiful young wife had been the cause of his death. Ian's beautiful white teeth gleamed as he described Maire Douglas and her attributes. Now, the lady divided her time between Edinburgh and London, following the court for amusement.

They dismounted at the rear of the house, leaving the horses in the care of a handsome young groom. Meg reached up to scratch the soft place behind Carnoch's ear and whispered a loving farewell as the black was led away.

A distinguished looking butler who could easily have been mistaken for a lord himself, greeted them at the door, and admitted them to a drawing room where a small fire burned sedately. Soon a young maid entered with a curtsey, setting a large silver tray loaded with scones and mulled cider on the low table before the fire.

Meg looked quizzically at the maid's comeliness and wondered to herself if Lady Douglas chose her servants on the basis of looks alone. Certainly the appointments of the house itself were impeccable, with ornately decorated plaster moldings at the high ceilings, and rich dark green satin wall coverings. Marble topped tables and green satin draperies all completed a carefully orchestrated atmosphere of lavish wealth. Even Glenlyon was not turned out so expensively. Meg hesitated to seat herself on the luxurious velvet chairs, realizing that Lady Douglas rivaled the Earl of Argyll in matters of taste and personal comfort.

She wished she had taken the time to bathe at the tavern. Now she would meet Niall's mistress in a state guaranteed to embarrass herself forever. Meg looked down at her rumpled clothing, and then, running a hand over her hair to smooth it, she caught sight of her reflection in a brass framed mirror.

Her face, pale and drawn with fatigue from travel and worry, was begrimed with road dust and sweat. *I look like a street urchin.* Her eyes sought Ian for reassurance, but he was engrossed in a whispered conversation with Fergus.

A musical voice interrupted her dismay, and Lady Maire entered the room on Andrew's arm, a fragrance of roses and freshness preceding her movement.

"Ian, my love, are these our eagerly awaited guests?" She held out a delicate hand to Ian, who bowed with an elegance Meg had not seen from him before.

The lady was taller than Meg, and dressed all in white except for the Douglas sash she wore across her bosom. Her hair was a soft black curly cloud, her eyes a deep dark violet. She was older too, well past twenty, and obviously accomplished and experienced in every way.

Lady Maire's face was quite friendly as she welcomed Meg. Seemingly uncaring of the possible damage to her own spotless attire, she opened her arms for an embrace, crushing Meg to her well endowed bosom. A sweet flowery scent enveloped Meg and she sneezed suddenly, three times in rapid succession.

"I beg your pardon." Meg was mortified at her outburst, but Maire Douglas laughed gaily.

"Don't fash yourself, dear. I have just the remedy for you. Agnes," she gestured to the little maid who stood behind Meg. "Please take Mistress MacDonald upstairs. I have given instructions that you are to have whatever you need to refresh yourself," Maire continued, smiling at Meg, "and when you are rested, we will get to know each other."

Meg looked at Ian mutinously. The redhead was trying to hide his amusement at the situation, and as she looked longer at him, Meg saw something else in his eyes as he stared at Maire Douglas.

"Thank you." Meg followed the maid from the room and up the wide thickly carpeted staircase. At the small landing between floors, she paused to stare at a stained glass window depicting St. Joan of Arc. Apparently the Douglasses were of the Roman Catholic faith like the

MacDonalds. It was a startling revelation, to see a relic of popery so blatantly displayed in the capital city.

Agnes opened the door to a large room at the end of the upstairs hall. It was a tastefully appointed bedchamber, heavy tapestry drapes hung on the window, and a matching rose colored coverlet covered the delicately carved bed. A copper hip bath filled with rose scented water waited before the marble fronted hearth. Meg went toward it gratefully. She shed her clothes without any hesitation, and entered the bath quickly as the maid picked up the discarded clothing and disappeared into an adjoining room.

The water was not warm but it was wonderfully comforting to enjoy the first true bath she'd had in weeks. Resting her back against the copper tub, Meg closed her eyes, allowing herself to luxuriate for a few moments of cherished privacy.

Inevitably, her thoughts returned to Niall, and suddenly she was remorseful for indulging herself so fully while he lay captive in Robert's prison. During the long ride to Edinburgh, there had been plenty of time to reconcile her feelings and plans. The important thing was to get him released. Personal desires were secondary, she told herself as she lathered her body with a bar of lavender scented French soap.

She washed her hair and rinsed it with a ewer of water that stood on a low table next to the tub. Niall must have enjoyed his tenure as Lady Douglas' special friend. The entire house, and the lady herself were apparently dedicated to comfort and convenience. Meg quelled the niggling jealousy she felt at the pit of her stomach. He was not her husband in reality, no matter what claims he had made, and no matter what sweet wild passion they shared. She had promised to exchange their marriage for his freedom. Meg shook her head to clear the drops of water from her eyes and the unruly thoughts in her head.

When she looked up, Agnes stood beside her, offering a large thick towel. Gratefully, Meg rose and stepped from the bath into the warm softness, wrapping it around her body like a shield. She sat before the fire and allowed Agnes to dry her hair and brush it with long gentle strokes.

"If you are feeling better, miss, m'lady wishes you to join her in her rooms for supper. The gentlemen will dine alone."

It sounded like a royal decree. Assenting, Meg rose and donned the pink satin dressing gown that Agnes had laid on the bed. It was a little long on her, the ends trailed on the carpet and she lifted it to slip into soft white satin slippers. It occurred to Meg that her hostess had sent some of her own clothing for the use of her guest. The thought was somewhat disquieting, since it was immediately followed by a mental picture of Lady Maire entertaining Niall in this same costume. Resolutely Meg threw off the image, and followed Agnes down the hall to the lady's private rooms.

Lady Maire was seated before her dressing table, her own maid coaxing the soft long black hair into becoming curls. "Thank you, Lily," Maire dismissed the servant, and the girl left, closing the door quietly behind her.

Lady Maire regarded Meg's reflection in the gilt framed mirror silently, and then smiled slowly before she turned around.

"We must not be enemies." Her perfect oval face was pleasant and open. "We both care for him. Niall must be our first concern and other issues must wait until he is safe." She rose languidly and drifted toward a tall open window beside the elaborately carved teakwood bed. A silk Oriental screen masked the dressing area, with colorful, feminine items of clothing draped over it.

After her first glance at the enormous bed, Meg averted her head, not wishing to visualize her husband with her hostess. She drew a deep breath, seeking to still the nervous flutters in her stomach. "I agree. I assume Ian has acquainted you with all our problems?"

"I believe so," Lady Maire replied. She reached up to close the window, latching it against the night air. "Your guardian has imprisoned Niall in retaliation for the abduction of you and your sister, which occurred as a revenge for the murders. And to protect you from the anger of the other men, Niall has claimed you as his wife?" She smiled and returned to sit on the divan, gesturing at the food lying on the table nearby. "You must be starving. We can talk while you eat."

Meg nodded her thanks and reached for a buttered scone. Still uncertain of Lady Douglas' true feelings, she determined to let Maire direct the course of the conversation. She was not left long in doubt.

Lady Douglas picked up a finely painted cup and sipped at the liquid it held. "These clan rivalries are so tiresome. Eventually we will end by killing each other once and for all, giving Scotland to the Sassenachs without the bother of sworn oaths." She smiled at Meg, her blue gaze curious. "Are you truly his wife?"

Better to be quiet than sing a bad song. It was one of Grandmother's favorite sayings. Meg smiled back at Lady Douglas. "That is a personal matter, Lady Douglas, and one which is not important at this moment. I am here to help his brothers get word to the other clans so that we may return to Fort William well equipped to free him." Perhaps that would still the questions Meg had no desire to answer.

"You may call me Maire, and I shall call you Meg. We must be friends, dear. After all, we have much in common. Come and sit here with me, while I tell you my plans." Maire patted the divan on which she was seated, and Meg unwillingly sat beside her.

"Ian assures me you know all about my relationship with Niall. You know also about the letter Lady Cathlan sent the last day Niall was with me?"

It was all out in the open now. Mistress and wife sat cozily together making plans about the man they both loved. Meg had difficulty believing that such civility was common, but it was a most uncommon situation they found themselves in.

"I know about the letter. I have not met Lady Cathlan, but I understand that she is a friend to the MacDonalds."

"And she holds the Queen's esteem." Maire's bright eyes had a triumphant gleam. "Lady Cathlan and I believe the Queen would be sympathetic to your plight. She has confided to several of her ladies that she is weary of all the Scottish intrigue, and she absolutely deplores the way the incident at Glencoe was handled." Maire pursed her lips in a pretty moue as Meg watched in fascination. "The Queen is very much in love with her husband, and blames Breadalbane for tarnishing King William's reputation in

Scotland." Maire rose and began pacing the wool rug in agitation, twisting one long black lock around a finger.

Meg could not take her eyes from the beautiful woman before her. Every gesture, every word uttered by Maire Douglas was entrancing. It was perfectly clear why Ian was smitten with her, and why Niall had chosen her for his mistress. Beside the elegant woman, Meg felt young and inexperienced. How could he have ever found pleasure with her, when Maire Douglas waited for him?

"Are you listening?" Maire's sultry voice was impatient as she stopped before Meg. "Lady Cathlan and I believe that the Queen can be persuaded to ask King William to pardon Niall and his brothers. Are you willing to go with us to try?"

"I will do whatever necessary to free him. Is the Queen in Edinburgh?"

Maire's smile was approving. "The court is here for a few days before they begin a progression through Scotland. It is to be a good will mission, whereby the king can get to know his subjects better. Lady Cathlan has arranged for us to see the Queen tomorrow, just after her morning prayers. Queen Mary always spends a few moments alone before receiving visitors, and Lady Cathlan will attend her tomorrow."

Apprehension raced through Meg's body, leaving a sense of helplessness in its wake. "Tomorrow?" She looked down at the satin robe she wore. "I have nothing suitable to wear to court. Only my riding dress, which is in laughable condition."

Maire patted her shoulder. "I'm sure we will find something for you from my wardrobe. I do not mind sharing. Do you?"

CHAPTER 21

"Lady Cathlan, may I present Mistress Meg MacDonald."
Maire Douglas spoke in a smooth husky voice as she made
the formal introductions. Although properly courteous, an
undertone of familiarity in her words belied the stilted
speech.

For this all important meeting, Maire had chosen to
wear a formally designed ivory colored dress, departing
slightly from her penchant for white. Jet beading covered
the bodice and accentuated the flowing sleeves,
complimenting the dangling black pearl earrings in her
small, slightly pointed ears.

Meg's costume was chosen with similar care from
Maire's extensive wardrobe. Hastily cut down to
accommodate her petite size, the outfit was of dramatic
black velvet, tight fitting across the bosom and hugging her
waist and the swell of her hips ever so slightly.

At Maire's insistence, the only ornament Meg wore was a
piece of dried white heather pinned to her collar. Standing
together in a small anteroom of Edinburgh Castle, Meg
thought that she and Maire presented quite a striking
picture.

Certainly heads turned on all sides as they made their
way down the gray stone flagged hall toward the Queen's
private chapel. Meg sensed the curiosity around her; it was
a tangible, breathing entity as the court sought to identify
the young woman in the company of the notorious Lady
Douglas. One courtier even followed them down the hall and
now stood quietly watching the unfolding scene.

Lady Cathlan, a woman of mature years and decided
authority, looked closely at the two young girls before her.
Her aquiline face was kind but cool as she appraised their
appearance and demeanor.

"Tell me what it is you wish to say to the Queen." The command was peremptory, almost royal in its abruptness.

Maire gestured gracefully toward Meg. "Meg is the wife of our dear Niall." She ignored the lifted brows of Lady Cathlan and placed a shapely hand on Meg's arm. "She has a petition for the Queen's mercy which is founded on Her Majesty's Scots blood."

Lady Cathlan's voice showed a faint twinge of bored exasperation. "'Tis not necessary to be dramatic, Maire. Let the young woman speak for herself."

The raven haired beauty reacted only slightly, lowering her arm. "As you wish," Maire murmured, her dark eyes sending a pointed message to Meg. *Keep your wits about you*, she seemed to be repeating her earlier instructions, *you must make every word and expression count.*

"Thank you, Lady Cathlan." Meg had rehearsed her speech all the way to the castle. Her voice was firm and strong, her gray eyes clear as she sought the help of the Queen's most influential lady. "Niall is held prisoner at Fort William, and I am come to ask the Queen to intercede in his behalf."

"And the reason for the imprisonment?" The question was sharp.

Meg took a deep breath. "Niall's brothers abducted my sister and me several months ago. After the attack on Glencoe last year, their plan was to ransom enough money to feed the clan and allow them to rebuild. Circumstances changed. Then Robert took Niall alone at the grave of his kinsman, and refuses to release him even though my sister is now safe here in Edinburgh, as am I."

"And you, I see, are working on behalf of your former captor." Lady Cathlan's voice carried a question. "'Tis a curious situation."

"He is now my husband. We are handfasted. And I believe that if His Majesty is apprised of the matter, he will act in the interests of peace and resolution, revoking Robert's orders to punish Niall and his brothers. And so I have come to you, my lady, and to the Queen, to beg clemency for my husband."

"Her Majesty places a great store on true love and fidelity." Lady Cathlan looked into Meg's eyes. "Do you love your husband enough to sever yourself from your clan and your sister if need be? For, be warned that it may indeed come to that. I doubt that Argyll, when he hears of the matter, will look upon your marriage with leniency. You stand to lose a great deal, Mistress MacDonald."

Acutely conscious of Maire's inquisitive presence beside her, Meg answered without hesitation. "Niall's welfare is the most important thing to me. Whatever comes afterward, whatever price is demanded, will be paid gladly, if I may see him returned to his Glencoe."

Lady Cathlan regarded Meg for a moment. When she spoke again, her voice was softer. "And are you aware of Niall's position at Glencoe?"

Meg tilted her head. "Why, he is their chosen chief, brother to Laurie who was married to the nephew of MacIaian."

Lady Cathlan's gaze flickered over to Maire and then back to Meg. "Indeed, he holds quite a strong place among the survivors. I will speak to the Queen and see if she will receive you. It may be that all shall be resolved as you wish. His Majesty has sought an opportunity to redeem himself with the northern clans. This," the corners of Lady Cathlan's eyes relaxed slightly, "may be the answer the Queen has been praying for. Wait here."

She was gone from them in a regal sweep of heavy dark green satin, and Meg looked at Maire for reassurance. "What do we do now?"

Maire guided her over to a seat in the small courtyard which adjoined the antechamber. "Why, we do just as she said." Maire seated herself carefully upon the stone bench, smoothing her skirts out in a becoming drape. "We wait."

Meg paced the small enclosed garden area fretfully. "I am tired of waiting. We should have ridden back to Fort William this morning with Andrew and stormed the gates."

Maire raised both eyebrows. "Stormed the gates? My dear, there are less strenuous ways of obtaining the results you desire, and far less bloody ones. Do allow Lady Cathlan to handle the matter. She is quite skillful at such intrigues, I assure you."

Meg paused in her pacing to send a sharp silver glare at Maire. "I hope Niall will approve of our waiting here. You do remember that he is in a serious condition?"

There was no smile evident on Lady Douglas' face. "Niall's well being is uppermost in my mind as it is in yours. Else you can be certain I would not be here, emphasizing my friendship with a group of outlaws who are in severe disfavor with the throne." Her mood changed quixotically, and Maire tilted her head to one side. "Tell me, dear, are you always so passionate? That must be what captured Niall's heart."

Meg's pent up energy exploded in a rush. "You know how I came to be his wife. Passion has nothing to do with it." The falsehood hurt her heart, but she was resolved not to come between Niall and the beautiful woman seated before her, the one whose love had caused him to turn his back on other women.

A loud sigh escaped Maire's lips. "Meg, 'tis time you and I came to an understanding. Niall and I have been friends for many years, close and good friends, and I hope we shall always be so. But our arrangement was not the romance that you have apparently heard it to be."

Maire's long fingers played with one of her dark black curls. "I would have married him in a moment," she admitted, "but he never asked me. There was something driving him even before the attack, and it prevented him from giving of himself completely to our relationship."

"I had not realized..." Meg did not know how to respond to this remarkable confession. "Are you saying that he did not love you?"

Maire dimpled. "They always love me, dear. Niall somehow managed not to fall in love with me. I'm sure you can appreciate the difference."

"But you were his mistress!"

"And we had some wonderful times together, and some intoxicating," Maire emphasized the word, "nights. But it was all very lighthearted on his part. Not in the least the kind of emotion I would have wished."

Meg thought this over, a tiny core of excitement beginning to grow in her mind. Was it possible? Had Maire been only a diversion for Niall? If so, there might then be room for Meg in his heart. "Thank you for your honesty. And for your help."

"I could do no less. Niall is still my dear friend, no matter what was once between us, and in spite of his marriage. Besides, it has been a wonderful opportunity to meet his brothers." Maire's eyes twinkled. "Especially Ian. Tell me, Meg, is he betrothed?"

"Not that I am aware of," Meg was fascinated by the other woman's ability to change moods so quickly. "Do you, er, like Ian?" It seemed slightly indecent for Maire to be thinking such things about Niall's brother.

"I'm sure I could like him very well." The arrogant complacency was back in full force. "And I shall be looking for the first opportunity to explore the possibility."

There was a stir at the door leading to the chapel, and Meg looked up to see one of the guards opening the door. Lady Cathlan emerged, beckoning to the two waiting women.

Hurriedly, they joined her, urgency evident in their footsteps.

"Her Majesty wishes to see you." Lady Cathlan was slightly breathless. "Do not speak unless she bids you to do so."

The Queen stood silhouetted before a tall multi-paned window of clear glass. She was not a tall woman, but her bearing would have announced her rank even without the trappings of royalty which adorned her person.

Meg and Maire stood in the shadows until Queen Mary turned to look at them. The Queen moved quietly toward them, stopping only a few feet away. Both girls made a deep curtsey.

"Rise." The Queen nodded at Maire, who was well known at court, but her gaze lingered on Meg's face. She seemed satisfied with what she found there, for a small smile curved on her thin lips. "Do you love your Highlander?"

Somehow, Meg was not surprised at the question. "Yes, Your Majesty, I do."

"I, too, love my husband. We must be vigilant in their interests, must we not?" Without waiting for a response, the Queen looked at Lady Cathlan. "Bring my prayer book."

When the small white book was placed in her hands, Queen Mary looked at Meg again. "You and your husband must promise to behave with dignity and respect toward the throne from henceforth. Another episode might be disastrous for the children of MacIaian." Her gaze did not falter. "Women have great power over the men who love them."

Meg lay her own hand upon the prayer book. "Yes, Your Majesty."

"You understand that I can promise only to try."

"Yes."

"God hold you safely." The Queen handed the book back to Lady Cathlan and, inclining her head graciously, walked from the chapel.

Meg turned to Maire. "Is that all?"

"Certainly. She has given you her word. Now we return to my house — and wait." Maire lifted her skirts and led the way from the Queen's chapel. "Perhaps on the way, you can tell me more about Ian."

Meg shook her head at Maire's retreating back. The young woman continued to surprise her. Perhaps that very inconsistency was what so charmed the men. But it was not a characteristic Meg wished to cultivate for herself. Oh, to be safe at home in the Highlands, with the clan at Blackwater. Things were so simple among them. No one pretended or sought to be anything other than what they were.

And then she realized that Blackwater was the first place she had felt at home since the deaths of her parents and grandmother.

Meg entered the coach behind Maire quietly, and turned her face away, seeking the impersonal view of the city streets as a veil for her thoughts. Fatigue and fear crowded in upon her, like the beating wings of carrion crows and she closed her eyes momently to fight the tears that came welling from her heart.

"We do not have time for despair." Maire's voice was soft in Meg's ear. "You must have faith, in God and in yourself."

The words sounded much like Elizabeth. Meg opened her eyes and smiled gratefully at Maire. "Do you think it would be possible for me to see my sister? I am feeling in need of a familiar face."

"'Tis not safe for you to enter Argyll's home just now," Maire's face was thoughtful, "but I shall see if something can be arranged. Perhaps we can send a note to your sister, and contrive to meet her at an evening amusement. I am sure Lady Cathlan would agree to act as Elizabeth's chaperone." Maire laughed lightly. "As I, of course, shall act as yours."

It was a humorous thought, and Meg joined Maire in her laughter. It was good to express merriment, the tension in her muscles relaxed, and for the first time since Duncan's death, Meg was at peace. Perhaps it would be only a passing moment, but for the non, it would do.

The footman opened the coach door and assisted them out on the pavement. Always gracious, even to her servants, Maire gave him a devastating smile as she brushed past, leaving a scented trail of rose cologne behind.

Ian and Andrew greeted them in the hallway. Andrew, bullying his way past his younger brother, was the first to speak.

"Did you see the Queen?" His broad face was pale.

"Let us discuss it in the drawing room," Maire suggested, sending a warning glance toward the butler. "Henry, will you ask Cook to prepare a small repast?"

The butler bowed and left the hall quietly as Maire paused before the French mirror that reached from floor to ceiling in the drawing room. With infinite care, she adjusted the collar of her gown, then turned and smiled at the two men who stood watching.

"We do not discuss the Queen in a hallway," Maire chided Andrew. She closed the massive double doors with a surprising strength. "But yes, we did speak with Her Majesty. That is, Meg did. And the Queen has promised to try to intercede."

Ian managed to pull his gaze from Maire. With commendable strength of will, he focused his attention on Meg. "Do you trust her?"

Before Meg could answer, Maire interrupted. Her voice was horrified. "Trust the Queen? Certainly we trust the Queen. Is she not one of the rulers of this realm?" Maire pointed a finger at Ian. "Even in this house, sir, there are limits to the freedom one's conversation may take."

Ian drooped like a small boy caught disobeying his parents. "Of course. I apologize. 'Twas ill said, and it will not happen again."

Maire smiled at him forgivingly, and Meg shook her head in amazement. The woman controlled them all, with only the barest expression. Even Andrew looked impressed.

Tiring of the word play and of Maire's continual performance, Meg put her hands on her hips. "Where are Fergus and Jamie?"

Relieved at the change of subject, Ian answered, "Jamie has gone to seek a position as stable hand at the house of Argyll. Fergus is obtaining provisions. He wants to be ready to ride immediately if need be."

Meg frowned at the words. "I hope we will not have to wait long. Too much time has passed already."

"Aye." Andrew nodded in agreement. "I should have stayed at Fort William and seen to the raising of the clans from there. I mislike all of us leaving at once."

It was a thought that crossed Meg's mind more than once over the past few days. "Perhaps Fergus should go ahead without us." She looked around the room for a consensus. "Alan would help him, and they could keep watch over Robert's actions."

"Alan already watches the fort," Ian told her. "It was the last order Fergus gave before we left. In the event that we do not return within five days, or if the Campbell tries to move Niall, Alan will act on his own authority."

Meg looked around at the earnest worried faces of the men who loved Niall. "I promise you," her voice was steady, "we will succeed. With the Queen's help or without it, we will succeed."

Henry knocked discreetly on the great wooden doors and Ian opened them. The butler set a silver tray down before

Maire and she thanked him in low cultured tones. As though drawn like suicidal moths, Andrew and Ian joined her.

Meg smiled with genuine enjoyment. Perhaps there was a thing or two that could be learned from a woman like Maire Douglas. Another old Highland proverb came into her head. Like the fox who stole the bagpipes, Maire demonstrated that there could be meat alongside music, did one but know the proper way to present it.

CHAPTER 22

The message penned by Maire was on its way to Elizabeth. Fergus insisted their visit be held in private, so the three women were to meet near the park. Lady Cathlan planned to call on Elizabeth that afternoon, inviting her for a drive. The reunion would take place under the ancient stone towers of Edinburgh Castle, in quite a commonplace manner.

After all, Maire remarked when once she and Meg were seated in the coach, ladies often met for impromptu visits under the tall oaks outside the castle. It was a convenient way to pass information among themselves without giving the gentlemen access to feminine activities.

Meg leaned forward, her nose pressed against the glass window of Maire's coach. Seeing Elizabeth was almost as important as freeing Niall. Never before had the sisters been so long separated, and the situation unsettled Meg's mind. The possibility of an even longer, more permanent separation chilled her blood, and she dismissed the idea quickly. Soon enough her sister would be in her arms and she would hear that loving voice speaking her name.

"Andrew speaks well of your sister." Maire strove to make light conversation, and Meg silently blessed her for the thought.

"Andrew is a bit taken with Elizabeth," Meg revealed with a grin. "He thinks her an angel lost among us lesser mortals."

Maire fanned herself with a lace trimmed rice paper fan on a long black wooden handle. "In the past, I've always found angels to be rather tiresome. I'm sure, however, that your sweet Elizabeth will prove the exception."

Meg leaned back against the soft leather upholstery. "You cannot help but love her. She brings out the better part of all of us."

Maire lifted one eyebrow, raising it to a dainty point. "Indeed? And what if one's better part is already revealed?"

Thoroughly enjoying herself, Meg smiled at Niall's former mistress. "I've never met anyone who could boast that state. Have you?" She reached to borrow Maire's fan, and watched the other woman react.

"Touché, my dear. The kitten flexes her claws. How refreshing. I was beginning to think you lacking in humor."

Meg laughed aloud. Maire was the most interesting woman she had ever met. It might just be possible for them to become friends when this was all over. She fanned herself a few times with a seductive flair, and then giggling, handed the fan back to its owner.

The coach slowed, coming to an unexpected stop. Maire rapped on the door with the handle of her fan. "John," she called to the coachman, "why have we stopped?"

Meg looked out the window again and was startled to see John standing in the street beside the coach. "Something is wrong." She pointed out the window and Maire bent across the seat to look.

"Something is very wrong," Lady Douglas said grimly as the coach began to move away from her driver. She opened the door to look at the man who now drove the coach.

"We're going to need a long spoon for our dinner tonight, my dear." With a sigh, Maire settled back inside the tiny compartment.

Meg could not believe the calm way in which her companion was reacting. "What do you mean?"

By the tight expression on her face, Maire Douglas was far from pleased at the proceedings. "That is one of Lord Breadalbane's men, my dear. I fear we are about to become guests of the devil himself."

"You are making no sense. Why would Breadalbane intercept us?"

Maire tucked her fan away in the sleeve of her dress. "We shall soon find out, I think, for the coach is slowing again. It is a shame we did not think to bring one of the men with us after all." She reached down and pulled up the skirt of her watered silk dress. A tiny enameled knife was strapped to the outside of her left boot.

"Do you have your dirk with you, Meg?" the question was offhand, but serious.

"I do, but I'd not have thought it of you," Meg answered honestly.

For the first time in their acquaintance, Maire responded without guile, her voice slipping into a heavily accented burr. "I was raised in the Highlands for half my childhood, ye ken, and will always be a good Scottish lass, no matter where I find myself. We must be very careful, Meg. Next to Stair, the king's advisor, Breadalbane is the most dangerous man in Scotland. Guard your speech as well as your emotions."

"He is a Campbell, too," said Meg, her quick temper beginning to rise. "I should not have to fear my own kin."

Maire looked at her curiously as the coach came to a halt. "You have aligned yourself with the MacDonalds now. Have you forgotten the reason you are in Edinburgh?"

She could never forget, but Meg's soul ached at the thought of choosing between her own clan and Niall's. For a moment, the insight she had received when Duncan lay dying returned, and Meg was bitterly glad that the clan system might also be passing. There was no more room in the world for these senseless feuds.

The door of the coach opened and the Earl of Breadalbane stood before them with a pleasant smile on his craggy face. "Welcome to my home, ladies."

He was tall and florid, with an uncanny resemblance to Robert, Meg noted. But whereas Robert's callousness was easily recognized, the Earl's was more craftily hidden. One would have to probe deeply behind the friendly facade in order to reveal the true nature of the man, and he wore a carefully maintained shield to prevent such intrusion.

Meg stepped out of the coach, disdaining the Earl's proffered hand. "Why have you brought us here?" The words echoed eerily in her head, reminding her of another time and place where she had uttered a similar question.

"My dear, let us reserve our discussion for more private surroundings." He assisted Maire from the coach, favoring her with an admiring smile. He wore English dress, tight breeches and coat, with his tartan sash thrown casually over his shoulder. There were heavily jeweled rings on most of his fingers, and the long wig about his shoulders was scented with perfumed powder.

Meg put a finger under her nose to ward off a sneeze.

"Thank you, sir," Maire turned the full effect of her dark blue eyes on the second most powerful man in the realm and fluttered her lashes. "'Twas unnecessary for you to apprehend us in such a manner, a simple invitation would have sufficed."

"Somehow, Lady Douglas, I doubt it." The Earl offered an arm to each of them, and Meg gritted her teeth before following Maire's example. Meat and music, she reminded herself. Meat and music. They climbed the steps to his townhouse, which was guarded by two massive stone lions next to elegant towers of sculpted rosebushes, and two menservants with swords at their sides.

The three entered the imposing home of Breadalbane quietly, and as the brass trimmed walnut doors closed behind them, Meg calmed herself with the knowledge that even Breadalbane would not dare to harm Lady Douglas. Maire was too visible a figure in the court, and she held the favor of many important people. But it was costing Meg the visit with Elizabeth, and the Queen might even now be sending word of a pardon.

Meg's frustration grew as the Earl handed them over to his housekeeper. "Mary will see to your needs while you are my guests, ladies." The housekeeper smirked and made a quick curtsey before opening a door off the main hall.

Meg fixed Breadalbane with a deliberately smooth smile. "Your guests? How long will we be stopping here, sir?"

"Only until Their Majesties have left the city." The Earl bowed deeply. "I regret the need to leave two such lovely visitors, but matters of state call me."

Maire touched her fingers to her lips pensively. "You hope that the Queen will be unable to contact us if we remain here."

"Why?" Meg asked sharply, facing the tall man with the bland expression on his face. "Why does it matter to you?"

He sighed, reluctant to engage in conversation. "Your mission has been known to me since your visit with the Queen. Let us just say that in the absence of the Earl of Argyll, I feel it incumbent upon me to provide guidance and protection for you in Edinburgh. Guidance that you seem to be sorely lacking, Mistress Campbell."

Meg stiffened, her eyes beginning to flash dangerously. "Campbell is no longer my name, sir. I am the wife of Niall MacDonald who is —"

He cut her off smoothly. "I am quite aware of who Niall MacDonald is, my dear, and that is exactly why you are here awaiting my pleasure and not at the Douglas home awaiting the Queen's. Now I suggest that you make the best of the matter, and wait quietly. It should not be more than two or three days before the court leaves Edinburgh, and you can spend the time constructively, by writing a letter to Robert Campbell and telling him exactly where to find your sister. We would not wish her to be harmed at the hands of desperate men when they learn their leader has died." The Earl bowed again, and left them to follow his housekeeper into a large drawing room.

"He does not know where Elizabeth is!" Meg cried.

"Aye," Maire hesitated, waiting until the housekeeper left. "And that may be our greatest weapon."

"How?"

"Lady Cathlan will know that something has happened and it will not be difficult for her to discover where we are. She will remove Elizabeth from potential harm, and if the Earl seeks to use your sister as a weapon against you, he will not be able to touch her. We are relatively safe from any threat. Breadalbane dares not actually hurt or imprison us, and servants talk, especially in Old Towne." Maire walked briskly to the large double windows which afforded a good view of the street. "Between Lady Cathlan and the boys," she smiled, "I am confident we will be discovered soon. And, I left my fan in the rosebush beside one of the stone lions at the door. Anyone who knows me will recognize it."

"So we wait again." Meg sat down at the piano which graced one corner of the Earl's drawing room and began to pick out a few notes of a lament she had heard Duncan play.

Maire settled cozily into a large overstuffed sofa under the window. "You are becoming quite accomplished at the art of waiting, my dear.

As is Niall, Meg's thoughts answered, but she did not speak them. *God in Heaven, let him still be alive.*

✧

Lady Cathlan carried a small envelope with the King's seal in her bag. The most fitting moment to bestow it, she had decided, was when Meg and Elizabeth were together. Elizabeth's excitement was quite adorable, the lady thought, watching the young girl as she studied each passing coach, carefully looking for her sister.

"Are you happy under the care of the Earl of Argyll, my dear?"

"Well, you see," Elizabeth answered, her eyes scanning the other people in the park, "we have been more in the care of Robert than the Earl. We were sent to Glenlyon quite early on, as the Earl is so often away from Argyll. He thought 'twas better for us to remain in one place, and so he appointed Robert to act as our temporary guardian."

"Indeed!" Lady Cathlan knew the reputation of Robert Campbell. "And does Glenlyon treat you well?" It was doubtful that he did, but one must abide by convention when dealing with such matters as the guardianship of young helpless girls. "Is his wife there to provide you with guidance?"

Elizabeth hesitated, not wishing to reveal that Robert's family had departed Glenlyon some months before, in desperation at his uncontrollable drinking. "He takes care of our needs, my lady."

Lady Cathlan smiled, pleased with Elizabeth's diplomatic answer. It was no secret that Glenlyon's family was currently in London and would probably remain there for awhile. This girl had great potential, as Argyll had foreseen. Too bad he had relinquished his control of her future.

"Shouldn't Meg be here by now?" Elizabeth grew impatient and was fidgeting in her seat.

Lady Cathlan looked out at the passing scenery. Spring was coming quickly to Edinburgh and the park was already renewing its famous green carpet under the trees. "They should have indeed been here by now." She patted Elizabeth's shoulder.

"We will wait a little longer. Tell me about your sister and Niall MacDonald."

✧

Robert Campbell swallowed a long draught of whisky and wiped his mouth with the back of his hand. "Would you care for a drink, MacDonald?" His face was amused as he studied the prisoner who stood shackled before him in his private office.

From some unsuspected depth, Niall was still able to walk and stand on his own strength. The chains on his feet and around his wrists chafed, but did not hinder the hatred that built steadily in his heart. Nothing could do that. His black eyes remained defiant as he returned Campbell's stare. "I do not drink with pigs."

Robert Campbell walked around his table, and with a flick of his hand, dismissed the two guards. "He can do no harm in his present situation. Wait outside until you are called."

When the men left, Robert drew himself up to his full height. A sneer came over his face as he approached Niall, taunting him with his nearness. "Did you know that your sweet wife came here to beg your release, MacDonald?"

Meg here? The pulse beat in Niall's throat and he looked at Robert Campbell with loathing. "And left, I am sure, in as good health as she arrived." His carefully enunciated words were a clear warning against the wrong answer.

"Indeed, she told me all about your marriage and her desire to remain with you. 'Twas most touching." Robert smiled, his words beginning to slur. "Of course, if she could see you now, I'm sure she would have second thoughts. My mark on you is plain for all to see."

Niall remained impassive. It was true that Robert had again opened the scar of the wound his sword had inflicted after their confrontation at the scene of the massacre last year. Flesh, however, would heal.

"I am certain that she will be much more open to the marriage Argyll has planned for her, when she learns of your permanent disfigurement," Robert continued, propping himself against the table for support. "Of course, I could put an end to any hesitation on her part by just killing you here." He looked at his sword which lay in its scabbard against the wall. "Did you know she is promised to an Englishman at William's court? Ah, I thought that would get your attention."

Niall made a convulsed sound and raised his hands, the chains rattling angrily. With a lightening quick step, his hands came down over Robert's head, pulling the chains down around his neck. Giving the chains a mighty wrench, Niall brought Robert's face up beside his own.

"Hear me well, you Dutch lapdog." Niall roared the insult and Campbell trembled before him. "Kill me now, for it will be your last chance. Afford me one opportunity and I will remove your head from your shoulders without a second thought." He jerked his hands upward again, releasing the terrorized colonel. Niall smiled pleasantly at the man. "Do we understand each other?"

"You are insane." Robert's voice shook and he moved to open the door and summon the guards. "Take him back immediately," he ordered. He did not look at Niall again as the guards led him away, but quickly reached for the consolation of his bottle. Argyll's orders should arrive at any moment, and it would be a great relief to finally put an end to the Glencoe affair.

Lady Cathlan tried to mask her concern at the failure of Meg and Maire to arrive in the park at the designated time. She reassured Elizabeth by telling her they must have confused their times. Attempting to instill confidence, she ordered the coachman to drive them to the castle.

"I should return to the house," Elizabeth fretted.

"That is exactly what you should not do, my dear. I will feel much better if you remain with me until we hear from your sister. Do not worry, I will send word to Argyll's staff so that they know of your whereabouts." That would be a great piece of news, Lady Cathlan told herself with satisfaction, picturing the resulting consternation among the servants. It was well known that Argyll held Lady Cathlan's enmity.

In her mind, the Queen's lady was already forming the petition she planned to make, to have the full and permanent guardianship of Elizabeth Campbell transferred to herself. Under the circumstances, she smiled as she thought of the pardon hidden in her reticule, the Queen was sure to agree.

In Breadalbane's drawing room, Meg and Maire played at cards. It was a lovely game of chance, and Meg's forehead wrinkled in concentration as she studied the hand she held. Maire lay a court card down and smiled across the tiny gaming table.

Triumphantly Meg covered it with a higher card and the two women laughed.

"Perhaps 'tis a good omen," Meg said, only half in jest. She rose from the table and walked over to the window as Maire began collecting the cards to reshuffle.

"It has been several hours already. How much longer do you think we will have to wait?" So much was at stake, Niall's life, Elizabeth's safety, the futures of them all. Meg looked out the window pensively. Two men stood across the stone paved street, apparently engrossed in a passionate argument. Arms flailing and voices rising, they shouted at each other in a most unbecoming manner.

"Maire," Meg kept her voice calm. "Would you come here for a moment? I believe that is —"

"It certainly is." Maire had joined her at the window. "We must be ready." She raised her skirt and withdrew her dirk.

As they watched the scene unfolding across the street, Breadalbane's two guards ran to stop the fight. In a beautifully choreographed movement, the antagonists turned on the guards, and the small altercation became a melee' of shouts and steel.

"Now!" Maire took Meg's hand quickly and they ran through the drawing room to the door. It took both of them to push the heavy doors open, and the effort was worthwhile. The first sight to meet their eyes was Ian and

Fergus standing with swords drawn against the throats of Breadalbane's guards.

"Now, lads," Fergus said politely. "Ye'll be returning to your post but without your weapons and wi'out a cry. Do ye ken my meaning?"

Both guards nodded, and Fergus nodded at Meg and Maire. "The coach is around the corner, and never fear, this time 'tis manned by Andrew."

The women ran without question to the waiting conveyance, and Andrew opened the door with a flourish. But when they were seated inside, he growled at them. "Another time you'll not be taking off without a proper escort. I near ran my feet to blisters following you."

Meg glanced at Maire and smiled conspiratorially. "Indeed we won't," she agreed, her face earnest and sorrowful when she turned back to Andrew. "We are fortunate that you were so alert. Thank you, Andrew. We are most indebted."

Maire clapped her hands with pleasure at the mimicry.

Andrew looked at her in puzzlement, and Meg laughed. "I truly do thank you. It will not happen again, I promise."

He shook his head at her mirth. "'Tis nothing to laugh about," he muttered, climbing back up to the driver's seat.

Ian and Fergus were already back at Maire's house when the others arrived. Two unfamiliar swords leaned against the wall of the reception hall, and Henry tried hard to ignore the ruffians who laughed and pounded each other on the back as they congratulated themselves on their able intervention.

"You have all done a great day's work," Meg agreed, casting a sly glance at Maire. "But how did Andrew know to follow us?"

Ian came to stand beside them. "Fergus was not sure of Lady Cathlan's dependability, not knowing her personally, and since Elizabeth did not know her either, we wanted to be certain all was well. Andrew saw you," he looked at Maire, "drop your fan, and I realized that you would never do that under normal circumstances."

"And 'twas a good thing he did." Andrew blustered. "Niall would have our hides if harm had come to either of you. You'll not leave here again without one of us. And what of Elizabeth? Is she being held somewhere too?"

"No indeed, she is quite safe and has been for several hours." The new voice boomed through the drawing room.

Lady Cathlan had bullied her way past Henry and stood dramatically in the doorway, Elizabeth at her side. "'Tis obvious that in the midst of all your scheming and nefarious following, none of you thought to see whether or not someone was following you." She paused to gauge their reactions, and smiled, well satisfied with her pronouncement. "My own man followed your carriage, Maire, as well as the big red-haired man who stopped traffic all over Edinburgh."

Meg stood with her arms around Elizabeth, uncaring of how or why the reunion had happened. Her sister was safe and within arm's reach again. But at Elizabeth's whisper, Meg broke the embrace and turned to Lady Cathlan.

"You have a message from the Queen?"

"I do." Lady Cathlan opened her reticule and handed the sealed paper bearing the King's seal to Meg. "'Tis not all we hoped for, I'm afraid, but 'tis a miracle nonetheless."

Her hands shaking, Meg opened the missive and her eyes quickly scanned the words written in King William's own hand. Tears sprang to her eyes and she looked up at the anxious faces around her.

"He has pardoned Ian, Andrew, and Jamie," she said slowly, "and all the others if they will swear the oath of allegiance and return us to Chesthill. There is no mention of Niall."

CHAPTER 23

Characteristically, Fergus reacted first. "That Dutch son of a dog! 'Tis not our necks that stand in danger. "

Lady Cathlan looked down her nose at the bristling man beside her. "If you can manage to hold your righteous temper for a moment, I will explain."

Fergus glared at her, but subsided, his chest still heaving with anger. He refused to sit down and stood with arms folded across his chest, his eyes trained on Lady Cathlan's face.

"His Majesty could not in good conscience grant clemency to an avowed outlaw who is already in custody."

The men around her snarled at the words, and Lady Cathlan raised one hand sternly. "To do so would be a slap in the face to His Majesty's advisors."

"I'll slap someone's face over this," muttered Andrew, but he hushed when Meg looked up at him wildly.

"Please, Andrew, let her finish." All Meg's fear was in her face as she faced Lady Cathlan. "Tell us what to do."

Elizabeth gripped Meg's hand, offering support as they waited for the rest of the explanation.

"As I was saying, because of the position Niall holds, His Majesty chose not to name him directly. If you noticed, the rest of the pardon reads, 'and all other survivors'. If you can get him out of Fort William yourselves, the pardon will apply to Niall, also. But the Crown cannot help you in that."

Lady Cathlan bowed her head apologetically. "Breadalbane and Argyll are too useful to the king's rule of Scotland for him to risk alienating them. They were the ones, with the Master of Stair, who convinced the northern clans to bow to William, and they have advised him well on many occasions. 'Tis all we could do. But Her Majesty, the Queen, offers you her personal regard, Meg, and bade me give you this in her name."

She opened her hand and showed them a tiny gold ring, delicately enough wrought for a child's hand. An ornate initial 'M' marked the oval top of the ring, and Meg slipped it on the little finger of her right hand.

It was a tremendous gesture for the Queen to make at such a time, and Meg could not find the words to express her gratitude.

She brushed away her tears. "Thank you, Lady Cathlan. You have aided us far beyond any expectation we held." She looked around at Niall's brothers and Fergus. "We must leave for Fort William now."

"Aye, lass, ye could wager your life on that and be sure of the outcome." Fergus strode to the door and flung it open. "Andrew, get word to Jamie to meet us at the tavern." He went quickly outside toward the stable and Andrew followed him.

Elizabeth put her arms around Meg, who had covered her face with her hands. "You will succeed."

Meg looked at her sister, anguish warring with determination in her face. "I must leave you again, though my heart is close to breaking over it. I have wasted too much time here already."

"You did not waste time. You hold a pardon in your hand that guarantees the lives of everyone. And it is not too late. We would surely have heard by now if —"

"I love him, Elizabeth. I cannot imagine living without him." She freed herself from her sister's embrace and stood up, the lines in her face smoothing with new resolve.

Lady Cathlan gave her an approving nod. "I have other news that I believe will be pleasant for you. The King has revoked Argyll's guardianship of Elizabeth. She is now in my care, and will remain so until she marries or until you have a place for her in your own home. You do not have to return her to an unpleasant environment."

Meg took the older woman's hands in her own. "You have been so kind to us. I can never thank you properly."

"You can thank me by rescuing that lad of yours." Lady Cathlan's eyes were moist. "And I know you will do it, Meg MacDonald."

Across the room, Ian's bright red head bent over Maire's dark one as she handed him a folded piece of paper. Their conversation was muted and intimate, and before he straightened to leave, Ian placed a lingering kiss on Maire's hand. In this moment of leave taking, Meg found it strangely comforting that Ian and Maire might have discovered each other.

Meg looked down into Elizabeth's wide blue eyes. "I will send you word as soon as possible." She kissed the tip of her sister's nose.

"Aye, you had better. But do not worry about me. Take care of Niall first." Elizabeth stood up next to Lady Cathlan. "I will be well looked after and will join you soon."

"Lady Cathlan has made it easier not to worry about you." Meg smiled at their benefactress again.

In the entryway, Fergus bellowed his readiness to leave, and the MacDonalds turned as one toward Maire, who sat dabbing at her eyes with a pink lace handkerchief.

"We must thank you, too, Lady Douglas, for your hospitality and your help, as well as for other things." Meg's voice was soft as she looked at the lovely woman. "I am forever in your debt."

"Just save him, and take care of each other. That will be thanks enough." Maire's indigo gaze lingered on Ian for a moment longer before she turned away. "God hold you in His care."

They waited only long enough for Meg to change into new riding clothes. Jamie and Andrew held the horses in front of the house and Carnoch tossed his head as Meg mounted him, exhibiting his eagerness to run.

"On the wings of the wind," Meg whispered to the black, and he was off at a full gallop, far ahead of the grim faced men who followed.

She fingered the tiny sprig of white heather in her hair, and decided that it was indeed the proper badge for a strong chieftain. When autumn arrived and the Highlands glowed with the flower, she would take Niall on a private search for the elusive white heather. She saw him in her mind, smiling arrogantly at her beside the burn.

There was need of a serious conversation between them when at last he was free. Meg could not live forever with the fear that Maire still held a place in his heart. And there were other matters to be resolved, questions and answers and confessions. She kicked her heels into Carnoch's sides.

Niall lay on the moldy straw pallet in the prison at Fort William and watched a spider spinning its trap for an unsuspecting fly. Except for his face, the wounds did not bother him much now. Although his reasoning was still clear, an uncaring stupor had settled over him, perhaps born of the poison he suspected they put in his food.

It didn't concern him much more than did the filthy state of his clothing and his body, which was another indication of how strong the poison must be. The important thing was for Fergus and his brothers to move the clan away from Glencoe. He prayed they would. But he knew his brothers well. Andrew and Ian would never allow him to die the traitor's fate of being hung, cut down before death claimed him, and dismembered before the eyes of the people who loved him.

He heard movement in the passageway, and the door to his cell opened. A tall, bent man dressed in somber black garb entered. Niall returned the man's stare quietly.

"MacDonald?" the question was uncertain, as if the stranger wished to disbelieve the identity of the prisoner.

With an effort, Niall marshaled his thoughts into coherency. "Aye." With difficulty, he raised himself from the pallet and stretched his long legs out before him. "And you?"

"Dr. Owen Kincaid." The man looked out at the impassive face of the guard who had led him to Niall's cell. "I have come to offer you spiritual counsel."

Niall looked at Dr. Kincaid without curiosity. "I am Catholic, born and bred, sir." He turned his head away disinterestedly and looked back at the spider on the ceiling.

Dr. Kincaid's eyes widened at the sight of Niall's wound. "Has your face been tended?" The skin had been crudely sewn together, but the flesh was puffy and proud. The entire side of the man's face was an angry red color, that bespoke an infection. Dr. Kincaid swallowed down his revulsion.

"I believe so," Niall answered vaguely. "I think the surgeon put a salve on it after he stitched it."

"I would hope he washed it before as well. But I am here to offer you hope, lad, Catholic or not, we all serve the same God."

Niall turned back to the minister. "I am slated to die a traitor's death, cut off from my family and clan. What hope do you have for me?"

"All men have the promise of paradise, if they will repent their sin and turn to God for forgiveness."

Apparently bored with the well known cant, the guard wandered away. His footsteps echoed down the passage, and Dr. Kincaid laid a trembling hand on the prisoner's shoulder.

"Have courage, lad," he whispered. "I have a message from Dora MacLean. You trust her?"

The familiar name penetrated the fog and Niall looked back at the fatherly figure before him. "Dora?" He brushed the matted black hair from his forehead.

"Aye, and one of your men named Alan?" Dr. Kincaid cast a nervous look over his shoulder.

A surge of energy cleared the last mists from his mind and Niall's black eyes were suddenly clear. "Alan sent you here. Quick, man, what is his plan?" His strong fingers grasped the minister's shoulders and Dr. Kincaid winced at the touch.

"We are to arrange things so that Campbell expects me to visit you again before he moves you to Edinburgh. For that last visit, I will bring you a bottle of wine, which I will first share with Robert." Dr. Kincaid was pale but firm as he recounted the way in which he planned to help deceive the colonel. "'Twill be an easy thing to reduce him to drunkenness. Unfortunately, that is a state he knows very well. Your man Alan will be waiting outside the gates with the others of your clan."

At Niall's look of skepticism, the minister sighed.

"You have no reason to trust me, I know, but I have prayed long over this, lad. Those girls were my pupils, entrusted to my care, and I see no other way to accomplish your release and secure their safety without bloodshed. Perhaps our Lord will forgive my sin." He bowed his head.

"Whether He does or not, sir, I surely do." Niall laughed with genuine enjoyment, startling the minister. "And I promise to buy a Mass for your soul, when next I see Father Michael." He laughed again at the startled look of consternation which crossed Kincaid's face. "You surely don't begrudge me the chance to assist you on your own way to Paradise?"

"As a servant of the true religion, sir, I deplore such erroneous practices. But I do understand that for one brought up as Roman Catholic, 'twould be difficult to renounce."

The minister cleared his throat, uncomfortable with the images of popery that flooded his mind. "The guard said that you will be moved in two days. I will plan to return here tomorrow evening."

He turned to leave, then turned back as a thought struck him. "Alan sent this for you." From the inside of his coat, Dr. Kincaid produced a small package wrapped in leather and tied with a thong. He watched with interest as Niall undid the knots and opened the flaps.

A good sized dirk with a staghorn handle rested lightly in Niall's hands and a slow smile spread over his face. He caressed the sharp blade and then carefully tucked the dirk into the back of his shirt.

"He said to tell you he will do all in his power to prevent you from having to use it." Dr. Kincaid was obviously perplexed by the message which accompanied the gift. "But why send it if he doesn't want it used?"

"It is my resource against the traitor's death," Niall said evenly, his face filled with a surprising calm.

Dr. Kincaid blanched. "Suicide is the devil's work, lad. 'Tis a mortal sin to take your own life. I cannot allow this."

Niall nodded. "'Tis not your responsibility, sir. I am the keeper of my own fate, and have always been."

"Blasphemy! Only God above has the right to decide the hour and method of our death."

"Perhaps He did decide. Perhaps this blade you delivered is His method." Niall smiled dangerously as the guard returned to unlock the cell door.

For a moment, Dr. Kincaid stood in the passageway, his mouth working speechlessly as he absorbed the meaning of the prisoner's last words. Realizing at last that he had no suitable response, he reached out to touch Niall's shoulder through the iron bars. "I will return tomorrow evening to pray with you, lad. Perhaps together we will discover His true will for your life."

✧

The small band of rescuers rode through the long night and into the day. At the small keep of Glen Larich, which lay close to Glenlyon and near to Glencoe, they stopped to rest and trade horses with Michael MacCurdy. Meg preferred to ride the black, and only gave him up because Fergus insisted.

"They will die on their feet do we not give pause," he argued, "I want to see Niall a free man as much as you do, but we canna kill the beasts to do it. Michael is our friend and will care for the horses until I send someone back for them later."

If there was a 'later'. Meg didn't voice the thought, not wanting to add to the growing weariness of the group. They ate well on hot porridge and goat's milk, and started the journey again.

The hills were touched with the morning sun, golden tips of barley beginning to dot the fields and glens, and at another time, Meg would have filled her spirit with the budding beauty around her. But each thudding hoof beat carried her closer to Niall and Robert, and her thoughts focused on the coming confrontation.

Fergus and Ian flanked her as they rode, with Andrew close behind. The pace was too quick to allow conversation, and no one was inclined to speak, anyway. From time to time, Meg glanced at Ian's profile, wondering what he was feeling in this frantic ride to save his brother's life. She grieved that he and Niall had been at odds before Duncan's death, and that she was the reason for the estrangement. She pushed her frustration away, promising Niall silently to do all in her power to reconcile him with his brother. Even if it meant she must leave Blackwater and Glencoe forever.

CHAPTER 24

Dr. Kincaid looked carefully through Glenlyon's well stocked wine cellar. Although an avid devotee of the usquebaugh, good Scottish whiskey, Robert Campbell prided himself upon his taste for exotic and rare wines. The minister himself rarely indulged in spirits, and the choice of a conciliatory bottle of wine was somewhat difficult for him to make.

Beside him, Dora shifted her weight. "It dinna matter which ye take, sir, 'tis the thought that matters."

"My dear girl, it does indeed matter which wine I take to Fort William." Dr. Kincaid reproved her. "We want to gain Robert's cooperation in the release of your chief, do we not? I believe that can best be accomplished by the gift of a fine wine." He looked back at the vast collection of vintages which stretched out before him. "Of course, he will not know that the offering came from his own store."

Dora sighed in impatience. "Get on with it then, if ye will, sir. Alan is about ready to split his trews. Tomorrow is the fifth day, ye ken, and he's fair aching to go in and rescue Niall. 'Twas a true battle to get him to agree to this."

"Yes, yes," the minister agreed. He reached for one dusty bottle and raised it up to look at the label. "Ah, yes, this should do well."

"Saints be praised," Dora muttered as she followed the old man back upstairs. Her own offering, a tiny packet of Annie's potion, lay concealed in the pocket of Dora's apron. It was not that she sought to deliberately mislead Dr. Kincaid, Dora smiled to herself, but sometimes men did not see the whole picture as well as women did. Even if he were plied with the finest wines in France, she did not think Robert Campbell would ever agree to release his captive. The herbal concoction in her pocket was merely a form of insurance.

"Now you will allow me to do the talking, Dora," Dr. Kincaid instructed as they rode from Glenlyon. "I recall that Robert banished you from the house, and he may not be pleased to see you."

"I'll keep quiet as a wee mouse," Dora assured the minister. At the moment, her mind was fixed on a more present trouble than her reception at Fort William. She was not accustomed to riding, and the stout Highland pony had a head of his own. "This beast is a pure divil, begging yer pardon, sir," she gasped as she fought to pull the pony's head back in the direction of the fort.

Dr. Kincaid smiled. "Just give him a swift kick, my dear, and he'll follow my own good Martha." He nudged his chestnut mare forward, and incredibly, Dora's hard headed pony followed. They rode quickly to the northwest, the wine securely packed in a leather bag strapped to the haunches of Dora's pony.

Alan and the other men waited for Dr. Kincaid and Dora a short distance from the gates of the fort. The clansmen were ready for battle, swords and ancient battleaxes gleamed in the fading sunlight. They spoke no more than was necessary, occasionally sharing a flask of water. No one voiced the possibility of failure; a handful of men against a fort of well armed and well fed soldiers could only hope for miracle to aid them in their efforts. Perhaps God, in His infinite compassion, would send them help.

Alan's stocky body was as tightly drawn as a bowstring, his speech short and clipped as he spoke to the minister. "If you do not return within two hours, we will come after you."

Dr. Kincaid bowed his head. "God in His mercy will surely aid us in our mission. We must trust in His will."

Alan looked sideways at the tall man dressed in black. "Aye, minister, but I maun also trust in myself. Dora, do ye yet carry the divil's breeches?"

She patted the leather pouch. "Right here."

"You will return to us with Dora, sir? Campbell will not thank you for interfering. He'll be sorely angry when 'tis done."

Dr. Kincaid was the essence of dignity. "I will admit my part like a responsible man." The minister's eyes began to glow with a soft fervor. "Even Peter worked to free those who were wrongfully imprisoned."

"Sir?" Dora sounded puzzled, and Alan shook his head.

"Quiet, lass, 'tis likely a teaching of his own."

"It is indeed, my friend. And before I go, I would offer a prayer on the behalf of all of us, if you are willing."

Alan held his bonnet in his hand. "Thank you, minister. We are not so full of the Lord's grace that we can afford to turn extra portions away."

Dr. Kincaid bent his head. "Our Heavenly Father and Protector," the deep voice, although strong in its faith, quavered slightly, "Have mercy on these, your children, who are about to enter into darkness for the sake of their kinsman. Grant unto them your protection and love. And at the end, Father, grant them your peace. In the name of our Savior, the Lord Jesus, Amen."

"Amen," the men shouted in one voice as Dr. Kincaid raised his hand in blessing over them.

"Thank ye sir, and God be wi' ye." Alan nodded to the minister, and Dr. Kincaid and Dora kicked their horses, riding quickly toward the fort.

"I have come to visit with the prisoner," Dr. Kincaid announced to the guards, "but would see the colonel first."

Assenting, the stone faced guard led them to Robert's office. He rapped on the door twice, and then at Robert's barely heard grunt, opened the door to allow the visitors' entrance.

"Dr. Kincaid," Robert turned from the dresser where he had just laid his wig. "I did not expect visitors this late. Is aught wrong?" His shirt front was opened, and the bony ridges of his chest were visible. He tried unsuccessfully to hide the empty whiskey bottle, but Dora and Dr. Kincaid saw it, and then exchanged a meaningful glance with each other.

"And Dora, lass, let me guess. You've come to ask for your old position back." He snickered at his own wit.

Dr. Kincaid banished the frown that threatened to appear on his face. "Is it true that your prisoner will be moved to Edinburgh tomorrow?"

"Perhaps yes, perhaps no," Robert eyed Dora uneasily. "Why should I tell you what my plans are?"

"I would offer the man comfort in these last hours before he meets his fate." Dr. Kincaid drummed his fingers lightly upon the top of the desk.

"I might be persuaded to allow a short visit," Robert said thoughtfully, "that is, if this lass has any information to trade for it."

Dora's round brown eyes grew ever wider. "Me, sir? What could ye be wanting from me?"

"I am certain you know the whereabouts of my ward, Mistress Elizabeth. Rumor has her in Edinburgh, but I don't believe it. Tell me where she is, and I may find it within my heart to grant you a visit with your former chief."

She looked at Dr. Kincaid, who nodded affirmatively.

"If you know anything, lass, you must tell him now."

Dora stuck her hands in the pocket of her apron. "Mistress Elizabeth, I did hear, is on her way to the Earl's own house, sir. She'll be escorted safe to Edinburgh this very day."

Unconvinced of Dora's sincerity, Campbell frowned. "I would surely have received word concerning such news. Are you certain of this, Dora?"

"Aye, sir, I saw her leave myself, on a little brown pony, in the company of some of our people who were leaving for another village."

Robert grinned. "Deserting the clan, eh? Understandable, that, since to stay would be to court certain death. I shall send a messenger to the Earl immediately to ascertain Elizabeth's safety. In the meantime, Dr. Kincaid, you may spend a few moments with my prisoner."

"God will bless you for your compassion," Dr. Kincaid thanked the colonel. "And, sir, in token of my hopes for the peaceful end of all this trouble, would you share a drink with me?"

"I would be glad too, if I had one to share. Unfortunately, I have run short on my stock, having recently exhausted my supply."

Robert sounded very regretful and Dr. Kincaid nodded understandingly.

"But sir, it was my desire to share a toast with yourself. See here," he triumphantly produced the wine from the leather pouch. "'Tis a rare tasting grape, from France, and I believe you will find it quite delightful." He smiled and turned to Dora. "Would you pour for us, my dear?"

Robert's eyes fastened greedily on the wine, and he waved a hand at the silver goblets on the dresser behind him. "Indeed, 'tis one of my favorites. Dora, do us the service, my dear. We will drink to peace in the Highlands and to King William."

Dora took the wine from the minister and with her back to the two men, pried the cork from the bottle. She emptied a pinch of the tiny packet of green mulberry powder into one goblet, then poured the wine in with it. She stirred the mixture with her finger, and wiped the member on her dress before pouring another good portion of the herbs into the bottle.

The men accepted the goblets gratefully, and Robert drained his at one gulp. "Fine, fine. Pour us another, lass. He held the goblet out for a refill. Ready for another, Kincaid?"

Dr. Kincaid sipped his wine. "I thank you, sir, but no. This one drink will serve me well. I do not, as you know, imbibe regularly."

"Then you won't be needing the whole bottle." Robert's eyes took on a crafty gleam.

The minister waved his hand. "Oh, by all means, Colonel, do keep it and enjoy it for yourself. Now if you will allow it, I should like to see MacDonald. 'Tis my duty to offer him solace." Campbell nodded agreeably, his hand on the wine bottle. "I won't need the goblet," he assured Dora, "since Kincaid has so generously made me a gift of the bottle."

"Aye, sir," Dora smiled sweetly.

"Guard!" Robert raised his voice, and the door opened.

"Sir!" the young soldier saluted.

"Escort the good doctor to the cell of the prisoner MacDonald and remain with him there."

"If ye don't mind sir, I'll go wi' the doctor. I'd fancy a last look at the chief." Dora gave the man a beguiling look and the young soldier smiled flirtatiously as she walked beside him.

They left Robert to his bottle and his rapidly deteriorating soberness.

Outside the fort, Meg studied the silhouetted hills in the distance while Fergus talked with Alan. Dark blue and purple under the starry sky, the high passes filled her with impatience to be done with the rescue and headed toward home.

Finally she turned to interrupt the two men. "We cannot trust to Dr. Kincaid's ability to outtalk Robert," Meg warned. "I must go inside myself."

"'Tis too dangerous, lass, I canna agree." Fergus' face was firm. "We will wait for Dora's signal and then go in together. They have it well planned."

Alan's good humor had returned with the arrival of his brother. "Besides lass, our Dora went ably armed with a particularly powerful offering of her own to add to the wine."

Meg smiled, guessing what Dora planned. "Even more reason for me to be there. Someone must distract Robert and the guards while Dr. Kincaid works for Niall's freedom."

"Ye canna go. I forbid it." Fergus ordered stoutly.

"Ye canna stop me. I will not wait." She kicked the horse away from them and rode through the gates of the fort.

Robert was reclining in the chair when she entered the room, and she could tell from his heavy lidded gaze that he was not physically able to rise to greet her.

"Meg," his mouth worked slowly over her name, revealing the quick work of the half empty bottle beside him. "You are looking exceptionally well this evening. Come to offer me a bargain for the life of your beloved husband?"

She walked lightly forward and sat on the edge of the table. "Good evening, Robert. You don't seem surprised to see me."

"I've had several visitors tonight, no big surprise, since word got out that MacDonald will be moved tomorrow." His wine glazed eyes were having difficulty focusing on her, and he took another long swig from the bottle.

She stifled her disgust and smiled at him. "Who were your other visitors?"

He belched. "You know quite well who they are. Your good minister," his inflection was sarcastic, "and your devoted servant. They came to offer solace to the man. As if prayers and tears can ease the knowledge of the death that awaits him."

She looked at her nails critically. "Is it to be the noose, then?"

"Aye," he smiled, and her blood cooled in her veins. "And a few other things."

She knew of what he spoke. The traitor's death of hanging, drawing, and quartering. Meg fought to control her rage. "Let us not play games, Robert. Elizabeth journeys to Edinburgh where she will be under the protection of the Earl. What else do you demand before you release my husband to me?"

He took another drink of the wine and looked at the tight velvet bosom of her riding dress. "You have never liked me, Margaret. Perhaps you could show a little friendship to me in return for his life."

"How?"

He wiggled a finger at her. "Come here and sit on my lap, my dear, dear ward."

She drew a deep breath. "Will you guarantee his life? Your sworn word of honor?"

He turned the bottle up and emptied it, gulping noisily at the wine made its way down his throat. His lips glistened with the red liquid as he smiled at her. "His life, I will guarantee. His freedom, however, is not within my scope to grant. I have always been quite fond of you, Margaret, and 'twill please me greatly to do this small favor for you. Come closer, dear." He patted his thigh invitingly.

She reached out her hand and ran it alongside his own, which lay on the table. "Do you find me attractive, Robert?"

The muscles in his hand quivered as he fought to control his words and his rapidly slowing motor control.

"You are quite exciting, Meg, especially when giving an impassioned speech. 'Tis no wonder the MacDonald wanted you." His pale, skinny fingers grasped her own and he stared up at her soft mouth longingly.

"Robert, can we be certain of our privacy?" Meg leaned toward him, her breasts thrust out temptingly.

He groaned with the effort to concentrate on her words. "Just latch the door, there, thass a good lass."

She walked over to the door, and opened it.

"Do you need anything, Mistress?" the guard asked, and looked inside at Robert.

The colonel waved a hand in negation. "Ever' thing fine, Ross, jus fine," he could barely talk by now. "The lady and I jus wan a little privacy."

"Aye sir!" The guard grinned knowingly and closed the door.

Meg gritted her teeth against an obscenity and squared her shoulders. But fate was with her, for when she looked back, Robert had sunk into his chair, his mouth was open and his eyes were closed. He was beginning to snore.

"Pig." She went quickly to his side and lifted his right hand, which bore a signet ring of the Campbells. She had to work to get it off, and she was frightened every moment, but at last the ring worked free and Meg slipped it over her thumb.

She opened the door and stepped out into the hall. A startled guard jumped to attention.

"The colonel is resting," she said. "He has given his permission for you to take me to the prisoner." She waved the ring in the guard's face and he led the way to the dungeon.

She tried desperately not to hurry down the long passageway, wishing to present an appearance of confidence and calm intent. At the end of the long hall, the passage made a t-shape, and the guard led her to the right past several small open rooms. There was a pervasive stench throughout the prison, and Meg pulled her plaid up to cover her nose. Decay and dampness were everywhere, and it was not surprising that most prisoners died here. Those who survived the squalor must surely be the exception.

The man ahead of her stopped to remove a large ring of keys from an iron bracket on the wall. The rattle of metal made a doleful sound as he held the ring under the light of a weak candle flame that sputtered and struggled in the thin air.

"Is it much further?" her voice was muffled by her plaid and she repeated the question before the guard heard her and gestured to a cell on the left a few feet ahead where they stood.

A few more steps, and they paused before a heavy wooden door. A low voice issued from inside the cell, a man's voice, speaking in a drone. The guard laboriously opened the huge lock and pushed the on the door. Meg stepped inside, her eyes searching out the dark interior of the prison.

Three people stared back at her, their expressions registering surprise.

She met Niall's eyes with an assuring smile and flashed Robert's ring so that it gleamed in the candlelight.

"My guardian has rescinded his order to keep you prisoner. The news of our marriage softened his heart, and he wishes to extend the protection of the family name to us both. He sends this token of his good will."

Dora was the first to react. "Och, miss, now ye're here to visit, perhaps this kind gentleman," she cast her eyes suggestively at the red-coated guard who still stood outside in the passageway, "would escort me back upstairs so I can take care o' some private business." She handed the small candle she carried to Dr. Kincaid, and picked her skirts up to show her ankles as she walked past the guard. "We'll return before ye have time to miss us." She winked at Meg and tossed her head.

"Wait just a moment, Dora." Meg put her arm around the girl and whispered something in her ear. Then she hugged Dora and looked at the guard. "I place her under your protection, as my husband and I are under that of your colonel."

The befuddled guard held out his arm and Dora took it with a flair that would have justice to Maire Douglas, gently removing the key ring from his hand and placing it back on the wall as they passed. "You won't be needing these, I can promise ye. And perhaps ye'll know where we might find a wee drop or two? This night air has made me that thirsty." She giggled and clutched his arm.

Meg waited until the sound of their footsteps receded, then she ran to retrieve the keyring. Her hands shook as she knelt before Niall, trying each key, searching for the one which would unlock the manacles.

"I cannot find the right one!" she cried. She looked up at Niall, who sat motionless before her. "Help me."

"Easy, *mo crigh*," Niall murmured, his eyes closed.

Dr. Kincaid reached for the keys and Meg sat back on her heels, allowing him to finish what her nervousness could not.

With a dull click, the cuffs sprang free, and Niall rose slowly from the bench. He staggered slightly, from weakness, and Meg reached out to steady him, biting her lip against the shock of the wound on his face.

She reached to touch it, but the minister stopped her.

"Not now," he whispered urgently. "We must get him out of here first, and it may not be easy. He has been drugged and is only now coming back to his senses."

They stepped back out into the passageway, and Dr. Kincaid replaced the keyring on its bracket. Together he and Meg supported Niall's tremulous steps as they walked down the long hall back to the staircase.

At the top of the stairs, a soldier stood stiffly against the wall. His eyes widened when he recognized Niall and he took a step forward.

Meg raised her hand to show Robert's ring. "We have Colonel Campbell's authority," she said, and the soldier fell back with a shrug.

"Aye, ma'am. I did see your maid before and she said summat like that." He saluted and returned to his position.

Meg's heartbeat raced as they progressed down the hall toward Robert's office. At any moment they might be stopped and the only pass they had was a ring.

As if reading her thoughts, Dr. Kincaid intoned impassionedly, "The Lord has given His angels charge over us."

Summoning courage from the minister's faith, Meg drew a deep breath and they passed Robert's guard, who was engrossed in the soft hair at the back of Dora's neck. Two down.

What was taking Dora so long? The final portion of their escape might depend on her. But Meg would not dwell on the fear. Better to take each moment as it came. And next was the outer yard of the fort.

They walked a few steps further and Dora caught up with them, her breath heaving noisily in the darkness.

"Here, miss," she said, and thrust a wadded bundle of cloth into Meg's arms. "Quick though, he may rouse at any moment."

Meg looked down at the woolen clothing in her hands.

"Dora! Thank God." She sorted out the tangled red jacket and Campbell plaid.

"It was not easy to get him out of them," the girl said impatiently, "and we must hurry."

Niall managed to help them pull the despised red coat over his chest, but he shook his head at the length of blue and green plaid.

"Nay, lass. I'll not exchange my own plaid for that bit of dung."

"Aye, husband, but you will." With a rapid movement, Meg wrapped the Campbell plaid around his MacDonald one, tucking the latter up above his knees so that it would not show under the outer skirting. "You married a Campbell who wore this same bit of dung, remember? This will ensure our safe passage from the fort. As God above is my witness, you will wear this plaid until we are clear, and you will keep your epithets to yourself."

He stared down at her for the space of a heartbeat and she almost wept from the strain. *We are so close to winning free! God, make him understand!*

"Niall," she put her hands on her hips. "Not everyone of the name Campbell is a devil. Many of those under Robert's command tried to warn your kin. Do not cover us all with the treachery of a few men. In the name of God, this is our only way out. Don't fight me."

At last he nodded, and somehow through the befuddlement of the past few hours, he managed a glimmer of a wicked grin. "Aye, lass. Ye are the one Campbell I know better than to fight."

Dr. Kincaid put one hand under Niall's arm. "Now, then, the main entrance is just ahead. We will go slowly and confidently. MacDonald, if you will just keep your head lowered, I believe all will be well. We must be careful, though. Do not speak to anyone."

"Can you make it?" Meg whispered to Niall.

He nodded. "Aye. I will. Tis your royal command, is it not?"

Each step seemed heavier than the last; time had slowed to a series of unbearable breaths that threatened to compress Meg's lungs. The clammy stone walls on either side seemed to stretch out forever.

Finally the massive wooden doors of the fort were before them. They stood open. The two guards beside the doors were engaged in a game of cards. They did little more than nod their heads in acknowledgement of the departing company.

Sweat dripped from Meg's forehead, but she paced her movements. *Don't rush, don't call their attention in any way. Another two steps. Good. Now two more. Take your time. One. Two. Three.* She thought her chest would crush from the effort it took not to gasp her dread aloud.

They were in the yard now, unmolested by any of the soldiers. Clearly, the regiment at Fort William expected no problems this night.

The ponies still stood tethered at the post, and Dr. Kincaid untied them quickly. He helped Niall mount, and Meg climbed up behind him.

"Alan gave me two dirks for ye." Dora opened the leather sack she carried and rummaged for something, but Dr. Kincaid stopped her.

"I think weapons are not necessary now," he told her softly. "Just as Daniel walked fearlessly from the lion's den, we too shall prevail through the mercy of our Lord."

"If ye say so, sir," Dora answered doubtfully. "But who is Daniel?"

"Another time, my dear, I will be delighted to tell you all about him." The minister's eyes glowed with religious fervor. "Let us rejoin our friends who wait for us."

It was indeed eerie to ride through the fort unharmed by the few soldiers who were visible. Those who manned the gate nodded respectfully to Meg and the minister and opened the gates wide for them to pass through. She sent a grateful look heavenward as they rode quickly away.

At the ridge, Alan and his men heard the approaching hooves. He restrained the men with difficulty, but there were only a few horses, not the number they would have heard had the soldiers been riding toward them. As the three horses drew closer in the misty night, Alan spied the red coat Niall wore.

"What is this? Has the wench betrayed us after all?"

He waited until they drew up even with him, then swept his bonnet from his head.

"God be praised!" his voice rang out. "He is safe."

Dr. Kincaid reined his pony in as did Meg and Dora. "You do not have time to linger," the older man warned. "You must leave quickly and go as far away as possible." He looked at Meg. "God will continue to look after you."

"Will you not come with us?" she pleaded. "Robert will be terribly angry when he learns that you have helped us."

Dr. Kincaid smiled. "I am sure he will. But I will wait for him to awaken, and restore his ring to his hand when he does so. You should be quite safe. Robert will never dare confess to the king that his drunkenness allowed his prisoner to escape." He held out his own hand and Meg dropped the gold signet ring in it without hesitation.

"There is one thing I still don't understand." Dr. Kincaid turned to Dora. "How did you take the guard's clothing?"

"Och," the girl said, glancing uneasily away from the minister. "I had me gran's blessing, if ye ken. I er, called on it while sharing a wee dram with the lad." She winked at Meg.

Niall reached out his hand to the minister, grasping the firm old one in his own. "I can never thank you for your help, sir." Although weak, his voice expressed a heartfelt gratitude.

"Give your thanks to the Lord who has guided us this night. And take care of yourself and your people." Dr. Kincaid turned his pony and rode with dignity back toward the fort.

Niall looked at the faces of his brothers and the clan who had been willing to risk their lives for him. He shrugged off the red coat and twisted the Campbell plaid from about his waist, then threw both pieces of clothing on the ground.

Bare-chested under the high night sky, he raised his right hand. "Blackwater."

"Aye," said Ian, confirming his brother's command, "and MacDonald."

The air was rent with the joy as the word burst forth simultaneously from the throats of the clan. "MacDonald!"

Their backs turned on Fort William, the clansmen rode triumphantly through the predawn mists, toward home and hope.

CHAPTER 25

"Most of Duncan's possessions have been distributed, but I kept this apart because I have always wondered about it. He kept it so carefully, it must have been precious to him. Would he mind us keeping his box, do you think?"

Meg slid the lid off Duncan's blanket box and removed the small rowan wood container that held other valuables; several pieces of gold, a curl of fine pale blond hair, a small stalk of dried white heather so ancient that it had darkened to a fine gray. Meg looked at the items respectfully, and touched the blond hair with an inquisitive finger.

"Duncan kept the history of the clan. He had particular charge over the things in this box. 'Twas thought they might one day be important. Mayhap, he was right."

Meg lifted the curl of blond hair and held it up inquisitively.

Watching her, Niall smiled and put his arms around her. "'Tis from my mother's last bairn, a wee lass who left the earth as quickly as she came to it."

"And the gold?" she looked up at him lovingly, secure in the intimacy of his embrace.

"'Twas the remaining portion of her marriage gift, sent with her by her mother. As long as she had it, she said, she felt protected against hunger and poverty."

Meg picked up the stalk of heather. "And this?"

Niall dropped his arms from around her and turned her slightly so that she faced him. "'Twas the first thing my father ever gave her."

Meg turned the withered stalk over in her hand. "But how strange, to give her the white heather of the MacIaian instead of his own larch of the Isles. Do you know why he did so?"

"Aye. 'Twas to be given to me when I came of age, to prove my parentage." Niall gazed at her, willing her to understand. "She died before that day came, but Duncan knew the truth and vouched for it. He kept the box for provenance if a question ever arose. He would hae brought the box out to show you all these things himself, if he had been spared."

Duncan. Meg's thoughts went back over all the questions of the past months, the clan naming Niall as chosen chief, his refusal to wear the white heather until Duncan died, the insistence of Fergus and the other men that Niall must be saved at any cost. Comprehension came to her suddenly.

"Aye," he nodded, his dark face still showing the effects of his torture at the hands of Robert Campbell. "Ian, Andrew, Laurie and I had the same mother. But their da was Arthur."

"MacIaian," she breathed, hardly daring to believe it.

Niall pushed himself up from the bench and walked to the door of Duncan's croft, looking out through the open door at the greening treetops. "Before her marriage my mother visited with her cousin at Glencoe. She caught MacIaian's eye, and Duncan told me she returned his interest. When she returned home for her wedding, she was already quick with child. Arthur, her husband, accepted it from the moment she told him, and never made any difference between Laurie and me and his own sons."

"But Maire and Lady Cathlan knew. And the Queen must have known too." Meg pressed her hand to her lips, remembering.

"Aye," he answered. "Knew and have kept the secret. Despite her love for the King, Queen Mary values the sons of Scotland."

Meg went to him and put her face against his back, nuzzling him with her cheek. "Did you know?"

"It was always in my mind. No one in Arthur's family had this hair," Niall tugged at the black curls lying lightly on his forehead. "But no one ever confirmed it to me until Laurie came here to be married. Duncan insisted that MacIaian send for me." His body was relaxed, belying the clipped way he spoke.

"Did he acknowledge you?"

"He would have. I refused. John and Alasdair, had grown to manhood thinking to inherit all this between themselves." Niall waved his hand at the landscape before them. "And now they are driven from this place, and I can no longer hold it for them. In truth, I doubt they will ever try to return."

"What will you do?" she asked as she ducked under his arm and looked up to face him.

He kissed her forehead and ran a finger along the side of her face. "For now I will take you and the clan and accept Maire's hospitality. We will go to Skye and govern her holdings for her. I have thought much over your words to me about blaming all the men of your name for the sins of a few. You are right, *mo crigh.* Not all the Campbells are blackhearted. Glenlyon's own piper played a lament to sound a warning. But I have no heart to linger at Glencoe with its ghosts. John and Alasdair may return someday. If they do not, perhaps I will. Maire's offer comes at a good time. On Skye, we can heal and rest."

Meg bit his finger teasingly. "Does it bother you that Ian and Maire are together? Mind how you answer."

He shook his head in denial. "That was over long ago. Ian is welcome to what pleasure he can find with her. Even should he choose to marry her. We will bide at Skye."

"And when Maire returns to claim her property there?"

He searched her eyes for any sign of hesitancy. "If the new MacIaian has no objection, perhaps we will return to the summer shieling when John and Alasdair reclaim those lands. But I am not ready yet."

"You will be," she told him confidently, "you will want a place to grow your own sons and daughters, a place of their own to hand on to them. I think that a home beside the river would be a fine place to do that."

The black eyes sparkled. "Have ye already started working on this, my silver eyed fox?"

"Nay, sir," She stood on tiptoe and kissed the soft curly black hairs at the base of his throat. "And I'm fair tired of waiting for you to do your duty by me."

"Are ye now? Then 'tis past time I remedied the matter."

He swept her up in his arms and strode outside to the soft green bracken covering the ground under Duncan's oak.

"I live to serve, my lady."

THE END

MUIREALL DONALD is the author of *Glencoe, A Romance of Scotland*, as well as several fantasy and paranormal novels that are forthcoming from Laughing Owl Publishing, Inc.

A native of southern Alabama and mother of two daughters, Muireall currently lives in an artists' sanctuary with her husband, three dogs, and six cats in a secluded area on the Gulf Coast.

Excerpt from

THE BELOVED

An occult novel
by

M.D. Gray

Shona didn't want to surrender to the man leaning over her. A distant warning burned in her belly. *Sinful. Evil.*

She turned her face away from the elegant hands that stroked her hair, brushing it back from her face. His fingertips lingered with delicate insistence over her lips. She ran her tongue over them, tasting the salty flavor his flesh left on her mouth. She was captive to his desire and at the mercy of her own. It was terrifying.

Deliciously so.

The flame in her lamp guttered and almost winked out as he bent closer to her, so near that his breath warmed her throat. A red gemstone hung from a leather thong around his neck. She stared at it, mesmerized by the pulsing light deep within the jewel.

"You will not deny yourself." His hands moved down over her wrists and pinned them to the bed. "Cease your struggle, beloved. Remember how it was."

She struggled against his grip, against his strength. Then he released her with a quick gentle pressure upon her arms. It was futile to deny him; his knowledge of her was an intimate, living creature.

Shona lifted her arms to embrace him and then, quicker than thought could take her, they were in her own big bed at Darkwood, the one that had hosted so many pleasures of love in the past. He was part of that urgent, hungry history; his face mirroring the sensuality of the carved gargoyles on her old oak armoire.

She had trusted him once, thrilled to his voice and his touch. It had led to tragedy. But he was here, *now*. Somehow, through the strength of his passion, he had found her again. This time it would be different. This time, there was no reason for her to resist. There was no one left to fight for against the darkness. Now she could stop mourning and begin to forget. Shona relaxed, opening herself to the intimacy time and taboo had so long prohibited.

A primal urgency forced her downward in a deep spiral of sensation that claimed her over and over again in a rush of heat and rapture. Her eyelids fluttered. She moaned, accepting the pleasure invading her body.

"You are mine, beloved. Never doubt it. You are bound to me through all time." His voice was soft and purposeful.

Minute wings flapped in the darkness over her bed. The gargoyles had come down from atop the armoire, descending to cover her. Their tiny tongues and teeth devoured her inflamed body. Shona twisted, writhing from the agonizing pleasure. Tiny hands invaded her secret places, pressing, pulling, torturing her with tiny pinches and tender slaps.

Her body arched in a frenzy of pain and exaltation.

LAUGHING OWL PUBLISHING, INC.

Call 1-334-865-5177 to order by phone and use your major credit card. Or use this coupon for mail order.

_____ **Song of The White Swan**
    0-9659701-6-7 $10.00 US   14.80 CAN
by Aleta Boudreaux
Historical Fiction. The people of Brittany have followed the old gods for centuries. Now the emissaries of the Catholic Church threaten the ancient ways and Antoinette Charboneau, Druid priestess and advisor to the Queen, must embark on a journey across the ocean, reclaiming her personal power and faith in her Goddess.

_____ **The Beloved**
    0-9659701-4-0 $8.00 US   12.00 CAN
by M.D. Gray
Occult. Adam was the man of Shona's dreams. But when the forbidden sensuality of their past lives came crashing into the present, she awakened to the terror of her lover's demonic possession and her own enthrallment to the ecstasy of his touch.

Name_____
Address_____
_____ State_____ Zip_____
Please send me the LAUGHING OWL books I have checked above.

I am enclosing $_____
Plus Postage and Handling $ 3.00
Sales Tax (Alabama residents add 6%) $_____
Total Amount Enclosed $_____

No cash or C.O.D.s.

Send check, money order, or credit card authorization to: Laughing Owl Publishing, Inc., 12610 Highway 90 West, Grand Bay, AL 36541.

Valid in the U.S. and Canada only. All prices and availability subject to change without prior notice.

To learn more about
Laughing Owl Publishing, Inc.,

visit our website at
www.laughingowl.com